A story of love
and Addiction —
Enjoy!

Esther's Race
By Mark Munger

Cloquet River Press
Publishing Stories from the Great Lakes Basin
www.cloquetriverpress.com

ISBN 978-09720050-9-8

Edited by: Scribendi
Published by: Cloquet River Press
                       5353 Knudsen Rd.
                       Duluth, MN 55803
                       (218) 721-3213
Visit the Publisher at: www.cloquetriverpress.com
Email the Author at: cloquetriverpress@yahoo.com

Printed in the United States of America
Cover Photograph though license with ShutterStock

ACKNOWLEDGEMENTS

The creation of a novel – especially one written in the first person and outside the author's field of personal experience – requires not only bravery on the part of the author; it requires the involvement of individuals called upon by the author to lend assistance to the project. Their criticism and commentary is the real story behind this book.

Writing about an ethnicity not my own and about events I didn't personally witness are things not new to me. My third novel, *Suomalaiset: People of the Marsh* (ISBN 0972005064), tells the tale of a fictional Finnish immigrant (I'm not a lick Finnish) set in the era of the Great War. Similarly, though I am one-quarter Slovenian, I'm too young to have experienced the events depicted in the first half of my debut novel, *The Legacy* (ISBN 0972005080). However, whereas both of those stories are set in the past and deal with issues and circumstances safely protected by a veil of years, *Esther's Race* does not enjoy such distance. It's a contemporary story of love, addiction, loss and salvation that hopefully rings true as a piece of fiction.

To create the world and characters for *Esther's Race*, the help of the following individuals was invaluable: Renata Skube; Assistant St. Louis County Attorney Mark Rubin; Reverend Cheryl Harder, Trinity Episcopal Church and Arrowhead Regional Corrections; Deb Cooper; Joel Cooper; the Honorable Natalie Hudson (Judge, Minnesota Court of Appeals); Assistant Wisconsin Attorney General Kelly Cochrane; Reverend Derrick Thomas, St. Mark's AMEC; Felicia Washington, Assistant Adjunct Professor St. John's (Minnesota) University; Reverend Howard Anderson, Canon, National Cathedral; Linda Pollock, RN, Miller–Dwan Hospital Burn Unit; Donna and Pat Surface, Spiritwoood Music; and Jill Lyman, CRM, Barnes and Noble Bookstore (Duluth). And as always, a special thanks to my wife Rene´ for her steady hand, keen eye and loyal heart.

Mark Munger

Esther did not reveal her race or nationality, because Mordechai had ordered her not to.
Esther 2:10

ESTHER'S RACE
By Mark Munger

Surely the day will come when color means nothing more than the skin tone, when religion is seen uniquely as a way to speak one's soul; when birth places have the weight of a throw of the dice and all men are born free, when understanding breeds love and brotherhood.
Josephine Baker

ONE

Del sat on the mattress in the dark, his once-photogenic teeth exposed, their enamel pitted, evidence of the drug's toxicity. He concentrated intently on tightening a rubber band around his left bicep. I watched – curious, a bit fearful, amazed – as he slid the tip of the syringe into the greenish-blue track of vein that bulged from his pallid skin. Del's right hand cradled the syringe as if it were a rare artifact. His thumb pressed firmly against the syringe's plunger. My boyfriend (for that's what I considered Delmont Benson) closed his eyes as fluid surged into his arm. Ecstasy swept over Del's face. His thin eyebrows furrowed. Release was clear in the quiver of his eyelids, in the pursing of his mouth, in the exhalations of breath through his lovely, full lips.

And then it was my turn, my opportunity, my first time to do meth.

Later, after the erotic rush of the drug had coursed through me, removing with it every constraint, every taboo and every hesitation, Del and I made love on the mattress in the basement apartment we shared in the Uptown neighborhood of Minneapolis. Our bodies moved and pulsed with frenetic energy. My peak was astounding. The meth seemed to direct energy along new and previously undiscovered pathways that lead to my epicenter. They say that you can become addicted to the stuff the first time you try it. That's not just a load of crap dished up by the DEA. I know it's true. It happened to me.

We stayed high most of the day. Del easily tolerated the long-lasting excitement meth infuses into its disciples. He'd used the drug routinely before I ever came along. I, on the other hand, found being high that first time akin to running a marathon. Oh sure, I'd drunk my share of beer and hard liquor when I partied as a kid. I'd smoked a little weed with friends in Bayfield, Wisconsin, where I went to high school, and in Marquette, Michigan where I went to nursing school. My experimentation with pot ended the moment I became a registered nurse. When I graduated and was pinned at twenty-one, I stopped smoking weed and dedicated myself to my profession, completely content to follow my father's example.

My father. Dr. Orville Theodore Xavier DuMont. There's a complex piece of humanity for you. On the outside, as striking a black man as you've ever seen, with chiseled cheekbones, finely detailed eyebrows, and the world's easiest-going smile. Tall, thin and fit even into late middle age (he's fifty-eight), Dad commands attention from folks – especially from women –even before they learn he's an orthopedic surgeon.

My twin sister Lilly, born fifteen minutes behind me, looks like a DuMont. She's slender, has an enigmatic mouth, and brown eyes – large, omnipresent discs of color set deep in her head, reminiscent of our father. Me, I take after our mother, Samantha Witta DuMont. She's half Irish and half Finnish, square of stature with thick hips, a significant bust, piercing blue eyes, and skin the color of clean straw. I didn't inherit her fair skin, blond hair or blue eyes, but I am an exact replica of my mother when it comes to physique, though I do share Dad's African heritage when it comes to abundantly nappy hair.

Using a needle wasn't a problem for me. As a nurse, I'd given plenty of hypos. Even in nursing school, we were always drawing blood on each other, inserting IV lines, and the like, so that part of the methamphetamine ritual didn't bother me at all. But the crash – now *that* was something that caught me off guard.

The problem with any good buzz, whether it's bourbon or meth, is that no matter how long the ride, it eventually ends. With meth, that first time, the end was cruel. Del hadn't prepared me for it; maybe, not knowing how my body would take to the stuff, there wasn't any way he could protect me from the abrupt crash that followed.

"Somethin' wrong?"

We were lying next to each other beneath a scratchy wool blanket on a clean white sheet in the cool dankness of the basement apartment we shared on Lake Street.

The floor of the bakery located above the apartment groaned from the weight of the "after work" trade: men and women on their way home from downtown Minneapolis stopping in to pick up a loaf of bread, dinner rolls or their kid's birthday cake. We'd spent the better part of a winter day exploring each other's bodies under the hazy, constant high of methamphetamine. I don't remember now all the twisted and unnatural things we did. I do remember I didn't want us to stop. But we did. The downhill slide began right around the time I first noticed customers stomping on the hardwood floor of the bakery.

"I think so."

Del wrapped his long arms around my shoulders and pressed his wet crotch into the small of my back. Inexplicably, my mind turned from the light, airy energy of the drug's high to something darker. It wasn't as if a massive cloud of depression descended over me. It was more like uncertainty had crept into my spirit, taking me down mental paths and trails I'd normally avoid.

"I've got another hit or two left," Del offered.

I shivered. The electric baseboard heaters were set on low to save money. Del hadn't worked much since I met him that one morning, six months earlier, in an all–night diner on University Avenue. My night shift at the University of Minnesota Hospital was over when I stumbled into Denny's for a cup of coffee and a ham and cheese omelet before heading back to my place, the apartment below the bakery, to sleep. Del was already at the lunch counter when I sat down heavily on a stool a few spaces away. His eyes engaged mine. I was instantly intrigued. His lips piqued my interest. And then there was his long blond hair. I've always been a sucker for blonds.

I'd been in the city for a year, and I'd given up dating. The bar scene wasn't for me. Creeps and married guys pretending that they're not – that's what you get in Twin Cities' singles bars. Madison, Wisconsin, where I first worked after graduating from nursing school, was different; it was friendlier, more laid back. In Madison, I had a few dates, almost all of them with white guys. You know, the curiosity factor: *What's a black girl smell like? Taste like? Make love like?* I didn't mind the attention. It was something I was used to, being the odd woman out, being a conversation piece, having grown up where I did. Anyway, some of my relationships in Madison looked serious at first blush, but nothing took. Not that I was in a hurry to marry, mind you. I wasn't. Back then, I didn't even think of myself as marriageable. The guys in Madison I dated were alright. We'd have a few drinks, go to a few shows, maybe catch dinner. But intimacy…well, because of the scars, that always posed a problem.

The scarring isn't *that* noticeable. I do a good job of concealing my defects. I mean, other than when I visit my doctor, disrobe in a locker room, shower at home or spend time in a bathing suit, who's going to know that my left side, from my hip bone to the hollow between my breasts and including my left armpit, is a ragged mess of scar tissue? Sure, I've lived with the scars for eleven of my twenty-eight years and I have, over time, come to accommodate my distressed skin and the fact that my left nipple is numb. Dead, in reality: dead to the touch – mine or anyone else's. The skin under my left arm (the armpit unnaturally hairless) is webbed, like that of a

9

bat's wing. Over the years, I've learned to protect my scars during the cold of winter or when I'm out in the sun.

It's during those first awkward moves towards intimacy, when a potential lover slips his fingers beneath my blouse or sweater in search of my bosom, that I tense, as if forced to watch an inevitable tragedy unfold. It's during those moments – moments in the mating ritual when the man attempts to explore my body based upon some time–honored instruction manual that requires hand–to–breast interaction before venturing into more "serious" territory – that I fall apart.

By the time Del came along, it'd been years since I slept with anyone. Actually, I'd only slept with one other person before Del. Kind of sad, isn't it? I mean, it wasn't like I didn't enjoy the experience. I'm not frigid or anything. Not in the least. But, like I said, I had a deep–seated phobia against intimacy.

Please understand: Delmont Benson was a lot of things. Some of Del's constitution I figured out right away; other parts took a while to percolate to the surface. But one attribute that showed itself right off the bat that first tentative evening in the front seat of his Dodge Dakota pick–up truck was Del's ability to suppress surprise when his fingers touched granulated skin. Most guys react, as I probably would if I were in their shoes, by withdrawing. It's human nature to recoil from the imperfect. I don't fault guys who respond this way. But, in my case, that's the crossing where the intimacy train always derailed. Before Del, my resolve, my declination, held firm and I abruptly ended every romantic encounter of my adulthood before consummation. Embarrassment had always manifested itself during intimacy. Not with Del. His fingers never wavered, never faltered in their attention to detail. I guess I must have instinctively picked up on the fact that he treated my left breast with the same respect, admiration and interest he gave my right. How he did it, I can't say. He just did. And that was all it took, thank goodness, for me to let him press on.

See, outside of the scarring, I'm fairly well put together. I'm not thin and angular like Lilly. Like I said, that's more my father's genetics. I'm built solid, with natural curves in all the right places and an attractive enough face. But despite making a positive first impression, nearly every man before Del had a problem with my scars. Granted, under the harsh light of the lavatory or in broad daylight, they are a wicked sight. But, God's honest truth, Del never once, in all our time together, made my scars an issue. Oh, he asked about them, and I filled him in to a limited extent. The difference was that once I stopped talking, Del didn't pry. Given the levels of intimacy Del and I negotiated for the better part of a year, that's pretty amazing.

"It'll cut the edge off the depression," Del whispered as darkness invaded my head. "Everyone tweaks a little now and then. It's like adjusting a carburetor," Del explained as he handed me a syringe loaded with another hit of meth mixed with bottled water.

"Thanks."

I closed my eyes and waited as my lover tied off a vein and reacquainted me with a world I had only once imagined.

TWO

Idyllic. That's the word that comes to mind when I think about my childhood on Madeline Island. History and magic abound on the little piece of sand, rock and clay rising out of the cool waters of Lake Superior. There must have been a lot of charm to the place on July 4, 1976. That's the date, if you count backwards from April 4, 1977, when Lilith Ann DuMont and I were conceived. Sure, it could've been a day or two on either side of the nation's bicentennial when Mom and Dad got together by deliberate resolve or through sheer carelessness. It doesn't really matter. Lilly and I have always insisted that July 4, 1976 was the day that Dad's seeds found their way to Mom's eggs for the first time.

You're sharp. You caught that I wrote "eggs," plural. You see, Lilly and I didn't happen into this world by having split off from the same ovum. We're the product of a shared uterine experience: fraternal twins, the result of two hard–working sperm fertilizing two tantalizingly available eggs.

Imagine my mother's surprise when, after pushing for three hours without success to deliver me, on the precipice of being wheeled on a shiny gurney into an operating room at Memorial Medical Center in Ashland (the same hospital where my Dad works), I finally popped my velvety black scalp out into the world. The fact I made it out wasn't the shocker. It was my physical appearance that created an element of hubbub. My face, so round, so fat, boasted an endless series of folds, like one of those wrinkle puppies, a face preserved for posterity in the first photograph ever taken of me. That picture shows me freshly sponged, mouth open in a primitive wail, my brown torso bare, the umbilical cord neatly clipped and tied, Dad leaning over Mom, his right arm draped around her shoulder, a big smirk across his face. Why would my appearance cause surprise, you might ask?

Well, my physical appearance must have caused no end of debate, once sister Lilly arrived and comparisons were made.

There's a photograph taken in the birthing room of the two of us in our swaddling blankets, tucked beneath our mother's bosom. The Polaroid showing Mom, her eyes tired from the labor, and Dad, the giddiness of successful procreation clear in his grin, makes such a comparison. I've been tempted to rip that family portrait out of the photo album, leaving only individual pictures of Lilly and me, taken on that day for scrutiny. Of course, my doing so wouldn't preclude comparisons, because the individual photos would still be right there, side by side, on page two of the scrapbook.

She's my sister. I love her dearly. Despite everything, despite all we've endured of each other and with each other, that much will always be true. But damn it, why does Lilith Ann DuMont have to be so physically stunning? To call her beautiful would be to do her a disservice. She's been that way since the moment her head crowned and the slime was wiped away from the evenly gold skin of her little face, revealing high cheekbones, a small nose pointed ever so slightly towards her eyebrows, and fine lips, lips seemingly drawn by God in imitation of a master artist sketching the portrait of someone famous. Like I said, the comparisons began the day we arrived. They've never stopped.

Our parent's house is modest: A robin's egg blue, three–bedroom, Craftsman–style bungalow. The master bedroom is on the main floor, and two smaller bedrooms in a second-story expansion attic, each with a little alcove covered by a gable. Dad put our desks in those alcoves so we could look out our windows while we studied. My desk stayed right where Dad put it. Lilly, well, she moved hers. Lilly preferred arranging her doll collection in front of the window so that she could play in the warmth of the sun on cold winter days.

On the main floor, a small kitchen adjoins a modest dining room, complete with built-in china hutches. Next to the dining room there's a brick fireplace surrounded by Mission–style bookcases with doors that are fully glass, their style identical to that of the china hutches; the fireplace occupies the north wall of the great room, a large atmospheric space boasting oak wainscoting from the top edge of the plaster walls to the peak of the ceiling.

The colors of the rooms are subdued. Mother has never been one to be demonstrative – in her life, in her love, in her decorating.

My parent's house is on the north side of Madeline Island, off the North Road, a tongue of well–worn gravel that provides access to the north shore of the fourteen–mile–long by three–mile–wide Island. Lilly and I walked to elementary school in LaPointe, a hamlet that sits on the leeward shore of the island facing Bayfield, a town located two-and-a-half miles away on the mainland. Every day school was in session, from grades one through five, we made the one–mile trek to and from the small school house in downtown LaPointe, through drifted snow and below–zero temperatures in the winter, around muddy puddles in the spring, beneath a canopy of scarlet and flame in the autumn when the oaks and maples tucked tight against the roadway showed their pre–winter glory. Fifteen to twenty kids made similar walks, rode their bicycles to town, took the island school bus, or had their parents drop them off at school. Why did we walk? Simple. Dad didn't believe in giving us rides, or Lilly and I taking the bus, except on days where we were dolled up for some special event. Besides, Dr. DuMont stayed in an apartment in Ashland during the week, Monday through Wednesday, when he'd come home, make love to Mom (the house was small enough and Lilly and I precocious enough to figure out why he came home), which meant that Lilly and I had to walk to school.

I mentioned the ferry landing. Madeline Island, named after Madeline Cadotte, the daughter of an Ojibwa chief and the wife of a fur trader, sits across the water, as I said, from Bayfield, an old Scandinavian fishing village. During late spring, summer and autumn, when Lake Superior is devoid of ice, ferries supply transportation to and from the island. The square–sterned black–and–white boats, their decks packed tight with trucks and cars, ply the waters between Bayfield and LaPointe every half–hour during the summer and less regularly when the tourist season ends. Once ice forms over the bay in sufficient thickness to allow vehicles to drive on it, an ice road is plowed between Bayfield and LaPointe. But the most interesting crossings, at least the ones I remember with the most fondness, occur when ice is in place but of dubious integrity, which requires travel by wind sled.

I've ridden the wind sleds – flat–bottomed steel prams powered by aircraft engines and propellers – more times than I can remember. Wind sleds differ from the airboats depicted in nature films of southern bayous, where passengers ride exposed to the elements. On a wind sled, you're inside, the passengers huddle together, and the noise of the big engine reverberates inside the thin walls of the metal cabin; your teeth rattle and your bones vibrate like so much brittle glass during the ten–minute trip.

Living on an island, any island, conjures up images of romance and reposeful days of reflection. That might be the case if the island is in the Caribbean, but not necessarily so if the island you're imagining sits in an ice field surrounded by winter nights capable of reaching thirty below zero. True enough, as I've already alluded to, I spent plenty of halcyon days as a kid on the island, during summer's height and during the occasionally pleasant weather of spring and fall. But winter on an island in Lake Superior, now that's an experience that few living in the lower forty-eight can claim familiarity with. You might want to know why my parents chose to live there. Good question. I'll try to give you an insightful answer.

My Mom, Samantha Witta DuMont, was born in Ashland, just a stone's throw across Chequamegon Bay, in 1957. That makes her forty-nine years old. She's what you'd call a Wisconsin native. An original. Her father, Elias Witta, was a logger, a drunk and a roustabout. Grandpa Elias didn't come home much and when he did, during the years my Mom lived at home – an only child kept safe from her father's impetuousness by the shadow of Grandma Mary McShane Witta's prodigious frame– he came home drunk and hell-bent on causing discord, but Grandma Mary didn't allow him the chance to disquiet her nest. She was capable with the business end of a baseball bat and always kept a sawed-off Louisville Slugger within arm's reach. Those few times, early on, when Mom was a toddler tucked behind Grandma's skirt, shivering in fear at the roar and thunder of Grandpa's arrival after an early evening of drink at one of Ashland's numerous watering holes, when Elias Witta tried his hand at dominance in the marital homestead, he lost. Lost in an ugly and bloody way. He lost so often that, by the time Mom was six years old, he stopped coming home. It wasn't that he left Ashland for a warmer place or a better life. He stayed around, renting a room from one of the single women he knew, doing to her what he couldn't do to Grandma. And Grandma Mary was just fine with the stalemate. She never sought a divorce, nor did she try to coax him back. "One man," she told her only child, "is more than enough for a lifetime."

Mom grew up near the ore docks along the eastern edge of Chequamegon Bay, in the shadow of the One True Church: Our Lady of the Lake Roman Catholic Church, Grandma Mary's church. Yes, Grandma was a Catholic. So is Mom. So is Lilly. Dad is a pragmatist – at least that's what he always says when asked about his faith. I don't believe he's ever found comfort in any particular brand of Christianity, though he does attend Mass on occasion.

Anyway, Grandma Mary left her home in Galway on the Atlantic coast of Ireland during World War II. She was a single girl of strong back and quick mind with overriding confidence. She left a girls' school run by nuns at thirteen to work full–time as a waitress in a dining hall and boarding house in downtown Galway. Her decision wasn't the result of some impulsive act; it was a calculated decision that allowed her to continue her studies during the evenings, live at the boarding house free of charge and save her wages for a one–way ticket to America. She spent a brief time in Baltimore, arriving two weeks after her nineteenth birthday. She had completed her secondary schooling by passing an equivalency exam and had enough money in her pocketbook for train fare to Ashland, where her cousin Susan Malone ran a coffee shop.

It was while waitressing in Ashland that Grandma Mary met Elias Witta, a stubborn Finn of few words but enormous physical appeal. Under the social constraints of the times, she was, of course, a virgin when she and Elias became, as they say, "an item." Their courtship, the way Mom describes it, was short, though not necessarily sweet – "sweet" being a notion that Grandpa Elias apparently never learned, right up until the day he laid himself down on the Soo Line tracks running through Ashland in a drunken stupor one cold winter's night in 1969, eight years before I was born. Cut in half, he was, by a locomotive pulling hopper cars full of iron ore mined in nearby northern Michigan. Mom says she mourned her father, though it's hard to figure out why. Grandma Mary apparently was less affected by her lackadaisical husband's leave-taking. If Elias Witta's sudden departure had any impact on Grandma, she never let it show.

Summers at Grandma Mary's house were a joy. Free of the claustrophobic geography of the island, Lilly and I spent most of each July at Grandma Mary's, occupying the walk-up attic in her little bungalow off MacArthur Street, given free rein by our very tolerant Irish grandmother to redecorate the space to our hearts' content. When we were little, Grandma Witta kept close tabs on us, restricting our sojourns to the two or three blocks surrounding her house. But once we started to sprout into womanhood, well, she just sort of cut us loose. After we turned twelve, Lilly and I were free to wander Ashland. Our first place of serious exploration was nearby Northland College. The old red sandstone buildings, the small knots of attractive young men and women, the serious nature of the discussions we heard as we scooted across the green lawn chasing Frisbees or Grandma's black poodle, Magnus, who often escaped from his leash to lead us on long and winding chases over the college grounds – all of these things made me want to be like the kids I saw. Not so with Lilly. She could've cared less about the educational part of the college experience we witnessed. She was more interested in the boys.

By the time we were fourteen, even college boys were taken with Lilly. By then, though I was older by fifteen minutes, Lilith Ann DuMont was nearly fully developed, and I...well, I was lagging behind in significant and troubling ways. At eleven, Lilly had her first period; my monthly waited awhile to make its appearance. Even before her first period, Lilly's little buds had sprouted, the nipples beginning to darken and enlarge, causing Mom to scurry to Duluth to buy an assortment of trainer bras in a variety of weird colors. I, on the other hand, stayed physically immature until the summer between the seventh and eighth grades, when, miracle of miracles, breasts seemed to grow out of nowhere. There was none of the gradual process associated with such development like Lilly had experienced, no slow ripening of childish flesh into a bosom. Instead, it was as if, one night I went to sleep, flat as a proverbial pancake, and the next

16

morning (I'm exaggerating a bit here, I know), there were size 34Cs awaiting discovery. I'll spare you details of the more intimate physiology of my change. Suffice to say, things happened there as well in very short and shocking order. It was as if some sort of alien being took over my body below my waist and replaced the known and comforting with strange, though intriguing, folds of flesh.

Anyway, about those college boys. During summers in Ashland, they were all over Lilly like bees on a flower. Oh, they cast a look or two in my direction as well, especially if I went braless and made sure the shorts I was wearing were skin–tight. I surely could turn a few heads and elicit catcalls and whistles, the boys shouting out things like, "Hey, little girl, how'd you like to get a college education?" or "Does your Momma know where you are?" Lilly didn't have to work to elicit such responses. I had a serviceable face and a nice figure, the kind of package that boys considered attractive, but I had to "close the deal" by revealing a little flesh and walking like I'd just left a fashion runway. My sister didn't need to stoop to such deception; she was, in a word, perfect. Halle Berry perfect. Angela Bassett perfect. Every tooth pristine and as white as snow. Every line of her body arranged in an agonizingly succinct order. She didn't get catcalls. She didn't get comments. She was so striking (and so natively aware of her primeval hold over men), when she walked the sidewalks of Northland College or downtown Ashland under the sweltering July sun, her presence evoked only awestruck silence.

I haven't said anything about Dad's family, the side of things that makes me a black woman. There isn't all that much to tell. Dad is sort of tight–lipped when it comes to his ancestry. In fact, Lilly and I never interacted with our grandparents on Dad's side, even though they were alive when we were born. They were living somewhere in Texas; Corpus Christi, I think. I've been told that Grandpa Emil DuMont was half Irish, half African American, and that Grandma Beulah Majors DuMont was the purebred by–product of former sharecroppers who traced their roots back to Africa. But, like I said, we never met. They died in a car crash three years after Lilly and I were born. The story is that they were killed driving north on I–35, somewhere near Des Moines. They were coming to meet their granddaughters – at least, that's the tale Dad told Lilly and I when we were growing up.

From Mom, I learned that she'd only met the DuMonts once herself, when she and Dad drove to Texas on their honeymoon. Mom had nothing bad to say about Dad's folks, other than they were quiet and relatively unemotional when presented with their new Caucasian daughter-in-law. The way Mom tells it, while the DuMonts were polite and deferential; there was a chill, an unspoken upset that descended over their

17

trailer house in Corpus during the visit. Mom figured it was due to her skin color and, to my knowledge; Dad has never dissuaded her of that belief.

Grandpa Emil DuMont had been a stoker in a steel mill in Gary, Indiana before he and Grandma moved to Minnesota in the 1950s, where Emil found work at another steel mill in Duluth. Dad was just a kid – an only child, like Mom. He was one of only four black children in the factory town neighborhood of Morgan Park. The way Mom tells it, by being black, Dad was expected to excel at athletics. Though coordinated, Dad had little interest in team sports. Mom played high school volleyball and basketball for the Ashland Oredockers. (I take after her, a woman who picked up golf clubs for the first time on her thirtieth birthday and out–drove Dad on the Ashland Municipal course's first tee despite Dad's practiced dedication to the game. Lilly, on the other hand, takes after our father. She's never had much use for competition, unless it's seeing if she could turn a boy's head before I could.) Anyway, the point I'm trying to make is that Dad didn't fit the stereotype of his peers, which, when he first moved to Duluth, caused him some problems with white boys who had hoped he would bolster their football, basketball and baseball teams. According to Mom, Dad had a rough first year of it, getting shoved around by an assortment of bullies and thugs – though once he fought back, doing little damage but at least defending himself, the white kids left him to his studies, which is how he became the only African American from Duluth Morgan Park High School to be accepted into Harvard University and later, into that school's medical program.

All of this information is to help you understand that, despite my physical appearance, it's unlikely that the person I am would meet your expectations. I'm not sure it matters much or that it will help you to understand what happened to me or why I'm the way I am, but I thought you should know.

THREE

I'm a fallen Catholic. Why that's so is something I'll let you in on, somewhere down the line. I have a Biblical name; Lilith and I grew up with Biblical names because our mother, despite looking pure Finn, takes after her Irish side when it comes to matters of the soul. Both my sister and I took First Communion at age eight in Grandma Mary's church, Our Lady of the Lake, in Ashland. That's where we went to Mass as we grew up, despite the fact that St. Louis Catholic Church in Washburn, Holy Family Catholic Church in Bayfield, St. Francis Catholic Church on the nearby Red Cliff Ojibwa Reservation, and St. Joseph's in LaPointe are all a lot closer. We rarely missed a Saturday night Mass, driving into town for a light supper at Grandma's and then walking to the church whatever the weather, whatever the season, together. I say "together" with this express omission: Dad rarely attended Mass.

Dr. DuMont makes a dedicated effort twice a year to attend church: Christmas Eve Mass and Easter Mass. He was raised African Methodist Episcopal but, somewhere along the line, his faith faltered. It wasn't as if Dad tried to infect us with skepticism. He let Mom have her way: she was given charge over family matters, including religion, and so that when, on Christmas Day 1992, Mom announced that she was going to have another baby and that arrangements for the christening had already been made, Dad diplomatically remained mute.

"So what do you think, Esther?"

Lilly and I were sitting up in her room, with Lil lying across the soft fabric of her down comforter and me sitting on the floor, my back propped against the maple footboard of her bed, watching a video. It was the newly released *Dances with Wolves*. Renting videos on the island back then was a pain. A few places rented videos in LaPointe in 1992, but the pickings were generally slim and the selection Puritan. *Dances with Wolves* wasn't my first choice of a "must see" film. It was simply the best I could do.

"About what?" I replied as Kevin Costner's commanding officer put a gun to his head and blew his brains out.

"About Mom being pregnant."

"It's all right, I guess."

Lilly paused. She was on her back, her head hanging over the edge of the bed and just a few inches from mine; her silky black hair, the fibers completely devoid of the kinks that make my own hair such a bitch, dangled loose, and her eyes were riveted on the flickering image on the screen.

"I was sort of blown away."

"Why?"

It was weird to watch a smile form on Lilly's upside down face in the reflection on the vanity mirror across the room.

"I hadn't heard any evidence that they were getting on like that anymore." She giggled and tossed her hair across my mouth and eyes. I brushed the offending mane away and turned to look at her.

"That's gross. Why do you say things like that?"

"Like what?"

"Like...you know."

Her hand reached across the comforter and tweaked my ear.

"Like you've never thought about our parents and what goes on when they say their 'good nights' right after the news."

I tried to concentrate on the movie. Lilly would have none of it.

"Do you think Mom has orgasms?"

My cheeks puffed as I tried not to answer.

"Do ya?" she insisted, poking my face with a finger.

"It's not something I dwell on," I muttered. "Frankly, I don't think it's any of our business."

"Miss Goodie Two Shoes doesn't wonder about whether our father is able to make it right by our mother? I don't believe a word of it."

Silence imposed itself while Lilly's mind conjured up the next unspeakable absurdity.

"Do you think they do oral?"

That one got me. I balled my hand into a fist and punched Lilith as hard as I could on the left shoulder. Given her build, there wasn't much bicep to cushion the blow.

"Hey," Lilly squealed, "that hurt!"

"It was meant to. Now shut up and watch the movie."

David Carver DuMont was born on May 25, 1993. Mom managed to conceal her condition from all of us, including Dad, for the better part of four months before her Christmas revelation. From the beginning, David

20

(we never called him Dave or Davie) was a source of controversy around the house. Mom wanted to name him Frederick Douglas DuMont, after the great African American abolitionist. Dad would have none of it.

"Sam," my Dad said with his bedside voice, the tone conveying seriousness, "we live in a white world, surrounded by the most Caucasian people on earth. I won't have my son carrying the burden of hundreds of years of slavery, poverty and cultural decay as his legacy, just because you want to name him after a black hero out of some misplaced sense of guilt."

Cultural decay. Dad liked that term. In his view of things, Black America, having become urbanized after its flight north following the Civil War, had devolved into a confused mass of humanity in search of heaven on earth. They'd never found it, at least not as a race, in the ghettos and slums of the cities. The advent of hip hop, drug culture, the reliance on sports as the young black man's Holy Grail, and the emergence of the ugly language of the streets convinced my father that many African Americans believed their race couldn't compete on an even keel with White America. He was thoroughly convinced that his people were abdicating morality and economic effort for sloth and the easy way. This thesis, if that's what you want to call it, was something he believed with near–religious fervor. It wasn't an opinion he bandied about at the hospital, on the golf course or at dinner with his Caucasian friends. Lilly and I rarely heard such talk from our father, but when Dad's opinions on race boiled to the surface, he had little difficulty expressing them.

Of course, you might expect that Mom, being white, would be taken aback by such oratory thunder. She wasn't. She was unusual that way, and different from most white folks I've met. She carried, at least to the casual observer, no trace of guilt for being in the majority. It wasn't in her nature to demarcate people by race. As a consequence, she didn't yield easily on the issue of David's name.

"Orville," she responded, her voice calm and her words concise (or maybe the word is "precise"), "you're being far too sensitive. I just thought that it would be nice for our son to walk the streets of wherever it is he ends up, his head held high before whomever he encounters, knowing that his name means something."

Of course, my brother was given a name that meant something. David, the King of the Jews. And Carver, as in George Washington Carver. The compromise was that "Carver" denoted a man of science; Dad could live with having a man of learning as a role model for his son.

Biblical names, as you can tell, are a big thing with Mom – which might strike you as odd, since kids raised like Mom, kids who went to Catholic school, don't receive their religious training with the Bible as a foundation. According to Mom, her religion classes were founded upon the specific doctrines of Catholicism, not the broad-based themes of

21

Christianity established in the Bible. But Mom's education in this respect was different from that of other Catholic kids. Grandma Mary was a reader and the book she read more than any other was the Holy Bible. Grandma's reliance upon the Word, and not upon some priest's extrapolation of the Word, set Grandma and my mother apart in their religion.

It's easy to see how this heritage played itself out in the naming of my sister and me. Lilith drew her name from one of the most cryptic myths of the Jewish faith, the supposed existence of a woman linked to Adam before the creation of Eve. Lilith, at least in legend, wasn't the most compliant of companions for Adam: she refused to copulate with him, and in fact, ran off when he approached her with amorous intent. As the story goes, God sent angels to retrieve Lilith. The heavenly host caught the reluctant girl and returned her to Adam, whereupon she ran off again. The funny thing is, my sister never really measured up to her namesake in terms of deviousness or aversion to subservience. In fact, as I think about it, Lilly is the most un-Lilith (if that's a word) woman I've ever met. About the only way Lilly seems to coalesce with the Lilith of mythology is that both, in the end, were treated like royalty.

My name is also derived from the Old Testament. Why Mom thought I'd end up being heroic and gave me the name of Esther – the Jewish Queen of Persia, helpmate and concubine of King Xerxes and rescuer of the Jewish people – I've never been able to figure out. Based on physical appearance alone, Lilly would have been a better choice to play the part of Esther. And, given what would later transpire, I would have made a far better choice to play Lilith, mother of demons.

FOUR

Moose had a plan to make us all rich. Not that money was something I really cared about. But Del, well, he'd been born poor and lived his whole life hand–to–mouth, a white kid from the projects who grew up surrounded by blacks. Del had stayed out of serious trouble his whole life, using his natural wit and his engaging smile to disarm folks, even those bent on doing him injury. Why Del hooked up with Moose to cook meth is pretty simple: money. Why I agreed to steal cold tablets for the pseudoephedrine they contain, the main ingredient needed to cook methamphetamine, is beyond me. I'd never even stolen so much as a pack of chewing gum before Del introduced me to crank. Not that I'm trying to play up my innocence, mind you – just telling the truth.

Del came from a family of eight kids raised by his mother Pearl, a woman who could count three Confederate generals and an assortment of Revolutionary patriots in her family tree back in Savannah, Georgia, where her father had been a judge. Pearl, who died of cirrhosis of the liver shortly after Del and I met, had long ago lost any resemblance to her jewel–like name. She was unattractive and cruel, and generally left her three boys and five daughters to fend for themselves while she entertained men. Despite an absence of consistent, gentle love from a parent, for the most part, Del and his siblings grew up straight. Only Jared, Del's eldest brother, ended up in prison. But Jared's failings didn't detour his younger brother. Once Del graduated from St. Paul Central High School and became a union carpenter, Del left home and never looked back.

Nathanial (Moose) Thompson was Del's best friend from their mutual comeuppance on University Avenue. They met on a basketball court where Moose, a fat ninth grader of ascending height (he was six–foot–six and still growing back then) and Del, a skinny five–foot–ten point guard in training, knocked heads over a loose ball at the University YMCA. After the two of them squared off, tossed a few errant punches and drew the wrath of Alvin Johnson, the YMCA's recreational basketball coordinator, a friendship formed between the boys. Actually, it was more like love, though I'm sure that neither of them, testosterone–driven as they were, ever used that term to describe their bond.

I was working at the University Hospital as a registered nurse in the neonatal unit when Moose, who hadn't had a decent job since he flunked out of Augsburg College, came up with his scheme. After crashing and burning in college, Moose found a place to live in the Cedar–Riverside neighborhood of Minneapolis. Moose was still living there when he and Del decided to cook methamphetamine. Like I said, we're not dealing with criminal masterminds here – just two guys down on their luck who needed something to keep the lights on and their bellies full while waiting for better opportunities to come along. Plus, the added bonus of being able to make your own drugs had a certain economic advantage over spending money on poorly constituted Mexican crank, stuff that barely touched the edges, much less peeled back the layers, like good old Minnesota home–cooked methamphetamine does.

"I've watched Carlos Rivera make the stuff plenty of times," Moose had said as he, Del and I sat in the backyard of a ramshackle duplex where Moose occupied the upper apartment. The duplex was located just a few blocks away from Sergeant Preston's, a well–known pick–up joint situated at the intersection of Cedar and University, near the West Bank Campus of the University of Minnesota.

We were sipping cold bottles of St. Pauli Girl, a treat I'd picked up and brought back to Moose's place. Our legs were stretched out and rested on a battered old wooden cable wheel, the oak planks weathered and beginning to warp; the sun was high but sliding to the west as a precursor to evening. My shift that day at the hospital had been an absolute bitch. We'd lost two babies, neither one weighing more than two pounds. There wasn't a doctor to be found to tell the two sets of parents what had happened, so it fell upon me, as the charge nurse, to break the news. The wailing and weeping was more than I could take. I'd have done a hit of meth the instant I walked into Moose's place if he'd had any to score, but he didn't and I certainly couldn't afford to buy meth somewhere else. I was down to my last fifty bucks. Del was totally broke. The union hadn't called Del back to work, even though there were signs of building, the clanging of steel on steel, the singing of cables and the steady drone of air compressors all over the Twin Cities. Whether it was Del's inability to show up for work on time or the fact that, when he was there, he was usually half-stoned, I'm not sure. The union just stopped calling.

"It's too damn dangerous," Del mused over Moose's plan, his mouth poised provocatively over the opening in the beer bottle, sweat beading on his pasty skin, his eyes closed against the bright sun. "This neighborhood's crawling with cops."

I didn't think Moose was serious. Moose was as kind a man as I'd ever met, not the sort of guy who'd fare well in the rough–and–tumble world of illicit drugs. I glanced at Moose's big face, the folds of black skin cascading down the back of his neck like an ebony bellows, and I knew in an instant that Moose wasn't joking.

"You're crazy," I said, point–blank.

If the two of them were crazy, I was insane. I had a college degree. A good job. The likelihood of promotion and, if I obtained a master's degree, perhaps the chance of becoming head nurse on the floor – or, better yet, of securing a position in hospital administration. How they ever turned me, and got me to steal Sudafed, the critical ingredient for cooking meth, I don't understand. I had everything to lose and nothing to gain.

It took Moose a couple of tries to get the formula right, but once he put it all together, the stuff he cooked up in the kitchen of his upstairs apartment kicked ass. The smell, of course, was atrocious. Del rigged up an exhaust system in Moose's kitchen to vent the fumes, but it didn't do much good. Stepping across the threshold into Moose Thompson's apartment was like walking through a chemical plant's smoke plume. When they cooked meth, the boys wore second–hand breathing apparatus they bought at a surplus store. There was little doubt in my mind that Moose's neighbors suspected something. It was only a matter of time before the Minneapolis cops would be called in to investigate the stench emanating from the duplex.

Moose was good at scrounging ingredients for his concoction: the lighter fluid, the drain cleaner, the lithium batteries. Del was the lookout, the distributor, the salesman and the go–fer, doing all that needed to be done to get the product to market and collect the cash. After a few weeks, Del managed to put two thousand dollars of pure profit into his checking account. Things were looking up for Delmont and me – at least if you discounted the edginess, fear and constant reliance upon meth in our personal lives to even out the rough spots and make things appear solid and manageable. Nothing could have been further from the truth; our world was, in fact, tilting dangerously out of balance.

I learned early on not to try buying the essential ingredient for cooking meth. With publicity about the drug at an all–time high, every pimple–faced clerk in every retail outlet was on high alert for folks trying to buy cold medicine in large quantities.

"I'm sorry, ma'am," a young man behind the counter at Walgreen's said during my first stab at obtaining Sudafed. "Our store policy limits you to two boxes."

"My fiancé has been fighting a terrible sinus cold for weeks," I implored, fixing my dark features into the best pout I could manage. "He can't even get out of the house to go to work. I'm a nurse. I know why you need to limit these things, sweetheart, what folks might do with them. But I can assure you, I'm just stocking up so I don't have to keep coming back," I said, my hands resting uneasily on the ten boxes of cold tablets I'd selected, my eyes batting coyly like a little school girl with a crush.

"You seem like a nice lady. And I believe you. But if I sell you these, it's my job. Two's the limit. Sorry."

I'd stormed away, humiliated and angry, but I'd acquired a clear understanding that I could not buy what we needed. I didn't formulate a plan to steal Sudafed that day. In fact, I came back to Moose's duplex empty–handed. The boys were disappointed, but they concealed any anger they might have had. Neither of them was made that way. When we ran out of meth later that week and the three of us, along with Moose's girlfriend, Angela Brown – a beet–faced white girl possessing buckteeth but wonderful boobs – wanted to get high, desperation finally compelled me to throw caution to the wind. I started pilfering cold medicine, so that Moose could work his magic.

I had no experience in shoplifting and knew that my race, despite my impeccable dress and the poise I carried as a seemingly responsible nurse, would likely target me for scrutiny. So I stuck to stores where blacks routinely shop. Always dressed to the nines, my gnarly hair brushed and tamed, my demeanor professional, I found it easy to slip boxes of cold medicine into my purse using other folks and the physical layout of the store to obstruct my thievery. At the slightest hint of security personnel, I'd walk away from the pharmacy section, slipping the purloined goods back onto any shelf that was handy, before leaving the store. Despite my heart racing, palms sweating and mind being assaulted with thoughts about the wrongness of my actions – with good old–fashioned Catholic guilt nearly overcoming my desire to feel the velvety excitement of a meth rush – I remained, at least to those watching my antics, a black woman of means who seemed hesitant as to what she wanted to buy.

Things were fine for a while. Despite my increased reliance on meth to keep myself on an even keel, no one at work seemed to suspect a thing. I became adept at using meth, having switched from injecting my fix to smoking it in a little glass one-hitter I kept between the front bucket seats of my recently paid-off Volkswagen Jetta. I kept my crank inside my purse in an old compact. I'm quite certain that no one at the University of Minnesota Hospital had a clue that the nurse in charge of the neonatal care unit during the night shift was a dope fiend. Sure, I missed a day or two of work here or there because of my habit. I even showed up late a few times.

But no one in authority at the hospital questioned my work ethic or my sobriety.

Things finally went south one afternoon. I was filling in for a nurse from Roseville whose little girl had the flu. Though I didn't normally work the day shift, the woman called in such a panic that I couldn't say no. It was that Saturday afternoon in September when Moose and Del were blown to bits.

FIVE

Billy Cadotte. Now there's a name from the past. Sitting in a holding cell, waiting for my arraignment on charges of Possession of Methamphetamine in the Fifth Degree, a low–level felony, other female prisoners asleep or bored out of their minds, there was no conversation, no camaraderie present. Our hair was disheveled, our faces puffy from tears and recriminations and demonstrative outbursts that we'd been wronged or that we'd really screwed up. All of us looked desperate in our jumpsuits, handcuffs and shackles. With this surreal spectacle going on, it was funny that my mind latched onto Billy's face as a savior.

I wonder why I didn't select Jesus instead. Maybe it was because, despite all my education in the One True Church, all the Masses I'd sat through and all the rosary beads I'd watched my mother and grandmother slide through their fingers, the things that had happened to me to that point made my belief marginal, a fragile sort of faith that didn't hold up well against adversity. But Billy Cadotte. Now *there* was an image I could latch onto.

I learned somewhere – likely from some long-forgotten book I scoured during solitary hours after my accident – that the place where Billy and I come from is very old. The landform beneath Lake Superior emerged billions of years ago. After the last of the glaciers slid across North America – thus scouring the ground, exposing the granite foundation of the Canadian Shield along Lake Superior's North Shore, smoothing out the sandstone of the South Shore into low hills and long beaches and depositing Canadian topsoil in southern Wisconsin as hills and eskers – there remained behind a woodland dotted with rivers, ponds and lakes, with the most prominent of the lakes being Lake Superior.

Even before the French and English began their exploration of Chequamegon Bay, a migration of the Ojibwa people –a journey necessitated by the harassment of the Ojibwa by the Fox and Sioux– brought the Ojibwa to Chequamegon Point, where the present-day village of Bayfield sits. After repeated attacks by their enemies, the Ojibwa sought safety on the largest of what would later come to be known as the Apostle Islands. Nearly twenty thousand Ojibwa occupied Madeline Island and the surrounding coast of the mainland until the early 17th century, when the Ojibwa moved north to the St. Mary's River. In time, the Ojibwa drifted back to Chequamegon Bay and lived peacefully alongside French, English and American fur traders. The French named the largest island in the Apostles after the daughter of an Ojibwa chief. The girl, Equaysaway, was also known by her Christian name, Madeline. Madeline married Michael Cadotte, a French fur trader, and the island where Michael Cadotte and his wife built their home came to be called Madeline Island. The French settlement on that island became the village of LaPointe, the place where I grew up – the place I call home.

Billy and I first met as teenagers at Bayfield Middle School. It was around that time, when I was twelve or so, that something strange happened: I discovered I was different. Oh, before I met Billy, I'd had inclinations that my ethnicity somehow set me apart from my friends – you know, the off– hand remark, the not–so–subtle racial slur generally whispered or said under the breath. But for some reason, like the other unsettling notion that hits kids around that age – you know, the sudden realization that you're mortal – I suddenly figured out that I was black. Funny, huh? You'd expect a smart black girl growing up surrounded by Scandinavians would have seen the discrepancy sooner. Well, I hadn't. I can't tell you when a similar thunderbolt struck my sister, though I'm certain it did. This realization lead me to seek out kids in similar circumstances – you know, kids designated, by virtue of their skin color, as belonging to some tribe "other" than the Norwegians, Swedes and Finns surrounding us. Opportunities for Lilly and I to connect with black children were absent, so I'm sure that's why we hung out with Native kids like Billy. There was a sense that they, like us, belonged to "the Other."

My first six years of schooling were, as mentioned, completed at LaPointe Elementary. In the September of our seventh year in school, Lilith and I began taking the Madeline Island Ferry to Bayfield every morning before eight. We also made the return trip every afternoon before four, except on those days when Lil had voice or dance lessons or I had basketball practice.

I won't lie: there's a certain romance in traveling to school by water. That enchantment evaporates when you're forced to walk from the ferry landing in downtown Bayfield to a school perched six blocks away on the side of a mountain. That's an exaggeration; there are no mountains in Wisconsin. Anyway, that damn *hill*, well, I'll never forget battling its steepness against blizzards in the winter or scrambling against its incline to take shelter from pulverizing spring rain.

Billy and I sat next to each other through all of sixth grade, and we became fast friends. He was a member of the Red Cliff Reservation located just north of town on Highway 13. He also had a "smidgen" of African American ancestry in which Billy took renewed pride, once he discovered me, the sort of human being not generally seen around Chequamegon Bay. He traced his African ethnicity to George Bonga, a *voyageur* whose roots were said to be the culmination of love between escaped slave Pierre Bonga and his Ojibwa wife. The Bonga lineage is linked to the Leech Lake area of Minnesota, where a large reservation of Ojibwa still remains. Billy's mother, Rose Bonga, met Billy's father, Emmett Cadotte, at a powwow in Grand Portage, Minnesota. Billy and his sister Margaret are the results of Rose and Emmett Cadotte's marriage.

Anyway, Billy and I became inseparable. There was an undefined (and likely unknowable, at age twelve) ethnic link between us that transcended Billy's awkwardness around girls. Though he didn't look black – on account of his sharp nose, hard–lined face and impenetrable brown eyes – there was a hint of our complimentary heritage in the spiraling texture of Billy's black hair. It may have been this primitive connection or our mutual ability to shoot the three-pointer that brought us together. To this day, I'm not sure which it was.

SIX

I hadn't known that the duplex was gone until my Jetta rounded the corner. Fire trucks and an ambulance blocked the street leading to the house and two police cars formed a barricade on Cedar. A female cop and her male partner were diverting cars into an alley. Firefighters dragged heavy hoses towards the duplex and the surrounding homes, all of which had suffered damage when Moose's meth lab exploded. I was in shock. I wasn't thinking straight. When the female officer approached the driver's–side window of my car, it never dawned on me what I was in for.

"Ma'am, you'll need to move along. Follow the detour into the alley," the female cop said in a firm yet polite voice. She was an attractive woman, totally Minnesota Scandinavian with her blond hair held tight against the back of her neck in a short ponytail. She was tanned, healthy and about my age. Her sky–blue eyes scrutinized the interior of my car.

"What happened?" I asked in a halting voice, trying to hide the reality of what I knew, and of what had likely taken place.

"Meth lab. Now, you really do need to move along."

For some reason, I didn't follow her instructions. It wasn't like I wanted to deliberately ignore authority; that has never been my style. I was slow to react, due to the grief welling inside me. My upset was caused by the realization that Del was, at the very least, severely injured, or more likely, dead, given the widespread destruction I now saw: the entire second floor of the duplex was open to the sky; the roof had been turned to splinters by the force of chemicals igniting; shingles, boards, papers, personal effects and garbage were scattered across the neighborhood. I didn't move. I didn't acknowledge the woman any further. I slumped in the driver's seat and began to cry.

"What's wrong, ma'am?"

31

The officer's badge indicated that her surname was "Holmquist." I remained mute. Tears rolled down my cheeks. The tone of the cop's inquiry shifted when she noticed the pipe.

"Step out of the car. Keep your hands where I can see them."

"What?"

"Step out of the car. Now!"

Officer Holmquist placed her torso against the rear of the driver's side of the car and requested back–up over the radio hanging from her shoulder. A burly male cop scurried across the hot pavement, his body shrouded in slowly–rolling smoke, until he was positioned to assist with my arrest. There's not much else to say. The officers found my stash in my purse and a bag of stolen Sudafed under the front passenger's seat. They pretty much deduced from this and my uncontrolled tears that I knew the victims. I admitted as much, which caused the cops' attitudes to soften a bit.

The officers had me identify Del and Moose as their bodies laid on gurneys, their singed faces lifeless and uncovered. That was horrific. Given what I'd already been through in my own life, with the burns and all, it was all Officer Holmquist could do to hold me up as I whispered the men's given names. I have to say that the officer, despite catching me red–handed, was truly fair and reasonable. When she asked me how I knew the dead men, and I explained that Del and I lived together, she allowed me some time to say goodbye. I didn't know it then, but it would be the last time I'd ever see Delmont Benson.

It's funny how the human heart works, how it searches and digs, in the face of horror and tragedy, for something to grasp onto that contains virtue and goodness. Billy Cadotte's face popped into my mind as I sat on a bench in the Hennepin County Government Center holding cell awaiting my first court appearance on the drug possession charge, sharing the cell with Wendy Newstrom, a neophyte prostitute, cocaine addict and overweight nineteen-year-old college kid who somehow thought that turning tricks wouldn't be that big a deal and would be the ticket to scoring more drugs. Thinking about Billy, it was as if someone had turned the pages of a scrap book to the photograph of a long–forgotten acquaintance. The truth was that, before that moment, I hadn't thought much about Billy Cadotte over the intervening years. Last I knew, when I'd been home for Christmas the year before Del died, Billy was still married to April Swanson, his high school sweetheart. They'd taken up seeing each other at the beginning of our senior year. April was a sweet, ordinary and somewhat quiet girl. A fine singer and even better piano player, April was as clumsy a girl as I've ever met, but she was caring to a fault and as nonjudgmental as they come. When it happened, the connection between them was mysterious, and something

I'd never anticipated. And given what Billy and I once had, it hurt something terrible.

A summer in the Apostle Islands isn't easily duplicated. The summer between my junior and senior years in high school, when Billy and I finally got together and advanced our relationship beyond friendship, was nearly perfect. There were few, if any, rainy days, and the sun warmed the shallow waters around the myriad beaches surrounding the unpopulated islands of the Apostles. Billy and I avoided the hordes of "pack sackers," our derogatory term for tourists, by staying clear of Madeline Island. Billy, a frequent hand on his father's wooden fishing trawler, *Bloom O' the Rose* (the boat was named after Billy's mother), had access to transportation whenever he wanted. There was no need for us to buck the crowds on the Big Island: we had an entire archipelago at our beck and call.

We spent time together – sometimes with friends, sometimes alone – just exploring. Basswood. Hermit. Outer. Bear. We visited all twenty–two Apostle Islands that summer, some more than once. Despite Billy's job as a night clerk at a convenience store in Washburn and the time he spent pulling nets for his Dad, and my job as a hostess at the Rittenhouse (an imperious Victorian restaurant and lodging house perched above Bayfield on Rittenhouse Avenue), we found ample time to traverse the jeweled waters surrounding the Apostles. My skin was not yet damaged. I had not yet experienced tragedy. It had been, in every aspect, until Labor Day of that year, a perfect summer.

Being close to someone, when the other person is of the opposite sex and you're both seventeen years old, usually leads to intimacy. At least, that's been my limited experience. Add to this mixture the hot sun, isolated beaches, bottles of apple and raspberry wine purloined from the stock Billy's folks put up every year to sell during Bayfield's Apple Festival celebration, and teenaged bodies clad in the strategically–placed strips of colorful cloth that pass for bathing suits, and the results are fairly predictable.

When we smoothed my Mom's old Hudson Bay blanket on the sand bar along the southwest tip of Oak Island, the *Rose* was safely anchored in shallow water, and waves were lapping at the boat's smooth oak hull. The *Rose's* white paint shone new and brilliantly reflective, and the red letters of her name were stark upon the stern. We talked and sipped wine straight from the bottle. We were wearing our bathing suits: mine, a little yellow one piece, the leg openings cut high up the thigh, accenting my broad hips; Billy's, a funky pair of red shorts, a drawstring hanging from the front, the cut identical to a pair of men's boxers, revealing Billy's hairless but muscular legs. I was on my belly, the straps of my suit falling from my shoulders; I rested the weight of my upper body on my left arm as I sipped wine, while the sun blazed overhead and the gulls circled the fishing boat in expectation of a free meal, their lazy glides set against a high sky of flawless blue. Billy was on his back, his eyes shut and his Ray Bans resting on the bridge of his wickedly angular nose. Little beads of sweat suspended below his hairline, unable to descend due to the tilt of his head. Perspiration formed inside my suit and clung to my chest, my naval and my belly. It was the day we had chosen to escape childhood; we had decided to discover whether "doing it" – a term we'd heard bandied about in the boys' and girls' showers at school – was all it was touted to be.

"Well," I finally said, my head slightly fuzzy from wine, my eyes looking at Billy over the frames of my department store sunglasses.

"That's a deep subject."

"Old joke. And not very funny."

I tossed the empty wine bottle. It landed next to Billy with a soft thud. He turned his head but didn't lower his glasses to meet my eyes with his.

"What are you thinking?"

"That you need to take off those sunglasses so I can see your pretty brown eyes."

I shifted my body until my face was hovering above his.

"Kind of forward for a good girl, aren't you?"

His right hand slipped between us as he removed his eyewear. His fingers wrapped slowly around the rims of my own sunglasses before removing them and setting them on the wool blanket next to his.

"You have the greatest mouth."

He rolled me onto my back and placed his body on top of mine. He was already erect. (Things work fast at seventeen.) We kissed. He fumbled with the stretchy fabric of my swimming suit before exposing my breasts to the warm air and the gulls. His hands and mouth moved quickly. My natural resistance melted. Then, with my suit unceremoniously dangling from one foot and sand gritty against my bare bottom, Billy removed his suit, pressed his body against my pelvis, slid inside of me, and began doing what I wanted him to do.

Sitting in the holding cell, the memory of that afternoon floated over me like a kind and comforting quilt. Having been with Billy later, on other occasions, and armed with the memory of making love to Del, I knew that there was nothing special about the physicality Billy and I shared that first time. But there is no comparing the emotional component of that first step into adulthood with anything else I've experienced. The sun, a boy's body, sea birds, waves: symbols of something mysterious and untamed, something you experience only once, and then, with the advance of understanding and responsibilities, you can't experience again.

34

I exhaled. The image vanished. I sat on the edge of the bench, facing the concrete wall of the holding cell. I fiddled with the ends of my untamed hair and wondered what Billy Cadotte was doing and what sort of life he and April had crafted for themselves, as I tried to restrain my grief.

SEVEN

Mom wasn't advocating promiscuity when she put both Lilly and I on the pill. She'd watched with nervous anticipation, I suppose, as the two of us matured, and as boys began to show interest by calling the house or taking the ferry from the mainland to Madeline Island for a chance to hang with the DuMont girls. She wasn't some "loosey goosey with the morals" parent; she was simply being diligent. Her staid and calm self naturally gravitated to providing us with the means to avoid pregnancy, despite the Catholic Church's theological position on the matter.

"This doesn't mean I expect you to tramp around like a pair of harlots."

In the summer between our junior and senior years of high school, Mom drove Lilly and me to Ashland for an appointment with her OB–GYN. It was my first visit to a gynecologist. I wasn't particularly fond of the stirrups and the cold hands. Lilly never mentioned what she thought of the experience. Why Mom had us dressed as if we were going to the prom, I'll never understand, especially since Mom knew that a strange man was about to stick his fingers into our nether regions. But we were. And he did. And we got through it.

My sister and I understood, I think – in some vague and girlish fashion – what having sex meant in the broader scheme of life. Lilly had been quick to confide in me after the Snow Ball in February, a dance she went to with Ben Stevens (a guy she'd had a crush on since she saw him slip off his football helmet after the Ashland Oredockers trounced the Bayfield Trollers on a chilly October evening at the Oredockers' home field), how she'd lost her virginity in the back seat of the quarterback's Ford Taurus. Lilith was a cheerleader; she had a great time shaking it for the crowd, and smiling like a mind-controlled beauty queen. (There I go again –

I can't seem to stop thinking of my sister in terms of royalty.) Anyway, word got out to Ben (whose biggest attribute on the football field, a quick release, turned out to be a less–than–stellar quality during intercourse) that Lilly was interested. They hooked up, did it, and that was pretty much the end of my sister's interest in the guy. Don't get the wrong idea. Lilly isn't fast or easy – not in the least. She's always been discriminating in her approach to men, but she figured – or so she related later that evening, after Ben dropped her off at the ferry landing and she caught the late boat home – that it was just time. It didn't really matter who it was that provided her with the key. She was determined to unlock that mystery and see what she'd been missing. It turned out that, at least with Ben Stevens, Lilly didn't uncover any secrets of life.

Of course, in a school the size of Bayfield's, the story of Lilly and Ben got around. Maybe it reached the ears of our mother as she worked at Gruenke's Restaurant in downtown Bayfield. Maybe not. Maybe Mom just figured that putting us on the pill was a natural step. In any event, there wasn't a lot of fanfare or lecturing that went with our trip to Dr. Evans's office.

"You girls understand that the pill doesn't protect you from venereal diseases?"

Lilly and I looked at each other as Mom negotiated the sharp curve on Highway 13, near the fish hatchery just south of Bayfield. Instinctively, we drew our hands to our faces to suppress the urge to snicker.

"I can see you two."

Mom's pewter eyes were riveted on our reflections in the rear–view mirror of the Saab.

"VD is not something to laugh about. You think the people who have AIDS are laughing now?"

Lilly and I struggled to contain our mirth. Our bodies convulsed – even though, beyond the last–minute timing of Mom's lecture on the drive home, there wasn't anything particularly amusing about what she was saying.

"I'm *serious*."

"Yes, ma'am," Lilly managed to say, struggling to contain herself by holding her face in her hands as she replied.

"We understand," I added, holding my gut to suppress laughter.

"You think having sex is all fun and games? There's responsibility that comes with such serious affairs."

The word "affairs" caused Lilly and I to burst into guffaws. We didn't stop laughing until Mom eased the Saab onto the loading ramp of the *Island Queen* and we were on our way across the water.

Labor Day, 1994. Billy navigated the *Rose* away from the Bayfield fishing dock, bringing Kevin Delmore, Jimmy Blackthorn, Katie Davis and my best friend, Amy Olson, across the channel for a barbeque at my parent's house. Mom and Dad were golfing at the Madeline Island Golf Course with three other couples; the women were in one foursome, and the men in another. Lilly and I were left in charge of our brother David, who was a handful.

Smoke from the stubborn charcoal in the Weber grill curled into the gray sky. It was the last weekend of summer vacation, and the sun was not cooperating. A chill blew in over Chequamegon Bay and stalled between the Apostle Islands and the South Shore. I was wearing a lined polyester shell over my swimming suit and tennis shoes on my feet as I scurried from the kitchen and out the back door, onto the deck. I was trying to make sure the grill stayed lit in the breeze. Lilly lounged around, offering scant assistance as I prepared chicken for the grill, put a potato dish in the oven and tossed a spinach salad. Our guests threw a Frisbee around the backyard. The *Rose* bobbed at anchor, just off the end of our dock. Mom and Dad had taken the *Samantha*, Dad's antique Chris Craft runabout and pride and joy, to LaPointe; they were planning on heading to Bayfield for dinner after golf. We had the place to ourselves and Billy had brought beer.

David trundled back and forth between kids playing Frisbee, his disposable diaper sagging, loaded and waiting attention.

"Can't you smell him?" Amy asked as I poured lighter fluid on the coals.

"Lil, can you take care of David?"

"In a minute," my sister responded, absent–mindedly twirling a strand of hair as she sat, her bare legs akimbo, in a lounge chair on the brick patio, a few steps away from the sliding door that led into the kitchen. "I'm talking to Jennifer."

Jennifer Wheaton was the only daughter of the richest family on Madeline Island. Her father and mother were divorced; both parents had remarried but continued to make LaPointe their summer home. The former Mrs. Wheaton occupied the elegant old log lodge that had been built by her father, millionaire Ernest Meeks, with her new spouse. Mr. Wheaton resided in a new Cape Cod that he'd built to accommodate his twenty-seven–year–old second wife. Jennifer was a snob; I never understood Lilly's connection with the girl. But then, I've never been as impressed with status as my sister.

"Get off the phone and do it *now*, please."

David's hands were wrapped around my ankles in a vice–like grip.

"Poo poo."

David's curly hair tossed in the wind, his Finn heritage clear in his sharp jaw and high cheekbones, as he tugged on me to gain my attention.

"Lilly will change you."

"Etter do," he cooed, missing the "s" in my name as he always did.

"Lil, take care of your brother." I placed David in front of Lilly. "I'm trying to get the food on."

"Gotta go, Jen. Diaper duty calls."

Lilly swept David into her arms and marched past me with an air of annoyance.

"Damn thing won't light," I muttered.

Billy walked across the lawn, stopped next to the Weber, and studied the coals. He brought a bottle of Leininkuegel's to his lips. I watched his Adam's apple expand and contract as he swallowed. I was truly, deeply and madly in love with Billy, and he knew it.

"Use gasoline. Use a small paper cup. Fill it up just an inch or so, and then toss it on."

A shiver interrupted my thoughts.

I'd witnessed my Dad's attempt to light a brush pile once when I was little. He'd created an enormous heap of old lumber, downed trees and brush in the center of our backyard one November day before the first snow. I don't remember all the details, but I do remember Dad grabbing me gently but firmly by my arm and escorting me off the lawn and onto the patio where Mom held onto me.

"You sure that's safe – I mean, the gas and all?" my Mom had asked.

"Samantha, I'm not going to stand next to the pile and light it," he said, exasperated. "I don't have a desire to have my hair and eyebrows singed. I'll stand back and toss a lit rag towards the pile."

For someone who had to take a lot of chemistry classes on his way to becoming a doctor, my Dad wasn't very practical in his application of science to everyday life. He'd poured two gallons of gasoline around the perimeter of the woodpile, far more than needed, though he'd been cautious enough to avoid splashing fuel on his clothing. Dad at least knew enough about gasoline to avoid becoming a human torch. But he'd seriously miscalculated what would happen when the lit rag he was holding was tossed in the direction of the pyre.

"Stand back."

Dad alerted Mom and me. Lilly was in the house watching a video. Too bad. She missed an impressive explosion. Dad hadn't taken into account the vaporous nature of gasoline (hence the nickname "gas"). No sooner had he lit the rag and tossed it into the air, the fumes exploded, knocking Dad on his ass and launching tons of debris several feet into the air. Despite his best precautions, Dad's hair and eyebrows *were* singed. The burning woodpile eventually returned to earth and Dad remained seated, admiring the masterpiece he'd created. I've always wondered, at the moment the gas ignited and Dad was knocked to the ground, whether he reconsidered his nonchalant attitude towards Jesus.

There was a can of oil and gas that Dad kept for his outboard trolling motor on a shelf inside the doorway of our home's walk-out basement. Against my better judgment, I took Billy's advice. I opened the wooden cellar door and removed the red metal can from its shelf. I poured gas into a paper cup, measuring out the fuel as Billy had instructed, and placed the cup on a black metal table on the patio before returning the gas can to the cellar. I remember placing the can back on the high shelf it came from and shutting the heavy wooden portal behind me.

At least, I think I do.

Billy was down at the *Rose*, fiddling with the boat's "kicker" or auxiliary engine. A flock of mallards flew overhead, their bodies seemingly defying the laws of aerodynamics. I stood a few feet from the Weber and tossed the cup and gasoline onto the smoldering charcoal.

Whoomp.

Flames leapt from the Weber and licked the black metal sides of the grill kettle. Lilly wandered back with David hanging heavily from her arms, his face smeared with mess.

"What did *he* get into?"

"Chocolate. I had my back turned for just a second and he made a beeline for the kitchen. I chased his fat little ass around the table a few times while he gobbled down a Hershey's bar someone had left on the counter."

David smiled a big chocolaty smile and wriggled in my sister's arms. He broke free of Lilly's grip and, in a heartbeat; he was the center of attention, making desperate moves to catch the Frisbee as our friends laughed and drank beer under the gray sky.

I'm not sure why I went back into the house just then. I can't remember all the details of what happened. I do remember that, when I left, Lilly was getting interested in Kevin Delmore, a lanky, good–looking kid from the mainland who was always hitting on her. Why she chose that day to return Kevin's attention, I'm not sure, but when I went into the house, Lil and Kevin were cozying up to each other on the front porch on a wooden bench. Between kisses, they watched David coast down the cement apron in front of the garage on his Big Wheel, his short fat legs working hard to push the tricycle back up the shallow rise so he could do it again.

Lil and Kevin were engaged in a soulful kiss. I didn't see the harm in it. I knew Lilly had a good grasp on the basics of leading a guy on; she was always open to exploration, but wasn't one to give a guy false hopes. She wasn't a prude, but she had a very strict pattern of behavior with respect to physicality. She rarely deviated from those guidelines. It didn't appear to me, as I went into the house, that Kevin was going to get much further with my sister that afternoon.

When I emerged from the house dressed in a pair of old blue jeans, the fabric shiny from wear at the rump and knees, the grill was roaring in flame and Lilly was walking pensively across the lawn towards the other kids. Kevin was sitting by himself on the patio drinking a Leinnie's, the bottle held tightly in his hands, his sandy brown hair hanging so that the bangs concealed the acne defining his forehead.

"Are you and Lil through?"

"Seems so."

Kevin replied as if someone had stolen his life savings.

"I should have warned you about my sister."

"I knew better."

He took a draw of beer and raised his eyes to watch Lilly float across the back lawn, a white sweatshirt covering her red one-piece swimming suit, her tawny legs exposed to the chill, as she chased after the Frisbee Amy launched against low silver clouds.

"Yes you did."

Then it dawned on me.

"Have you seen David?"

"Nope. Last I knew, he was with your sister."

I looked across the lawn. No David.

"Lil," I shouted, my voice calm, as there was no reason for it to be any other way. "Have you seen David?"

"I thought he was with *you*." Lilith leapt into the cool air but missed the flying disk.

I walked towards the front yard, thinking that David might still be playing with his Big Wheel. When I passed the yellow tea rose bushes bordering the back of the patio, the cellar door came into view. The door was open.

I thought I closed that, was the last thing I remember thinking as I stepped down the concrete stairs and entered the dark basement.

I learned later that David somehow got hold of the gasoline can and tipped it over, spreading gas across the unpainted cement floor of the cellar until the liquid pooled beneath the propane hot water heater. I don't remember the explosion. They say I screamed and dove into the darkness, and that I found David's tiny body engulfed in fire. They say I grabbed the burning child and that I did what I'd been taught in school: stop, drop and roll. The doctors said later on, when I came to, that my burns weren't so much from the fire itself – which, once the gasoline was consumed, pretty much extinguished on its own. Instead, they were caused by the polyester warm–up I wore that melted from the heat and stuck to my skin like sizzling glue. My parents, when they made it to the burn unit of Miller–Dwan

Hospital in Duluth after chasing the Life Flight chopper carrying David and me away from Madeline Island – well, there was nothing really for them to say. David slipped into a coma and died three days later.

The doctors tried to tell my hysterical mother (her staid demeanor had finally met its match) and my stubbornly scientific father that my brother's swift demise was likely for the best. David sustained third–degree burns to over eighty percent of his body – burns that had turned his pliant baby fat and lightly pigmented skin into something more like over–done bacon. I wasn't awake to hear the telling of it, of course, but that really didn't matter. Words of solace weren't going to change the fact that my carelessness had killed my brother.

EIGHT

When I was fired from my job, I had to be satisfied with a public defender representing me. As it turned out, that was the least of my worries. The State Board of Nursing in Minnesota suspended my nursing license; Wisconsin, where I was also licensed, followed suit. I was twenty–seven years old and jobless. It really didn't matter that much when they took away my car.

You see, under Minnesota law, a vehicle used in connection with a drug crime can be seized. The cops took immediate possession of my car even though there had not yet been any finding of guilt. My Jetta was towed when I was taken into custody and I was given a form advising me that I could challenge the seizure. I crumpled the paper and tossed it on the ground before I was put in the squad car. I never saw the Volkswagen again.

So there I was, sitting at a table in the arraignment courtroom of the Hennepin County Government Center, a bargain–basement attorney by my side. I'd used my one phone call to talk to Lilly. She was in the back of the courtroom, along with a host of other folks concerned about their family members; most of them were black, Native American, Hmong or Hispanic. Lil was dressed in an Armani suit and two-hundred–dollar–heels; needless to say, she didn't fit in. I, on the other hand, was decked out in a beat–up orange jumpsuit with the county's moniker silk–screened across my back in bold black letters, and I was wearing someone else's tennis shoes.

Despite my circumstances, when my lawyer sat down next to me, I nearly broke out laughing. My attorney, Cherise Bennett, bordered on the ludicrous. She – and I use that pronoun only after much reflection – was obviously a man. Oh, I'll grant you that Cherise was dressed in a nice skirt, blouse and jacket combination, complete with an orange silk kerchief wrapped around her spooky white throat for flare, but behind all the hormone pills, recently acquired breasts and breathy feminine speech, Cherise still possessed, at least at that time, a penis.

I later learned that she'd been born Charles Martin in Calgary, Alberta, but had moved to Minneapolis with her folks when she was a child. The way Cherise told it, she'd always had an inkling that things weren't right in her chromosomal universe. She gravitated towards dolls rather than trucks at an early age. Nail polish and mascara held more of an allure for her in her teens than Brut cologne or Edge shaving cream. By the time she'd completed her undergraduate work in sociology and a Juris Doctorate at the University of Michigan, she was seeking significant bodily remodeling. She was on the sex–change waiting list at the University of Minnesota Hospital. The big day was a month away, and it was all Cherise could talk about when we weren't discussing my case.

Lilith was in court to pony up five hundred dollars to Bernie Silvester, the bail bondsman; it was Bernie's ten percent on the five-thousand–dollar bail Judge Lester Patrick, the arraignment judge, had set on my case. Because I'd agreed to participate in drug court and signed supervised release terms, the money wasn't needed. A quick change, a "thank you" to Cherise – whom I would see a *lot* of as my case wound its way through the court process – and Lilith was ready to drive me home.

"What were you thinking?"

Lilly talked as we climbed into her bumblebee–yellow BMW Z3 with black leather interior. My eyes misted over as I considered her question.

Lilly's diction, the result of years of practice, was both urbane and ethnic, befitting the African American wife of a quarterback–turned–neurosurgeon who had once captained the University of Iowa football team.

"I *wasn't* thinking; that much is clear."

My eyes were riveted on the passing scenery: the wrecked cars, the crumpled buildings, the smoggy sky of urban Minneapolis.

"What's going to happen to your job?"

"Already gone. This was the straw that broke the camel's back."

"What about the union?"

My eyes teared up. The truth was, I hadn't bothered to contact my union steward, because I felt too defeated to contest my termination by Fairview, the health conglomerate in charge of the University Hospital that fired me. I didn't know how to explain my meth use in terms my sister would understand, so I kept my mouth shut and let her prattle on.

"Of course, you'll stay with Richard and me. You've got an appearance in drug court tomorrow, right? And a pee test immediately before that, to make sure you're clean?"

I nodded. Supervised release could also have included an ankle bracelet (an electronic monitor that would keep track of my whereabouts via a land phone line). The probation officer, Julia Frisk – a lean, tall and nearly bald black woman whose demeanor meant all business, and who didn't smile once during our brief meeting in the small dank conference room adjoining Judge Patrick's courtroom – didn't believe the monitor was warranted in my case. I would've had to pay for it and I was, as you already know, no longer employed.

Lil became quiet as she drove towards Apple Valley where she, Richard and my niece Abigail live. Thankfully, Richard and Abby weren't around when Lil's BMW pulled into the cul–de–sac in front of the masonry and redwood mansion, an edifice that oozed pretension. Lilly pushed a button. A wood paneled garage door opened, whereupon she parked the Beemer in the garage and pushed the button again. The chain drive rattled as the door shut. A weak auxiliary light illuminated our path as we exited the car and entered the house.

"You can stay in the extra bedroom next to Abby's room," Lilith said quietly, placing her purse on the kitchen table before ushering me towards the stairway. "I'll get you some clean undies, a pair of my jeans, and a top. You can use Abby's bathroom to clean up."

As Lilith spoke, I realized that it had been forty–eight hours since I'd bathed. I was wearing the same bra and panties I'd had on when I was arrested. My clothing was also unchanged, but given that I'd spent thirty–six hours in a jail jumpsuit, my slacks and top weren't quite as smelly as my underwear. Lil disappeared for a moment and returned with an armful of clean clothes, things I'd never seen her wear – likely extras for working around the house. I stood dumbfounded and empty at the bottom of the stairway leading to the second floor of the house and accepted the clothing in silence.

"It'll be all right." My sister's eyes were quick and appealing, with no hint of pity or judgment showing as she touched me briefly on the cheek with a bony finger.

She's always been a good actress, I thought to myself. *Appearances mean a lot to Lil. Having her sister arrested in a drug bust that nearly destroyed Cedar Riverside is not something she can, in her wildest imagination, relate to. But she's trying, God bless her. She's trying.*

"Thanks," I mumbled, before turning to climb the hardwood stairs.

At the top of the stairs, I turned right and followed the hallway leading to Abby's bathroom. The thought of soaking in hot water eased the emptiness gnawing at me. I entered the lavatory, undressed in silence and filled the tub, pouring bath oil into the tub and checking the water with my fingers to make sure I didn't scald myself. Naked and unwilling to look at my body in the wall mirror, I stepped over the tiled enclosure surrounding the tub and slid through the suds. Soaking in the bathtub with my body hidden by white bubbles that pillowed above the water like a feathery iceberg and my head resting on a terrycloth bath towel wedged behind my neck, I couldn't stop crying. My parents, despite all their faults, didn't deserve to learn what I was going to have to tell them. There had been, as far as I was aware, no hint or inkling to them of my drug use that would prepare them for the rapidity of my descent. My eyes blinked. I tried to bat away the tears seeping down my face. There was no danger of smearing my mascara because I wasn't wearing any. I flicked a wayward tear from my nose with a finger and closed my eyes, shutting out the pale light of the overcast late summer day that filtering through the bathroom's solitary window. The lights were off. The house was quiet. My heart beat slowly and anxiously inside my chest as I reclined and allowed my ears to slip beneath the surface of the water.

I remembered the joy I'd felt when Lilly and I were finally allowed the luxury of separate baths. I'd sink beneath the water and listen intently to my heart, wondering how long the organ would hold out, and whether there was some unknown defect lurking inside the chambers of that mysterious pump – like with my friend Adrian Olcott, whose leaky valve required two corrective surgeries before she was able to run and skip with the rest of us in third grade. When I was little, I wondered whether Lilly slid beneath her bath water to consider similar thoughts. I don't know. Even when we were kids, I never saw her as being that way. But maybe that's unfair; maybe my sister's intellect is capable of more than I give her credit for.

My face broke the soapy surface of the bath water as I came up for air. Del appeared to me. He wouldn't leave. His eyes, the shape of his hands and the smell of his body demanded my attention. Realizing that I'd have to face Del's family at his funeral and that I'd have to make that long walk from the back of the funeral parlor to Del's casket and place my hands on the smooth wood of his coffin, I hyperventilated. I crossed my arms, my damaged skin smooth and slippery from the bath oil, and sank beneath the water in hopes that I could find the courage to drown.

NINE

Human flesh comprises three layers. The epidermis, or outer layer, is the veneer that's injured when we're out in the sun too long. Epidermal burns involve the cornified cells that are in the last phase of life. Beneath the epidermis is the dermis, an amorphous layer containing vascular and nerve networks, infinitesimal glands and connective tissue. Finally, as I learned during my anatomy classes in nursing school, there is a third level to skin: the subcutaneous tissue. Most people know that the severity of a burn is rated in degrees, from the least onerous first–degree burns to the most serious third–degree burns, the type of burn experienced by David and me. Third–degree burns, as all burns, are the product of the combined effects of temperature, time (duration of skin contact with heat or flame) and the age of the victim. Young children and older folks suffer worse in terms of burn severity, though the number of serious burns is highest, regardless of degree, in young adults. Most burn victims under age two sustain injuries because of scalding, like the tipping–over of a coffee pot or the dripping of bacon grease from a frying pan. The most serious burns across all age groups come from open flame.

David's body, protected from that cool day by a onesie, a long-sleeved shirt and blue jeans, was burned from the tops of his bare feet to the middle of his chest. His clothing and his diaper were saturated with gas, and by the time I made it to the ball of flame that had once been my brother, the plastic of his diaper had melted, and exacerbated his injuries. Only David's neck, head and face escaped trauma. His hands sustained severe burns due to his futile attempts to beat down the flames. I only remember snippets of that afternoon. I do remember David's face. I'll never forget it.

David was fair–skinned, his complexion something between copper and bronze. He had brown eyes. When I saw him on fire that day inside the

47

cellar, his eyes showed terror. I grabbed him and tucked his smoldering body under my left arm, my feet covered in tennis shoes, my legs protected by blue jeans, before racing outside, dropping to the ground, and rolling across the lawn. As it turns out, "stop, drop and roll" doesn't do the trick when an accelerant like gas is present. I didn't know that then. I know it now, but that hindsight doesn't do David much good. Eventually, after the melted fabric of my pullover seared my own skin, my efforts did extinguish the flames. I have no clue how we made it onto the Life Flight helicopter. I do recall bits and pieces of the flight: a nurse comforting me and sliding the tip of a syringe into my bare right forearm; the diffuse, distant relaxation of morphine as the narcotic took over. I don't remember David being in the chopper. I later learned that he was next to me, on a separate gurney. My last memory of him is from the fire. I wasn't even there when my parents buried him.

Third–degree burns destroyed the subcutaneous layer of my little brother's skin. Smoke inhalation damaged his lungs. He never regained consciousness. He never opened his eyes. I learned these things from eavesdropping while the medical personnel in the Miller–Dwan Hospital Burn Unit attended to me – or, later on, from Lilly, when she came to visit. I certainly didn't learn these things from my parents. Even after David passed, having lingered three days before his soul left this world, my parents said little. When they did, my folks made perfunctory admonitions such as "get better" and "do what the doctors say," and little else, which caused me to conclude that they'd formulated their own views on my culpability in the matter.

From Mom's behavior, one could conclude – with good reason – that she was operating on autopilot. Lilly related during a bedside visit that Mom never shed a tear during David's funeral Mass or at his grave. At first, I attributed this reaction to fortitude. But as Mom's silence extended, I became convinced that she blamed me for David's death. Normally cool and curt but capable of subtle warmth, Mom displayed none of her more endearing traits when sitting in my hospital room. She was there. I was her child. It wasn't like she had disowned me, but the emotional ties between us were made brittle, like raw spaghetti, ready to break apart. For his part, Dad dealt with the loss of his only son by releasing serious sighs when seated at my bedside, only to recover and assume the role of physician, ever curious and demanding of the staff's protocols in "healing his little girl." He sat with me for hours while I slipped in and out of morphine–induced dreams. He displayed such tenderness and kindness towards me that, given what had occurred, I believed in redemption.

If God can do this – take this man who has lost his son, and allow compassion to fill his heart, I thought at one point as Dad slumped in the chair next to my bed, his feet propped up on a metal visitor's chair, his eyes closed; his snores audible to me even over the drugs, *God must be powerful.*

I was in the Miller–Dwan Burn Unit for over a month. Forty–three days, to be exact. Once my body stabilized and I recovered from shock, the staff began treating my "major burn injury." More than 25 percent of my Total Body Surface Area (TBSA) had been injured, hence the "major burn injury" designation. The first step to treating me was to begin fluid resuscitation: the replacement of the water in my body. A nurse hung an IV to supply fluids and pain medications, then inserted a Foley catheter to eliminate urine. Shortly thereafter, someone snaked a nasogastric tube down my throat to evacuate fluid and air from my stomach and to feed me for that first week in the Burn Unit. I remember hints and fragments from that time, but none of what I experienced during those first days at Miller–Dwan stands out as remarkable, because narcotics sedated me and I was emotionally numb.

As treatment progressed, nurses used antibacterial surfactant to clean my charred skin. Doctors snipped away dead tissue. Dressings were applied and replaced daily. All the folks who treated me must have been very good at their jobs, because I never became infected. Dr. Porter, a handsome plastic surgeon no more than thirty–five years old, was in charge of my care. He removed grafts of uninjured skin (my buttocks, from where he harvested the needed tissue, bear evidence of his work), and applied the grafts to my left thigh, left flank, left chest wall and left armpit. We became friends. How else do you view someone who removed pieces of skin from your ass and attached them to your breast?

Dr. Porter made constant conversation with me as he removed and applied the dressings and splints that kept the grafts protected and in place during healing. I listened more than talked, studying his quick blue eyes and thick lips, completely enthralled by his beauty and his Southern accent. He told me he was from a little farming town near Richmond, that he'd attended the University of Virginia, and that he was single. I think I fell in love with Dr. Porter, a–not–so–uncommon transference of emotions that I witnessed later, from the perspective of a nurse. I think Stanford Porter recognized my girlish infatuation and, in a kind way, redirected it, though his efforts did little to dissuade my narcotic–induced fantasies.

Once the grafts adhered, I was plagued with itching that can only be described as something that happens when an entire village of mosquitoes becomes trapped with you inside a tent that you can't leave. Even prescriptions for atarac, periactin and benedryl couldn't stop my skin from crawling. By then, I was off morphine and taking pain pills, but the weaker narcotics did little to dull the general distress I was experiencing. There was little I could do, immobilized as I was, captive in bed and surrounded by medical appliances, splints and tightly wrapped dressings to alleviate my agony. I couldn't scratch myself, for that would destroy Dr. Porter's careful work. It wouldn't relieve the itching anyway. This is the majority of what I do remember from the hospital once I was taken off morphine: every square inch of my skin, whether damaged in the fire or not, felt as if it had been afflicted by poison ivy. I was fighting this misery when it dawned on me that I was missing my senior year at Bayfield High School.

Before the fire, I packed a well–muscled one–hundred–and–fifty pounds on my five–foot–eight frame. I'd come into my own during my junior year, breaking into the starting line–up in a home game against Mellon. Coach Ebert put me in after Amy Olson went down with a sprained ankle. I hit a trio of three–pointers, had four steals and blocked two shots before rounding out the night with a pair of free–throws to win the game. Amy came back the next week to play small forward. I stayed in the line–up as power forward and ended up averaging twelve points and six rebounds per game for the season. It wasn't until I was three weeks into my stay at Miller–Dwan that it dawned on me I was unlikely ever to play competitive basketball again.

TEN

Meth addiction is one of the hardest compulsions to treat. That's the message Julia Frisk browbeat into me when we were talking about options available to me, if I pleaded guilty. My lawyer, Cherise Bennett, told me that I could contest the police having stopped my car, and argue that the pipe wasn't in plain view, and that all the evidence seized after that point, including the meth, had been wrongfully obtained. But she also told me that the best advice she could give was to fess up, come clean, lay it all out for the judge, and turn the negatives of my situation into positives. The fact I had no job meant I had ample time to enroll in treatment; the fact that my parents had sufficient resources to fund a long-term program meant my chances of success were all that much better. On the down side, my health insurance would only cover thirty days of treatment. The program Ms. Frisk was interested in using, New Beginnings in Panora, Iowa, required a minimum stay of six months.

"Your body needs at least six weeks of detox," my probation officer advised. Ms. Frisk's icy courtroom demeanor melted somewhat as we spoke in her office the day before my plea. "A thirty–day program doesn't work for meth addicts. The timeframe is too short. You're not even off the drug and they're sending you out the door, proclaiming what was broken is now fixed."

Broken. I hadn't thought of myself like that, not even when I walked timidly down the center aisle of Brown's Funeral Parlor on University Avenue, where Del's family and his few friends gathered to say goodbye. All of them, I was certain, were unnerved by the sobbing black woman who wouldn't leave the closed casket at the front of the room. It took Del's younger sister Cheryl, the only one of his siblings I spoke to and the only one who considered me worthy of Del's attention, to guide me back to my chair and break the horrible spell of the moment. What I got from the other members of the Benson Family – the cold stares, the unkind reception – might as well have included the word "nigger." It was clear that Del's kin, with the lone exception of Cheryl, blamed me for Del's death. I didn't have the strength to defend myself from such opinions, and Cheryl didn't have the spine to speak out against the family's universal disdain for me.

You might think that, growing up black amongst a majority of whites and a small community of Native Americans, that Lilith and I heard the "N" word routinely. That's not the case. There were a few times back home in northwestern Wisconsin when we heard the word, but I can honestly say that any prejudice that folks living where we grew up held towards African Americans was pretty well hidden.

Oh, don't get me wrong. I felt the chill of indifference creep into my bones every now and then when a white boy would introduce me to his parents before going out on a date, or if we showed up later at his house to watch the tube or kick back. But overt racism? It wasn't expressed in my presence very often. As a consequence, despite the fact that I saw the distinctions in my features – the pink of my mouth, or the lightness of my palms, set against my blackness every day when I got ready for school and later, for work – I rarely, if ever, worried about being different. Understand: I *knew* I was. I mean, I already explained how I'd had *that* epiphany when I turned twelve. But my skin color, my blackness, wasn't something I dwelled on; it wasn't something I lamented or worried over to such an extent I couldn't focus on getting on with my life. I knew enough to be wary. But the infrequency of racist incidents lulled me into the belief that I was the same as everyone else.

In a very real sense, due to my father's quietude about who he was and where his people had come from, I didn't really have a comprehension of who *I* was, at least not in terms of *my* African heritage. I guess I never really thought about such things before Del died and I was arrested. Once that all happened, I found myself with plenty of time for self–evaluation and introspection.

"New Beginnings *is* expensive."

My lawyer repeated this fact, her thin fingers nervously tapping the top of a photographic wood desk in Ms. Frisk's office.

"How is Ms. DuMont going to pay for it, presuming she pleads to the charge and the judge goes along with a stay of adjudication?" Ms. Frisk asked.

Cherise and I had talked about Minnesota Statute 152.18 and the fact that first-time offenders are entitled to a period of probation and treatment – which, if successfully completed, keeps a felony conviction off their record. If I stayed clean, I'd have a good chance at getting my nursing license back. Granted, I'd be suspect goods and I'd likely have a difficult time finding work, but at least I'd have a license. Cherise had approached the Minnesota Board of Nursing on my behalf. They agreed to suspend my license, rather than revoke it outright, if I got help for my addiction.

The cost of New Beginnings is five thousand dollars a month. Six months. Thirty thousand dollars, of which, only the first month was covered by insurance. I knew Lilly and Richard would lend me the money, but that wasn't right. They had a daughter to take care of and their own set of problems in paying for all the trappings of success they'd quickly accumulated once Richard became Board–certified and opened his own practice in Lakeville (another suburb of the Twin Cities). I knew, despite the flashy cars and the big house, that much of my sister's lifestyle was propped up with credit and borrowed cash. She and Richard were living on other people's money. Asking them to pay for my stupidity – or, more correctly, my avarice – made my stomach turn and my heart uneasy.

That left my parents. Lil hadn't tattled on me yet, like she was apt to when we were kids. There was a myriad of times when her quick mouth got me in trouble, like the time Johnny Morton and I went skinny–dipping in my next–door neighbors' hot tub while they were out of town. There wasn't anything for Lilly to gain by sharing this confidence – information she'd gleaned during one of our late–night chats over marshmallows and Oreo cookies in her bedroom. Yet, for some unexplained reason, she felt compelled to share this secret with Mom. Then there was the time I dented the passenger's side of Mom's Saab while taking a turn onto the ferry ramp too sharply. I parked the car so that Mom had to approach the Saab on the driver's side, keeping the dent completely concealed from her. When Mom came back from shopping lamenting the fact that some idiot had dented her car without leaving a note, there was no reason in hell for Lil to tattle – yet she did. Maturity apparently caused Lilith to refrain from calling Mom or Dad and giving them a heads–up regarding my arrest. Of course, this left the disclosure of my sin up to me.

"That's a lot of money."

"Can you borrow it?" Cherise asked.

"Maybe from my folks."

"There's no 'maybe' about it, Ms. DuMont. Without funding for a long–term, in–patient program, I have real concerns that you'll be right back here, in sixty or ninety days, looking at the workhouse – or worse yet, prison."

A period of quiet ensued once the probation officer quit talking. Coffee percolated in a pot sitting atop a file cabinet in Ms. Frisk's office. Clients and correctional officers bustled past the glass window that looked out into the hallway. My eyes scanned the room. I focused my gaze on a small picture of Julia Frisk and her husband that hung on the wall behind her; their African American faces were dark and expressive.

"I can ask."

"You can use my phone."

"You mean right now?"

"Yes, I mean right now."

"You have to tell them sometime," Cherise counseled as she touched the back of my right hand with her soft palm. "You might as well get it over with."

I released a deep sigh and nodded my head. I was left alone in the room. I dialed my parents' number. The conversation I had with my father was not an easy one.

ELEVEN

Father Michaels was the angel that God sent to me in the horrible days after the fire. I explained before that I am a fallen Catholic. I wasn't at the time. I was a believer, one of the devout. It's only been as I've aged – as I've considered the Church's stand on birth control and marriage for priests, the absolute lack of women in the hierarchy of the Roman Catholic faith, and my own tragedies and experiences – that I have fallen away. Don't misunderstand me: I still believe in God. I still believe in Jesus. I just don't believe that one man, one human being, could have such a direct connection with God and be in charge of the souls of almost a billion human beings. But back when I was a patient at Miller–Dwan Hospital, I still considered myself a loyal Catholic. In some ways, I wish I could go back to that simple belief system, but it's too late. Too much has happened to retrieve what's been lost.

Father Tom was young. He was twenty–three years old that autumn, and the youth pastor of Our Lady of the Lake Roman Catholic Church. I met him during the summer of 1994. He'd come to Ashland directly from the seminary, assigned by the Bishop of Superior to work with the youth of Our Lady of the Lake, under the direction of Father O' Rourke, who was a hard–line Vaticanist. For years, there was virtually nothing but an occasional bowling outing available to the youth in our church. When Father Tom arrived, bringing his acoustic guitar and his zealous ability to entice teenagers to commit themselves to God, he upset the decaying applecart that had been the youth program at Our Lady. Within two months of his arrival, kids were flocking to Sunday night Youth for Christ gatherings in the church's social hall. Some came for the music; others came for the food – piles of tacos; platters of spaghetti and serving bowls of mac and cheese. Some came for the spiritual excitement: the kids put on the majority of the evening Mass by assisting Father Tom with the Eucharist, giving the homily and choosing the hymns. A few of the girls, like me, came because we lusted after Father Tom.

How a gorgeous young man like Thomas Michaels could profess celibacy was a puzzle to those of us who coveted him. He was, in a word, handsome: thick curly black hair framed his narrow head and cascaded to his shoulders. Deep blue eyes – eyes that mimicked the color of the waters off the Apostle Islands on a cloudless day – demarcated his movie star looks: feline lips; a sculpted jaw; and a lean and muscular body that was the product of an obsession with karate. Father Tom reminded me of an icon adorning the sacristy of my church – the one of St. Thomas touching the wounds in Jesus' hands. It was as if whoever had created the stained glass window over the baptismal font had used Reverend Thomas Michaels as a model.

From the behavior of the older women in church, including Grandma Mary, it was clear that the admiration of Father Tom's beauty wasn't limited to adolescent girls. The flirting was shameless. That these outlandish displays weren't observed by Father O' Rourke and nipped in the bud was likely due to the old priest's failing eyesight and escalating deafness.

It was evident, from watching Father Tom interact with his parishioners, that he was gloriously happy being a priest. It was also clear, by how handily and easily he rebuffed these childish advances – whether from schoolgirls or from women the age of my grandmother – that he had a good handle on his vow of chastity. I was aware of Father Tom's resolve on this point when he appeared at my bedside at the hospital.

"How are you doing?"

Father Tom stood alongside my bed, dressed in his cleric's uniform and collar. My body was wrapped in gauze. The process of healing prickled my skin as he spoke to me.

"I've been better."

The guilt of David's death hung over me. My brother's passing caused hefty remorse, and that weight was aggravated by the belief that I'd taken my eyes off my little brother and left the gasoline can open to his curiosity.

"Are you in pain?"

"I itch like crazy."

"From the grafts?"

"Yes."

Father Tom reached for a visitor's chair.

"Mind if I sit a while?"

"That would be nice."

My cheeks flushed, though given my skin pigment, I doubt Father Tom noticed. The priest slid the chair across the linoleum floor, sat down, reached into his shirt pocket, pulled out a small gold crucifix, and handed it to me.

"I understand you lost yours while trying to save David. This was mine when I was a teenager."

My fingers wrapped around the small metallic figure, and I held the chaplet in my right hand. I studied the diminutive Jesus at the end of the chain, beneath the unnatural light of the hospital room. I was lucky. I was in a private suite. I had the place and Father Tom all to myself. Tears formed in my eyes. Fingers closed around gold. I brought the crucifix to my chest.

"There, there, Esther. What is it?"

I shook my head.

"David?"

I nodded.

"Ah. Guilt, I suppose."

I lowered my eyes in shame.

"There's no reason to dwell on what happened. God has a path for all of us. Some paths are rocky and steep and lead to places that we can only imagine. Other paths seem well defined, but the ultimate destination is still unknown. We cannot possibly know what is in store for us as we walk through life." He paused. "Our duty is to place one foot ahead of another and choose the path that seems morally right. David's death was an accident and a tragedy, but one seen and understood by God. We will likely never know why some things happen the way they do, at least while we live on this earth. But it's not our role to understand everything. It's our role to continue forward, always striving and looking. Only in God's face will we likely find the answers we are seeking. Only when standing before Jesus will we experience such an awakening. Don't destroy yourself with recrimination. Don't allow self–blame to defeat you. David needs you to remember him and to stay strong for him."

My eyes misted. It was hard for me to focus as Father Tom leaned over me and brushed hair away from my forehead. My heart pounded. My chin tilted towards his lips. But Father Tom knew the danger and my fragile emotional state, and pulled away.

"Get some rest, young lady. I'll be back in a day or so to check in and see how that itching is doing."

As he spoke, a narrow smile crossed Father Michaels's lovely lips. He patted my arm with his hand and placed his chair against the wall. I couldn't take my eyes off the priest as he opened the door and walked out into the hallway, leaving me alone once again.

TWELVE

The telephone call was excruciating.

"How could this happen?"

My father's tone betrayed hurt, as if he'd been struck in the gut with a crowbar.

How indeed? I asked myself. *What was the real and true reason, the motivation that brought me to methamphetamine? Was it as simple as the fact that I was seeking something beyond faith, God and physical love, to deaden the constant aching I felt? Why was that? What mechanism had caused my inner being to drift aimlessly, unbridled and burdened, since the day David and I were burned? Remorse? Grief? Guilt? Bits and pieces of all of these?*

A long–distance telephone call made on a probation officer's phone to your father without warning, where you unleash a torrent of upset and failure upon him, isn't when you should attempt self–psychoanalysis. Perhaps that's something I should've done after the fire – gotten some counseling from a professional. No one suggested it, surely not my Mom, who maintained her steady composure and never asked me to relate the details of what happened that day. Certainly not Dad, who placed his faith in the curative powers of invasive medicine, not the "touchy–feely" approach favored by mental health therapy.

"I have no idea." It was the best response I could come up with. "I never meant for this to happen." *Of course not*, I thought to myself. *No one plans on getting caught.*

There was a slight pause. I could tell my father was weighing whether to voice disappointment over my fall or to advance support. Luckily for me, it was the latter.

"What will happen next?"

"I'll plead guilty. It's a felony but if I make it through probation, it won't be on my record. I'll be able to get my license back."

"And your job at the hospital?"

"Gone."

A pause.

"Can't you grieve that?"

"I could but I won't. I needed a change anyway. I may go back to school. Earn a master's degree in nursing or something else. I'll take some time while I'm away, getting better, to figure it out."

"Away?"

"New Beginnings – it's the program my probation officer wants me to go to in Iowa."

"Sounds expensive. How will you pay for it?"

My father had cut to the chase. He knew there was a reason, beyond confession, for my call. He'd guessed that it had to do with money. With kids, no matter the age, it always has to do with money.

"Insurance will cover the first month. I'll need help after that."

"How much help?"

"Five thousand a month, for five months."

"Haven't you any savings?"

"Gone."

I said the word quietly, the shame of having depleted my meager savings to fund my drug habit made clear with that single word.

"Gone?"

Tears began.

"Yes."

"The kind of money you made? No house, just a little VW for a car, and you've got nothing?"

"Nothing."

"Can you take out a loan against your car?"

The car, I thought. *I don't even have a fucking car.*

I began to sob uncontrollably.

"It's not important." Paternal love softened my father's voice. "We'll help you."

My throat closed. I felt unable to breathe. Words wanted release, but my mind wouldn't let them form.

"Esther?"

I pushed unruly hair out of my eyes and nodded, as if to buck myself up. The interlude reminded me of the differences between Lilith and me. Lilly: slender, gorgeous, and blessed with velvety, straight black hair; married to a surgeon; and now, a mother. Me: thickly built, nappy headed, recently single, unemployed, and a drug addict. The comparison didn't make what I had to say any easier.

59

"There is no car. They took it."

"The bank?"

"The cops. Part of the procedure. It's called a forfeiture. I could fight it but, as part of the plea bargain, I can't. They won't charge me with aiding and abetting Del and Moose in making meth and in return, they keep the car."

"How in God's name did you ever get mixed up with that SOB? Didn't your mother and I warn you? Didn't we tell you, you could do better, that you were a DuMont, that you had no reason to lower yourself to his level? I knew that boy was nothing but trouble from the day you brought him home last summer."

You don't know, I thought. *You can't understand that Del wasn't like that. Not really. Behind his addiction, he was thoughtful and kind and good. More so than most men I've been around. You wouldn't understand. I can't make you understand. He was the best I could get. The best I was entitled to.*

"Del wasn't like that."

"Hell he wasn't. It was that boy who got you all turned around and confused about who you are and where you came from. It was that piece of riff–raff who turned you into a junkie. Can't you see that, daughter? Can't you see what he's done to you?"

Who I am? What the hell does that mean, coming from you, Dad, a black man pretending to be white? What have you done to ensure I know who I am, where I'm from? Nothing. That's what. Nothing. I bit my tongue.

I'm not stupid. I didn't unload my cultural anxieties on my father at the very moment I was asking for help. I kept my thoughts to myself.

"Did."

"How's that?"

"Past tense, Dad. Del died when the meth lab blew up."

Another pause.

"If you expect me to offer my condolences, well, that's not going to happen. I don't wish any man ill, but I certainly won't grieve the passing of Delmont Benson."

"I'm not asking you to."

An unsteady, unspoken truce was reached in our conversation.

"Dad, about the money...."

"You know we'll help you. You're our daughter. We love you. We'll get through this."

"You'll break it to Mom?"

A deep exhalation.

"I will."

"Thanks, Dad."

"You get well, child. Does Lilly know?"

60

"I'm staying with her and Richard."

"Good. Times like these should be spent with family. Your sister's a good woman. Despite her airy ways, she's smarter and deeper than you might think."

"I know that."

"I'm glad you do. I've got to get back to work. Give Lilith and that beautiful daughter of hers my love."

"Okay."

Tears erupted as I hung up the phone. The emotional impact of my father's love, his unwavering support, was simply too much for me to handle.

THIRTEEN

When Billy Cadotte came to see me in the hospital, I knew it was over. Billy was a sweet kid. We'd had a lot of fun. Okay. It was more than that: he was my first love, my first experience in wading into the tidal pool of romance, of letting emotional waves lap at my heart, of intimacy floating my soul. Add to this that Billy was part of "the Other" – a minority kid, someone who looked different, like me – and you'll understand what a blow it was to have him create distance after all the closeness we'd shared.

Billy didn't come right out and say we were through, but his body language said it all. And, truth be told, I should have expected it. We were kids, and modern connections don't work that way. The number of high school sweethearts that get married and cobble together a strong and steady bond in the face of all that today's world tosses at them – well, that's more fantasy than reality.

There wasn't really anything of substance said between us. I know that's strange, but it's true. I'd been conscious for a week or so. Lilith told me that Billy had spent time in the hospital waiting room before I came to, driving up from Red Cliff with some other Indian kids, but he couldn't see me, what with the risk of infection and all, for quite a while. It wasn't until after the skin grafting started that Billy and I had the chance to talk.

"How's it going?"

Billy's almond face was lined with concern. I'm sure I was quite a sight. I had bandages wrapped around my upper body and left arm like a mummy, IVs and tubes running this way and that, monitors blinking, pumps humming, nurses wandering in and out on a near-constant basis, and this sweet boy stood next to me, trying to comprehend what I'd been through, not having any benchmarks in his life by which to measure my pain, sorrow or loss.

"Okay. Could you hand me that water?"

I nodded towards a small glass on a nightstand next to my bed. Billy's hands trembled as he held the glass and watched me suck water through a plastic straw. I drained the glass in a few gulps. Billy put the empty glass back on the stand before sitting in a chair near the windows.

"Does it hurt?"

"Not so much. Itches like hell."

Billy sighed. "About that day…"

"Billy," I interrupted. "Don't. I know you would have risked your life to save David and me. I know that."

I crossed my hands over my chest, the cotton of the white sheets stiff and formal against the bare skin of my right wrist.

"I just wish I could've done more, been there to help you. But no, I was screwing around with that piece of shit boat."

I smiled. "Your father wouldn't like that. And neither would your mother. The *Rose* is a good boat, named after a good lady. I don't think you should go around knocking either of them."

"I guess you're right." He studied me before continuing. "You gonna be all right?"

I nodded. "They say I'll have some nasty scars, but everything still works. Only thing is, with therapy and such, I won't be getting out of here for another two or three weeks. Then I'll have to take it easy. Looks like my senior season is shot to hell."

"That sucks."

"There goes the scholarship."

I'd been close to getting a full ride at Northern Michigan. The coach there couldn't make a commitment, but things had looked promising; She had been holding a spot open, and she was set to come down and watch another game or two during the upcoming season before deciding to make an offer. It was up to me: play well, and I'd get a full ride. Play poorly, and I could try to make the women's basketball team as a walk-on. But that opportunity went up in smoke on Labor Day.

My high school coach, Lois Ebert, a Northern Michigan grad, visited me in the hospital. Coach Ebert said there was still a chance the college would find a way to offer me scholarship money based on my grades – even though I couldn't play ball. Some sort of pity fund, I guess. She was true to her word. Northern found the money. I didn't want to accept the help, but once I got out of the hospital, I changed my mind. I saw no benefit in being unreasonably stubborn and refusing the kindness of strangers.

But I didn't know about the pity fund at that point, and Billy didn't say anything in reply. He just sat there, his black Ojibwa eyes staring at me. His Native quietude was disconcerting. It wasn't long after that exchange

63

that Billy kissed my forehead and walked out of my room. Oh, he came back a few more times, twice with Amy Olson, I believe, and once with April Swanson, the girl he eventually married. When I saw them together, I knew whatever we had was kaput. Done. Toast. Like my skin. Billy and April didn't do anything overtly; they didn't waltz into my room holding hands, but the chemistry was clear. I knew. And I think they realized I was on to them. I held my breath and battled the realization that this boy who looked like me – who had a mixture of Africa and tribal America flowing through his veins – had fallen for a girl as white as the driven snow. It was a very short and perfunctory visit.

Without Father Tom, I'm sure the loss of Billy Cadotte would have been a catastrophic blow to my frazzled ego. As it was, the hurt was genuine and deep, despite my understanding that we were only kids, and that things couldn't be set in stone at such an early age and be expected to weather time. Still, I'd hoped we could hold it together for our senior year; go to the Snow Ball and Prom as a couple, then perhaps take separate paths to whatever destinations awaited us. Without Billy, I was lost. There was no one willing to approach me, ask me out, or take me to dances once I was physically healed, or even to take me to a flick in Ashland or Superior or Duluth.

I'm not blaming the boys. My scarred skin was not the only part of me hardened by the fire. If the boys found me unapproachable during that year, it's because I was. My God, if you'd have seen what my left side looked like as it healed, you'd understand my urge to hide in my bedroom and avoid human contact unless absolutely necessary. I felt like a freaking monster. In retrospect, that's a little over the top, but at the time, as a senior in high school, the reaction had merit.

The only moments I recall feeling alive and open to male companionship then were when the plastic surgeon, Dr. Porter, Father Tom or Dad came around. Of course, the reasons behind my being open to their company were different for each of them. With Dad, well – he's my Dad; unconditional love, and all that. With Dr. Porter, it was simply a teenaged infatuation coupled with my attachment to him as my doctor. With Father Tom, I latched onto his spirituality like he was a life preserver and I was a survivor from the *Lusitania*. There's something I would have never known about, if not for Father Tom: the sinking of that ship. I know about the *Lusitania* because Father Tom encouraged my love of books. He knew I was a voracious reader.

"How's Miss DuMont today?"

Most of the gauze had been removed. The skin grafts were solid and adhering to my body like glued patches on a punctured inner tube, the tissue knitting together, forming one, if somewhat distorted, contiguous surface. It was during this time that, when taking a shower, I discovered that I'd lost all sensation in my left nipple. I could feel pressure on my breast when I washed my skin, but I could not feel detail. It was as if someone had injected my boob with Novocain. When I made this discovery, I wasn't concerned about the romantic implications; I was concerned about whether I'd ever be able to nurse a child.

I thought about this discovery, something new and disquieting, as I watched Father Tom sit down next to me in a soft chair in the Burn Unit waiting room. Bright autumn sun bathed the space. We were alone. The air was pure and clean, completely absent of dust motes, which allowed light to wash over the room in surreal fashion. Father Tom was dressed in priest's black and a white Roman Catholic collar. I was trying out a new pair of sweat pants and a loose blouse my mother had bought at Younker's in Duluth.

I think buying me clothes was Mom's attempt to reconcile. There was hurt between us, a rift I felt but which Mom never verbalized. I figured Mom blamed me, and me alone, for David's death; I sort of shared her view. I mean, I had been the one watching David on the day he was burned. Of course, Lilly was supposed to be helping me. But Lilly, well, she was, at least back then, far from responsible. Her mind was on her looks, her body image and boys. I wanted to believe that it was as much Lil's fault as mine for what happened, but I knew that wasn't the case. I was the one Mom trusted. I was the one who let her down.

Anyway, it was the first day I'd donned real clothes and ventured out of my hospital room on my own. It felt good, now that I look back on that day, to be up and about, to see the sun rising over Lake Superior, the steely water so familiar, the South Shore standing clear and dark across the flat pan of fresh water. I smiled as I took in the priest's handsomeness and, for the first time since the fire, I felt lucky.

"Best I've felt in a month."

"It's great to see you up and about."

Father Tom smiled and patted my right arm.

"Thanks for coming by to cheer me up." I shifted my gaze.

"I have something for you."

"Oh?"

He was holding a large bag from Bookworld, the chain bookstore located on Ashland's main street. I knew the store intimately, as I had visited the place nearly every week. As a child, I went with my mother and sister to pick out the bedtime stories and nursery rhymes Mom read to my sister and me. Once I learned to read, I begged Mom to drop me off at the bookstore whenever she took Lilly to dance or voice lessons or ran errands. I learned to savor the smell, feel and atmosphere of the place as I searched the shelves for novels, biographies and short story collections to defeat the boredom of school–less summers or the cold and isolation of deep winter.

"Here." The priest withdrew a leather–bound journal from the bag. "This is so you can write down your thoughts – the bits and pieces of life that interest you that you might want to use later on."

"Use later on?"

"When you write."

"Write?"

The priest smiled.

"Most folks who read end up becoming writers. Maybe poetry. Maybe memoirs. Maybe something more weighty and time–consuming, like a novel."

I laughed.

"I'm the world's worst speller," I revealed as I thumbed through the volume's blank pages.

"So am I. That's why I also got you this."

Father Tom removed a copy of *Webster's Unabridged Dictionary* from the bag. My right arm strained accepting the heavy book.

"You shouldn't have."

"There's one more."

Father Tom withdrew a copy of Margaret Walker's novel, *Jubilee*, and handed it to me. I didn't know what to say.

"It's a little presumptuous of me, I know. I mean, my only connection to African American heritage is that I've seen *Roots*. Twice."

Race, I thought. *What an odd topic for my priest to bring up.*

"I bought the book because of the title. I've not read it myself."

"The title?"

"In the Jewish faith, Jubilee involves a time of forgiveness, a time when all households recover what they've lost, when land taken through legal processes is returned to its rightful owners, when slaves are granted freedom and when all debts are deemed satisfied."

"What does that have to do with me?"

This wasn't some smart–ass remark. I had no idea why my priest believed I should learn about Jubilee.

"Without stating the obvious, I thought you, as a young black woman, might be interested in learning how the Jewish concept of Jubilee became engrained in the lore and spirituality of African Americans."

"I'm black?"

Father Tom didn't rise to the bait. His grin merely widened.

"There's also a Roman Catholic concept of Jubilee. It's a religious ceremony where the Holy Father knocks on the Basilica door, which has been walled up, exemplifying man's inability to enter into heaven due to sin. The Pope knocks the wall down and enters the Basilica, symbolizing faith's triumph over sin. It's impressive to witness; I'm sure, but not all that interesting to a young lady such as you. What might be interesting to you is the connection between the Jewish concept of Jubilee and the beliefs of your ancestors."

Up until that moment, the only time I'd ever seriously contemplated my African ancestors was when kids at school would look at Lilith and me as if we were supposed to be experts on Dr. King and other luminaries in black history. We knew about as much as the other kids did, so we were, I guess, a bit of a disappointment to our classmates and teachers in that regard. Of course, as I said, I'd experienced intermittent moments of revelation and understanding that Lilly and I were different. Those fleeting pangs of angst caused me to gravitate towards friendships with Billy Cadotte and the other Native Americans in school. But there was, somewhere inside me, I guess, a desire, a pent–up need to understand the differences between my sister and me and the white kids surrounding us, even if I didn't know the details of our ethnic history. I tried to get my Dad to open up and share what he knew about his ancestry. He was noncommittal, indicating he didn't really know all that much. I let it drop. It wasn't something I felt compelled to push given Dad's blasé attitude about his African forefathers and foremothers.

"I'm listening."

"Faith, it seems, was one of the rare comforts that slaves in the American South enjoyed, oftentimes without the knowledge of their masters who forbade their slaves to learn how to read and write. But where there's a will, there's a way. And through surreptitious readings of Leviticus, slaves became acquainted with the idea of Jubilee: the belief that eventually they'd be set free. This of course, happened – at least on paper – with the Emancipation Proclamation. Later, the day of Confederate surrender, June 15, became known as Juneteenth: the day of Jubilee, the day of freedom."

I was stunned. A white priest from a little town in northwestern Wisconsin knew more than I did about my own people. My fingers rubbed the slick surface of the book's cover as I read and reread the title: *Jubilee*.

"Thank you."

"It's the least I could do."

I remember there being a very tortured break in my thinking process at that moment, as I tried to gauge if a further response would be appropriate. Eventually, my heart overwhelmed my head and I gave Father Tom a very serious hug. It was at that moment, when the priest did not chastise me, when he made no strenuous objection to my embrace, that I sensed Thomas Michaels was not entirely chaste.

FOURTEEN

Foxy Brown's "Broken Silence" resonated from the kitchen of my sister's house as Lilith loaded the dishwasher with cereal bowls and juice glasses. The music moved my sister to grind her hips as she worked. I sat at the kitchen table, a mug of coffee in front of me, ready to bust a gut at her antics. No steam rose from my coffee. I take my coffee lukewarm, a quirk of mine that always drove Del nuts.

Del.

Thinking about how we got together, how he died – well, that was something I'd been avoiding since his funeral and the chilly reception I'd gotten from his kin when I showed up to say goodbye. I don't know where they buried him. I left the service before learning Del's final resting place, chased from the chapel by ugly stares and ill feelings.

Sitting in Lilith's kitchen, I tried to remember how it was that Del and Moose talked me into participating in their little scheme. I couldn't understand my surrender. I was unable to get past the fact that I was raised different, that I had no reason to hurt so badly that I needed meth to make me feel good. And yet, that's how it was. I felt bad. Del and the drug made me feel good; they made me feel better than anything I'd experienced since I left Madeline Island for college.

"Whatcha thinkin'?"

Lilly's words were so Midwestern, so at odds with the lyrics and voice inflection of the singer she was listening to.

"Trying to figure out how I messed up so bad."

"There's no easy answer for why we do the things we do." Lilith said as she turned off the stereo. "Best to just chalk it up to life experience and move on, head held high, walkin' proud."

A small laugh escaped me.

"What's so funny?"

"You."

"How's that?"

"You're in no position to empathize with your fallen sibling, now are you?"

"'Fallen sibling.' That's rich. Sounds like someone's feeling mighty self–pitiful this morning."

"I'm not sure 'self–pitiful' is a word."

Lilith sat down across the table from me, smiled and pulled hard on her coffee. Abigail bounced in a swing suspended from the doorframe between the kitchen and the dining room, her chubby brown arms and legs jiggling as she pushed against the tile floor with little feet. The child let out a laugh as she bounced, her milky blue bonnet eyes, a residual of Mom's bloodlines, seeming odd against her dark skin, as she waited for Lilly to react.

I looked at my hands.

"She's precious," I said.

"You won't feel that way when I make you change her diaper. She pees on the toilet. But for the life of me, I can't get her to poop in the hole."

I laughed again.

"We'd best be heading to the courthouse," Lilly advised, her dark eyes locked on a wall clock hanging over the sink. "Richard," she called out. "We need to go."

My brother–in–law sauntered down the stairs from the master bedroom and slid across the quarry tile floor until he stood, stocking–footed, a six–foot–three tall handsome black man, his physique cloaked in a flannel bathrobe, his ebony hair tight to his scalp, a hint of morning stubble on his face, in the center of the kitchen.

"Morning, Abigail darling." Richard pecked his daughter on the cheek as he lifted her free of the swing. "Has she eaten?"

"She has. Changed too. She's ready for a Daddy play day."

Richard sashayed, holding Abby away from his body with long arms, out of the kitchen.

"See ya," Richard said, "and good luck, Esther," he added, his voice echoing off the walls of the hallway as he disappeared.

Lilith rose with exaggerated grace from her chair, opened the door to the dishwasher, and placed her coffee mug on a stainless steel rack. I dumped the last of my coffee into the sink before handing Lilly my mug. She put it next to hers, closed the door, and started the dishwasher. Water surged into the unit. I cleared my throat.

"Thanks for doing this, Richard."

My brother–in–law popped his head back around the corner.

"Nothing to it, Es. You're family. Families need to help each other out. You'll be fine. In six months' time, you'll be back working at the hospital, like none of this ever happened."

"We need to scat," Lilith insisted. "I'll be back sometime later this morning." She gave her husband and daughter a kiss goodbye.

"Do what the judge says," Richard admonished as I picked up my sweater, put on my dress pumps, and followed Lilith out the door.

"I intend to."

Judge Lester Patrick, a rotund black man with no neck and seriously deranged white hair, presided over my sentencing hearing. I'd already entered my plea and met with Julie Frisk, my probation officer, for the pre-sentence investigation. The recommendation was as agreed: I was to be given a stay of adjudication on the charge. I'd do no more time and have no conviction on my record, provided I completed probation. I'd be supervised by Ms. Frisk for three years, reporting to her on a weekly basis by telephone while at New Beginnings, and in person once I was back in Hennepin County. I also had to remain drug– and alcohol–free, attend Narcotics Anonymous meetings twice a week, pay a five–hundred–dollar fine or do one hundred hours of community service, and have no similar charges. If I made it through the three years without a problem, I wouldn't be a felon. If I messed up, I'd go to prison.

After Ms. Frisk made her recommendation, Judge Patrick asked me if I had anything to say. I didn't. I mean, what was I going to tell him? I didn't understand at the time what had compelled me to use meth; I'm not sure I know the whole of it even now. No, there wasn't much I could've said that day with Lilith sitting in the back row of the gallery. I figured the less I said, the less notoriety I'd bring to my already–embarrassed family.

Silence, I thought, remembering something I'd learned as a child from my Mom, *is a virtue.*

"No, your honor."

Judge Patrick looked at me as I sat next to the soon–to–be gender–modified Cherise. As I waited for the Judge to say something provident and wise, my lips curled into a grin at the realization that my attorney was about to become all lady.

How do they do that? I wondered absent–mindedly. *How do they make an 'outie' into an 'inie'?*

Of course, I couldn't very well ask Cherise this while sitting in a courtroom, and it really wasn't any of my business, but it sure brought a smile to my face as I waited for the judge to speak.

"Ms. DuMont, you are the rare exception to the folks that I have had in front of me. You have all the advantages. A supportive family. An education. Intellect. A positive outlook. But I want you to realize that methamphetamine addiction is the hardest addiction to beat. You've made it this far. I hope you make it all the way to being free of the drug," Judge Patrick advised. "Good luck to you. I hope we don't see each other in this context again."

Me neither, I thought, my mind absurdly fixed on the operation my lawyer was about to endure.

FIFTEEN

Billy Cadotte and I never had it out. Even after I was well enough to return to school for my senior year, Billy and I never discussed his betrayal. I don't want you to get the wrong idea. I experienced hurt – deep injury caused by his rejection. But in my case, that harm took a back seat to the devastation I felt being considered the cause of David's death. Both aspects of injury were there, just beneath the surface, as I tried to slide my way back into the routine of school and my part–time job at the Rittenhouse Inn. And though folks around me marveled at how well I was adjusting to my circumstances, the truth is, I wasn't really dealing with any of it.

I maintained a semi–conscious ability to smile and say "hello" to Billy whenever we met – which, given the claustrophobic nature of the place in which we lived, was nearly every day. I handled these encounters best when I prepared my mind, when I closed off my heart by anticipating Billy's presence and steeling myself as if I were going to shoot free–throws to win a big game. Chance meetings threw me. Absent the ability to gird myself, it was difficult to maintain my composure. But through prayer and a little fakery (studying how Lilly put on false airs helped), I got by. I'm sure, given what Billy knew about me, he knew I was ready to explode whenever we were near each other. Thankfully, he was smart enough to avoid setting a match to the fuse. He kept his mouth shut, forsook demonstrations of affection towards April when I was around and, his duplicity aside, behaved admirably. I won't say that I forgave him; I certainly didn't forget. Many were the times that, standing on my weary feet in the Rittenhouse, memories of our time together on the *Rose* would storm back into my mind, obliterating any other line of thought or reason, no matter how hard I concentrated my prayers to the Blessed Virgin to block out such dead–end visions. Folks in the Rittenhouse dining rooms would whisper as I muttered

72

petitions to the Holy Mother like some dark–skinned Joan of Arc. I understood their pointed critiques of my sanity; it didn't matter. The scenes came back and stole me away – transfixed as to time and place, on something precious, something dear, something forever lost.

A memory. We're standing at the railing on the observation deck of the Raspberry Island Lighthouse. The sky is open and clear. To the north, Bear Island rises two hundred feet above Lake Superior. Oak Island is close at hand to the east, its steep sandstone cliffs appearing pink beneath the blistering sun. Canada Geese strut and stroll and occasionally honk as they feed on tufts of grass poking through the sand. Gulls swoop and screech loudly for no discernible reason. Billy's black eyes stare out across the water. He holds my hand. We stand, completely silent, watching the world, feeling as if nothing could ever defeat our bond or us.

We had made love dozens of times by then, the Friday night before Labor Day. It wasn't always perfect. Billy sometimes rushed, and sometimes didn't give me the proper time and attention before he entered. But on other occasions, he was marvelous. His fingers. His tongue. His touch in all the right places, finding all the right edges. Most often, he was on top. That position made me giggle. Consider the scene: a black woman and an Indian having sex in a manner prescribed by Christian missionaries. How rich! But despite the unimaginative – innocent, really – nature of our explorations, we surely had something. Even today, the distant imagery of it all sends a shudder into my womb. One thing is for sure: I remember the waves crashing and the surf rising, both on the beach and inside me!

Lusty daydreams of these trysts still haunt me, but they aren't nearly as important as what happened at the Raspberry Island Lighthouse that Friday before Labor Day. For it was then, as we held hands and watched summer parade by, that Billy Cadotte told me he loved me. How was I to know that his expression of devotion would vaporize in a few weeks' time? I can't really say it was Billy's fault. I mean, we were seventeen years old and he, suddenly and without preparation, was confronted with the horrible realization that I had been rendered less than perfect; that I was now damaged goods. Billy's inability to endure such a test is something that I began to consider while standing on my tired feet in the dining room of the Rittenhouse. And though I worked our parting over and over and over in my young mind, I couldn't offer Billy any semblance of forgiveness until years later, after I fought my battle with meth.

That senior year, I wandered through school, doing the bare minimum needed to graduate. Coach Ebert asked me to be the student manager of the girls' basketball team. I declined; I didn't see the point of sitting on the bench keeping stats for Amy and the other players when I longed to be out there, stealing the ball, pulling down rebounds, shooting the three. I didn't make it to a single game that season. I couldn't bring myself to watch. On game nights, I stayed at home. I didn't devote much time to my studies, though I did read. No, that's not quite right. I *devoured* words, is what I did. Books seemed to be my therapy, my solace. The first novel I opened when I came home from Miller–Dwan was *Jubilee*. I would've read it in the hospital, but I just couldn't concentrate on large projects while I was there. Oh sure, I read magazine articles and the newspaper. But a novel? That had to wait until I went home, though even after reading the book, I missed the point of Father Tom's gift. It wasn't until recently, after I reread the priest's scribbled inscription to me inside the novel's front cover, that I finally understood what he was really getting at.

SIXTEEN

Panora, Iowa: a little hick town west of Des Moines in the virtual, if not the actual, middle of nowhere. That's where I landed for treatment. By the time Lilly and I arrived at New Beginnings, an enormous farmhouse located on the north end of Lake Panorama (I'm not making the name up) in Lilly's BMW, I was fighting the deepest, darkest depression I'd ever encountered.

See, the thing is, meth works like the devil himself. The reason that it's so damn devastating is the way it impacts the brain. Meth is masterful at stimulating brain cells and getting them to release massive quantities of dopamine, a neurotransmitter that, when it courses through our bodies during sex, or is released during our admiration of a sunset, or is set free upon our recognition of a loved one in a crowd, produces euphoria. Imagine being in the throes of the best orgasm you've ever experienced, while free-falling from an airplane, as you eat chocolate ice cream. If you can conjure up such an imagined experience, you'd approximate the rush you achieve doing meth. I say approximate, though not equal. Meth, so far as I know, has no equal when it comes to heavenly immediacy. Any wonder why I – along with thousands of other smart, educated folks – fall for the stuff? And I stand by my observation that meth shares attributes with the devil. I say this because, just as with the dark master, who, scripture says, can grant his followers riches, worldly recognition or power, the trade-off for achieving such treasure is the loss of one's soul. So it is with meth.

Unlike cocaine, which prevents dopamine from being recycled back into the brain cells, methamphetamine actually enters cells and triggers the release of excessive amounts of dopamine. What happens next, once meth is inside the cells in the brain, is where the analogy to Satan rings most true. You see, once methamphetamine enters a cell, it damages that cell's ability to manufacture dopamine. The destructive process is similar to what happens when you're afflicted with Parkinson's disease. Scary stuff? I wish someone had explained these attributes of the drug to me. Maybe, just maybe, such knowledge would have had curbed my behavior. Maybe not. We'll never know, now will we?

They call what was happening to me anhedonia. You've heard of hedonism? Same root word. Instead of being bent on pleasing oneself as a hedonist would, when you suffer from anhedonia, you suffer, quite literally, from the inability to experience pleasure. The dopamine–producing cells shut down, becoming incapable of releasing the chemical and leaving a person unable to feel anything. That's the trade–off with the devil I was talking about: immense transitory pleasure that results in the destruction of one's ability to feel everyday joy. I made that bargain the day meth first traversed my veins while laying with Delmont Benson in our basement apartment in Minneapolis. By the time I was sitting in the intake room at New Beginnings, my sister already gone, on her way back to her perfect little life and her perfect little family, I was so deep in depression, it was all I could do to give my name to the lady across the desk from me.

The woman, licensed social worker/therapist Maggie Prescott – a rotund and billowy lady who stood no taller than five–feet and weighed in at close to three hundred pounds, her hair an unnatural shade of magenta, her skin, so pink, so strangely alien next to my own – didn't waste time. That first day, Ms. Prescott met with me from eleven o'clock until noon. The programming protocol at New Beginnings was for each patient to talk to Ms. Prescott three times a week. The objective of these one–on–one sessions was to seek out the root of why I became a meth user, what voids I was trying to fill, and what hurts I was attempting to salve over with the drug.

I was also scheduled to attend cognitive–behavioral group sessions, the sort of thing you see on television: you know, the scenes where everyone sits around in a circle on hard plastic chairs, introduces themselves and shares their pain. Those sessions were five days a week, from two to four in the afternoon, with a fifteen–minute break at three.

Like I said before, New Beginnings is an expensive proposition. With a total of twelve patients staying at the farmhouse during the six–month treatment cycle – some leaving early of their own choosing, while others were discharged for messing up – all vacancies were filled to keep the house full. The place was making good money, considering there was only five staff on duty.

The director, Dr. Rebecca Hodges, a sternly countenanced black woman – a psychologist with enormous, flabby breasts, a constricted waist and spidery varicose vein–tracked legs that seemed incapable of holding up her torso – had battled her own demons (rumored to be crack cocaine) before getting clean and going back to school. She ran the group sessions where, in the close quarters of the meeting room, her impregnable façade melted away and she became the consummate facilitator. But magically, once the group session was over, and once she returned to her role as administrator, she was all business, cocking her stiletto chin at you, and staring over her bifocal glasses in your direction with unwavering eyes.

Another integral member of the staff was Harry the cook. Being the cook at the place meant more than simply making meals for twelve drug–crazed women. Oh, did I mention that New Beginnings is a women's–only program? Well, I should have, if I didn't. Anyway, Harry Bjorklund, a tall, quiet, very pale and bald man in his early forties, was so shy that he barely spoke two words to me during my first three weeks of taking meals in the dining room. Harry wasn't overtly interesting but, I must confess, as the only male in the place during the workweek, there was a certain lightness in all of our steps when we were able to catch a few moments alone in the same room with Harry.

Mason Erickson, a farmer in his mid–thirties, short, fairly stout, with cloudy hazel eyes and thick blond hair, filled in for Harry on the weekends. At first glance, Mason wasn't an eye–catcher, but after some study, his features became more attractive, his mannerisms unquestionably quaint. Word was that he'd bought his father's farm west of Lake Panorama and was a dairyman. I knew nothing about dairy farming at the time, other than holding some fuzzy notion that dairy farming entailed immense dedication and work. My suppositions on that score later turned out to be accurate.

My first session with Ms. Prescott was a total waste of time. She had me sit in a raggedy–ass armchair, the kind that sort of, but not really, reclines. (I'm not a fan of doing things half–way, as you can tell; my aversion to people and things that are partial, that don't make solid commitments, includes recliners that don't allow a person a full repose.) Anyway, my initial interview with Ms. Prescott led nowhere. Oh sure, she got me to relay the fact that I'd been there when David was burned up and that I'd sustained physical trauma, but that's sort of obvious, isn't it? I mean, those things happened and there was a burden, a cost, associated with them. Ms. Prescott seemed unduly pleased she was able to wrangle bits and pieces of that ancient tragedy and its aftermath out of me during the hour we spent together. I didn't see the cleverness in it, nor the point. Then, little by little, as I felt more comfortable in therapy, and after I began to really listen to the other girls during group – especially my roommate, Wanda Jones, a middle–aged black lady from Rapid City, South Dakota who'd stolen over forty thousand dollars from municipal accounts under her care and control as Rapid City's Finance Manager, to pay for a very secretive but very real meth habit (she used the drug to boost her energy and keep her weight down) – something happened to me. My self–constructed barriers to self–reflection began to weaken. Strictures of guilt and loss started to loosen.

That's when David's and Del's faces came into focus. They began to haunt me, visit me, during quiet moments spent in the old farmhouse located in the middle of nowhere.

SEVENTEEN

It wasn't as if Mom outwardly accused me of causing David's death, but her silence spoke volumes once I came home from the hospital and tried to reintegrate myself into life on Madeline Island. Mom isn't a chatterbox, but she'd always been interested in what Lilly and I were up to, consistently inquiring into our daily routines at school and work and monitoring our social lives with a light but parental touch. That all changed once David was gone. To be honest with you, I think the situation would have been healthier if she had railed and screamed and cried when I came home from the hospital. I mean, I carried the guilt of what happened with me anyway; bringing my failings out into the open and kicking them around a bit couldn't have done more damage to me than leaving my culpability locked up, tight as a drum, inside me. But that's not the way Mom played it. Maybe her love for me prevented her from attacking me. Maybe she was too exhausted from warding off her own demons of self–doubt regarding religion and faith to enter into a dialogue with me about what had happened. I'm not a psychiatrist. I'm just a nurse who's been through hell. How would I know what my mother was thinking?

In other ways, my return home from Miller–Dwan Hospital was routine. Lilly chattered her usual schoolgirl nonsense, clearly not forgetting our brother, but determinedly dedicated not to let his passing destroy her senior year in high school. She made captain of the Bayfield High School cheerleading squad, became Homecoming Queen, and continued to fend off admirers at the rate of one or two new beaus a week. Boys from as far away as Superior and Duluth came around to court her. The phone rang so often, and she was on the line so much, that Dad was forced to put in a second line. Of course, no one called me. It was pretty much Lilly's line.

Dad, for his part, immersed himself in work. Wednesday nights? He spent fewer and fewer of them on the island. The emotional separation that occurred between my parents after David's death was unheralded. It wasn't like Dad abandoned Mom and took up with some twenty–year–old medical technologist; I'm quite certain that Dad's morals wouldn't allow that to happen. It was subtler than that. It was more like a slow erosion of time spent together. Later on, the situation seemed to right itself. I never knew whether Dad saw trouble coming, or Mom put her foot down. But eventually, they returned to the pattern of life they'd crafted before David passed. How they retrieved that balance and saved their marriage is something I wasn't privy to.

Still, Mom's silence, the unnatural way she moved around the house, was unnerving. It began to eat at me and bother me more than it probably should have. Talking to Lilly about it wasn't an option; like I've said, Lil's solution to dealing with grief and loss was to create a whirlwind of social involvement. It's not that my sister is so empty–headed that she can't serve as a sounding board. She may appear to be a ditz at times but she's got a solid heart and a reasonably well–attuned mind. I knew how badly David's death hit her, being her twin and all, even when she was loath to articulate her feelings. Opening my big yap and unburdening my own pain didn't seem, to me, to be fair to Lil, since it was obvious that my neglect was the root cause of her downheartedness. So I turned to the one person I believed would listen: Grandma Mary.

By the time of David's death, Grandma had moved out of her house in Ashland and into an assisted–living apartment in Superior, which meant we didn't see each other that much. Once a month, Lilly and I took a trip into Superior to see Grandma. After the fire, I preferred going alone, but I couldn't figure out a polite way to shed Lil. Even so, every so often, I managed to make the hour–long trip alone, which gave me the opportunity to talk seriously with Grandma Mary.

"Sure it is now, little lady," she'd start off, Galway Gaelic plain in her diction, "that God works in mysterious ways."

"Gram, I'm not too keen on God right now."

"That's to be expected, child. But David's with our Lord and the Holy Mother right now, smiling down on us, don't you see? He was baptized in the water of the River Jordan in the One True Faith and he's in glory, as sure as I am breathing. 'Tis not a myth or a belief, child. 'Tis fact."

Her spiritual strength was remarkable. I felt its power, the magnificence of two millennia of faith behind her words, when we sat in her apartment and talked about what had happened. And yet, there was doubt inside me – evil forebodings of disbelief that even her soothing calmness couldn't defeat.

On one of my visits to her, during Christmas break that year, Gram suggested that I talk to Father Tom. He was still the youth pastor at Our Lady of the Lake, and though my attendance at church youth events became infrequent after the fire, Lilly still saw him. Mostly, Lil went to youth group only if she knew a particular boy was going to be there. It wasn't ever the same boy, you understand; she was more interested in variety, in the flavor of the week. Gram's suggestion that I talk to Father Tom caught me off guard, dredged up feelings for the young priest that were wholly incompatible with seeing him as a parishioner.

"He's a bright young padre. You need someone close to your own age to confide in. Who better to confess to, if that's what you be needin', than a priest?"

I considered my grandmother's suggestion but made no commitment.

"Besides, granddaughter, he's not hard to take in the looks department, is he now?"

"*Gram!*"

"Oh hush, child. I'll not be telling you something you haven't already deduced yourself, if I point out to you that Father Michaels is one God-crafted handsome man of the cloth."

I smiled. In fact, I believe I laughed. No, thinking back, I'm sure we both did. I know this to be true, because I'll never forget that exchange. I'll never forget it, because it was the last time I visited Grandma Mary. The tough old bird passed away just two days later. She keeled over dead from a sudden heart attack, just as Mom arrived in Superior to bring Grandma back to the Madeline Island for Christmas Eve.

EIGHTEEN

Time crept by. Each hour, each day, inched along. I felt like I was stuck in some sort of surreal slow-motion video of someone else's misfortune. The one–on–ones with Maggie Prescott were insufferable – not that Maggie didn't try to enlighten me, engage me and prod me into revelations that would unburden my melancholy and release me from the demons of my past. Oh, how she wrestled, how she fought with my hardheaded reluctance, my ingrained (DuMontish, if you will) refusal to allow a stranger into my personal vault of doubt and angst. It was as if she were Mary Magdalene herself with a grip on Ol' Beelzebub, trying to strangle the life (or is it the death?) out of Jesus' archenemy. Turns out, I'm a hell of a lot more stubborn than the devil. That's a fact Maggie Prescott would verify if you chanced across her.

Group, on the other hand, was immediately beneficial. Talking things over with eleven other women whose personal stories, their own versions of the inky pit, caused the hair on the back of my neck to stand on end, reduced me to tears. And shedding tears had a profound impact upon me. Dr. Hodges saw this right away, and knew just how to use my weepy predilection to her (and my) advantage.

"In the hospital..." Dr. Hodges began one day as we all sat on chairs in a circle, our faces starting to show glimmers of sanctification, our eyes beginning to clear from the dull, lifeless glaze of addiction compounded by withdrawal, the faint sunlight filtering through the windows lining one side of the conference room, the light fractured by a passing sun shower.

"Yes?"

Everyone's attention was riveted on me. I felt the other women inspecting every nook and cranny of my face.

"Have you ever talked to your mother about what happened?"

A lump formed in my throat. I struggled to swallow.

"No."

"Why?"

Good question. I searched for a good answer. Not *the* answer – just an answer that would placate Dr. Hodges.

"She never brought it up."

The incredulity on the psychologist's face was clear.

"*Really?* She never once asked you what happened? Never hinted, through a question or a gesture, that she might want to know your side of the story?"

Had mother, in some oblique way, tried to get me to talk as I rehabilitated in Miller–Dwan? Once again, I searched my memory. Nothing came to mind.

"I don't think so."

"Don't you find that strange?"

Delores Pufall, an emaciated Native American woman in her late fifties who had a dark complexion and was battling a career of lost family, lost jobs and eight in–patient treatments for alcoholism, posed the question. I sincerely liked Delores. She was generally quiet, minding her own business and causing no trouble. She wasn't one of the women you had to be wary of or had to protect your secrets from. Now, here she was, asking probing questions about my life, examining facets of my past I wanted left buried.

How dare she! I thought. "How so?" was what I said instead.

"I mean, if it was you who had lost a child, and your daughter was involved – either as the person to blame or as the person who tried to save the child – wouldn't you ask questions? Wouldn't you want to know?"

Delores's inquiry stopped my mind dead.

Yes I would, I said to myself. *I surely would.*

Hazel Edwards, a suburban housewife my own age fighting a serious infatuation with ecstasy (something she'd learned to use to "loosen up" when she and her girlfriends went barhopping in Council Bluffs, where she lived) pushed a strand of limpid peroxide–whitened hair away from her eyes. Her unrestrained breasts shifted beneath her yellow t–shirt as she stretched her legs and took up the inquisition.

"There must've been some point in the hospital when your mother tried to break through. It seems weird she didn't try to reach out, to save her connection to you."

Damn it, I thought. *Damn it to hell. I don't remember Mom trying to talk to me about David or the fire. I just don't remember anything like that happening.*

"There's nothing," I whispered, tears sliding down my cheeks. "Nothing."

My roommate, Wanda Jones, was sitting next to me. She handed me a tissue. I dabbed my face, sopping up evidence of my self–deception: there *was* something. Something I couldn't bring myself to tell. At least, not in front of those women. It would eventually come out, weeks later in a one–on–one with Maggie Prescott, and it would catch me completely unaware.

NINETEEN

There are two things I need to come clean about. During my therapy, I came to grips with these simple truths: that I am not, by and large, an envious person, and I really only have one regret. In terms of envy, I have rarely coveted my neighbor's house, car, lifestyle, lover or wealth. I've already admitted that, at one point in my youth, I coveted Father Tom. I'm certain that I've experienced other, transitory flirtations with envy over my twenty–eight years of life, but there is only one thing, one earthly treasure that I have consistently dreamed of snatching from its owner and possessing – hoarding, if you will, for myself – and that's Lilith's beauty. As soon as we were able to stand side–by–side and brush our teeth each morning before school, our faces reflected in the big mirror in the bathroom, I became jealous of Lil's looks. I coveted, even at that early age, the finely crafted lines of her features. I wanted her silky, straight, easy–to–manage hair. I resented that my own head was covered with disorganized swirls that, for the life of my mother and me, we couldn't tame. I instinctively knew that Lilly's beauty was something that would make life a snap for my sister; I wanted that easy road for myself. If there had been some way to steal Lilith's beauty without killing her, I would have done it in a second.

In terms of regrets, as I say, I have only the one. The lamentation I am still troubled by emerged during my treatment, at nightfall, as I neared the edge of sleep. At that time, my eyes were heavy and Wanda Jones had slipped into a slumber, her light snores echoing faintly from her bed across our shared space like the beat of so many dragonfly wings navigating the heavy summer air.

I watch him toddle across the cool concrete of the basement floor, his diapered rump sagging as he moves. He toddles unsteadily towards the metal can. He stops next to the container, places his pudgy fingers around the metal spigot, and rocks the gasoline can back and forth, back and forth. Gasoline sloshes from the air hole on the top of the can. He discovers that, by pulling on the spigot, he can make the can dance on its metal edge. David coos and giggles as the container rocks. The can balances precariously on its steel rim. The child's fat upper arms flap and wiggle as he relishes his game. And then it happens: the can teeters and David gives the spigot one final tug. The can falls. Gasoline spreads across the floor. The child sits in the puddle of cool liquid, completely oblivious to what is about to happen. In my mind's eye, I watch my baby brother splash fuel with his hands and feet as the gasoline flows across the basement floor. A propane hot water heater stands in one corner of the basement. The child kicks, spraying gasoline into the air and coating his clothing with fuel.

I'm watching this scene voyeuristically, in wonderment, as if I don't appreciate the danger. I'm curious to see what will happen and powerless to intervene. I utter no words of warning. I make no move to stop the tragedy. The fuel spreads beneath the hot water tank. Though the pilot light of the device is burning, its faint heat isn't enough to ignite the gasoline. There is still time – time to rush in and save my brother from what must happen – but as I am only watching this in a dream, there is no rescue. When someone on the main floor of the bungalow turns a spigot, water surges. The pilot ignites propane and then, after a slight hesitation, the fumes trapped beneath the hot water tank burst into flame. David stops, tilts his head towards the noise, and watches as the fuel he is sitting in becomes a sea of fire. It is only then, after flames engulf David, that he understands things aren't all right. He releases a single, panicked wail. I hear him. In real time, I race into the basement as the fire burns David's clothing and consumes his skin. I try to intervene. I try to save my brother, but there is nothing I can do.

When I reach him, though his face is contorted as if to scream, there is no sound. His initial cry had alerted me to the disaster and sent my feet slapping against the ground, propelling me to his side. But once I was there and leaned my body into the pyre to snatch him away from the gasoline's power, he was silent. I stole him away from danger and rushed outside. I stopped, dropped and rolled in a futile attempt to extinguish the flames. Someone grabbed a fire extinguisher and sprayed us with foam. David's eyes were fixed. He whimpered, but did not cry. I don't remember anything after that, after his eyes locked on mine. There was a hint, a trace of something in his gaze that suggested betrayal. That's what I was left with as my body shut down in response to my own burns.

So you ask: what is your one regret, Esther Mary DuMont? My one regret in life, the only lingering disappointment that isn't petty or easily remedied, is that I did not die in the fire. My baby brother was sent, all alone, to meet Jesus. I should have gone with him.

TWENTY

Maggie Prescott finally broke through. It happened during a one–on–one session the week after Thanksgiving, three months into my stay at New Beginnings. It happened because I'd been granted a leave to go home to Madeline Island to spend the holiday with my family.

The entire Culver family – Richard, Lilly and Abigail – picked me up from the treatment center in Richard's black Dodge Durango the Wednesday morning before Thanksgiving. There was a dusting of new snow on the ground. A negligible crust of ice had formed on Lake Panorama, and the sky was unremittingly gray. The air was brittle from the cold as I followed Lilly out to the car.

"How's it goin'?"

"Okay."

I'm not sure Lilly heard me given I had a wool scarf wrapped around my mouth.

"What's it like?"

"Whaddya mean?"

"Treatment."

"Okay. I'm clean," I said plainly and without conviction. I had no desire to get into the nuts and bolts of my program with my sister between the front door of my treatment center and the door of her husband's SUV.

"That's a start."

Lilith's mittened hand grasped the door handle of the Durango's rear passenger door and she opened it for me.

"Thanks."

I raised my left leg to get inside. Abby was sitting in the back seat, behind the driver's seat; amidst a sea of black leather, smiling like she'd just won a guest spot on *Blue's Clues*. She was dressed in a dark blue woolen coat, black leather boots, a matching blue felt hat and blue wool gloves. Her deep brown features were barely visible inside the contours of the hat – a sort of Annie Hall affair that covered most of her face in shadow.

My niece leaned against the restraint of her seat harness to peck my cheek. I wrapped my arms around her – as much as the child restraint would allow – and squeezed tight.

"I missed you, Abs."

I righted myself and fastened my safety harness.

"How's it going?" Richard asked.

"Great."

"You look like a million bucks," he added convincingly.

Having backed the Durango out of its parking space, Richard stepped on the car's accelerator. The big SUV pulled onto a blacktopped two–lane and headed east, towards Des Moines.

"Thanks. I feel like I'm making progress."

We loaded the Durango onto the *Island Queen* for the twenty-minute trip to Madeline Island. Wind whipped the water between Bayfield and LaPointe into whitecaps. Water sprayed my face as I stood outside, exposed to the weather. My sister's family remained inside the ferry's cabin during the crossing.

The reality of coming home overwhelmed me. Standing at the iron railing, I looked back at Bayfield: the town's yellow, red and white lights had sparked to life against the barren early winter hillside rising behind the settlement. The oaks and maples lining the steeps were devoid of leaves. Their colorless shapes merged with the overcast sky. I sobbed. My tears were a mixture of upset and relief.

Del's face, his haunted eyes, came to me as I turned my attention towards Madeline Island. His appearance was only a fleeting, ghostly specter against the slumbering woods of the island's shoreline. He was there for a moment, then he vanished, replaced by the mist, cold and fog.

Mom and Dad were fine. There were no deep discussions, and no lengthy intrusions into my personal life during our two days together. The weather was awful: a November rainstorm swept over the South Shore of Lake Superior for the entirety of my visit, requiring us to stay inside and bond. I felt comfortable sleeping in my childhood bed, surrounded by my own things. Even the pounding of the rain against the gable window in my old room didn't disturb my sleep. I ate too much, slept too much and drank pots of coffee during those two days at home. Lilly and I laughed out loud, telling old stories that we'd told many times – stories that everyone had heard before – though we waited until Dad was out of the room before we retold the story of Mom taking us to the doctor for birth control pills. It was a tale Dad hadn't heard, and one he really didn't need to know about.

It was only when, for reasons I can't quite recall, I ventured into the basement that I came unglued. Like I said, I'm not sure why I went down those rickety old stairs and into the unfinished cellar of my parent's house. Maybe I needed to put something in the wash. Maybe I was looking for an old board game, Scrabble or some such thing. The "why" isn't important. What is important is that, once I stepped onto the cold, cement floor beneath the dim glow of the light bulb hanging from the unfinished ceiling, the exposed floor joist holding up the first floor of the house over my head, furious dread overcame me. The speed with which my mood changed from light and lovely to dark and forlorn, shocked me; it crippled me like a poisoned arrow had been fired into my heart.

Please understand: this was not my first time back into the cellar since David's death. I'd been able, after a time, to venture down the stairway and into the basement to do laundry and the like at my mother's behest. I won't say it was easy, but I was able to do it. The more times I made the descent after coming home from Miller–Dwan Hospital, the less onerous the trip became. In the end, I don't recall feeling anything in particular once the initial trepidation wore off. To have feelings of anxiousness and fear rise up after descending those stairs a decade after David's death was totally unexpected. And, despite all the time spent at New Beginnings, I was unprepared for the experience. Anguish trapped me. I was unable to stand up, unable to retreat, for the better part of twenty minutes. There was something down there – something in the dank recesses of the cellar – waiting for me, trying to get my attention. It was something so large and all–encompassing that I dared not move towards it. My legs refused to work, so I simply sat down on the last step, closed my eyes and tried to will myself to forget. I couldn't. An image, very faint and remote, asserted itself. I strained to rid myself of the thought, and struggled to filter out the image so that I could rise and flee the darkness. But the picture was too strong: its power over me was simply too great.

Now, I know what you're thinking. You believe that I was held captive that Friday in the basement of my parent's home by a vision of my baby brother's demise. One could assume such, but one would be wrong. No, the image chaining me was not one depicting David's agony. It was simply a short sequence, shown over and over in the theater of my memory, of *me*: me walking into the basement through the cellar door, placing the gasoline can on its shelf, too high for David to reach. The image was grainy and jerky, like an old silent movie. There was no mistaking the person portrayed in the scene. It was me. I had done the right thing.

The reason I was laid low by the image is that I could not remember, before that day, the details of what had happened. It wasn't like I hadn't searched and searched my memory for some scrap of vindication, some small piece of alibi. But until that moment, when the scene suddenly resurrected itself, I hadn't been able to recall my movements immediately before David's accident, at least not with the crucial detail needed to assuage my guilt.

Is this for real? I thought, sitting on the bottom stair, my bare feet numbed by the cold concrete. *Or is it just wishful thinking?*

The door to the upstairs opened. Lilly descended. She expressed concern. I passed my condition off as nothing, as simply being overcome by nostalgia. We retreated to the upstairs, to the light. And that was all – or so I thought.

"We've never been able to break through the barrier you've erected around your time in the hospital, after the fire, when your mother visited you," Maggie Prescott reflected during a session in her office once I returned from my Thanksgiving leave. "Why is that?"

Why indeed, I thought. "I'm not sure."

"You blame yourself?"

"That's stating the obvious."

"Your father has absolved you."

I nodded.

"And then there's your mother...."

It was then that the proverbial light went on. I had experienced the same revelation – the slow, labored depiction of me placing the gasoline canister in its proper place, the flammable liquid clearly out of David's reach – on one other occasion. *Why hadn't I remembered this before?*

"You seem preoccupied."

I remained quiet as I mulled over another long forgotten scene from the past.

Mom is in my hospital room, sitting on a chair next to my bed. Her hands work at a knitting project of some sort, though I don't really care about its exact details. It's after the IVs and other tubes have been removed; the debriding of my skin is complete, the grafts are set in place and I'm itching like hell. My eyes are closed. I don't remember sleeping, but I might have been. Something – a sound, a movement – catches my attention and forces me to open my eyes, and to come back into the room. I remember my mother. I remember watching her put needles to wool. There is an omnipresent contentment about her during that instant, when she doesn't know I'm awake and looking at her, that promotes understanding. I realize then that she is no longer angry with me.

Why not? I ask myself. *Why isn't she angry?*

Knowledge surges across me as I watch Mom purse and unpurse her lips. Instantly, her position on the matter becomes clear: she isn't angry with me, because she knows I'm not to blame.

"It wasn't my fault."

"How's that?"

"My mother. She knew it then. I did too, but for some reason, until I returned home last week and went into the basement, my mind was a blank."

"And?"

"I know I put the gasoline can away."

Releasing those words – words that had been irretrievable for over a decade – overwhelmed me. Maggie Prescott's chubby pink fingers plucked two tissues from a Kleenex box on a nearby table. She handed me a tissue, kept one for her own use, and the two of us had a good cry.

TWENTY-ONE

I went into treatment at New Beginnings in August. By December, the good doctor and Ms. Prescott had pulled what they could from me. Using cognitive retooling and self–examination, they coerced my psyche into deconstructing my craving for an altered reality – a reality lacking the anguished cries of the departed. I began to feel whole: a complete woman, a daughter, a sister, an aunt.

I'd started working outside New Beginnings as a waitress. My status as a registered nurse was on hold pending my completion of the program. Even then, a period of intensive supervision would be required if I were allowed to return to my profession. There was no way, until I proved to people who mattered that I could stay clean, that I'd be allowed back into nursing. I felt a longing to do that, to go back to helping others. In early December, I began a part–time job at the Town's Edge Café in Guthrie Center, the county seat of tiny Guthrie County, which is located seven miles west of Panora, and ten miles west of Lake Panorama. Maggie Prescott found me the job. (Her brother–in–law, Earl Prescott, runs the place.)

Before my Thanksgiving revelation, both Maggie Prescott and Dr. Hodges vocalized fears that I was regressing. I understood their concern: I spent my free time in the big lonesome house by myself, and the only thing I did with regularity was read. That's why Maggie suggested the part–time job. She and the good doctor got tired of me sitting around, being anti-social and all, my eyes glued to a book. I wasn't too keen on the idea, but given that I needed to appease those in charge of my destiny, I took the job.

Wanda Jones is the best–read woman I've ever met. She brought a collection of her favorite novels with her from Rapid City. The literature she favored was a welcome respite from the Danielle Steele and Ken Fowlette novels on the shelves of the New Beginnings library. Not that I'm a snob,

93

but I prefer complexity in what I read. I love books with intricate plots and detailed characters. A mass–market story is a good summertime diversion, but generally, I need more. God bless Wanda Jones, is what I say, for letting me share her books. Of course, when she handed me the novel she claimed was her favorite, it didn't come without a price.

"This is one of my most cherished books, a story written by an African American woman, back when African American women didn't write many books."

"How's that?"

I wasn't paying attention as Wanda pulled the book out of her satchel. We were sitting next to each other on battered rocking chairs in the second–story library of the treatment house. I was sipping coffee. Sunlight, oddly white and brilliant for December, penetrated the room. Wanda handed me a trade paperback from her knapsack, the seams of the canvas bag stretched to their limit from the weight of Wanda's traveling literary collection. I accepted the volume, a modest book by size, the pink of my palms flashing in the early afternoon sun.

"You haven't read Hurston?"

"Hurston?"

"Girl, what school did you go to?"

"Northern Michigan University."

"A fine school like that and your English professors didn't have the common sense to have a black girl read Hurston?"

When Wanda got on her soapbox, there was no stopping her, and I knew better than to interrupt. The inflection of her voice – normally plaintive Midwestern – changed dramatically, harkening back to her being raised in the darkest (cosmetically and literarily) neighborhood of St. Louis. Only Catholic school had saved Wanda – at least that's how she told her story – from a life on the streets. The meth she fell into later in life, once she'd survived the chaos and danger of the slums, was a trap of her own making. It was created, she says, by her need to remain thin and attractive.

"What can I say? I've never read anything by her. Never heard of her, to tell you the truth."

"You've read all the white boys – Hemingway, Faulkner, Fitzgerald – writers that don't have much in common with you. Am I right?"

I nodded in agreement.

"And I suppose you've spent time acquainting yourself with James Baldwin, Langston Hughes and, lord of all mercy, Alex Haley?"

"I've read them all."

"Then, sister, you need to read this book."

My fingers received the slim volume as if accepting diamonds.

"Thank you."

"You read it. All those crazy questions about who you are and where you come from – well, they'll vanish once you've read *Their Eyes Were Watching God*."

Wanda smacked her lips in utter satisfaction as she released the edge of the book and nodded her skinny head with certifiable supremacy. There were few times when Wanda Jones lectured me during our months together in treatment. She was naturally laid back and unassuming, rarely allowing her keen intellect and eight years of college to shine. Even in our room, with the lights dimmed and night approaching, we generally spoke as equals, not as a superior to one still trying to learn. This talk was different. She had noted something, seen some defect in my character that she felt needed addressing.

That night, after an exhausting evening at the café, I plunged into the novel. Barely two hundred pages long, I devoured Janie Crawford's story. It is a brilliant gem of a tale that swept me back to a time and place I'd only heard snippets of from my father, in unguarded moments around the dinner table. It was in those moments that our family's history innocently seeped through his filter and pronounced itself, albeit in a discrete way, for Lilly and me to retain.

As the early morning sun crept over the farm fields to the east, when magenta and red light cast black shadows across the acres of dry rows of neat corn awaiting harvest, the stalks and leaves chafed by the wind, I remained riveted. I couldn't put the novel down. I couldn't abandon Janie or her story of persistence and strength, until I read Hurston's last poetic words:

Then Tea Cake came prancing around her where she was and the song of the sigh flew out of the window and lit in the top of the pine trees. Tea Cake, with the sun for a shawl. Of course he wasn't dead. He could never be dead until she herself had finished feeling and thinking. The kiss of his memory made pictures of love and light against the wall. Here was peace. She pulled in her horizon like a great fishnet. Pulled it from around the waist of the world and draped it over her shoulder. So much of life in its meshes! She called in her soul to come and see.

As I served the girls, taking my turn as waitress to eleven seriously fractured women, I slipped my hand into the deep pockets of my apron. The garment's embroidered admonition, "Shut Up and Eat What I Cook," had faded from countless cycles through a washing machine. I returned the book to Wanda.

"Thanks," I whispered.

Wanda Jones looked up, fried egg dripping from her fork and her mouth poised for another bite, as I slid the paperback across the polished top of the oak table. Our eyes met. I'm sure she understood that mine were on the verge of weeping. I know this to be the case because, uncharacteristically, Wanda Jones didn't say a word. She simply smiled. Her big white teeth filled up the entirety of her small face and her tongue pressed hard to the roof of her mouth as she pulled the book towards her and nodded, all the knowing and all the understanding clear in her eyes.

TWENTY-TWO

I remember Father Michaels's kindness after the fire. I saw him intermittently, on the rare Sunday evenings when Lilly dragged me to Our Lady of the Lake. Like I said before, I wasn't much interested in church and rarely attended youth group after David died, but when I did, those Sunday evenings were the only social life I had. Not so for Lilith, of course – she was constantly dating. I admired her. She was able to flirt and maintain romances with a variety of guys without being promiscuous. She drew a line in the sand that, I truly believed, no suitor, despite the fact she continued to be on the pill, could cross. (I'd gone off the pill after the fire; there being little danger I'd become involved with a boy.) While I mooned over Father Michaels, Lilly remained aloof to the Catholic boys invariably surrounding her – boys who circled her beauty like bugs inspecting a Venus Fly Trap, impatience and longing clear on their earnest faces.

"How are you?"

Father Tom and I were doing dishes in the parish kitchen one Sunday evening, a month or so before my graduation from Bayfield High School. It was just after my eighteenth birthday. (Lil's too, as if you hadn't caught on.) The priest was washing dishes and I was drying them.

"Okay."

"You know," the priest observed without looking at me, "you'd feel better if you'd stop blaming yourself for what happened."

I didn't respond. I simply stacked a plate and reached to pick up another dish.

"There's no sin in what you've done, Esther. None at all. You're not scarred because of something you did or didn't do."

I became uncomfortable.

I'm scarred because I failed my brother.

97

It was as if he could read my thoughts.

"Not true, young lady. You were not burned as punishment. God has no interest in meting out corporal recriminations. The fire was, very simply, a thing that happened. It was an accident, nothing more. There is no deep moral message, no underlying revelation in what took place."

Father Tom smiled and rinsed his hands with cold water from the tap. Soap slid off his skin and dolloped into the stainless steel sink as water circled the drain.

"What you need to understand," he continued, "is that Jesus himself recognized this to be true. Remember your scripture? The Gospel of St. John? Jesus, on one of his walks with the disciples, was asked this question: 'Rabbi, who sinned, this man or his parents, that he was born blind?'"

I had to admit, I didn't recall the verse. Thomas Michaels looked at me intently before replying to his own query.

"Jesus answered: 'Neither this man nor his parents sinned. He was born blind so that God's works might be revealed to him.' It's the same with you, Esther. God is watching and waiting to see how you handle what's been given to you, how you come to grips with what lies ahead."

"Seems to me there are better ways to send me a message than to kill my baby brother and turn me into a freak."

Father Tom's fingers reached out and touched the bare skin of my arm. The contrast between his fair complexion and my own was distinct under the harsh fluorescent lighting. The reality of his flesh upon mine caused me to blush.

"You're no freak. Whatever the scars you've been left with, do not let the loss of David scar your inner beauty."

I averted my eyes.

"Do you remember that famous photograph from the Vietnam War, the one where the little girl is running naked down a dirt road, her clothing burned away by napalm?"

"No."

"We're both too young to have seen the picture when it was first published, but that little girl, Kim Phuc, is now a middle–aged woman. She lives in Canada with her husband and her young son. She is a private person cast into the public eye by one unfortunate day in her life."

"I'm not sure I understand what this has to do with me."

"Simply this: Kim Phuc suffered burns over thirty–five percent of her body. Thankfully, like you, her hands, face and neck were spared. She could easily 'pass' as having never been injured. She could easily slip into a crowd, never to be heard from or seen. Instead, she's publicly forgiven the American pilot who dropped napalm on her village and she's become an advocate for child victims of war."

Thomas Michaels wiped his hands on a nearby dishtowel and motioned for me to join him at a small table in the far corner of the kitchen. He pulled out two chairs, poured us each a cup of hot cocoa from a thermos, and sat down. The priest was dressed casually, in faded jeans, a plain teal blue sweatshirt, white athletic socks and well–trodden Nikes. He wasn't wearing his clerical collar. I sat across the table, quietly admiring his beauty. I was certain he was the loveliest man I'd ever met.

"Kim Phuc, though I don't know her to be a Catholic, epitomizes the Church's doctrine of receiving grace through faith and good works. It's not just what you believe, Esther – it's how you live your life that entitles you to God's grace. You cannot find peace or obtain forgiveness without good works. We don't receive grace as some treat, like some sacred doggie biscuit, just for recognizing Christ's divinity. That's the false hope Protestants, God bless their souls, adhere to. Without sanctification through hard work and effort, you cannot come into God's grace. Understand?"

I remained silent. The conversation had taken on a preachy tone I hadn't anticipated.

"I'm boring you, aren't I?"

I smiled shyly.

"Not at all. It's just, well, I've never thought about such things."

"Ah, I forget myself. You're a young lady in the throes of fighting off suitors. You've little patience for such deep discussions. But that will change."

The priest's fingers pressed lightly against the skin of my left arm. Embarrassed and confused by his gesture and uncertain of his intentions, I smiled awkwardly and lifted the cup of hot chocolate to my lips. But I did not remove his hand. Silence imposed itself upon us. Thomas Michaels's eyes stared intently at my face. I didn't mind the attention.

The door to the kitchen opened, and Lilly pranced into the room, her chin lifted regally and her long black hair flowing sensuously behind her. Instantly, she noted the priest's hand resting on my forearm.

"Oh, was I *interrupting* something?"

Father Tom grinned. "Just a little pep talk. Your sister seems down in the dumps."

Lil stopped and placed her hands on her hips.

"Father, you've got to do something about Joe Nelson. He's impossible. He tried to kiss me while we were getting the missals out for service. I told him to knock it off, but I'm not sure it did any good."

The priest removed his hand from my wrist.

"You're a pretty young lady, Lilith. He's a young man. These things happen."

It was at that moment that the light went on. I knew for certain, watching Father Thomas Michaels and my sister interact, that there was

99

something going on between them. How serious, how deep the connection went, and whether it included physical intimacy, was something I would later come to understand.

TWENTY-THREE

Mason Erickson's farm was the first place I ever milked a cow. Well, I really didn't milk it so much as squeeze the animal's teats. It was just before my Christmas leave, and Mason had convinced Dr. Hodges and Ms. Prescott that an afternoon at his farm might be a good diversion for those of us who'd been following the program. There was a momentous snowfall during the week that, once the roads between Lake Panorama and the Erickson farm were plowed, formed the perfect base for a sleigh ride. There wouldn't be any outsiders at the farm, and no men (other than Mason, of course) for us to ogle or swoon over. (I'm writing like my Grandma Mary here.) It would be a safe excursion for the five of us who qualified for a momentary respite from rehabilitation, by virtue of adhering to Dr. Hodges's rules.

Mason Erickson is an interesting man. As careful in his speech as in his movements, he is as cautious a man as I've ever met. At first, given his penchant for introversion, I thought he was just another hayseed from Iowa. Don't get me wrong: I wasn't judging his intellect. This was simply my impression of the man. Turns out, once I completed a few shifts on the weekend kitchen crew, I learned some things about Mr. Mason Erickson that weren't obvious to the casual eye. Like the fact he graduated *summa cum laude* from Iowa State with a master's degree in agricultural economics. This information slipped out one evening after supper, as Mason wrapped leftover pork roast in plastic and I scrubbed pots in the kitchen sink. He related how he'd tried his hand as an economist at Cargill in Minneapolis and then, when his parents announced they were selling their dairy farm, Mason realized that he was, at the core of it all, a dairyman: a man who lived for his cows. Okay, so I ad–libbed a bit there. He never said it quite that way. But having watched Mason work, and having seen the care he puts into even the most mundane task, I'm certain my characterization is accurate.

He revealed enough during these talks for me to come to the conclusion that, if Mason had any say in it, he'd live his life tending cows and riding horses until, one day, he'd tumble from his saddle due to a stroke, or he'd die from a heart attack pitching bales of sweet Iowa alfalfa into the loft of his barn. Either scenario, I believe, would allow Mason Erickson to depart this world a satisfied man.

Don't get the wrong impression here. Mason Erickson doesn't wear cowboy boots or a cowboy hat. He's a dairy farmer who happens to own horses. I've never seen him wear a bolo tie or saunter like a man who's been in the saddle too long. He is, when all is said and done, a shy, thirty–three year old Iowa dairy farmer with a stern belief in God. There's no chance in hell that he'd be caught impersonating a rancher.

The afternoon we crowded into the New Beginnings Caravan to drive over to the Guthrie Center for a tour of the Erickson farm, it was a sunny early winter day. The newly fallen snow had been plowed into neat hedgerows along the shoulders of the highway. High vapor trails from jet airplanes extended east and west across the boundless sky. The sun's embrace could be felt, though it remained cold enough that the distant sun did not impact the snow. There was an air of excitement amongst the group from New Beginnings as the van bounded over the rough grade of the gravel lane leading to the Erickson place. The women – with the exception of our chaperone, Ms. Prescott – were giddy. Other than working our menial jobs or visits home, the trip to Mason's farm was our first real interaction with the world outside chemical dependency treatment.

Mason greeted us on the front porch of the farmhouse that had been the shelter for his ancestors and family since the place was built by his maternal great–grandfather, Nels Nelson, in 1876. The house was red brick, with chimneys at both ends, and a covered porch running the length of the building. Slender wooden posts boasting new white paint supported a green metal roof that protected the weathered decking of the front porch. The corrugated steel roof of the house was also green. The old wooden double–hung windows of the house were small. The window trim was painted the same brilliant white as the posts. A huge red barn, its gambrel roof rising to greet the aquamarine sky, stood behind the house. A chicken coop, its tired frame leaning hard to the left, was situated next to the barn. Inside a fenced run, several dozen hens and a solitary rooster scratched at the deep snow in expectation of food. Two gigantic Belgians stood patiently in a corral behind the chicken coop, seemingly impervious to the cold, their coats thickened by winter; their great nostrils flaring as they studied our arrival. Also in the same paddock – a space enclosed by a split–rail fence turned gray by the Iowa sun – was a black–and–white mare eating green alfalfa from a worn–out tractor tire. A roan gelding stood towards the rear of the enclosure, aloof and seemingly uninterested in strangers.

"Welcome," Mason Erickson said. "I hope you're bundled up. Thermometer on the barn reads five below."

Maggie Prescott's plump mitten–covered palm grasped Mason's bare hand in greeting. The farmer was wearing an Iowa State Cyclones sweatshirt and boot–cut blue jeans as he stood stocking–footed on the cold porch.

"Thanks for having us out. I know the girls could use a little diversion."

"You got that right," Wanda Jones blurted out. "How's about finding us something hot to drink, Mr. Erickson?"

"Wanda, where are your manners? Maybe Mr. Erickson wants to show us around a bit before we go into the house."

"No, ma'am, that's fine. I've got some hot chocolate and decaf coffee on the stove. Some pumpkin bars and fresh sweet rolls, my Mom's recipe, to go with the hot drinks. The ladies can surely come on in and get warmed up before we take a look around the place."

Wanda Jones, Delores Pufall, Hazel Edmunds, Etta Nyquist (a fifty–something pot smoker from Brule, Wisconsin, a little town just down the road from where I'm from) and I followed Ms. Prescott up the front steps and through the open front door. Warmth from a wood fire hit my face as we entered the farmhouse. We unbuttoned our coats, slipped off our winter boots and milled around the spacious living room; we held the palms of our hands towards the fire raging in the big stone fireplace as Mason Erickson escorted Maggie Prescott to the facilities. I separated from the others, and as I explored the first floor of the house, my eyes took in a myriad of photographs – some old, some more recent – all neatly arranged against patternless cantaloupe–colored wallpaper down a hallway. A snapshot of a strikingly beautiful young blond woman and a little boy caught my eye. The faces were repeated in a more formal portrait, in which Mason Erickson's left arm encircled the blond woman's waist and the boy stood in front of the couple. Mason's right hand rested on the child's shoulder. I was struck by the familial love captured in the portrait.

"That's my wife, Virginia. And my son, Jacob."

I hadn't heard Mason come down the hallway. His words, spoken without warning, startled me.

"They're beautiful."

"Yes, they are. The others are taking their coffee and treats in the living room."

"I need to use the bathroom."

"Next door on the left. You'll have to wait for Ms. Prescott."

103

I looked at the farmer. His wind–roughened face boasted a slight smile, and yet there was a hint or inflection of sadness as he looked past me and studied the photograph.

"Do they live here, with you?"

"They live in Saskatchewan."

There was a period where neither of us spoke.

"Divorce?"

Mason nodded. "She found someone. Someone who made her happy. I couldn't do that, couldn't make her happy," Mason volunteered.

A lump formed in my throat. There was nothing for me to say. He wasn't a close friend. I had no advice – no wisdom to offer to someone who was only a peripheral acquaintance, someone I'd met while working the program at New Beginnings. I moved closer to the bathroom. The sound of an enormous fart escaped the lavatory, followed by the urgent flush of the toilet. The red–faced fat woman hastily emerged from the chamber; as she passed by, Maggie Prescott declined to acknowledge me. From her demeanor, it was clear she realized I'd heard the prodigious release of gas from her bowels. I smiled, and then glanced down the hallway. Mason Erickson stood a few feet away, his blond hair swept to one side, his indigo eyes riveted upon the portrait, loss and disillusionment plain on his face.

TWENTY-FOUR

Memorial Day, 1995. Lilly and I were set to graduate from Bayfield High School at the end of the month. A church youth retreat at a resort owned by a parishioner from Our Lady of the Lake was held over the holiday weekend. Twenty–three Roman Catholic high school seniors from Ashland, Bayfield and Hurley, Wisconsin gathered together. Altogether, there were eleven boys; twelve girls; four priests, including Father Thomas Michaels; and four adult chaperones. I remember bits and pieces of that retreat – fragmented memories distorted by the gauze of time. I'm sure Lilly recalls the events of that weekend far more clearly than I do.

An Ashland School District school bus, rented for the occasion by the sponsoring churches, brought us to Bennett Lake. After stowing our sleeping bags and luggage in guest cottages, we arranged picnic table benches in a circle around a roaring bonfire. Sparks shot up against the endless night sky to merge with a plethora of twinkling stars. There was no moon. There were no clouds.

Father Tom has an ordinary voice, high–pitched and limited in range. My own singing is limited to following the melody without vibrato; Lilly, on the other hand, can wrap her voice around a song like melted butter on French toast. She has the ability, though she rarely displays the talent, of both intensity and accuracy in her voice. While Father Tom punched out the melody, allowing others to follow his lead, Lilly, once the fire warmed her heart and her vocal chords, added texture, ultimately owning each tune, making it surge and soar with vitality. Despite her slender build, Lilith's capable of instilling a sense of God-fearing old–time holiness in music, reminiscent of Dad's AME upbringing. Given the lack of hymn–singing in our own church, Lil had little opportunity to display her pipes at Mass, but that night, with the world warming to the promise of

105

summer and adulthood just a few weeks away – and with a handsome Roman Catholic priest finger–picking a ravaged Martin guitar – Lilly let it all hang loose.

"Wow," Father Thomas whispered as the last line of "Shall We Gather at the River" echoed across the oaks and willows surrounding the fire pit. "Where in the Lord's name did you ever learn to sing like that?"

I recall Lilly's eyes fluttering and her face flushing; her breathing was heavy from the effort of the singing, and I remember her body, a mere shadow across the fire from me, as she conjured up an answer.

"She's always been able to sing like that," I offered, tossing a branch into the fire.

"It's a shame we don't do more singing in church. You'd be wonderful as a soloist."

Lilly's cinnamon face flashed color against the darting light of the fire. Like I said, as I'd suspected, and to the devastation of my own heart, Lilly and Thomas Michaels were attracted to each other. At that precise moment, I realized that their affection was desperately seeking fruition. Don't ask me how I knew this, or how I came to fashion images of the priest and my sister locked in lovemaking, their lust finally consummated. The details of this connection were, I'll admit, fuzzy. But there was no mistaking their desire for one another.

We sang a few more hymns and a couple of old folk standards, ending with a highly sentimentalized version of Dylan's "Blowin' in the Wind." Lilly's voice hit an octave above her normal range, the edginess of falsetto only a note or two away. It was well after midnight when the boys followed the male chaperones back to the main cabin. We girls traipsed after the two mothers assigned as our guardian angels to our lodging place: a small guest cabin. I remember walking with Lilly, her gait seemingly tireless and her frame upright and strong; the patterned sound of waves lapping against the lakeshore was audible over the scuffing of tennis shoes and the snapping of flip– flops against the dry ground as we moved towards sleep. Lilith still hummed the Dylan tune. It was obvious that she was supremely and undeniably at peace with herself. I was envious. No, I was more than that. I was wracked with jealousy over the extent of her beauty and the ease with which she was able to enthrall a man who professed to love his God more than his humanity. But I didn't voice my complaint; I simply, as I always did, acquiesced to Lilith's power.

I awoke later that night and went for a sleep–impaired walk to the biffy. The painted wooden toilet seat was cold against my ass, and my underwear and my gray sweatpants were bunched around my ankles as I peed. I clenched and pushed hard, urging my bladder to empty quickly so I could retreat to the warmth of my sleeping bag. I finished and gently lowered the toilet seat lid so as not to have it slam loudly in the deeply silent night. Emerging from the outhouse, my eyes adjusted to the evening. My flip–flops popped as I walked, like the way gum snaps when you chew with your mouth open. Silence cloaked the resort. Stars gleamed silver, and waves lingered along the shoreline. A dog barked from across the lake. And then, I heard them.

At first, I thought it was only the rustle of new spring leaves in the breeze, but as I stopped and listened, I came to understand. Though their indiscretion was partially concealed from view by an alder thicket, the sounds of Father Thomas Michaels and my sister making love were unmistakable.

TWENTY-FIVE

My fingers fumbled with the teats of one of Mason Erickson's Guernsey heifers. Try as I might, I couldn't coax a stream of warm milk from the animal. The women from New Beginnings stood around me in a circle, their teeth chattering against the cold and their arms wrapped around their bodies in an attempt to stay warm. Their observations were lewd and unkind but advanced with humor.

"Work that tit," Wanda Jones cracked, the whites of her wide brown eyes the only part of her face not covered by the red wool scarf wrapped around her head. "Haven't you paid attention to your man when he's doing his work?"

My face flushed. The other girls chortled. The barb didn't help my efforts.

"Here, let me show you."

Hazel Edwards, her pale complexion luminescent beneath the fluorescent lighting of the barn, gave me a gentle prod with an elbow. I vacated the three–legged milking stool, a remnant from an era when cows were milked by hand, and allowed the skinny woman to sit in my place. Hazel spread her lanky legs beneath her paisley skirt, removed her leather gloves, and began to work the cow's nipples. Warm milk spat into the bottom of the pail. The cow chewed last summer's hay, her large head bowed to the feeding trough; her tail swished slowly with contentment.

"I thought you were a housewife," I remarked.

"I am. But my ma grew up on her daddy's farm in Cresco. Used to have Jerseys. They're all gone. Granddad switched to hogs. God, how I hate pigs."

The other girls laughed.

"Nothing wrong with pigs," Mason Erickson observed. "If I had any common sense, I'd convert this place to pork myself. But there's something about milk cows that seems more ancient, more tied to the land, than slopping hogs."

After ten to fifteen minutes, Hazel stopped working the udder and lifted the bucket off the floor. There was at least a gallon and a half of warm milk in the bottom of the pail.

"Nice work, Mrs. Edwards."

"Miss. The divorce came through last week. George got the kid, the house and his pension. Everything but my car."

Hazel's reply was matter-of-fact, as if losing a family and a way of living wasn't all that big a deal. I glanced at the woman. I was certain I'd see sadness in her eyes. I was wrong. Hazel Edward's face bore no such emotion. The woman handed the pail to the farmer. Mason gestured for us to follow him. He led us into the milk house, where he poured the contents of the bucket into a stainless steel pasteurization vat. A cat scatted across a rafter above my head in pursuit of a field mouse; the mouse didn't make it to the end of the beam.

"Gross!" Maggie Prescott blurted as the cat sauntered down to proudly deposit the dead rodent at Mason's feet.

"She's the best mouser I've ever seen. Just don't get between her and her kittens – she's not very discriminating when it comes to being protective."

The farmer opened an adjacent door and kicked the dead mouse outside. We exited the barn. The sun was setting and a pall had fallen. Shadows undulated across the pastoral landscape. Beyond a barren field, a line of frozen oaks bearing dead leaves demarcated the banks of a distant creek. Mason led us towards a hay wagon hitched to his Belgians. Though cold penetrated my bones, I had a desire to ride across the snowy fields of the Erickson Farm in the company of the quiet farmer.

"Climb aboard."

In the wink of an eye, all six women were sitting on hay bales in the wagon. Our feet and legs were wrapped tightly in wool blankets Mason provided. I sat next to Maggie Prescott, my teeth chattering and eyes wide with anticipation. I'd enjoyed a hayride or two as a child. In the October of my eighth grade, I'd even fooled around with a ninth grade boy (whose name I can't remember) under loose straw while a hay wagon rolled lazily around an apple orchard in the hills above Bayfield. But it'd been years since I sat on hay bales as a team of horses patiently plodded around a farm.

"That's Brushy Creek."

Mason gave us the lay of the land as the wagon's rubber tires bounced over a roughly plowed path. The trail divided a snow-covered cornfield in half, and the black ice of the frozen creek divided the snowy landscape like a tear in a bed sheet.

"The pond used to have a saw mill on one end. My grandfather harvested oak and maple. He built most of the farms within ten miles of this place."

My eyes strained. The stone foundation of what I presumed to be the old sawmill poked above drifted snow at the far end of the pond. Winter birds wove patterns against the close sky as if they were of one mind. Cows mooed. I stood up and shook loose the hay from my corduroy slacks. My scars became sensitive; the damaged nerves tingled in objection to the cold. Without knowing why, I moved towards the front of the wagon where Mason Erickson stood, his thick body covered in tan Carhart overhauls and a matching jacket stained from years of working the farm. Mason was hatless, and his blond hair rustled in the frigid air. He braced himself against the front wall of the wagon and clucked at the team, commanding the horses more by understanding than by force of will.

"Hi."

I didn't reply. I was unsure of why I'd decided to join the farmer, and why I'd left my sisters in rehabilitation congregated on hay bales behind us. Mason Erickson and I had little in common; he was, so far as I knew, not interested in me. I was damaged goods – a meth addict with serious deficits and a long, long way to go. Hell, I didn't know if *I* was interested.

In a farmer?

What was there about him, about his way of life that meshed with my way of being? A farmer living in the middle of a flat, lonely place, in a house occupied by unhappiness, and who filled his days up by caring for livestock, certainly didn't seem to be someone I would've fallen for, had I not been bruised and injured by life. That's what I thought as I stood next to the Iowan, watching the great horses sway from side to side in their traces.

110

TWENTY-SIX

"What am I supposed to do?"

Lilith's voice was torn apart by sobs. I had a difficult time understanding her when she called. I was in my dorm room at Northern Michigan University, studying for the first exam in my advanced anatomy class. The Resident Assistant, Lucy Bates – a tiny waif of a girl from Houghton, Michigan in her third year of the nursing program – knocked on the door of the room I shared with Amanda Priest, a squat but brilliant black girl from Detroit in her first year of nursing (like me), to let me know I had a phone call.

"Lil, what are you talking about? And why are you crying?"

There was nothing but constrained weeping from Lilly's end of the phone.

"Look, if you need my advice, I need to know why you're calling."

"Thomas."

The name didn't strike a chord. The last person my sister dated the summer I left home for Marquette was Alonzo Gurtes, a Hispanic kid from the south side of Milwaukee who had been sent north by his parents to keep him out of trouble. My take on Alonzo was that, no matter where he lived, he was trouble. He was a royal pain in the ass, so far as I was concerned: way too immature and demanding, and controlling in a scary sort of way. My sister and Alonzo parted on bad terms, after a loud fight inside the Bay Theater in Ashland. They had disrupted *Forrest Gump* during Forrest's jog across America. Alonzo didn't respect the word "no," an objection made by Lil to thwart Alonzo's attempt to sneak his fingers under her blouse during the movie. That's my understanding of the matter, anyway. But "Thomas"? I couldn't recall her dating anyone named Thomas.

There was no response to my question other than more crying.

111

"Lil, I'm in the middle of studying for a God–awful exam. The RA pulled me out of my room to answer your call. I need to get back to work."

In hindsight, had I known the enormity of what Lilith was facing, I would have shown more sensitivity.

"Thomas Michaels...." She whispered the name with such deference; it was as if she were mentioning God Himself.

"Yes?"

"He's the father."

It was early September – three months, give or take, from that night at the lake. Three months from the moans, the furtive motions, the noises of passion. Lil's message was obvious. I didn't need details.

"Shit."

More sobs.

"What will you do?"

Lilith blew her nose. I visualized her standing in the cool autumn air beneath the street lamp in the convenience store parking lot half–way up Rittenhouse Avenue, her body willed smaller to prevent passers–by from seeing her face and knowing who was making that horrific call. She would've told our parents that she needed to go into town, taken the ferry across the bay, and walked desperately up the steep hill to use the phone.

"It's no good, Esther. It's no good."

"You've told him?"

"No."

"Why not? It's his baby; damn him."

She choked up. "Don't say 'baby.' And don't put all the blame on him. It wasn't like *he* seduced *me*."

Lilly paused.

"I'm not ready to do this, Esther."

You sure as hell were ready to spread those hellaciously fine legs of yours for a priest. You sure as hell sounded like you knew what you were doing as I eavesdropped on your liaison with the good Father. Ready? When is any woman ready to have her belly scarred by stretch marks, her legs blotched by varicose veins, her breasts engorged? To be responsible for bringing another person into the world? When, Sister Lilith, when?

Of course, I kept my thoughts to myself. There was no point in lecturing Lilly when she was falling apart. She needed my help, not my piety.

"I still think he needs to be told. I'll bet the son of a bitch hasn't talked to you since the end of the retreat, has he?"

"You knew about the retreat?" There was astonishment in my sister's voice.

"I saw you that night. With him."

112

There was silence on the other end of the phone as I thought back to some sage advice I'd learned growing up. "Men won't buy the cow when they can get the milk for free," Mom always admonished, trying to make us understand that sex carries with it consequences and commitments that aren't easily escaped.

"He's tried to see me. The guilt of that night is just damn too much. I know, I know. You think your sister simply trots through life like some happy–go–lucky mindless twit. That isn't true, it isn't so. I've got depth to me, you know. I've got standards. It just happened. Sometimes, you can't stop yourself from doing a thing you shouldn't."

I didn't understand what she meant then. I do now. I learned my lesson about compulsion the hard way.

"The last thing I wanted to have happen was to become pregnant."

"But you were on the pill...."

"I missed one. Plain and simple. A mistake."

You got that right.

Lapping water. Oaks and willows swaying in the late spring air. Me standing beside the outhouse, my spine pressed against the clapboard siding, becoming invisible so that I could watch – watch the most private of all human acts. His face was buried in her stomach, and her naked back was pressed against the harsh bark of an ancient willow. Clothes littering the ground, shed quickly and without a plan. A faint expression of defense – the word "no" repeated softly during intervening moments. The disregard for the objection – not through violence, but through persistence. Stars twinkled overhead. My eyes were riveted, focused and amazed. Again, the word "no"; again, the priest, his skin gleaming white beneath the starlight, ignored the pleas of my sister.

I hadn't stayed for the aftermath. I'd seen things I wasn't meant to see. I didn't need to invade their connection further. I slipped away while they retrieved their clothing and dressed. I was curled up inside my sleeping bag by the time Lilith slithered back to the cottage, the serpent and Eve all rolled into one.

"You stopped seeing him?"

"I was never with him again after that night. The weight of it was too much. Oh, he tried to hook up with me. He slipped a letter and a poem into my backpack one Saturday evening Mass at church. I'm surprised you didn't see me reading it back at the house. The words were full of love but I knew what happened was a mistake. Why'd I tempt a priest? I made a priest break his vows, Esther. I'm bound for hell for sure."

Other girls lined up behind me to use the phone. I turned and grimaced. With my face clear of make–up and my hair was snarled in a curly mess of blackness, I must have been a fright. The other girls backed off.

"You could keep the baby. Mom and Dad would help. Or give it up for adoption."

A sigh.

"I told you: I can't do this. I'm not ready to carry a child, not ready to watch my body – the only thing I've got going for me – be torn to shreds by something that isn't right, isn't holy. I need to find someone to take care of it."

Abortion. The word slammed into my mind like a fist striking a plaster wall.

"No way, Lil. Think of what you're saying. Think of what the Church teaches about *that*."

Sobs interrupted our dialogue.

"I am *not* having it." There was firmness and finality in Lilith's words. "Will you help me?"

A lump formed in my throat. "How?"

"There's a place. In Duluth. But I need four hundred. I only have two."

My mind assessed my savings, the money I'd earned working at the Rittenhouse.

"I can help with the money part."

Another interlude.

"Es, I can't do this alone."

I exhaled and drew in a deep breath of air.

"I'm right at three months. If I wait much longer, they won't take me. I can't hold down a thing. I'm worried Mom is suspicious. I'm starting to show. She's gonna know sooner or later. I can't face her and Dad. Can't you hear me, Esther? I just *can't*."

"Okay."

"Can you come home? Thursday night? I'll set it up for Friday morning."

Visions of a seedy storefront on some forlorn street on the Duluth hillside, a smarmy–looking white man wearing a doctor's smock covered in blood, and a waiting room crammed full of Native American women, poor white women and young black girls, crowded my thoughts.

"My exam is on Thursday morning. I'll be home by ten Thursday night," I said quietly.

"Thanks, Es. I knew you'd be there for me."

I hung up the phone and turned to face the college girls waiting to use the telephone. I saw nothing in their eyes that remotely approached what I was feeling.

TWENTY-SEVEN

Who would ever think that a baby–killing doctor would be, or could be, a woman? When Lilly and I snuck out of our parents' house, the last thing I expected when we walked through the security doors of the Women's Health Clinic in Duluth was to meet up with a lady abortionist – a black one, at that.

"This is Dr. Samuels," a nurse with a severe case of acne had said, introducing us to the physician while my sister lay on the clean white linens of the examining table, her lanky brown legs bare below the hem of the thin hospital gown. Her naked feet dangled over the far edge of the bed and were not yet secured by stirrups.

"And this is Lilly DuMont."

Dr. Samuels stood ramrod straight, narrow of hip and absent any discernible femininity other than the rouge on her cheeks and the artificial color on her lips. Her stork–like body leaned over Lilly. The doctor extended spindly fingers in greeting. My sister accepted the tall doctor's hand in silence.

"Pleased to meet you, Lilly."

"And this is her sister, Esther."

"Likewise, Miss DuMont," Dr. Samuels said, shaking my hand in turn.

The doctor's grip was unassuming, as if she did not want to frighten folks compelled by circumstances to seek her power, the power of life and death.

"Can Esther be in the room during the procedure?"

Lilly's request was a surprise. We hadn't talked about such a thing being possible on the trip from Bayfield to Duluth. We'd limited ourselves

115

to chitchat in my car, a 1984 Dodge Horizon with over a hundred thousand miles on it. It was my high school graduation present from Mom and Dad.

"Esther?"

Being a nurse in training, I could, if I so desired, participate in the procedure at some time during my clinicals. This was different. My niece or nephew was about to be torn from my twin sister's body. I was eighteen years old and absent the tools needed to nonchalantly stand beside my sister while she underwent an abortion.

"I'm sorry. I don't think I'm up to it."

Dr. Samuels nodded, her face devoid of empathy. I guess she'd watched the same scenario play out hundreds, if not thousands, of times.

"Have a seat in the waiting room. I'll come get you when the procedure is over."

The nurse escorted me out the door. Lilly wept when I left. It was a half–hour or so before Dr. Samuels appeared in the lobby. Unlike the steely demeanor she displayed in the examination room, the doctor's eyes conveyed understanding as she sat next to me. Lilith had been the first patient. There were no other women in the room.

"Everything went fine. She'll rest another half hour or so, to allow the local to wear off, and then you can take her home."

I looked at the doctor, a woman of shared heritage, and wanted to question how she could take one of her own, and how she did the job she'd chosen to do. I didn't have it in me. I was just a girl, fresh out of high school, who'd learned very few lessons about life beyond the sadness of David's passing, and perhaps an inkling about the cruelty of love (namely, Billy's leaving me after my accident, tossing me into the trash like some unwanted piece of clothing that no longer pleased him). These things circulated through my mind as I studied the tall woman sitting on the hard plastic chair next to me. I thought these things – oh yes, I did – but my mouth never opened. I simply accepted her words as if I agreed that what had just happened to Lilith was a good and necessary thing.

"Thank you."

My reply lacked sincerity. I'm not sure the doctor noticed, though I believe she cared deeply for the women she met. How that was possible, given why they were at the center, I'm still at a complete loss to comprehend, even after having been a nurse for over seven years.

Afterwards, I gave Lilly my arm. We walked across the vinyl flooring of the lobby and past a uniformed guard. The heavy metal frame of the security door slammed behind us. The city, which had been dormant when we arrived, was now alive. Cars and trucks whizzed past the building. As my eyes adjusted to daylight, I saw them: a group, a small crowd really, of men, women and young people holding signs and pacing on the sidewalk. Protesters. Right–to–life types – some were likely Catholic, like my sister

116

and me. Lilly's eyes grew wide as a disheveled middle–aged man in a dirty green Mackinaw scampered up to us, holding a placard with a color photograph of a dead fetus. The edges of the sign flapped as the man advanced, clearly intent upon saying something untoward.

"Sinners," he shouted. "Murderers."

Lilly ducked into the hollow of my right armpit and wailed. I walked faster, intent upon ignoring the man. Two women carrying signs that read: "Holy Rosary Catholics for Life" with the word "Abortion" encircled, a red line slashed through the word like a European traffic sign, came at us from down the street. The man quickened his pursuit. The women blocked our retreat. I wanted to scream, to tell the protesters that we were there because my eighteen–year–old sister had been impregnated by her Catholic priest. I wanted to ask those pious asses where the Lord stood on such a thing, whether their clear and unequivocal lines between right and wrong applied regarding the inappropriate conduct of a Catholic cleric, but I was too afraid, too morally frightened of my sister's complicity in the sin, to speak. My rhetoric slipped on the moral quicksand of my sister's laying with a holy man. I could find no sure footing in the matter, and Lilly was in no shape to argue the point.

"Hold on there, folks." The young man working the security desk exited the clinic, his right hand demonstrably resting on his waistband, near a set of handcuffs, a canister of mace and a black wooden baton. His blue eyes scrutinized the situation. "You need to let these women get to their car. You know what the restraining order says: fifty feet from the door and the parking lot. No closer. Now move on back or I'll call the police."

The protesters stopped dead in their tracks.

"Murderers, that's what they are," the unkempt man spat back. "Goin' to hell, they are. Straight and sure. Goin' to hell."

"That's fine, Marty. We all know your position on it. But the fact is, unless you step back, I'll arrest you myself and hold you until the police get here."

The protesters made space. The security guard stood near us as I opened the passenger door and helped my sister into the front seat.

"Thanks."

"Just doing my job. You ladies have a good day. Try to put this behind you; not everyone in Duluth is an asshole."

I couldn't tell from the guard's comment whether he supported the work of the clinic or whether he simply empathized with our situation. I closed the passenger's door, walked around the car and opened the driver's door. As I turned the key in the ignition, protesters gathered to confront a woman and her adolescent daughter sheepishly approaching the clinic from the east.

TWENTY-EIGHT

Group continued to go well. Dr. Hodges was adept at taking what we revealed – snippets of truth colored with lies, deception and self–righteousness – and turning our words inward. Over time, we began to see, to varying degrees, that our addictions were not the result of an impossibly fractured infrastructure; they were the result of gaps and holes needing filling. Repairs were possible; the flaws in our psyches simply needed corrective action.

My own "holes" included the pit of guilt I carried regarding David's death and the unconscious desire to be physically complete, to be beautiful in the way that Lilly was. Of course, I knew, deep down, that Lilly wasn't the apex of perfection she appeared to be. I'd seen her performance with Father Michaels. I'd watched her flit empty–headed from boy to boy like a curious moth discovering flowers. But now, in her late twenties, Lilly had what I seemingly couldn't attain: contentment, a solidly handsome husband with a prestigious job and a pedigree; a black man of substance and position who knew the line of his ancestors on both his mother's and his father's side, an unbroken chain of men and women stretching all the way back to Africa. And she had a daughter – a child conceived and born of love, evidence of their clear and dedicated passion for each other.

I read the books, the Alice Walkers, the Toni Morrisons, the Maya Angelous and all the others that Wanda Jones placed in front of me. I tried to understand what it means to be a black woman in today's America, and tried to fathom the connections between my pigmentation and those folks who bore witness to tragedy, turmoil and unrest during the 1950s and 1960s. Coretta Scott King, Rosa Parks and all. But it didn't feel right. I didn't seem to fit in – for, as I've noted before, I am a child of water, a woman from northwestern Wisconsin born to a Finnish–Irish mother and an

African–Irish father. Though my skin color, deep brown eyes and hair may cry out "inner–city Milwaukee," my soul, my very being, was founded on the soft sandy beaches of Chequamegon Bay. What I learned in group, listening to and talking with Dr. Prescott and the other women, is that I needed strength to be at peace with that heritage, to be at ease with who I am and where I come from.

Christmas, 2004. When we pulled up to the Bayfield ferry landing in Richard's Durango, with Lilly sitting primly beside her husband in the front passenger seat and Abby next to me in a repeat of our Thanksgiving sojourn, I felt healed. I felt like I had very little left to accomplish at New Beginnings. As I watched my sister and Richard interact, the jealousy, the coveting of her existence that had boiled up inside me just a few weeks earlier, seemed to be replaced by an acknowledgement that each of us – Lilly, me, Richard, my parents, Mason Erickson, Wanda Jones and even skinny–assed Hazel Edwards – deserves tranquility in our lives. None of us, not even the philandering priest, deserves to experience conflict and turmoil that tosses and turns us over and over within the confines of human existence, churning us indiscriminately like floating sticks in a Lake Superior storm. My eyes were seeing clearly that December afternoon. My head was thinking right thoughts, and yet I felt the need for distance.

"I think I'll walk into town for a soda. You guys take the ferry; I'll call you from LaPointe for a ride when I get in."

Lilith turned and locked her eyes on me.

"You're gonna what?"

"I'm just gonna have a soda and think some things over. I need some alone time, out in the real world. Haven't had much of that since Del passed."

"You sure you're up to that? I was given strict instructions. Dr. Hodges said it plain and clear: I'm to keep careful watch of you."

"Lilly, if I wanted to screw up, I could have done it long before now. I'm telling you, plain as that cute little button nose on your face: I'm just going to have a soda and think a little. That's all."

"Richard?"

My brother–in–law turned the Durango's heater up a notch.

"Esther will be fine. She needs space. If she's not on the next ferry out, I'll personally drag her sorry black ass back to the island, okay?"

"You be at the landing in LaPointe no later than six, you hear me?"

"No later than six, Lilith. Scout's honor."

I opened the door and hopped out of the SUV.

"Scout's honor? You were never a Girl Scout," Lilly smirked. "Never acted like one neither."

I smiled and let the double negative slide. She was right. My life hadn't been the model of propriety. But whose has?

"Always wanted to be one, though. Mom never seemed to have the time. See ya at six."

It was four o'clock, and two days before Christmas. The streets of Bayfield were nearly empty. Wrought–iron street lamps cast their pale light over the town. Infrequent cars negotiated tortured asphalt. I tightened the drawstring of the new down parka Mom had mailed to me. My hatless hair bounced, its wildness finally tamed by chemicals. My hiking boots displaced snow as I walked. This was home. The sound of storm–stirred water battering the village pier, the echo of the arrogant wind rushing between rickety buildings, the muffled banter of customers inside my destination growing louder with each step I took – these were all indicators of my belonging.

I stopped in front of a restaurant and studied the people inside through a frosted window. Parkas, jackets and coats hung over the backs of chairs and on bar stools as customers chatted with each other, their forks and spoons poised over meals. I recognized a handful of faces. When I entered the place, I was greeted by odors of fried food and spilled beer, and I spotted Billy Cadotte and his wife across the room. My inclination was to flee, avoid Billy, avoid envying his happiness – his love for someone other than me. But I didn't leave.

It's time to stop running.

"Isn't that Esther, Esther DuMont?" Billy asked in a loud voice, waving his hand as he spoke.

"Hi," I replied sheepishly, my response limp and noncommittal.

"Come join us," Billy urged as he stood and gestured for me to sit at their table, oblivious to the apprehension clear on his wife's face.

I fixed my mouth into a smile and stepped forward to confront my past.

TWENTY-NINE

Diaspora: the scattering of a people.

I don't understand why that word and its definition manifested in my thoughts as I entered the restaurant. Maybe it was seeing Billy with April. Or, perhaps, the word was prompted by a fleeting memory of Del, sleeping next to me in our shared bed, the contrast between our skins obvious, creeping into my head.

Making my way towards Billy and April Cadotte, I day–dreamed of sailing ships plowing through the West African surf, filled with black–skinned men, women and children – people of many dialects, a disparate collection of unrelated tribal cultures, prisoners bonded together by pigmentation and someone's desire to sell them for profit. They fought the stench of feces, urine and vomit, not to mention the threats of dysentery, influenza and fever, as they crowded together in the holds of slave ships, sharing meager water and spoiled food. The prows of the slavers speeded westward, towards North America, South America and the Caribbean. In one of those ships, my father's people had come. In another, Billy Cadotte's African ancestors came to the New World. Why these thoughts hit me as I stood before my ex–lover and his wife two days before Christmas, I have no idea.

"It's great to see you, April."

April Cadotte smiled but didn't reply, prompting me to remember that April is a quiet woman. Her lazy green eyes fixed on me, as if she were trying to discover my intentions. I sat down across the table from Billy, and realized that April hadn't aged much at all. Her face was still smallish and round. Her once–auburn hair was now blond and cut short, the ends flipped up and tacked in place with hair spray. She was eating a sandwich when I sat beside her. From the look of the woman, the thinness of her, I figured she'd be taking most of her meal home in a doggie bag.

"Order something. We've just started," Billy said.

"No thanks. Mom's expecting me to eat when I get back to the island."

"Beer?"

God, I'd love one right now. No, can't do that. Soda. Think soda.

"I'll pass. I'll order a Sprite when the waitress stops by."

"That's right. How stupid of me. You're in treatment, right?"

Same old Billy. Cuts right to the chase, he does.

"For a few months."

"How's it going?" April asked demurely.

"So far, so good."

Without thinking, I rapped my fist on the oak surface of the table. My eyes took in Billy, mentally gauging the man I'd known as a boy. A holstered semi–automatic pistol peeked out from beneath his tan sport coat. The polished black plastic of the gun's grip reflected light. Billy caught me staring at the handgun and smiled.

"Sheriff's Department. I got on a few years back. Made Undersheriff this year."

I nodded.

"Billy's been working hard on the meth problem." The political incorrectness of April's remark caused her to blush. "I'm terribly sorry."

I'd had far worse things come up in conversation. I was a meth addict. The whole Town of Bayfield and all of Madeline Island knew that Dr. DuMont's headstrong daughter had a meth problem.

"No offense taken. It's no secret what my troubles have been."

"How's it been going – treatment, I mean?" Billy interjected.

The *Bloom O' the Rose*. Billy and I are retrieving a gill net from the lake, near Stockton Island. The net runs along the island's rocky coast, perpendicular to the shore, stretching twelve feet between the lead weights at the bottom of the net and the plastic floats riding the surface. Every two or three feet, we come upon silvery bluefin herring, fish between twelve and fifteen inches in length, some approaching a pound or more; their gills are caught in the squares of the net. We work silently, pulling fish free of the mesh. When we're finished, we reset the mile–long net, anchor the boat, and begin gutting several hundred herring. We stand in virtual silence, on opposite sides of a twenty–foot long wooden table in the boat's hold, working as a team, fillet knives slicing the bellies of the fish, removing entrails; heads and skin left on; before tossing the cleaned fish into metal tubs of ice. It's hot down in the hold, but there's a wind. The flies don't find us. I can hear the gentle "thwap, thwap, thwap" of Lake Superior's embrace against the old boat's wooden hull. Herring gulls circle the *Rose*, cognizant of the bounty we're creating, coveting fish guts as a hungry dog covets beefsteak. The cries of the gulls are constant. I am happy; probably the happiest I've ever been. Billy taught me to clean fish – not to fillet them like Dad does for the frying pan, but clean them quickly and efficiently *en masse*. I envision our connection becoming permanent. I dream of marriage, of the little Ojibwa–Irish--Finnish–African babies that we'll one day have together. Instead, there is Labor Day. There is a fire. There is April. And two little girls with blond hair and fine Caucasian features who call this woman sitting next to me "Mommy."

"If you'll excuse me," April said, interrupting my melancholy, "I need to use the restroom."

"How have you been?" Billy asked when his wife was gone.

"I'm doing well," I shrugged. "If I'm lucky, I'll be out of treatment by February and, with God's grace, I'll be back in nursing by summer."

"That's great."

There was something lingering beneath Billy's statement. I had no idea what it was.

"Esther...."

"Yes?"

The noise from the other patrons swelled to a peak, then settled down to a modest hum.

"I am so sorry."

"Nothing to be sorry about, Billy. I made some bad choices. I got pointed in the wrong direction."

I refused to say that I'd met the wrong people. Del and Moose weren't "wrong." They were simply people hooked on a drug that wouldn't let go of them. They didn't rob or steal (unless you count shoplifting as stealing but that's not the kind of thing I mean), and they didn't sell their stuff to kids. They made and sold drugs to satisfy their own habits. And I fell in with them. Our actions were undeniably wrong. But that, in my mind, doesn't make me, or them, "wrong" people.

"I'm not talking about the present. I'm talking about the past."

The waitress took my order. She returned with a glass full of fizzy soda, ice and a plastic straw.

Oh, oh. Confession time. He waits ten years to begin a dialogue? The nerve of the guy. My mind is tired of dredging up old memories. Nothing good can come of this. Nothing.

"I'm not sure this is the time or place to go down that road."

If Billy caught the cautionary inflection of my words, he ignored it.

123

"The way I treated you, the way I left your side when you needed me, was just plain unkind. I don't want to dwell on the past either, Esther. I simply want to say 'I'm sorry.'"

I mulled over Billy's apology. The door to the ladies' room opened and April moved towards us.

"I'll have to consider a response," I whispered. "I'm not sure I can accept your apology. Seems to me, the time for apologies passed us by a long time ago."

Billy's brow furrowed. He took a sip of beer. April sat next to me. I smiled, a perfunctory gesture.

"Catching up?"

"Somewhat," I replied. "I really need to get going."

"You haven't finished your Sprite," Billy noted.

"Gotta go," I replied, rising from the table, arranging my jacket so I could close the zipper.

"Have a good Christmas," Billy added.

"You too. Make sure you spoil those girls."

"You know he will," April responded, her gaze locked on my face.

As I turned to leave, a vision of two beautiful little girls – girls sired by Billy Cadotte but carried and born of my womb – invaded my mind. That vision stayed with me all the way to LaPointe.

THIRTY

Lilly had her first period four months before I got mine. From then on, once I caught up, our monthly cycles have coincided like clockwork. Whether we are together or apart, you can put money on the fact that our periods are in sync. Both of us having PMS on Christmas Day was probably not in the best of form, but it was beyond our control and it's what happened as we opened packages on the braided rug in the great room of my parent's cottage on Madeline Island. It's likely that the PMS is what led Lilly and me to fight about religion.

Lilith Ann remains a staunch Roman Catholic. She, Richard, and Abby attend All Saints Church in Lakeville, a suburb of Minneapolis adjacent to their home community of Apple Valley. I've been to All Saints a few times with Lil. It's a mammoth church, beautifully appointed. The priest who conducts Mass there seems sincere, but for me, there's something missing. Since the night Lilly spent time with Father Michaels, I've felt there's something wrong with the Roman Catholic Church. My judgment on this point isn't just based upon what Lilly went through; it has more to do with the subjugation of women within the Church and the fact that, given all the female African American writers Wanda Jones compelled me to read, I came to appreciate the position of black women in American society – how they've been the strength and the core of preserving families and dignity, often times engaging in skirmishes with the male leaders of their own race over issues such as equality and social justice. Blind obedience to male–dominated power structures, following dogma without question, without challenge, is not what they – the Oprah Winfreys, Maya Angelous and Alice Walkers – stand for. And neither, having thought long and hard on the issues, do I.

Lilly, on the other hand, seems content to remain a compliant parishioner. Despite the hypocrisy of her position, she is vehemently pro-life. I know, I know. Seems a bit revisionist, doesn't it? But that's how Lilly thinks, how she views the world. I normally refrain from discussing such topics with her, knowing, as I do, that I could cut Lil's arguments to the bone with the blade of historic truth. I'm not out to hurt my sister or to cause a wound that can't be mended, simply to win an argument. But when I learned she was enrolling Abigail in Catholic preschool, I couldn't help myself.

The two of us were sitting cross–legged on the rug in the great room with half–full mugs of coffee at our sides, watching Abby open packages beneath Mom and Dad's beautiful Scotch pine Christmas tree. Its needles were still supple, and the aroma of the freshly–cut tree was overpowering. I had a headache: my brain felt like someone had hammered on it with a baseball bat. Lilly was in similar distress. Richard, his body's leanness discernible beneath the two–piece Nike running suit he was wearing, sat on the couch next to Dad, his dark eyes riveted on his daughter. Despite having just arisen, Richard's hair, teeth and appearance were *GQ* perfect. If I hadn't felt so crappy, I might have felt unforgivable lust for my brother–in–law. Dad was perfectly composed; his small black eyes expressed joy as he watched his only grandchild dart from package to package, Abby's long black hair trailing behind her, and the hem of her nightgown floating above the hardwood flooring as she ripped wrapping paper from boxes to discover the measure of love hidden inside each present.

Mom sat quietly, looking tired. She seemed as old or older than Dad, despite the ten–year gap in their ages that should have favored her. She held a glass of whole milk (she'd already consumed her one cup of coffee – her daily limit, as recommended by her doctor, to deal with hypertension) tightly in one hand. Mom's hair, so luxuriant and golden in her youth, seemed limp and lifeless. I think she was upset that I had missed Mass with the family. No, I *know* she was upset with me over that. But true to her Finnish heritage, she never said a word. One would have thought that, over the years, her fiery Irish blood would have bested her Nordic stoicism, which would have allowed her to let me have it. But that never happened. She has never, in all my years around her, allowed her Irish dander its release.

"Hey," I said to Lilly between gulps of coffee as I followed the hectic progress of my niece, "Abby's not wearing a diaper."

Lil smiled.

"She's been working on that since you went away to treatment. I told her she needed to be out of her diaper by the time Santa came. And last week, right on schedule, she figured it out; like she knew Christmas was coming and she needed to take care of business."

"That true, Abby? You poopin' in the hole now?"

"Esther, is that really necessary at seven in the morning?" Mom wasn't really upset with my language. She was more annoyed than anything, I guessed.

"Lighten up, Sam," I replied, knowing that Mom hated it when I called her by her first name.

"Daughter, you know your mother doesn't like it when you do that," Dad interjected. "You trying to vex her, on Christmas morning no less?" Dr. DuMont was in good humor. He wasn't angry; he was just pulling my chain.

"Sorry, Samantha," I said.

Mom flapped her lips but refused to be drawn into a petty disagreement.

"So Abby, I hear you can go on the big potty."

My niece stopped demolishing a box of Duplos long enough to respond.

"I go poo poo."

I smiled and was immediately smitten by the color of Abby's eyes, a blue so unusual and so at odds with her African skin it nearly took my breath away.

"Now she can start pre-school. All Saints takes two-year-olds, as long as they are out of diapers."

Now, I have no real idea why my sister's comment, so seemingly innocent and innocuous, started my mind churning – especially since it was Christmas Day, a day set aside for joy, family and tolerance. But, for some reason, the revelation that my niece was going to start her indoctrination into Catholicism caused me to spout off.

"What the hell?"

"Pardon me?"

"Lilith, what in God's name is wrong with you? You're really going to allow your baby girl to be infused with a religion that, because she has a vagina, she can't fully participate in?"

There was nothing but silence in the room as my words settled over us. Only my mother had the wherewithal to challenge me.

"Hush your mouth, Esther Mary DuMont. You've no right taking the name of the One True Church in vain, no right whatsoever."

"She's right, Es. What's gotten into you? You're still a Catholic, aren't you? You've not taken up being a Buddhist or anything weird like that, have you?"

I smiled dementedly. I was always so much better than Lilith at debating. She's a sweet woman, but she doesn't have the mental horsepower for discourse.

127

"I'd rather be Hindu, Muslim or Jewish than Catholic," I said confidently.

"That's enough, young lady. Matters of faith are personal, not something that lend themselves to family debate."

There was a stern rebuke in my father's words. I didn't normally challenge Dad. Whether it was a hormonally–driven lapse or simple defiance, I plowed right ahead.

"That's rich, coming from a man who hasn't been inside a church for twenty–five years, except to attend Christmas and Easter Mass. When was the last time you gave confession, Dad?"

Richard shifted uncomfortably on the couch. His jaw quivered, as if he wanted to say something downright nasty to me. Richard Culver is a faithful man, a true follower of Rome; I had stabbed at the very heart of his beliefs with my diatribe. Yet, he remained silent. I was outnumbered. He seemed content to let my sister and my parents handle my heresy.

"Esther, what is wrong with you? What has the Church done to you to provoke such venom?"

Mom stood over me, her hands on her wide hips and her nostrils flaring.

"Samantha," I replied, "don't get all bent out of shape. If Lilly wants to torture Abby by sending her to a Catholic school, she has every right to do so. You're right. It's none of my damned business."

I stood up. My face reddened. I was dangerously close to saying more, to disclosing the thing that could not be disclosed. I brushed Mom's shoulder as I tried to pass her. Her eyes widened. I think she believed the gesture was deliberate.

"Sorry," I whispered.

I had a desire to wax histrionic, but instead I held my tongue and climbed the stairs leading to my old room, with Abigail's whimpers haunting my every step.

THIRTY-ONE

Blowing up at your family on Christmas Day isn't the most Christian tack to take. I spent most of the rest of my leave taking reflective walks with Skipper, my parents' golden retriever. I was fairly certain that no one wanted to accompany me on my sojourns after my insensitive performance. Thankfully, Abby recovered from the shock of seeing her female relatives engaged in a verbal catfight. I had done wrong, but that was in the past. The blow–up was erased from Abby's brain by the selective recall of near–infancy, a trait adults wish they were blessed with during their later years.

It was the last day of my leave. I was pulling my winter jacket over my arms, having already laced up my hiking boots; the leather was sleek and well oiled, the result of Dad's particular care towards footwear. My father appeared in the back hallway of the house.

"Mind if I join you?"

Dad's voice startled me. It took me a moment to recover.

"Sure. Skipper and I were just going to hike into town."

"It's ten below zero."

"You don't feel the cold as much when you're walking."

Dad didn't reply as he dressed for the weather. I grabbed the dog's leash, opened the door and called for Skipper. The retriever loped across the backyard. Water dripped from the dog's jowls. He'd obviously found an opening in the lake's ice from which to drink.

"Sit."

Skipper obeyed. My father shut the back door and joined me in the frigid morning air. I snapped the metal latch of the dog's leather leash onto his choke collar.

"Ready?"

Dad nodded. We began to walk, and it wasn't until we left the gravel surface of the North Road and our boots were clambering over the frosted tar of County Road H, heading westward into town, that he spoke.

"What's going on?"

By then, my period was full–blown. I was packed so tight, my legs bowed outwards like I was riding a horse. Even though Dad's a doctor, my monthly dilemma is not something I discuss with him – I didn't as a teenager, nor would I now as a mature woman. Besides, there wouldn't have been any point to it. My PMS had abated. I was no longer sore at the world, just physically uncomfortable.

"Nothing."

We walked some more.

"You know, you had at least one thing right when you went off on your sister – not that she deserved what you hit her with."

The wind came from the northeast, straight down the corridor of open water between Madeline and Stockton Islands. Twenty–mile–an–hour gusts infiltrated my parka and chilled my bones. If the cold affected Dad, he never let on. Skipper seemed similarly oblivious to the weather, protected as he was by unruly reddish brown fur over every inch of his body.

"How's that?"

"You had me pegged right, at least as far as my commitment to God."

Please understand: my father and I had never once, to that point, talked seriously or in depth about religion. Oh, I'd heard him talk to Mom, casting out the odd aspersion against Catholicism from time to time or challenging Christianity – at least the fanatical adherents of the faith, whether Protestant or Catholic – on occasion, throwing off–the–cuff disparagements against televangelists and right–wingers who invoke the name of God when typhoons wreaked havoc on the Islamic or Buddhist regions of the world. But Dad and I...well, we'd never had a one–on–one concerning matters of the soul. So you'll understand that, during our casual walk, I was taken aback by the direction of the conversation.

"Might have told you this. On my mother's side of the family, the Majors side, we come from a long line of preachers. My mother's father, Albert, was an AME preacher in Gary, Indiana. His cousin, William, was a preacher in Duluth. St. Mark's, I think. Consequently, Beulah, your grandmother, she was one Bible-thumping lady, she was."

I was surpised. Dad had provided little more than a smidgen, a small inkling, of his religious heritage during my childhood. The story of his African American roots had been closely guarded. They weren't really secrets, as hints and bits and pieces of the family story leaked out over time. Like the fact that Grandpa Albert's father, Edgar Majors, had fought in the Civil War, losing his left arm in some unknown skirmish. Fragments of

130

knowledge surfaced from time to time, but given Dad's solemn nature and his desire to get along with others, he shared precious few details of his African lineage with Lilly or me during our childhood.

"So what happened to you?"

My father kept pace, his tan leather hiking boots matching my boots, stride for stride. A red squirrel skittered from a ditch onto the snow-dusted asphalt. Skipper strained at his leash. I yanked, closing the choke collar and reining the dog in. The squirrel stood on its hind legs, caught sight of the dog, and scolded us before scampering into a thicket of raspberry canes.

"Wasn't just one thing, I guess. It was a lot of things. I don't want you to think I don't believe. I do. There's a Creator, a God; of that, there's no doubt in my mind. And I have a sneaking suspicion that Jesus was, or is, who he said he was, sent here by God. His Son? I'm not too sure about that. Prophet? That seems too lightweight a label. Something more. Maybe akin to the way Muslims think of Him: right up there, next to God, but not necessarily kin. You know what I mean?"

My mind swam with images of Jesus sitting on a big throne up in heaven, and God himself sitting next to Jesus on a slightly elevated chair of His own.

"I think I understand."

St. Joseph's Catholic Church, the first significant building at the north end of the village of LaPointe, came into view. Early morning sunlight reflected from the roof of the little church – a church that, despite my Mom's religious roots, we attended sparingly. Mom didn't trust the priest who served the parish when Lil and I were kids. She had no specifics, mind you, just maternal instinct. As it turned out, her intuition was right: Father Benovance was later outed for abusing little girls. Twelve girls, now grown women, came forward with claims of abuse against the priest years later. It was too late. There was no retribution, beyond money, to be had. Father Benovance was gone, having died in Arizona before any lawsuits were filed. He left this world with an unsullied reputation. I never realized why Mom insisted we go to church in Ashland, why we didn't go to St. Joseph's on the Island, until Father Benovance's predilection made the news.

My father studied the church as we passed by. If he was thinking about the pedophilic tendencies of the dead priest, he didn't elaborate. Dad's eyes, clear and showing no age, took in the building as if he were a tourist on his first visit to the island.

"I think the real break for me, why I avoid going to Mass with your mother unless absolutely necessary, came when my cousin Aaron died."

"Aaron?"

131

The name was unfamiliar. In fact, except for Grandma and Grandpa DuMont, my Dad's side of the family was pretty much a mystery to me.

"Aaron DuMont. My Dad had three brothers: Edward, Charles and Benjamin. Edward was twenty years older than my father. Charles, fifteen or so. Benjamin, at least twelve. They were all gone by the time you and Lilly were born. Aaron was Benjamin's only child. He was a neat kid, and smart as a lick. But he took to the bottle at an early age, and by the time he was twenty, Aaron was ruined. He tried to get straight– he worked the program and found a good job with the public works department in St. Paul. He got married – he was the only one of my kin I really connected with. I was in his wedding as a groomsman. He and his wife couldn't have kids; they tried to adopt, but had no luck. Then, in their early forties, they finally adopted a little Korean boy, Julius. Then suddenly Aaron's wife, Estelle, got pregnant with twins. So there they were, going from having no kids, with Aaron sober for years, then boom, three kids under the age of two."

The wind picked up. I shivered. A snow squall blanketed us as we passed the museum.

"Time to turn around?"

My father nodded; we spun around without stopping. A black–and–white cat dashed across the street. Skipper eyed the animal without commitment. My face ached from cold as we walked into wind–driven snow.

"How does that tie into your lack of faith?"

Dad smiled.

"Oh Lilly girl, I have faith. I'm not an atheist. Not even really agnostic. I believe – with certain, stringent restrictions."

"Objection noted," I said.

My father let fly a laugh. It was heaven to see him happy.

"Anyway, Aaron and Estelle were Catholic. Don't ask me how that happened. They just were. Anyway, something went on between them after the twins were born. Maybe Aaron had an affair, maybe not. The details never made it this far north. In any event, they grew estranged and Aaron went back to the bottle. He ended up getting a couple of DUIs and found himself in the Pine County Jail."

A big sedan passed us. The tires of the Buick kicked up snow. The driver seemed to recognize Dad and waved. Dad waved back. I had no idea who the guy was.

"Sounds familiar," I whispered after a few minutes.

"Didn't mean to bring your situation into this. Just telling a story, Es," Dad said. He stopped to hug me; the embrace was welcome and warming against the cold. We continued our walk.

"Aaron was despondent. Estelle left, and went back to her mother's house in Appleton with the kids. Aaron couldn't make bail. I'd have loaned

132

him the money if he'd have asked. But he never called. I didn't even know he was in jail, or that he'd hung himself in his cell with his shirt, until Estelle called and asked me to be a pallbearer."

A lump formed in my throat. Nothing I'd experienced had pushed me anywhere close to suicide. I tried to comprehend what it would take, what mechanism would have to be triggered, for me to seek out my own death. I wasn't able to envision anything that could send me down that path.

"How horrible."

"It was. And that's where the Church comes in. Now, of course, because Aaron committed suicide, his soul was in jeopardy. That rubbish was hard enough on Uncle Ben and Aunt Mercedes, but the clincher for me came at the funeral. A packed church in downtown St. Paul – not the cathedral, but a neighborhood church near the capital. What happened during that service turned me off, completely and unalterably, from the Roman Catholic faith."

A raven landed in a birch tree above us on the leeward side of the road. Skipper's nose twitched but, once the dog was confident the bird wasn't a grouse, he pranced forward.

"Must've been something terrible."

"Terrible and unholy, in my book. Because there was a full Mass, Communion was prepared. While the deacons made ready, the priest turned to the mourners and, without missing a beat and while understanding and knowing the depths of the loss felt by all of us in that church, he advised that any non–Catholics were welcome to *watch* while the *faithful* received the body of Christ."

"No!" I gasped. "He didn't!"

"Yes, he did. It was right then and there, with your mother sitting next to me, pregnant with you girls, that I told myself I was no Catholic, that I wanted no part of a religion that would do such a thing – denying God's blessing to people! Understand, most of the folks there were AME, Lutheran or Episcopalian. Very few of the mourners were Catholic. In a single moment of insensitive superiority, that priest tried to cut faithful people off from God. I vowed right there that I wasn't going to be a party to that."

We walked on. The only sound, other than the rustling of marsh grass and dead oak leaves clinging stubbornly to trees, was the noise of our boots crunching against frozen snow. We turned onto my parent's driveway. I knelt down and let Skipper off his leash. The retriever bounded towards the house.

"I've never discussed this with your mother," my father continued. "It would do no good. She'd argue that the priest's intentions were honorable, that the Catholic Church requires certain protocols be followed – that only through order and structure can the True Faith be protected. She thinks I stopped believing. That's why when you and Lilly went after each other; I tried to stay out of it. I would likely have ended up taking your side, Esther, and no good would have come of that."

I nodded but said nothing.

"Try to hold onto whatever faith you have. Whether you follow the faith of your mother or find your own way, that isn't important. But try and be sensitive to your sister and your Mom's views. If you don't respect their faith, are you any better than that damned priest?"

I wanted to answer my father. I wanted to tell him he was right, and that I needed to focus my tolerance on those I loved – and those who loved me. But he was already inside the house, looking for his granddaughter.

THIRTY-TWO

My craving for methamphetamine died a lingering death. My longing to get high didn't vanish like a miracle you see in some feel–good Hollywood movie; it dissipated slowly, over time, the way cold rain evaporates off sun–baked asphalt. Inklings of anhedonia remained for a period of time, but once the meth was out of my system, my brain began to right itself.

By early February, Dr. Hodges was talking about graduation. My weekly urine tests, including those completed after my visits home, came back clean. I was working the program and participating in group. Even though the progress of my individual therapy sessions had plateaued, I was doing fine. I wasn't on anti–depressants like some of the other girls. I'd worked the twelve–step program, received my six–month sobriety pin, and was on my way. I felt like there was nothing that could lay me low. I was on top of the world – at least in terms of my dependency – but I still felt the heartache of losing Del. As bad as that boy was for me, I missed his smile and his weird sense of humor. Most of all, I missed his body.

Men come in all shapes and sizes. The sum of their parts – and the parts themselves, for that matter – aren't always equal. Talking to Billy Cadotte at Christmas reminded me of that.

When I first saw Billy naked, laying on his back on the sandy beach of Oak Island on a borrowed blanket, I thought he was the most beautiful being I'd ever seen. Oh sure, I'd caught a peek or two of Dad naked as a little girl, back when I was real young, at an age when it's still kosher to take a bath with your father. Lil and I did that all the time, up until we were four years old. But that time passed, and modesty suddenly reigned. I never appreciated the difference between Dad's uncircumcised penis, and one that had been clipped, until I saw Billy's. Del, like Billy, had gone through the

135

ritual but that's where the similarities ended. Del was built long and powerful, like a Cadillac. Billy...well, God love him, was constructed more along the lines of a Chevrolet.

My memories of having sex with Delmont Benson include clear and distinct moments of pleasure. When I pondered what Del and I'd shared, there wasn't much I could do to reenact that intensity, confined as I was with eleven other recovering female addicts and watched by staff twenty–four seven.

Self–gratification? Please. Even after Father Michaels's debauchery with my sister, which caused me to mistrust my faith, I've maintained Catholic–instilled hesitations. Oh sure, I'd managed to make do a time or two in a pinch. But the guilt, the overwhelming shame that always followed – unreasonable as it is in this modern age, but present nonetheless – loomed in the back of my mind as a deterrent. And then there was the risk of discovery, the risk of someone barging into my room, or worse yet, someone walking unannounced into the lavatory where the lock on the door worked intermittently at best. Being caught in the act was one scene I didn't want preserved in someone's remembrance of Esther Mary DuMont.

I'm not certain when or how it happened but, at some point during my stay at New Beginnings, I realized Mason Erickson was attractive. Mind you, I wasn't infatuated with him. I simply realized that he was a decent–looking guy with a pleasing personality and an interesting outlook on life. During those times we worked together in the kitchen, Mason and I connected. We talked about politics (me, the brazen liberal; he, the moderate Bob Dole conservative), both lamenting the idiot president the Supreme Court had foisted upon the country. We were pretty much in accord that the war in Iraq made no sense. Mason's take (being the economist that he is) was that the war was a fiscal cesspool. My thought on the subject was that we'd sent young men and women onto foreign soil to protect America's self–evident right to drive gas–guzzling SUVs, at the expense of innocent Iraqi women and children. Two very different objections to the same conflict, yes, but there *was* the consensus that the man leading America is a dolt.

We had some spirited conversations, Mason and I, about how to change things. We didn't share the same view as to who should take over once Bush had served his time. I'm partial to Russ Feingold, the senator from Wisconsin, a man who had the foresight to oppose the war from the start. Mason is a John McCain man, though he's admitted, when I've cornered him on his choice, that McCain's chances of being endorsed by the uber–conservatives in charge of the Republican Party are next to none.

"You're crazy."

"How's that, Miss DuMont?"

"The party will never support McCain. He's too independent. He's got as much chance of being endorsed as I do of being elected Mayor of Bayfield."

"You'd make a great mayor," Mason had replied, stacking the dishes I passed to him as we stood in front of the stainless steel sink in the New Beginnings kitchen.

"How so?"

"Well, you're obviously feisty enough. You've got smarts. You're attractive."

At that point, Mason realized that he'd revealed more than he'd wanted to. I felt heat climb the back of my neck as I pondered his compliment.

"I guess I should say 'thanks'...I think."

The awkwardness passed. We went back to our banter.

"I doubt that the good folks of Bayfield are ready for a black woman to be in charge of their little Scandinavian fishing village. Besides," I added, "I'm from Madeline Island. I'd have to run for Mayor of LaPointe."

"Even better. You could secede and form your own country. Call it 'Estherville,' a haven for wacky, mixed–blood liberals."

There was audacity in Mason's comment but I knew he meant no offense. I chuckled.

"You've got guts."

"Politically incorrect, am I? Hell, Miss DuMont, who among us isn't a mix of something? Finns married to Swedes. Italians married to Jews. Norwegians married to Germans. Native Americans married to Englishmen. Hispanics married to Blacks. This country is one big cauldron of cultures and races and tongues brewing, simmering and steeping. That's the beauty of America."

"Sort of sad, don't you think? I mean, each of those cultures, those tribes of people, have certain attributes, beliefs and customs that make them unique. I'm not too sure that losing those differences is the best thing."

"Maybe you're right. Maybe there are things, such as language – like the Native Americans preserving stories and songs in their own tongues – that need to be kept. But isn't it better mixing our blood and joining together, over the long haul, than standing apart from one another?"

Of course, given my being raised in northwestern Wisconsin, I'd never really been a part of Black America in terms of culture or language. But Mason had a point, I thought. Though I wanted to clarify and articulate that there were still things about my ethnicity and the ethnicity of others that might be beneficial if they were to be preserved, the moment passed and we moved on.

Something came to mind after we went our separate ways that afternoon. It was this: as pointed out by the female African American authors I had been reading, those of us with African blood shouldn't forget the heritage that formed us. Not that we need to hold slavery over the white community as a guilt–edged sword; I'm not much for reparations or anything like that. But young blacks like me need to embrace history to understand our community and its attributes – most particularly, the closeness of black women to their children, children that only a few generations ago were in jeopardy of being separated from their mothers and sold, never to be seen again. I wish I had been quick enough to bring this to Mr. Erickson's attention on that February afternoon. I wasn't.

When Mason asked Wanda and me out to his farm a few days later, I sensed that my attraction to the stout Norwegian bachelor farmer was mutual. Day passes for personal excursions, other than time to work paltry jobs, were rare at New Beginnings and were always encumbered by caveats and cautions, not to mention the mandatory urine testing that was required once you returned. Girls were always failing urine tests. Consequences for using while on leave included adding a month to your "out" date. That was for a first offense; there was the possibility of jail, or, worse yet, prison, for repeated violations. There'd been a girl or two during my six months at New Beginnings who ended up in the Big House. I was a month away from completing the program, and I wasn't about to screw up and find myself sitting in the Hennepin County Jail waiting for Judge Lester Patrick to throw the book at me.

Anyway, Wanda and I left New Beginnings for the Erickson Farm early on a Friday afternoon. It was cold – twenty–two below zero, to be precise. Maggie Prescott had arranged a ride for us. Her cousin Albert, one of the drivers the Center relied on, would drop us off just after noon and pick us up at five. Dr. Hodges approved our passes, seeing how both Wanda and I had toed the line, but cautioned against any monkey business. It sort of galled me to be lectured by her. What did she think Wanda and I were? Two promiscuous teenagers infatuated with a farmer? It wasn't likely that either of us were going to do anything to or with Mason Erickson that we'd regret. And that wasn't even taking into account his position on the thing. Sure, like I mentioned, I think he'd expressed an interest in me; I drew that conclusion from his comment about my looks and all. And then there was the way his eyes shifted when I'd walk into the kitchen and interrupt his work. I could feel power and intensity in his gaze. A girl knows such things from a lifetime of dealing with men – that slow and steady look they use as they assess your physicality. Their eyes linger here and there as they take inventory of your attributes. Mason Erickson had looked at me like that on more than one occasion. I had, for better or worse, never encouraged it. And I certainly hadn't reciprocated – at least not consciously.

So, when I tell you that Wanda and I were dropped off at the farm around noon, stayed until five, and were driven back to New Beginnings by the ever–charmingly dull Albert Bechom, and that nothing of consequence took place between Mason and myself, you'll just have to trust me.

There were a few times during the visit when Mason's blue eyes looked at me and I blushed. Wanda got a real charge out of how easily I got flustered. Whenever Mason would wander out of earshot, I gave her a good stab in the ribs to get her to stop making rude comments under her breath, but Wanda's so damned bony, I expect the blows hurt me more than they did her.

About the only thing noteworthy that happened is that Mason showed me the car. It was stored in a machine shed located off the dairy barn. We were in the shed helping Mason attach a bucket to his big John Deere tractor; his normal snowplowing rig, an ancient Oliver narrow front, had gone on the fritz. Wanda was the one who saw tires peeking out from beneath a canvas cover. She nudged me and we both stopped short in our lift, leaving Mason in the unenviable position of holding up one end of the tractor bucket while we gawked.

"What are you gals looking at?"

"The car," we said in unison.

"Aw. Used to be my wife's. Hasn't run since she left, which is going on three years this summer."

"What kind is it?" I asked.

"Saab. 1972 Sonett."

My folks are partial to Volvos and Saabs. I expect if the Finns or the Irish manufactured cars, Mom would own one, but the best she could do was buy cars made in Norway or Sweden. Why Dad went along with Mom on this point remains a mystery, but go along with her he did. Ever since I came into this world, my family has owned nothing but vehicles made in Scandinavia.

"Mind if I take a look?"

Mason lowered his end of the bucket to the ground.

"Feel free. I'm thinking of selling it come spring. You interested?"

I walked slowly towards the car and lifted the tarp.

"Pretty awesome. I didn't know Saab made a sports car."

Mason came to my side. Wanda rolled her eyes. She had no interest in the car, because it wasn't big and powerful and noisy, and it didn't have all the doodads. Not her cup of tea, I suppose. Mason pulled the canvas cover off the Saab.

"The light in here's not the best," he offered, standing next to me as I opened the driver's door. "It's butterscotch, sort of a burnt yellow color. Tan interior. Everything's here but she needs new struts, brakes, tires and a manifold."

The two–seater was slung low to the ground with a wedge–shaped front end and a square butt. Soccer–style wheels and stainless steel rims covered in dried mud and grain dust hinted at agility and speed.

"Go on and sit in her."

I looked at the farmer and smiled.

"Doesn't seem like the sort of car a dairy farmer's wife would drive."

The cold vinyl seat crackled as I slid into the cockpit behind a myriad of gauges. I dreamed of a day when I'd have my freedom. Driving is one of my passions; it's one of the ways I tried to stay away from meth. I'd race my Jetta through the flat farmland west of the Cities, or east through the bluffs overlooking the Mississippi and the St. Croix Rivers, hoping to replace the euphoria I attained doing meth with physical speed.

"That was part of our problem. Virginia wasn't happy being a farmer's wife. It wasn't that I didn't want her to work outside the home; I had no problem with that. But she just has no affinity for farm life, for the day–to–day labor it takes to run a place. I bought her the car after Jacob was born, in hopes she'd stick around. The car didn't close the deal. She left and told me I could sell the Saab and use the money for child support. I couldn't see doing that – don't know why. Just couldn't. But, well, the thing is, it's a fun car to drive, but I'm not the sports car type. Someone should be driving it rather than it sitting here, gathering dust."

Wanda poked her head inside the car.

"Our ride will be here any minute. You about done pretending you're Jeff Gordon?"

I smiled.

"Don't sell this car until I've had a chance to make you an offer. I'd love to take it for a test drive in the spring."

"You've got my word on it. I won't sell it until you've taken it for a spin."

"There's just one problem."

I fingered the leather–covered stick-shift.

"What's that?"

"I don't know how to drive a stick. My Volkswagen was an automatic."

I hadn't made that disclosure so that Mason Erickson could make some sort of commitment to me. I really hadn't thought of it that way. Still, I won't say I wasn't flattered by his reply.

"I'd be more than happy to teach you."

There was an awkward pause.

Now, I want you to know, I'm not the sort of girl to lead a man on. As I've said, I had some interest in Mason Erickson. How deep and how genuine that interest was at that moment, I wasn't in a position to commit to. I should've said something, and somehow let him know that I appreciated the offer. Instead, I stared out the windshield of the car and tinkered with the dials on the dash. Thankfully, the farmer moved on.

"It'll take me some time once the snow is gone to get 'er ready. By then, you'll likely be back home. How'll I find you?" He paused. "To let you know about the car, I mean?" the farmer quickly added, his interest in things other than motors, grease and oil made clear by his question.

"I'll give you the address of the halfway house I'll be staying at," I said as I took one last look around the interior of the car. "I'd best get out of this thing before Miss Jones and I miss our ride."

I exited the car and closed the car door behind me. Mason covered the Saab as Wanda Jones and I left the machine shed to wait outside for our ride. Assailed by winter, I longed for spring – for sun, and for the day when I'd be free of treatment and constraint.

THIRTY-THREE

I thought a lot about Billy and April as I completed my treatment. What is their married life like? Is their physical relationship as emotionally deep and wide as the one I'd had with Del? Or is that part of their relationship perfunctory, their connection based more on the emotional tie that comes with having children together?

Children. God, how I want to have kids. Someday. While I was in the last days of treatment, I realized the foolishness of that occurring any time soon. Kids weren't in the cards for me then, as I worked to get straight. But someday…someday, when I'm thinking clearly and my goals are set, I'd love to be a mother. I'm not afraid of stretch marks or the birthing process. I've seen all that as a registered nurse. Will I feel pain? Will I whimper as the baby's head crowns, as the razor–sharp contractions rip through my insides? Probably. Even with pain meds, most women yelp to some degree when giving birth. Nothing to be ashamed of, mind you. Just a thing that's true, is all.

Sitting in the library at New Beginnings, contemplating Billy and April and their life in northwestern Wisconsin – including her teaching music at the Red Cliff Tribal School to dark–skinned elementary school kids, and him enforcing the law for Bayfield County – it all made sense to me. How it is, and how it should be.

One day in late February, Wanda Jones upped the literary ante. She walked into our bedroom a week or so before our discharge date and handed me a book. Her elongated fingers, the palms of her hands lightly pink and the cuticles of her nails trimmed and neat, held out a modest trade–size paperback for me to accept.

"Here," she said quietly. "It's about time you knew the truth."

I looked with one eye at the woman standing at the edge of my bed. She was dressed in blue jeans so tight you could see the outline of her underwear. Her feet were bare. She wore a wildly patterned purple and orange chemise top that wasn't tucked into her jeans. Her coarse black hair was piled on top of her head, held in place by a purple Nike headband. She wore no earrings, which was unusual, since she favored oversized hoops. Her face was accented only by a hint of purple eyeliner. Wanda Jones was equal parts starkly beautiful and serious as she handed me the book.

"The truth about what?"

"About how African women are treated."

We'd already talked about our families. I had confided how little I knew about my dad's ancestors, how tight–lipped Dad had been over the years as to his heritage. I knew little more than what he'd revealed to me during our Christmas walk on the island. Wanda and I had discussed Africa, and about being black professional women in America. Since she could trace her lineage – pure as it was on both sides of her parentage, back to Mandikan tribal roots in Senegal on the coast of West Africa – her perspectives were different from mine. She had a grounding, a basis, in Africa. I had only theories, wisps and murmurings of ancestry to speculate on.

"What about it?"

My fingers wrapped around the glossy cover of *Possessing the Secret of Joy.* I'd never heard of it, and I had no idea why Wanda was so insistent that I read it.

"I'm not about to tell you what you should believe or know," Wanda explained, sitting on the edge of the bed as I rotated my legs to make space, my bare feet coming to rest on the dusty hardwood floor. "But here's how I see it: this book…well, it says all that needs saying about things that need knowing."

I opened the cover, scanned the introduction and immediately grasped the subject matter of the novel.

"Female circumcision?"

"More like mutilation."

My innards tensed.

"The old women have been doing it for centuries. They take girls who are no more than eleven, and butcher their privates in a way that ensures they'll behave."

I swallowed hard.

"I'll read it. I'm just about done with the one about the lynchings in Duluth."

"Those three boys had nothing to do with that white girl. She lied through her teeth and those white men, well, they ate it up. They hanged Elias Clayton, Elmer Jackson and Isaac McGhie without evidence or proof."

I nodded but said nothing in response.

"Well, you got a week to read this and get it back to me. You'll get it done, fast as you read. Isn't much to it in terms of size, but Miss Walker's words – now that's a whole 'nother matter."

Before I could thank her, Wanda Jones rose from my bed and left the room, not bothering to close the door on her way out. I pondered the woman: she was steady, kind and intelligent, but I worried about whether she'd make it on the outside. Unlike me, she hadn't taken a job while she was at New Beginnings, though she had the opportunity to work retail, as a cashier, under close supervision at a convenience store in Panora. She'd rejected the job without giving a reason. My guess is that Wanda had no interest in reintegrating herself into the job world at a level lower than the position she previously held. Wanda Jones seemed too prideful to return to a rung on the economic ladder she'd passed years before. That's what worried me about Wanda: her pride, the way she held her chin up – not in aloofness or superiority, but in self–assuredness. That was something I thought would come back to haunt her when she tried to make a go of it in the real world. But there was nothing I could do for her. Wanda is who Wanda is, and no twenty–eight–year-old registered nurse–*cum*–meth addict is going to change that.

I reached across the bed and placed the Walker book next to the paperback copy of *The Lynchings in Duluth* I'd borrowed from the Panora library. The lynching story was one of the few books Wanda told me about that she didn't own. A name I'd come across towards the end of the book, Reverend William Majors, had struck a chord. According to a tidbit of oral history Dad had shared with me over Christmas, William Majors was a distant relative. Though the reverend wasn't integral to the lynchings, he was mentioned because, as the pastor of St. Mark's African Methodist Episcopal Church, he voiced the anger of Duluth's black community at the tired way the justice system dealt with the killings.

I rose from my bed. The quilt was rumpled from use, and I smoothed the bedding as I reflected on this familial tie – however thin and distant it was – to the lynchings, as I left my bedroom in search of lunch.

THIRTY-FOUR

My running shoes – once clean, shiny and just out of the box (a Christmas gift from Lilith) – were now beaten and tired from wear. I was five days away from discharge. My immediate future was set. I was to live in a halfway house in northern Minneapolis – Castleman's, it was called – for three months immediately following my stint at New Beginnings. I had a job lined up as a nurse's aide at the Hennepin County Medical Center. The Minnesota Board of Nursing insisted on a year of abstinence before they'd clear me to go back to work as a registered nurse. Even then, I'd have to meet certain restrictions: no dispensing of medication and no access to controlled substances. Which hospital or clinic would hire me with those prohibitions was anybody's guess, but that was the deal. I had to take it or leave it. What choice did I have?

I was running with determination. I'd spent a month breaking in the new shoes and conditioning my lungs and legs. Being clean caused me to gain fifteen pounds. Trust me, it wasn't the food at New Beginnings that made me put on the weight; it was the fact that I was no longer artificially suppressing my appetite with methamphetamine. Even though I'd never used the drug for that purpose, weight loss was a welcome side effect of addiction. What girl wouldn't want to stay a size ten? I surely did. So when my gut started expanding, my boobs drooping and my ass growing, it was time to run. And run I did.

New Beginnings is located on the northeastern shore of Lake Panorama on a dead–end dirt road off Panarama Drive, the roadway that encircles the lake. It's open country away from the lake. The Iowa landscape is virtually flat – much easier terrain than what's found in northwestern Wisconsin, where I used to run to get in shape for basketball. I'd thought about playing some round ball in the Panora adult league. There were quite a few women playing hoops, but the logistics of getting to and from town were too complex. It was easier to lace up my New Balances and head out the front door of the treatment center, all the way down Panarama Drive to Rose, up Rose to 180th Trail, and then west back to Panarama. It was a good route through friendly terrain. I had feared being chased, but to my joy, I discovered there was an absence of free–roaming dogs along my route.

By the time February came around, I was in a groove. I'd lost eight pounds. My legs were strong. My wind was excellent. I was closing in on doing three miles in less than twenty–one minutes. I'd never run a mile in less than seven minutes in my life, not even when I was in my best shape. I was pushing myself and it was paying off.

My feet pounded asphalt. My nylon running suit flapped, the result of a hard wind coming from the north, out of the Dakotas. Since the early storm in November, there'd been little snow; the landscape consisted of shades of gray and black, monochromatic and monotonous beneath the light turquoise sky. There were no clouds that day, at least none that I can remember. As I ran, words from a Tracy Chapman song, my favorite song at the time, filled my head. As the lyrics and tune of "All You Have Is Your Soul" spun round and round in my mind (my brain is capable of carrying a tune in perfect pitch, even if my vocal chords aren't), I pondered the most recent session with Maggie Prescott. We'd talked about my mother. It had not been an easy discussion.

"You think she's forgiven you?"

The question was asked earlier that morning in Ms. Prescott's office as I sat in a chair in front of a window overlooking Lake Panorama. I knew what Maggie meant. I just didn't want to blurt out a bunch of confessional crap I'd regret later. Even if Mom had no way of learning what I said about her, how in the world was I going to face my mother if I derided the love and generosity she'd shown me over three decades of life? *Wasn't gonna happen*, was what I was thinking.

"For what? What are you talking about?"

"For David's death."

I exhaled like a bull waiting to charge a matador. I'd become certain, after the revelatory vision in my parent's basement, that I wasn't to blame for the tragedy. And even though I believed Mom suspected the truth, I never confirmed my supposition with her.

"How in the world would I know that?"

"Well, you say you and your mother have a good relationship, right?"

"*Had*. We were getting along fine, even after my arrest, until I got into it with her and my sister at Christmas. Why? What's my mother got to do with anything?"

Maggie Prescott adjusted her blouse to release creases of fat that were trapped by the fabric. She was dressed and accessorized in royal blue, right down to her eyeliner.

She looks like a giant blueberry! I thought to myself. I must admit, I felt a sense of superiority over the out–of–shape woman. I was young, well toned and healthy. I mistook her obesity for mental sloth. I should have known better.

"There's no reason to parry and thrust with me, Miss DuMont. I'm not here to critique your mother. I'm only here to make you understand yourself."

"Uh huh."

Ms. Prescott's brow furrowed. We stared each other down.

"Well? Have you thought of an answer to the actual question I asked?"

"Which was?"

"Do you think your mother has forgiven you for David's death? You've made it quite clear your father has. You said back around Thanksgiving you saw signs of forgiveness and understanding in her. Have you talked to your mother about those perceptions?"

I shifted my butt on my chair. *Why won't she just leave it alone?*

There was a protracted interlude in our conversation. Maggie Prescott stared me down with her audaciously blue eyes.

Damn, she's insistent.

I exhaled before answering.

"No."

Ms. Prescott nodded smugly and jotted a note down on her pad of paper.

"But you do talk? There's still a line of communication open between you?"

"Yes."

"So why not put it on the table? Ask her if she's still angry, if she still considers you responsible for David's death. You were, after all, only a kid. And your sister – Lilly, isn't it? – wasn't she helping you keep tabs on your brother? Why isn't the burden of David's death shared equally between you and Lilly?"

Because folks think I'm the one who didn't do what needed doing. We've gone over this, Ms. Prescott. What more can I say? Of course, I didn't express this thought. Our time together came to an end. I had one more session remaining with her. I knew that she'd come after me about bringing David's death and my role in it out into the open. I wasn't looking forward to our last session together.

But if it helps me heal, I relented silently, *and keep me off meth, maybe it's worth the anxiety, the tears and the hurt feelings – both Mom's*

147

and mine. I know Mom loves me. Beneath that cool exterior lies a loving heart. Maybe Prescott's right; damn her, anyway.

I turned my face into the gale. My cheeks grew numb. Sweat accumulated under my clothing and caused me to shiver. My fingers remained warm inside leather choppers and wool liners. I glanced at a stopwatch hanging from a tether around my neck. I was bucking fifteen–mile–an–hour gusts, but was on pace to beat the twenty–one–minute mark. An Allied moving van zoomed by. The truck's passing sucked yellowed newspaper into the air. The debris swirled around me as I increased my speed. A silver Dodge van filled with squalling children raced by. Tracy Chapman's lyrics slid through my mind. I thought of Billy Cadotte leaving me in my hospital bed. I thought of Del lying in his coffin. And I thought of Mason Erickson, an honest farmer who had done nothing wrong, nothing to deserve his wife giving up and deserting their future. Betrayal. Sadness. Loss. The totality of it all made me mad. It downright pissed me off.

   Is this all there is?

My question remained unanswered. I ran on. Daylight was fading as I turned onto the gravel drive of the treatment center, the rusty orb of the sun suspended above the ridge of trees demarcating the far shore of Lake Panorama. I stopped in front of the house, doubled over with exhaustion. I place my hands my hips. Clouds of vapor spewed from my mouth and my heart beat like a bumblebee's wings. My eyes steadied on the snaky dimensions of Lake Panorama and the wind–polished ice that dissected the land like a scrawling streak of black crayon on a vast sheet of white paper.

   You call yourself a lake? You're not a lake – just an artificial widening in a river. The Raccoon River: who's ever heard of the Raccoon River? Lake, smake. I grew up on a real *lake – a lake with tides and surf and danger. And fishermen dropping their nets into cold, blue water. And ships docking in harbors. You're not a lake. You're a disgrace.*

Pain stabbed at my left side. A light from inside the house cast a yellow glow across the ground, but no sound emanated from the building. I was all alone, just me and the God–awful excuse of an Iowa lake I'd just insulted. *Insulting an inanimate object?* I rolled my eyes and looked at my stopwatch. I shook my head in disbelief: I'd done my three–mile loop in 19:45.

THIRTY-FIVE

In retrospect, taking a road trip with Hazel Edwards three days before our graduation from New Beginnings wasn't a wise choice. Why I agreed to co–pilot Hazel's beat–up Lumina sedan from Panora to Council Bluffs, Iowa, where Hazel wanted to retrieve her things – things she claimed she'd need for the halfway house in Minneapolis, where we were both headed – I don't know. The bigger question is: why did Dr. Hodges put her stamp of approval on such a cockeyed plan? The good doctor's blind trust, given Hazel's minimal compliance with the program...well, *that* surprised me. But Hodges knew what she was doing. At least, that's what I thought at the time.

I hunkered down in the front passenger seat of Hazel's garbage–infested car as she propped up her snaky body behind the steering wheel. She insisted on listening to a heavy metal station as the car sped down the road, her murky green eyes riveted upon the pavement, the morning sun behind us. There was scarcely anyone on the freeway. Go figure! It was six o'clock on a Saturday morning; sane folks were sleeping in, catching up on rest they'd missed during the week.

I was supposed to be at work for my last shift at the diner, but I'd switched with another girl. I was slated to work the following day, Sunday afternoon. It would be my last shift at the Town's Edge Café. I was hoping that Mason Erickson, who'd taken the weekend off from the treatment center to medicate some sick heifers, would stop at the diner after his quarterly visit to First United Methodist Church in Guthrie Center. Mason once confessed to me that he'd have gone to church more often if it weren't for his weekend schedule at New Beginnings. He also revealed that he'd been baptized into the Evangelical Lutheran Church of America but there wasn't an ELCA church close by. The local Missouri Synod Lutheran

149

church, the nearest Lutheran congregation, wasn't an option for him; it was too dogmatic, he said – too rigid for someone like Mason, even taking into account his decidedly Republican bent. His parents had insisted on toting the family to Council Bluffs for services at Emanuel Lutheran during his formative years, but he'd put a stop to such long–distance worship when he came of age. As a compromise, he'd hung his hat with the Methodists.

Thinking about Mason coming into the diner reminded me that I had his address and telephone number in my purse, along with the note about the asking price for the Saab being three thousand cash "as is," or four thousand with everything in working order. The little car intrigued me and, as I surveyed the dismal confines of Hazel's Lumina, a ride utterly devoid of style, I was certain I'd find a way to buy Mason's car.

"You're nuts. No good can come of you and that little white girl traipsin' off to her hometown."

Wanda Jones had objected to the road trip. She had no interest in tagging along, despite Hazel's invitation that Wanda come with. She was convinced that Hazel Edwards was headed for disaster and would bring me down with her.

"I need to get away," I said half–heartedly. "Hazel's got her shit together. There won't be any problems."

"With white people, there's always problems. Didn't you read that Maya Angelou book I gave you? The one with 'Christmas' in the title? Miss Angelou tells you, plain as day, that you can't ever really trust white folks. She says there's a world of difference between sharing a laugh and sharing a bed with a white man. I say: same thing applies to sharing a ride with a white woman to someplace you've never been."

Wanda knew, from our past conversations, that I'd spent my life living among whites – my mother was one, after all – and that my most intense love affairs had been with white men. If all my blood were emptied and measured, drained out like old oil from an automobile, it would be confirmed that I really was more white than black. Oh sure, I had enough blood quantum, if African Americans were to be measured like Native Americans, to be a member of *the* tribe. Similar calculations for Native Americans determine whether they're entitled to tribal benefits, and with Indian gaming casinos picking the pockets of the retired, this means entitlement to money. Historically, less beneficial ramifications flowed from discovering that one has a quantum of African blood. One drop of black heritage, no matter how small, was usually enough, under the laws of the Old South, to enslave a person for life. Quantum for blacks granted membership in *the* tribe all right, but unlike Native Americans, that computation was a means of exclusion, not a means of inclusion. In my case, despite my dark skin, my African blood never defined my relationships or me: I was born, raised and lived nearly all my life in the company of my mother's people. I was comfortable with them. Wanda, given her pure ethnicity and her prideful African–ness, just didn't understand how this could be.

"You're wrong. Hazel's a little touched; I'll give you that. But she's clean as you and me now. Nothing's going to happen."

"You're as crazy as that bitch is," Wanda said, leaving me alone to dress.

I thought about Hazel's story as she drove, and how it was she'd come to be at New Beginnings. Hazel started taking X when she was in high school, when she went to raves to listen to her favorite local bands at supposedly chemical and alcohol–free clubs across the Missouri River in Omaha, Nebraska, Council Bluff's immediate neighbor to the west.

"I'd never felt much when I was with a boy, before doing X…I mean," she'd said in group more than once, "the drug left me with a powerful glow. I wasn't driven to take the drug because my mind or my body demanded it. I did X because it made sex so much better."

Given my own meth–induced ribaldry, I figured I understood Hazel Edward's compulsions better than most. I guess this bond between us was one of the reasons I agreed to tag along with her.

Hazel's Lumina chugged up Huntington, a quiet street traversing a knoll containing Fairmount Park, a large green space in the middle of Council Bluffs. Pamela Bunt, Hazel's Mom, lives in a small green–and–white 1950s style bungalow on Huntington. We pulled up to the house a little after eight in the morning. It was my understanding that we were staying until early afternoon. We would load the things Hazel wanted into the Chev, have lunch, do a little shopping and be back to New Beginnings before dark. It didn't work out that way. In hindsight, I think I knew something weird was going to happen. I mean, after all, Hazel *is* an odd woman.

Hazel's manner of speech – stopping and starting sentences without finishing them, like her brain works two tracks at once and neither track ever quite makes it into the station – is off–putting. Her constant nervous fidgeting, a trait driven not by energy but by frayed nerves, causes her thinking to sputter like a bad electrical connection. She was on meds for these deficits; on that day, it didn't seem like the meds were working.

Pamela Bunt greeted us at the door. She was a fragile looking woman in her early fifties. Her face and posture displayed decay and use far beyond her years. Her hair had been dyed so many times, and likely so many shades of red by the looks of her roots, it appeared lifeless and dead, done in by chemical torture. Mrs. Bunt's cheeks retreated into her face; she wasn't wearing her dentures. Her eyes were the same pale, non–committal gray--green as Hazel's; in fact, as I think back, the daughter may have been named for the eye color the two women share.

Pamela – or "'Pam," as she insisted I call her – held a burning cigarette in her right hand, a cheap off–brand by the look of the packaging balled up in her left fist. The smoke framing Pam's face didn't improve the woman's appearance. "How's my girl?"

Pam gave Hazel a peck on her cheek. Hazel responded with a slight hug, a gesture that looked forced and unnatural. There seemed to be cool affection, if not genuine love, in the mother's response to her only child, the result of an affair between Pam, a legal secretary, and her first boss, a prominent Nebraska attorney. The affair went on for years after Hazel came into the world, with the attorney paying child support out of guilt and a sense of moral obligation. I'd heard the whole story, as everyone in group had, multiple times, in slightly disparate versions. The details of Hazel's past became clearer in my mind, more connected with reality, once I crossed the threshold of her mother's modest house.

"This is Esther DuMont."

"Pleased to meet you, Esther," the woman said, shoving the cigarette package into a pocket in her flannel bathrobe before offering me the wrong hand.

I took the woman's cold left palm, the skin dry and alien, and shook it.

"Likewise."

The woman studied my face. I got the sense that she hadn't entertained many black folks. She didn't make me feel uncomfortable or unwelcome. It was just an inkling, a premonition, that I was an unusual specimen for Mrs. Bunt to consider.

"Have a seat at the table. I made Hazel's favorites: chocolate chip pancakes and sausage."

"Mom, you really didn't have to," Hazel said, shifting her eyes like a schoolgirl sharing a secret. "We're gonna go shopping at the mall after we load up the car. We'll likely get a bite there."

"My little girl needs to keep up her strength, now doesn't she? Come sit down. You know how much you like my pancakes."

We followed Pam through the house. The place was, in contrast to its owner's personal hygiene, neat as a pin. There wasn't a hint of dust or dirt anywhere. At least in terms of housekeeping, Pamela Bunt was nothing like her daughter; the New Beginnings staff was constantly reprimanding Hazel about her room. Clothes on the floor. Make–up tubes scattered in every corner. Dirty underwear hiding under the bed. Hazel had stubbornly resisted all efforts to reform her ways. I thanked my lucky stars that she and I were not going to be roommates at the halfway house.

It wasn't until we were loading the car after breakfast that I found out about the party – a "coming home" celebration, cooked up by Hazel's mother, was apparently planned for the early evening. Hazel hadn't said a word to me about it until her Mom tossed it out there like a hand grenade.

"We can't stay. We're supposed to be back by five. Our day pass is only good until then," I said as Hazel backed the car – its rear seat and trunk filled with clothes, childhood mementos, stuffed animals, and assorted junk that I really couldn't see Hazel needing at a halfway house – down the cement driveway to Huntington Street.

"Lighten up. We'll be back by ten. I'll phone ahead and say we had car trouble. I'll get my cousin Donald– he'll be here tonight– to write out a repair ticket from his garage. Hodges will never know. Mom's been planning this thing for months. You don't want to see the old bat cry, do you?"

I pursed my lips and stared straight ahead as the car bounced down the precariously steep road.

"Don't be like that."

"Like what?" I muttered.

"Pissed off. We'll have a few laughs, listen to some music, and be back before anyone gives a damn."

"I'm pissed because you didn't bother to tell me about your little party. It's the least you could've done. I thought we were friends. Friends don't keep secrets from one another – not ones like this, anyway."

Secrets. Hazel and I, we've…well, had our share of them. Mine, you've heard most of them. Not all of them, I'll grant you, but the ones important to this story. I'd witnessed the dark and scary edges of Hazel's life through her eyes and through her mouth, during group. In fact, when we were at the house on Huntington, I looked (cautiously, so as not to get caught) for evidence and verification of what she'd revealed, memorialized in the photographs in Pam's bungalow. I didn't see any pictures of the bastard. That's Larry Bunt, Hazel's stepfather, the man who picked up the pieces of Pam's life after she miscarried the second kid sired by the lawyer, after Pam's spirit was broken when the attorney took up with another mistress, leaving her with little but the monthly payments he made as child support to assuage his guilt. It was after the lawyer had broken that time– honored promise made by all philanderers: "I'll leave my wife just as soon as I get things settled." It hardly ever happens; it certainly didn't in Pam's case.

That's where, according to Hazel, Larry Bunt fit in: he started dating Pamela when Hazel was nine or ten – just as she was on the verge of budding. He apparently liked that. He had in fact been convicted in Lincoln, where he'd taught elementary school, of acting on that propensity with other pre–pubescent girls. The thing that caused Hazel no end of angst and heartache and trouble – beyond what one would normally expect from having to give your stepfather back rubs and blow jobs at the age of ten years – was that her mother *knew* of Larry's past. That, of course, came out later, when he was charged in Iowa, after Hazel spilled the beans to her high school counselor about what Larry had done. It was tough to hide, seeing as how Larry had gotten her pregnant. It was a good thing, she confided to us in group, that she'd miscarried the child.

"Imagine," she said during a teary–eyed group session, "giving birth to your own step–sister."

Anyway, it all came out during Larry's trial. He wouldn't do the right thing, and confess; he wouldn't fess up and take the five years. Instead, he got ten. And Hazel learned, at age seventeen, that her mother had knowingly brought a convicted pedophile into their home.

The discovery of that betrayal – a daughter's discovery of her mother's willingness to place her own pleasure ahead of her love for her child – has a lot to do, I thought as the Lumina pulled into a downtown parking lot, *with why Hazel is so damned screwed up.*

That evening, I realized that it was all wrong. The place. The people. Me being there, in Pamela Bunt's house on the bluffs overlooking the Missouri River in far Western Iowa. There wasn't a right thing about it, not a one. I knew it before Pamela Bunt pulled out her meth pipe. I knew it before Cousin Donald unwrapped the cellophane package he'd removed from the front pocket of his jeans and showed Hazel that he'd managed to score some X. I knew it before the music peaked and I became surrounded by twenty strangers with body piercings, scruffy faces and desperate eyes: the men, tall and angular, hungry in as many ways as one can be; the women, unhealthily gaunt, their faces painted messily with rouge and eye–liner and their hair wild and tall, reminiscent of something out of a bad '80s flick. When Pam's guests crowded into the place, I knew I was in the belly of a beast, sort of like old Jonah in the whale, and that I was likely to drown, not be spit onto shore and saved by God. When I saw Hazel toss back two hits of X and follow them with a chaser of beer, there was no doubt in my mind: I was in trouble.

I was holding a can of Sprite, sitting on a love seat in the hallway and contemplating how in the hell I'd gotten myself into this mess. I watched the clock above the fireplace tick off the minutes; I wondered if, when the clock struck seven, I'd still be sober. As I considered my predicament, a girl named Angel and a guy named Vince staggered over and sat down on a plastic–covered couch across from me. When Vince pulled out a rock of ice from the front pocket of his western style shirt and clumsily loaded it into a pipe, the desire to get high – the desire to know the delicious flow of meth into my essence – grabbed hold. I was like a penniless child coveting candy for sale in a jar on a counter in a corner store.

THIRTY-SIX

Outer Island is the last of the Apostle Islands. Beyond it, Lake Superior spreads out to meet the distant shores of Minnesota, Ontario and Michigan. Billy Cadotte and I spent a night on the northern–most beach of Outer Island, snug in a canvas pup tent, mosquitoes buzzing at the mesh behind the door flaps. Our breathing formed condensation inside the tent; water dripped onto our sleeping bags once the morning sun rose to heat the canvas.

We embraced that night, a week before David's death, unaware that a spark and a pool of spilled gasoline would change it all, would vaporize our future. I slept after we made love and I dreamed that Billy's body was behind mine, my face pressed into the fluffy stuffing of my sleeping bag; Billy was inside me, pushing hard. I saw stars and colors. I shuddered and shook. I felt joy. I remember it. I really do.

Joy. Sitting on the love seat in Pamela Bunt's little bungalow in Council Bluffs, joy seemed distant and foreign as my eyes took in the gyrating men and women, all of them bounding and moving to music, with smoke thick in the air. I looked into the faces of the two human beings occupying the love seat with me, Cousin Donald and that wreck of humanity, Pamela Bunt. Pam had put make–up on and slithered into a silk dress that was one size too small. Her saline implants squished together, and her dentures were aligned, polished and gleaming white against her powdered skin. I knew I was in hell. The vision of Billy and I was replaced by an image of me doing someone, anyone, in the room. Images of decadence rolled through my brain like something out of Dante or *Eyes Wide Shut* – you know, that weird Tom Cruise movie – and sent a shudder through me.

"Where's Hazel?" I asked.

Vince, the trucker, was passed out next to Angel on the love seat across from me, a full bottle of Old Milwaukee in his left hand. He'd lost it before he could rejuvenate himself with meth. Angel hadn't waited for him to come around. She'd already smoked a bowl.

"She's in the bathroom, hurling. Crazy bitch took four of those pills Donald gave her. One was all she was supposed to take," Pamela said, shaking her head.

Four hits of X, I thought. I'd never done the drug. I had no idea what was considered the norm. I found my way to the lavatory and knocked on the door.

"Go away."

I tried the doorknob. The door was locked.

"It's Esther. We need to get out of here."

There was no answer.

"You okay in there? I asked. "Hodges will have our asses if we're not back before ten. We'll be lucky to graduate on Tuesday."

"I don't feel so good. Give me a few more minutes."

A Coldplay song, "God Put a Smile on Your Face," boomed out from the stereo in the living room. I rapped on the hollow-core door.

"We need to get out of here," I repeated, desperation sinking in as someone turned up the music. I heard retching and the sound of liquid dripping from inside the bathroom.

Panic overwhelmed me and self-preservation took over. I walked away. I know, it doesn't sound gallant or brave. But understand: I was near the point of yielding myself, my soul, to crawling back onto the couch and inhaling pungent smoke. What would happen then would have been anybody's guess. Would I end up with the tall muscular blond standing off by himself, watching the others dance, his quiet blue eyes and cleft chin handsome and seemingly out of place against the ugliness of the room? Or would I simply smoke until I'd had enough, wander back to New Beginnings sometime on Sunday, only to fail my urine test and find myself back in front of the judge? I took one last look at the blond guy and made my decision.

I walked into the kitchen, picked up the cordless phone and went out the back door. On the rear porch of the house, the night was black and open; stars were sprinkled across the sky above me, their light defuse and faint due to the interference of streetlamps. I opened my purse. My fingers shook as I withdrew a wrinkled scrap of paper and dialed Mason's number. I prayed to God that he was home. My heart pounded. My anxiousness increased as the phone rang. Once. Twice. Three times.

"Hello?"

THIRTY-SEVEN

I waited for Mason in Fairmont Park. I pulled my choppers over my hands, sat on a wooden picnic table covered with ice, and studied the cityscape that spread out below me. When I began to shiver, I left the table. I walked to get warm, following obvious paths worn into the frozen soil. The lights of Omaha dotted the horizon. Freight trains rumbled through the river valley and shook the ground beneath my feet. Train whistles echoed from below, the sound too regular to be considered mournful.

What the hell am I doing here?

The thought ended there. My mind explored images I hadn't seen but could imagine: Hazel, her limp brown hair plastered to her sweaty cheeks; her emaciated body slumped on the ceramic tile floor; her white hands gripping the porcelain toilet bowl; her eyes glazed and frightened, as she up–chucked the last of her lunch, the food reduced to bits and pieces of spittle as it passed her shaking lips.

I'm a nurse, Goddamn it. I should've helped her.

She was likely dehydrated. The heaves would deprive her brain cells of moisture. If the process continued, she'd fall unconscious. She'd die. What the hell was I doing walking around a city park three blocks away while my friend slipped away?

Friend? Hazel really isn't much of a friend. Would a friend lead you on, use deception to bring you to a place of abomination and ruin?

I chuckled, which was odd, given the circumstances. In the depths of my internal argument, I was talking to myself as if I were a character – perhaps my namesake from the Old Testament. I found a picnic table, cleared the bench of broken ice and sat down. The air grew colder. Revelry escaped from Pamela Bunt's house down the street. I pulled my navy blue watch cap down over my coarse hair and tried to disappear inside my jacket.

Strains of indie music, a song by Tomorrow and Forever, filtered up the street. Drumbeats and bass thumps resonated from the house I'd escaped. As I waited, I thought about the people in the house, and how they'd looked at me and had taken in my blackness as an exception to their world. Even Maria, a nicely put–together young Latina dancing with abandon in the living room, critiqued me with her Hispanic eyes.

Like I've said before, I rarely heard or saw obvious racism while growing up. Maybe that has to do with the fact that Lilly and I are the daughters of a respected physician. Maybe it has to do with the fact that folks in our part of Wisconsin are used to dealing with Native Americans and consider my sister and me just slightly darker versions of the same. I don't really know why we didn't encounter more catcalls and whispers. Actually, I can only think of a couple of instances where race became an obvious issue during my childhood.

Lilly and I were playing on a co–ed basketball team. Dad was our coach, the one and only time he attempted that role. He did a reasonable job of mentoring, but his lack of court sense, well…it showed even at the fourth–grade level. I was a big girl for my age – not fat, but solid and tall. Lilly, of course, was slender, cute and a klutz. We were playing in a Christmas tournament at South Shore Elementary School in Port Wing. Now, understand that, in these contests, a score of ten to eight or something similar was not uncommon. Most fourth–grade girls and boys have trouble throwing the ball anywhere near the basket; in fact, I don't think Lil made a single shot in the seven games we played that season. I, on the other hand, was big enough and strong enough not only to shoot lay ups, but I could routinely make free–throws. I used the square on the backboard as a target to bank the ball off the glass and through the net.

I was playing center. Sandi Niskanen, I think, was one of the guards. Sandi was a fireplug who knew how to dribble better than I did. She was the one who brought the ball down the court. I'd stand as still as a house in the paint (they don't call three–second violations at that level), catch Sandi's pass, spin around and bank the ball off the glass and into the net. It was a play that worked nearly every time.

We were playing the host team, South Shore Elementary. South Shore didn't have anyone tall enough or savvy enough to defend against me. By half time, I had eight points and we were up fourteen to two. An incident happened right after we took the floor for the second half. Understand, though I'd heard the word "nigger" on television and at the movies, I never understood the depths of the hatred and loathing behind the word until that day on the elementary gym floor, when the otherwise normal–looking white father of the center of the other team took issue with a block I'd laid on his

159

son. I'd slapped away the ball so hard that it bounced off the poor kid's nose, opening up a spigot of blood.

"Damn it, ref," the man had yelled as he scurried down the wooden seats of the bleachers, "that little nigger girl is out of control. You gotta get her out of the game before she hurts someone else."

The import of the "N" word didn't register with me at that young age, other than I knew it was an insult and that it was wrong to say it. Dad, on the other hand, took immediate offense. He left the team bench, where Lilly was contentedly playing with her hair, and walked to the scorer's table.

"Sir, there's no call for language like that – not aimed at my daughter, not aimed at *any* child."

The ref acknowledged my father with a nod and stepped between Dad and the other parent. The other parent's face was red and his hands clenched. The game had stopped; the injured kid's mother had made her way onto the floor, tilted the boy's head back and sopped blood with a towel. I felt bad. The boy was a full head shorter than I was and he was crying.

"Jerry," the ref said in a calm voice, "there's no call for that. You should be ashamed of yourself. The little girl didn't do anything wrong."

The boy's father stood toe to toe with the ref, as if he was going to bowl the man over, despite the fact that he was giving up thirty pounds and five inches to the official.

"Their kind shouldn't be allowed to play against our kids."

Their kind. What kind is that? I recall thinking in my ten–year–old mind. *What kind am I, if not their kind?*

"That's enough of that," my father interjected. "Either this guy leaves or we do. I won't have him disparaging my daughter, or anyone else, with such low talk. It's either him or us."

It was obvious even to someone of my young age that the ref and Jerry were friends; that they both lived in Port Wing and had grown up together. I watched as the ref held out his hands to keep the irate parent off Dad as he considered Dad's ultimatum.

"There's no call to get your dander up, Dr. DuMont. I'll talk to Mr. Harris and calm him down. You're a doctor; why don't you tend to his son?"

This last suggestion was a huge mistake.

"No nigger doctor is going to touch my kid."

My father had already started towards the injured child. At the "N" word, he stopped dead in his tracks. I expected, given what I knew about my father up until that point in my life – how genteel and professional he talked and acted – that he'd simply turn on his heels, collect our team and leave. It was a complete surprise to me when he reached across the referee and grabbed the white man's shirt. I remember Dad using words I'd never heard him use, words I knew both he and Mom would wash my mouth out with soap for, if I so much as *thought* let alone said. I remember the other man trying to bring his hands up to strike Dad in the face with little fists; the problem was, my father was too strong. His rage had injected so much adrenaline into his veins that I doubt Governor Arnold could have beaten him down.

The man's wife sat on the gym floor consoling their son, saying absolutely nothing – nothing to support her husband, and nothing to rebuke him, either. Mom, of course, now *that* was a different story. She scrambled down the bleachers just as soon as the good doctor looked like he was ready to commit a felony, and she began talking in that quiet, straight way she always does when Dad is upset. It was a combination of the referee and my mother that settled Dr. DuMont down and convinced him to release the quivering mass formerly known as Jerry. Needless to say, the game was over and, despite winning our first two games, we forfeited the tournament.

When we got back home that Saturday afternoon, Dad didn't say much. Mom did. She explained to us the animus behind the word that the white man had used in front of a gym full of parents and kids. I think Lilly and I both got it, and understood why Dad went off like he did. We knew from that day forward that some folks were never going to give us a fair shake, simply because of the color of our skin.

The second time I heard the "N" word, I was working at the Rittenhouse. It was before my accident. Two drunks wearing motorcycle leathers stumbled into the foyer of the old mansion, looking for lunch on the Saturday of the Apple Festival weekend, the busiest weekend of the year in Bayfield. In an average year, 40–50,000 tourists crowd into the village's tiny downtown to buy apples and apple pies, view booths filled with crafts for sale, window shop the stores lining Bayfield's streets, listen to music and celebrate the harvest. These two white guys, loud and obnoxious as they were, became my problem because, at sixteen years old, I was working as the hostess. When the men elbowed their way through the crowd waiting to be seated and asked me how long it would be for a table, and I told them it would be an hour, they didn't take the news kindly.

First, the older drunk – short, heavy–set and with dark wavy hair, dark eyebrows and a full beard – said something I took to be discourteous. Though I couldn't hear what he said, the tittering between the two drunks led me to assume that the short guy had mumbled a sexual insult or something similarly deprecating about me. Then the skinny guy leaned into me with his chest, making a point of grabbing my ass with both his hands while asking me if there wasn't some way we could work it out so that he and his companion could get special treatment.

"I don't think so."

What the thin man said didn't leave much to the imagination.

"I like chocolate. Joe, don't you like chocolate? Sweet, firm, new chocolate, right out of the wrapper?"

I started shaking. I pushed the man off me, and one of the other patrons – a guy as tall as the offending drunk but significantly heavier – put a hand on the skinny drunk's shoulder.

"Get your fuckin' hands off my brother," the shorter drunk said.

The man stopped advancing and released his grip.

The drunk had moved his leather jacket away from his belt to reveal the distinctive handle of a Buck knife, resting in a sheath. I gasped. The taller brother smiled. His right hand touched my left cheek. I shivered.

"I bet she a hoe, Joe. What you think? A nigger hoe?"

"I think so."

The crowd of customers opened up. Two beefy Bayfield County Deputies swaggered in. Within seconds, both drunks were in cuffs and headed out the door. I'd never felt physically threatened on account of my race until that day. To be challenged like that, with at least fifty people standing around me as witnesses, was unnerving.

I glanced at my wristwatch, a cheap throwaway I'd picked up at the convenience store in Panora for five bucks. It had been an hour and a half since I made the call. The noise from the party had lessened. The glare of headlights interrupted my melancholy. I recognized the throaty rumble of a diesel engine. Mason Erickson's green Ford F–250 King Cab crested the hill and rolled into Fairmount Park. The truck's headlights dimmed as I walked towards the truck. I stopped next to the passenger–side door. Waiting for Mason to unlock the door, I started to sob. I didn't weep because I was sad, or afraid. I cried because I was relieved: supremely relieved that someone cared enough about me to save me from myself.

THIRTY-EIGHT

Maria Morales blocked the road. The woman, not much more than a slip of a girl, stood in the middle of the dark street, her miniskirt flapping in the wind. Maria held the hem of her skirt against her thigh with one hand in an attempt to keep her thong underwear from showing. Her upper body was wrapped in someone else's jacket. Her black eyes were frantic. The Ford rolled to a stop.

"You know her?"

"She's a high school classmate of Hazel's. Maria Morales. I just met her tonight."

Maria's body shook from the cold as she approached the passenger side of the truck.

"You're a nurse, right?"

I nodded.

"Well, you better get your ass inside. Crazy motherfucker is in the bedroom, passed out, with Donald and her momma doing God knows what to her."

My mind raced.

"Who's passed out?"

"Hazel, the stupid bitch. She's passed out in her momma's room, with her momma and Donald in there. Door's locked and no one's sayin' nothin'."

"We'd better see what's going on," Mason said.

Mason parked the truck on the street. As we walked through the front door of Pam Bunt's house, it was obvious to me that the theme of the event had gone from getting high to making out. Every available seat was taken up by couples embracing, hands moving, lips pursing, clothes shedding. It was one massive orgy of drug– and alcohol–induced passion.

The smell of booze, pot, meth, sweat and cheap perfume and cologne greeted us as we followed Maria through the house. The blond guy with the chin, the guy I'd had my eye on earlier, was curled up in a corner with a redhead who looked to be no more than fifteen. As we passed them, the guy's hand slipped inside the redhead's tattered blue jeans. I averted my eyes, wondering whether or not her mother knew where she was.

Probably told her old lady she was at the mall, hanging out.

We stopped at the door to Pamela's bedroom.

"Hazel, it's Esther. You okay in there?"

No one responded. Mason stepped to the door and banged on the cheap wood panel with a fist.

"Hey, Esther's a nurse. She needs to take a look at her friend to make sure she's all right. Open the door."

Bed springs creaked and music in opposition to the Led Zeppelin playing in the living room leaked from the bedroom. The song was familiar – an old blues tune by a black singer, the sort of music Dad likes.

The door lock clicked. Cousin Donald, wearing only boxer shorts decorated with pictures of the Tasmanian Devil, opened the door and stared at Mason.

"Who the fuck are you?"

Mason was sober. Donald was high.

"A friend of Esther's. She wants to take a look at Hazel and make sure she's okay."

"Sorry, no can do. Little Hazel's busy right now."

Mason used his broad shoulders to shove the door and Cousin Donald out of his way. Donald retreated into the shadows as Mason, Maria and I entered the bedroom. Gobs of iridescent goo rose and fell in a lava lamp on a nightstand next to Pamela Bunt's king–sized bed The headboard and footboard were covered in black leather, and the black satin sheets and black blanket were disheveled. Pamela was propped up in bed, her bare breasts sitting perky and unnatural on her chest, her nearly colorless nipples aroused. She had a lit cigarette in her hand as she adjusted her black silk pajama bottoms; her tummy flab was exposed, and the skin was pale and ugly in the muted light. Hazel was passed out in the bed next to her mother, her face buried in the sheets. A pillow was under her stomach, and her narrow bare ass was propped up, as if poised for an enema.

Mason eyed Cousin Donald. Donald stood precariously in the shadows, his balance poor; he was on the verge of toppling. I moved towards the limp form of my friend. Maria whimpered like a puppy and hid behind Mason, her eyes wide with shock. I knelt by the bed and checked Hazel's pulse.

"She's alive. Barely. What the hell did you do to your daughter?"

Pamela Bunt waved her lit cigarette in the musk–tainted air. My eyes caught the outline of a dildo on the nightstand, next to the empty plastic case for a porno movie. The television across the room was on, the audio muted, the tape rolling. Two white women were doing a black man in a hot tub, with one girl sitting on the guy's lap. Her legs were spread around him, water was bubbling between them, her head was slung back in mock pleasure, while the other girl fondled the first girl's breasts from behind. I looked around for Hazel's clothes and found them in a pile at the foot of the bed.

"What the hell did you do to your daughter?" I repeated.

"Nothin' that hasn't been done before," Pamela Bunt said, her words slurred and nearly incoherent.

Satisfied with her reply, Pamela blew smoke rings into the air above the lava lamp.

"She needs to go to the hospital. She's dehydrated and unconscious. She's likely depleted the electrolytes in her brain. If she doesn't get help soon, she'll die."

"She ain't goin' to no hospital. She'll be fine once she sleeps it off. No hospital, you hear me? There'll be too many questions. Cops'll show up. Then *I'll* be the one with trouble."

Mason bent to the floor, retrieved Hazel's bra and panties and tossed them to me, all the while keeping an eye on Cousin Donald.

"You leave her be," Donald muttered as I turned the woman over to dress her. "We'll take care of little Miss Hazel."

I used the edge of a sheet to wipe puke off Hazel's lips and semen off her ass. She was lucky: her head had been turned just enough to allow the vomit to seep out, keeping her airway open – otherwise, she would have asphyxiated while Donald and Pamela went about their business. I sat Hazel up; her breathing was shallow. I had a premonition that she wouldn't make it.

"Maria, get over here and help me."

The Latina hesitated. The blond guy stumbled into the doorway.

"Who the hell are you?"

The blond's eyes locked on Mason. Mason didn't answer. It looked like there'd be trouble.

"Bobbie, Hazel's sick. She needs a doctor," Maria said softly, a hint of pleading in her voice.

"You a doctor?"

"Nurse," I said.

"Is she gonna be okay?"

I shrugged and lifted the stricken woman so Maria Morales could slip Hazel's bra over Hazel's tiny boobs. Maria and I pulled Hazel's panties over her legs and hips before dressing the woman in her own jeans and a sweatshirt.

"Hey, that's my shirt."

"Shut the fuck up," Bobbie, the blond guy, said, sticking his finger in Donald's face. "I always knew you were a bastard, Donny O'Hara. What kind of sick fuck screws his cousin?"

The red–haired girl wandered into the room.

"What's wrong?"

Bobbie turned to the girl.

"Nothin'. Just crazy Hazel whacked out on too much X. This lady here's a nurse. Everything's cool."

Maria Morales and I lifted Hazel Edwards and supported the unconscious woman between us. Pamela Bunt looked beyond us, beyond the inert form of her child. The woman's attention never wavered from the television screen as her comatose daughter was dragged from the room.

THIRTY-NINE

Hazel Edwards didn't die. Mason drove his pick–up truck through the darkened streets of Council Bluffs with Maria Morales sitting in the front passenger's seat, giving directions. I struggled to keep Hazel upright in the rear seat of the truck's club cab as the F–250 swerved around hairpin corners on the descent from Huntington out onto East Graham. I know we took a left onto South 6th and a right on US No. 6 before coming to Mercy Drive and Mercy Hospital. The trip took less than five minutes, but the ride, much of it on two wheels, is something I'll never forget. The emergency room staff took over once Mason's truck stopped in front of the entrance doors. I gave them a brief assessment. No one questioned my credentials.

"You saved her life," the ER doctor on duty said softly as he held Hazel's wrist to measure her pulse. "Another twenty minutes, and she'd have shut down completely. I see way too many young people doing ecstasy, tossing it down like candy. I've called four of 'em myself since I came here from Wichita last June."

I mutely accepted the doctor's praise.

"You a nurse?" he asked.

The doctor stood up. An orderly pushed the gurney carrying Hazel towards an open room.

He's a young one, I thought studying the physician's diminutive eyebrows, the Asian aspect of his face, his pliant skin. *Can't be much older than me.*

"Dr. Yang" was imprinted on the plastic nametag pinned to the physician's neatly pressed white dress shirt. His tie was conservative, blue with red stripes. He was, as Grandma Mary would say, a natty dresser.

I nodded.

"Registered?"

I didn't want to reveal that my license was under suspension for being a meth addict, so I simply nodded again.

"Well, ma'am, if you ever need a job, give me a call. We could use someone with your smarts."

I had nothing more to say. Mason, Maria and I waited for the Council Bluffs Police to arrive. I'd vowed, as the pick–up truck tumbled down the steeps from Fairmount Park, that Cousin Donald wasn't about to skate out of what he'd done to Hazel. Consent? There was nothing consensual about what Donald O'Hara had cooked up in Pamela Bunt's seedy little bedroom, at least insofar as it related to Hazel. When the cops came, both Maria and I gave our versions of what had happened. Maria, luckily for her, wasn't holding when they patted her down, though it was pretty clear to everyone – by virtue of her glazed eyes, slurred speech and the sweet herbal smell imbedded in her shoulder–length black hair – that she was high on more than just life. Still, the cops didn't test her. Once they learned that I was on a pass from a treatment center, they asked for my consent to do a drug screen. I agreed to a blood draw – which, of course, when the results came back several days later, confirmed I'd maintained my sobriety.

No one, not even Mason, knew, as we stood in Mercy Hospital Emergency Intake, how close I'd come to blowing six months of sobriety. The nearness of my descent was something only God and I appreciated, and I was pretty sure neither God nor I would spill the beans.

Sometime that night, Mason called the on–duty tech at New Beginnings and gave her an abbreviated version of the evening's events. I'm certain that the tech relayed the message to Dr. Hodges within the hour. I wasn't worried about repercussions. I was worried that Hazel wouldn't pull through – but, as I've already revealed, she did.

It was after eleven when Hazel came to. She asked for me by name. Not her Mom. Not Maria. Not anyone else that had been at the party. Certainly not that disgusting wretch of humanity, Donald O'Hara.

"How are you feeling?" I asked when I entered her room.

Understand, Hazel's usual complexion brings new meaning to the term "white." What I witnessed, in terms of her post–trauma coloration, was beyond pale. She was downright cadaverous. Asking her how she felt was done purely to provoke dialogue. It was pretty damn obvious she wasn't feeling so good.

"Like shit."

Hazel sounded parched, a result of the ecstasy. I reached for a glass of ice water and held the plastic straw and tumbler beneath her lips. She shook her head. I put the glass down and sat in a chair that I'd pulled up next to her bed. Hazel's pale eyes studied my face as if she wanted to understand – to comprehend me and my essence. It was a deep and thoughtful gaze, something I'd not witnessed from Hazel in all our time together at New Beginnings.

"What?"

My question didn't prompt a response only a more concentrated focus from the girl. The steadiness of her scrutiny was unnerving. I blinked and looked away.

"I wanted to die."

"What are you talking about?"

She coughed and sat up in bed, supporting her back with two pillows. We were upstairs of the ER, in a regular room now, her condition having stabilized, the emergency having dissipated.

"I took too many."

I forced a grin. "No shit."

"You don't understand. I took too many...on purpose."

"Why? You were almost home free. Why didn't you tell me or someone else about the party? That's what we're here for. That's what Prescott and Hodges get paid for – to keep you sober. Keep you clean. I would have talked you out of coming back to Council Bluffs, had I known."

She hacked phlegm into a paper tissue that was balled in her right hand.

"Wasn't like that. I didn't go to Pam's thinking I'd use. But there's just somethin' about being in that house. Creeps me out so bad, I needed to escape. Not just the house, but the whole works: my life, this planet, my existence. When Donald gave me that look, I knew it was hopeless. He was going to find a way to get to me, just like my step–Daddy did, and make me do things. Things I don't want to do but can't stop from doing."

I was at a complete loss. I had no understanding, no landmarks in my sexual history by which to comprehend such yielding, such helplessness. I'm certain my eyes betrayed my disconnection with what Hazel was saying. It wasn't that I didn't believe her. I just couldn't believe that such suppliant behavior was possible without physical force.

"You must think I'm nuts."

"You're not nuts. You've been mistreated."

Hazel smiled. "Ain't that the truth. By more than one man. Cousin Donald? It wasn't what it looked like. I let him do it. What the hell; I thought I was going to die anyway. Before I passed out, I said to him, 'Bring it on.' Momma, that crazy lunatic, she was going to town on her own nephew, with me nearly passed out next to the two of them on her bed, the bed she once nursed me in. Disgusting shit. That's 'love' in Pamela Bunt's house. I figured that I might as well join the fun. After all, I was minutes away from the Big Sleep, until some do–gooder black witch showed up, spoiled all my plans, and ruined my front-page exit. 'Former High School Homecoming Queen Dies Screwing Cousin in Her Mother's Bed' was how the headline would have read. Well, maybe not in the *NonPareil*. Wouldn't do to have such trash exposed in this little shit–hole of a town, would it?"

Hazel asked for the water. I held the glass while she sipped noisily through the straw. She drained the glass, leaving only ice chips at the bottom.

"I ever tell you how I became Homecoming Queen?"

"I don't think so."

"I did the entire offensive line of the football team in the boy's shower. No weird shit – just straight missionary–style sex. Condoms required, of course; I didn't want to repeat the fiasco of what happened with my step–Dad."

The vision of the white girl in front of me, her body seemingly barely past puberty, her eyes wide and absent, like she was famished – which, in the case of real honest–to–goodness love, she was – running a train on a bunch of muscle–bound football players, upset me. Stomach acid found its way into my throat and nearly caused me to gag.

"You okay? Didn't mean to gross you out. But that's me. That's where I come from."

I regained my composure and switched topics.

"You tried to kill yourself?"

"Hell, who wouldn't? I took those mother–fucking pills. I was sure my brain would seize up and I'd die in bed between Momma and old Cousin Donald. Think of what that would have done to Pamela? But you, you bitch," she smiled as she swore at me, "you, that hayseed honey of yours and that ditzy Mexican chick spoiled it all."

I nodded.

"The nurse told me they got Donald and my Mom locked up."

"Yes."

"Well, it won't last."

My mouth opened.

"Save it. They'll get whatever's coming to them on the drug charges, but I won't testify against them for anything else."

I shook my head. "That's just not right, Hazel. That asshole – your own cousin – sodomized you while you were passed out and nearly dead. That's rape, any way you want to color it."

"Maybe so, but I ain't pressin' charges against him. I told you: I let him have his way with me. That's how low I've sunk. I let my first cousin screw me – in my mother's bed, with my mother watching. Still think the time I spent at treatment did some good?"

I stood up, walked over to the window, opened the drapes, and looked out across the highway at a vacant hillside. Beneath the artificial light of the street lamps, trees swayed in a rising wind, causing shadows to dance over a darkened land. My mind searched for something poignant to

170

say. I was at a loss as to how to convince Hazel that her life was salvageable: why suicide was not the way to leave this world. Why she should value herself more than she did. I knew her story. I understood, at least as best I could, the depths of her sorrow, and the horrors she had lived. A tear fell.

"You don't have cause to cry, Esther. You did what Christians do. You saved me. See? I'm alive, breathing and still capable of redemption. Isn't that what you wanted, to redeem me? The job ain't finished but, now that I ain't dead, it's still possible."

I sighed. "I still think you should press charges against Donald."

"Not goin' there. I've been forced to do lots of things in my life. Being passed out while Donald gets his rocks off isn't even in the top ten. I'll take a flyer on being humiliated in court, on telling the entire city of Council Bluffs what a useless piece of shit my momma is. Maybe the judge will see it clear to send me back to treatment. Who knows, more time spent with the entertaining duo of Prescott and Hodges might just be the cure."

At least she's open to going back. Maybe the judge will send her back, if New Beginnings will take her.

I couldn't think of anything else to say. I walked over to Hazel, stood next to her bed, and watched an IV bag drip clear fluid into her arm. Hazel's bony fingers found my forearm.

"I'm tired. You need to get back to the Center. You're likely going to have hell to pay. Tell them it was my fault. Have Hodges call me. I'll tell her. I'm sorry I dragged you into this."

I nodded my head noncommittally before leaning over to kiss Hazel Edwards goodbye.

FORTY

We maintained silence as the pick–up truck's tires whined. The lights of the F–250's dashboard cast an alien glow as we listened to an old radio episode of *Gunsmoke*, starring a guy named William Conrad. I'd watched reruns of the television show when I lived in the dorms in Marquette, but I'd never heard the radio version of the western. One of the black guys on the men's basketball team I knew, Curtis Lovell, he was big on the TV show, and loved James Arness. I can't say I was enthralled with Mason's choice of programming; I'm a child of the VH1 generation, and radio, in my mind, is for music, not drama. But being as I like to read, the story, spoken as it was, created enough imagery in my head to keep me interested.

After *Gunsmoke* ended, I slept the last fifty miles of the trip back to New Beginnings. I awoke as the truck pulled onto Panarama Drive. My hands were sweaty. My face, pressed as it had been into my jacket – which I'd taken off and rolled into a pillow against the passenger door window – was flushed. I had drooled a little, something I hoped the man riding next to me hadn't noticed.

While I slept, I dreamed about my parents. Why they occupied my mind, after the ordeal I'd just experienced at Pamela Bunt's bungalow, I'm uncertain. Maybe my mind needed grounding; maybe it needed to reach back into memory and find something stable and loving and consistent that I could draw upon for strength. Whatever the reason, I found myself considering my parents and how they met.

My father had just finished his orthopedic surgery residency and had taken his first "real" doctoring job in Ashland. It was 1975, and my mom was eighteen, having just graduated from Ashland High School. The way Dad tells it, Mom was working as a waitress at Gruenke's, and my dad

172

happened in one summer Saturday morning. He was in town to go charter fishing with two other doctors. They were setting out from the Bayfield Marina, in search of German brown and lake trout, but they had an hour to kill so they walked into Gruenke's. Dad was ten years older than Mom and not looking to settle down. He'd just finished a long and difficult indoctrination into his chosen profession, including sleepless rotations as a resident, so he wasn't ready to fall in love. But that's what happened.

Samantha Witta had, and still has, a rare combination of aloofness, native handsomeness and deeply imbedded sensuality. The way Dad tells it, and I have no reason to doubt his word, when he and his two friends sat at the lunch counter on the round stools that morning in Gruenke's, his first impression of Samantha Witta was simply: "wow." Not "wow" in a Charlize Theron or Uma Thurman sort of way. Those women sport looks more based upon statuesque beauty. This "wow" was more like a base inkling that this particular female human being has really something, by the way she moves, the way she handles herself, and yes, because of the way she looks – a "total package" that men universally desire. I can see these qualities in my mother: her sculptured jaw; her high cheekbones; her squarely solid figure; her calves, much like my own, well–toned and striking in high heels. And her enchantingly Scandinavian blue eyes and blond hair – attributes that I, like my father, seem drawn to. Of course, as Mom is always quick to assert, Dad's infatuation would have vanished if she wasn't intelligent. But she *is*. Intelligent, I mean. That she never went to college and has worked as a waitress and manager on and off for more than thirty years in a little restaurant in a little town, doesn't mean she can't put thoughts together. She can. Like she says, if a pretty bird sings like a crow, the bird's not all that pretty; that day, she didn't sing like a crow. She was able, once Dad warmed her to the concept of talking to a black man, to express her thoughts and hold her own with Dr. DuMont, despite her lack of formal education. Love at first sight? I think it was for Dad. For Mom, given her native caution, I think it took some convincing on Dad's part. But in the end, she fell for him.

Mason's truck pulled onto the lane leading to the treatment center. My mind returned from scenes my father had painted for me. I looked at the man driving the truck, a man willing to leave whatever he was doing to respond to a desperate plea from a woman he didn't know all that well. There was obvious kindness in Mason's face, a solid and quiet strength that was comforting and peaceful. Mason hadn't made the same sort of immediate impression on me that my Mom had made on my Dad, but I'd come to think of him as handsome. And he had saved my life. I guess that's why I did what I did.

"Pull off to the side of the road. We need to talk."

Mason eased his truck onto the shoulder of the entrance road and came to an abrupt stop. The diesel idled in the cold.

"About what?"

I slid across the cloth bench seat of the pickup.

"You."

My eyes searched Mason's face. He blinked. He was clearly uncomfortable with my candor. I drew back, creating space. Truth be told, I was as nervous as Mason, but something inside me – something that had been dormant since Del's death – made me press on.

"What do you mean?" he asked.

I felt that familiar rush of excitement one gets from a first date, though what Mason Erickson and I had just experienced in Council Bluffs, Iowa, could hardly be considered a date.

"You saved my life."

Classical music played softly in the background as clouds covered the stars and the moon. The only light outside the cab of the truck came from a porch light at the treatment center a good distance away.

"I'm glad you called me."

The comment seemed, when viewed in connection with the softness that came over Mason's face, to be an opening. I took a chance: I leaned over and gave him a hug. It was all it took to melt the dam of his resistance. Instantly, our lips were locked and our tongues were probing. I could feel, through the rough texture of his blue jeans, Mason rising. His hands worked the buttons of the cashmere sweater I was wearing; there was the usual fumbling of fingers, banging of foreheads, and confusion over zippers until he pressed his broadly naked chest into me, his fingers working the clasp of the well–used orange bra that I'd thrown on that morning when all I thought I was going to do was take a road trip to a mall. Despite the raggedy nature and the obscenely bright color of my underwear, I liked the look. The stark contrast between the orange fabric and my brown skin intrigued me. Why? It's the look that every white woman envies, that every white woman seeks by sunbathing: the contrast of dark skin against vibrant color. It's easy for me. I don't even have to work to get it.

Mason's free hand massaged my nipples. I'd never told him about the scars. He knew a little about David and the fire, but not the extent of my injuries. But there was no hesitation when his index finger encountered my damaged left breast. There was only the steady pulse of blood, the gasping for breath, the clouding of the windows.

"You sure you want to do this?" he asked.

I nodded. *Yes*, I thought. *I'm about ready to explode from wanting it.*

"I don't have anything with me – protection, I mean."

This pregnancy advisory was uttered by a man who was pulling my brown corduroys off my legs as I leaned against my jacket and the passenger's side door. The man said this to me as his hands slipped inside the waistband of my orange panties and slid them down my thighs – thighs that quivered with the anticipation of feeling something that I hadn't felt in a very long time.

"It's okay. I'm at the beginning of my cycle."

Of course, millions, if not billions, of wee folk, as Grandma Mary would say, have been conceived after such statements – statements which have been tossed out by deliriously negligent women over the millennia of humankind's existence. Be that as it may, my panties flew into the back seat. I worked at the zipper of Mason's jeans. Things were percolating right along until the sheriff's squad car pulled in behind us. When the lights from the deputy's rig, a high–profile Chevy Suburban, erupted inside the Ford, we were completely engrossed in each other. In retrospect, Mason's reaction, sitting upright, wasn't well planned.

"Shit!"

"The cops?"

"I think I cut my head."

Indeed. By the time the deputy wandered over to check us out, flooding the cabin of the truck with a flashlight, Mason was bleeding like a stuck pig. He'd broken the mirror off and slashed a three–inch long gash into his scalp. Head wounds bleed; his certainly did. I'll spare you the dialogue that Mason had with Deputy Alder. Once you got past the smirk on the officer's face – likely there because he'd gotten an eyeful of a young black woman's naked body as she scrambled to get dressed – Deputy Alder wasn't insensitive. The night security technician at New Beginnings, Alice Salveson, had called it in; she had seen the truck parked on the lane. There wasn't anything we'd done wrong, other than try to make love in an idling vehicle on a private driveway. The officer said his goodbyes, chuckling to himself as he turned to leave, surely storing up memories of what he'd seen for conversation at the department water cooler the next time he was in the office.

"That went well," Mason said as I held one of my white athletic socks against his head.

We dressed in a flurry. The farmer put the truck in gear and drove slowly towards the front door of the Center. My body was excited and under the mistaken belief that it was going to attain nirvana. I didn't respond to Mason's comment.

"Probably for the best. What the hell were we thinking?"

My heart fluttered.

"I just wanted to say 'thank you.'"

175

Mason's head turned; my fingers were tangled in his hair, holding the sock on the gash.

"That's an interesting way to thank someone: getting him so excited that he whacks himself in the head."

We laughed.

"There's a butterfly bandage in the house," I said once my nervous giggles had subsided. "You need one or you'll have to get stitches."

Mason nodded.

"I'd ask you in, but I think Ms. Salveson would have *way* too many questions. Put pressure on the cut while I go get a bandage."

Mason parked the truck and applied pressure to his wound. I opened the passenger–side door of the Ford and got out, leaving him bloody and horny in the idling truck. As I walked towards the treatment center, I thought about the scene that had greeted the deputy: my legs spread, and my nether regions exposed; my gut hanging slightly, the few extra pounds I was working on still there; my bare boobs resting on my chest. It was as I stood next to the door, one hand on the doorknob, the other adjusting the knitted watch cap sitting cockeyed on my head, that I came to understand the hilarity of it all. The deputy would indeed have quite a story to tell. He'd seen me, in my buck–naked splendor, making love to a dairy farmer in the front seat of a pick–up truck with a stocking cap on my head!

FORTY-ONE

Sister Flora Washington convinced me to come back to God. Flora and I worked together at the Hennepin County Medical Center in downtown Minneapolis. We both worked in OB. I'll spare you the details of all the ladies' asses I washed, all the puke I mopped and all the bedpans I changed, during my three–month stint as a nursing assistant.

But before we get to talking about how Miss Washington convinced me to come back to Jesus, you need to know what happened after Mason and I got caught naked in Mason's truck. The plain and simple truth of it is that Dr. Hodges and Ms. Prescott believed me – about the happenings in Council Bluffs, that is, not what happened in the truck. That part, they weren't privy to (at least not until they read about it here!) Mason and Wanda Jones laid it all out for them – how I'd never intended to stray, how Hazel Edwards sprang the party on me, how I'd saved Hazel's life. After the blood test from Mercy Hospital came back clean, the folks in charge of New Beginnings were convinced that I deserved to graduate.

The last Tuesday in February, I, along with ten other clients of New Beginnings (Hazel was in jail, awaiting her fate) sat in metal folding chairs in the living room of New Beginnings, listening to Dr. Hodges pontificate. When she was done, each of us walked up to her, received our certificates, and returned to our seats. There was a smattering of applause, a whoop or two from family and friends in attendance, and it was over: six months of intensive introspection were done, kaput. Once the ceremony finished, I left my seat, rolled up diploma in hand, and walked towards the back of the room to a table crowded with lunch, the celebratory cake and a glass bowl of Hawaiian Punch mixed with 7-Up. Mom, Dad, Richard, Lilith and Abigail met me by the food. Mason was there, too, though he stood off by himself, daunted by the presence of my parents.

"You did good, Es," Lilly said as she hugged me.

"Thanks."

My sister released me, and Mom, usually blasé in front of strangers, hugged me tight, tighter than I ever remember her doing as a child. I studied my mother's face. Her eyes were closed. We both battled tears.

She's showing her age, I thought, cognizant of the laugh lines around my mother's mouth and eyes, the slight weight gain around her neck that was creating creases that hadn't been there a year or so earlier. Her eyes remained clear and slate blue, but there was no question she was beginning to show her years. Dad interrupted us to embrace me so hard I thought he'd break my ribs. Time seemed to stop as his love – love that I'd always taken for granted, but now, after doing what needed to be done, I felt I'd *earned* – flowed over me like a warm ocean tide. Abby grasped my hand, her tiny fingers in mine, squeezing like the dickens. Richard simply planted a brief, tender, brother–in–law's kiss on my cheek. I welled with pride and happiness. The moment emboldened me.

"Mason," I called out. "Come meet my family."

The dairy farmer was dressed uncharacteristically in a neatly–pressed, navy two–piece suit, a light blue tie neatly tucked into the buttoned–down collar of a crisp white dress shirt. His black shoes were so shiny the entire scene was reflected in their gleam. He approached me with hesitation, red punch sloshing dangerously near the rim of the elegant cut–glass cup in his hand. Dad stood beside me, equal in height to the farmer, eyeing the white man with the butterfly bandage on his head up and down as if scrutinizing a new car.

"This is Mason, Mason Erickson. He works here on weekends as a cook. He's also an agricultural economist and farmer. Mason, this is my Dad, Orville DuMont."

Mason extended his hand to my father.

"Pleased to meet you, sir. Esther's told me so much about you and the rest of her family."

My father was gracious but cool as they shook hands. Mason's meaty palm enveloped my father's slender hand.

"Likewise," Dad said.

"This is my mother, Samantha."

The gesture was repeated. Mom was every bit as circumspect as Dad.

"Ma'am."

"...and my twin sister Lilly Culver; her husband, Richard; and their little girl, Abby."

Mason was spared any further awkwardness; pleasantries were exchanged without physical contact.

"Pleased to meet you," he said to my family members. "You have a wonderful daughter, sister and aunt."

I beamed with pride. Love? I'm not sure about that. Mason and I didn't know each other all that well – not enough history and depth for that emotion, in my mind. But I felt something, something akin to the ignition of flames inside me.

"Mason saved my life," I said quietly as we all retrieved cups of punch and glass plates of sandwiches, and found an empty table to sit at. "I was close to back–sliding. Mason helped me stay clean."

My father ate without comment. Mom looked deep into my eyes before she replied.

"How so?"

I didn't want to share the details of the sordid events of that night in Council Bluffs with my family as they ate celebratory food. I'd fess up my sins – or near-sins – to Lilith later that night, when I stayed at her house, waiting for a bed at the halfway house in north Minneapolis. (Ms. Frisk said it might take a week or more for me to get situated. Until then, I would stay with Lil and Richard, bolstered by daily calls to my probation officer. I was to start my nursing assistant job the following Monday. Whether I'd be at Castleman's by then or not, I had to start work. I needed to fill time. Even the menial tasks of a nursing assistant would be better than sitting around and contemplating my navel. Besides, as much as I love Lilly, I'd go absolutely nuts if I had to spend an inordinate amount of time listening to her prattle on about suburban life.)

Anyway, I digress.

"He just did. I called, and he came. Simple as that."

"So what sort of a farmer are you?"

Richard's question was well timed. Mason stopped eating and smiled.

"A good one."

Richard chuckled.

"Sorry. Couldn't resist. Dairy. My family's had a farm for generations a few miles to the west of here, near Guthrie Center. A little over 300 acres. 40 head."

"It's a beautiful place," I interjected. "Sits right on a little creek, with big oaks and willows. It's very pretty – for Iowa, I mean."

Even Dad laughed.

"You've been to *his place*?" Lilith asked with interest.

"Miss Jones and I – the lady I introduced you to earlier – we were there once to help milk the cows. I was also out there with four or five other girls for a tour."

Lilly's eyebrows rose. *"Oh,"* she said airily, having finally discerned there was something more going on between Mason and I than just friendship.

After I finished eating, I said goodbye to Wanda Jones. Wanda was heading back to South Dakota to work as an assistant stock manager in a Wal–Mart store. Her new position was devoid of any opportunity for her to dip her hand into Sam Walton's till. Wanda and I shed quite a few tears. She lent me some new books to read. I promised to mail them back to her when I finished them. I also promised to keep in touch, and to visit Wanda in South Dakota. I did read those books, and I returned them just like I'd promised, but I never saw Wanda Jones again.

Mason? Well, what can I say: we snuck a few moments together in my room at the treatment center, after he offered to help me with my things. The things that I wanted help with, we really didn't have time for that day. But once we were safely behind the closed door to my room, our lips did meet and blood pulsed and rushed as we embraced. I was dressed in a red and black skirt and blouse, the heels of my black pumps high and dangerous, and my make–up (cosmetics I'd bought mail order from a specialty shop in Minneapolis, a place that caters to black women) perfect. Mason was, as I said, decked out in a blue business suit. I could feel our hearts pound as our hands followed the contours of each other's bodies. But my family was waiting downstairs. There was no time to consummate our connection. Looking back, I don't really know what I felt at that moment and I'm fairly certain Mason hadn't yet labeled his own feelings.

"I'll email you. They have a computer at the halfway house," I whispered into Mason's right ear.

Mason smiled.

"For a while – then you'll meet someone else. The emails will dwindle, then stop."

"That won't happen."

"Sure it will."

I didn't acknowledge his premise. Instead, I challenged his intentions.

"Will you email me?"

Mason nodded.

"Promise?" I asked as I wrote out my email address for him.

He nodded and wrote his own email address for me before picking up my suitcase and garment bag. We joined my family in the ornate foyer of the old mansion that housed New Beginnings. Mason followed me to Richard's Durango and settled my luggage into the cargo area before shutting the tailgate with a loud "bang" that seemed utterly and completely final, like a punctuation mark at the end of a sentence. Mason offered me his hand. I took his bare palm in my mittened one and shook it perfunctorily. My parents migrated to Dad's Volvo station wagon, while Lilly and Richard took their seats in the Durango. Abby was already firmly belted into her car seat.

My eyes locked on Mason's; there was something between us that was not yet defined, not yet clear. Whether it would survive our separation, was unknown. I bowed my head and ducked into the Dodge.

The week at Lilly's came and went, and I moved into Castleton's without ceremony. My new digs weren't bad as halfway houses go, though who was I to make comparisons, being a bit of a neophyte to these things?

Castleton's is located on the corner of Hennepin and Pierce, and I had my own bedroom on the third floor of the frame house with peeling sky--blue paint and mismatched raspberry red shingles. I was supposed to have a roommate, a young black woman named Isobel DeWitt from St. Paul, but she never showed. She had relapsed, was what I was told. By the time her replacement arrived, I was ready to move out, ahead of schedule, due to the intervention of my public defender. But that part of my story comes later.

Like I said, Flora Washington and I worked together at the hospital. We slid into conversation during my first shift and hit it off. She's a black woman in her late forties, about my Mom's age, with small black eyes, a squat nose, stands no more than five feet tall and weighs less than a hundred pounds. A sprite, I think the Scandinavians would call her – a leprechaun to the Irish and an elf in Tolkien lore. She wore a large gold chain and a prominent gold Protestant cross every day she worked. I doubt, given what I learned about her spirituality, that she ever took the icon off; she likely wore it when she bathed or showered. The size of Flora's cross echoed the largess of her faith. Similarly, the tiny Roman Catholic crucifix I wore – the one I got from Father Michaels that displayed the anguished body of Jesus nailed to the cross – also seemed appropriate because, after David's death, Lilly's escapade with Father Michaels and Del's untimely end, my faith in God had been shriveled to the point of disappearing altogether. It hadn't completely vanished; I hadn't followed my father into skepticism, but I was darn close, I'd have to say, to taking that route. Flora worked on me nearly every day, chipping away at my stubbornness and assaulting my defensive veneer, until at last, one Sunday in March, a few weeks after we'd started working together, I agreed to go to St. Francis's AME church with her.

The church was only a three–block walk down Hennepin from Castleton's. The aging structure had once housed an Episcopal congregation, but the Anglicans got uppity, merged with another congregation and built a brand new worship hall somewhere out in the suburbs. The folks from St. Francis's begged, borrowed and scraped together funds to buy the old church, renovate it and redecorate it according to their own tastes and sensibilities.

Stepping through the newly fallen snow that covered the sidewalk, I realized my black pumps were a foolish choice for the weather. I wore a conservative blue and white dress beneath my parka, and my straightened hair (the result of another extremely painful perm) was anchored soundly to my scalp as I moved along at a Sunday crawl. I never had my hair straightened while growing up. Mom kept my hair natural, restraining my mane with strategically placed ribbons, bits of yarn, berets, pins and twists of innumerable varieties (the Senegalese twist, Nu–locks, yarn locks and dreadlocks were just some of the styles Mom had subjected me to). Once I'd done it – once I'd had my hair straightened – I came to the conclusion it wasn't for me. It didn't feel right. I know, I know: I told you that I'd coveted Lilith's silky, straight hair for years. That's true. But I came to the conclusion, upon studying my new 'do in the bathroom mirror, that taming my hair with poison couldn't approximate what my sister had been blessed with. That said, I had to live with what I'd done, at least until the perm chemicals washed out over time.

The work week bustle along Hennepin Avenue was noticeably absent. In contrast to weekday traffic protocol, Sunday drivers patiently allowed vehicles to turn in front of them with impunity. I smiled and returned "hellos" to couples, families and single folk I met on the sidewalk. The sky was gray but the snow had stopped. A slight wind, noticeably humid and warm, embraced my face as I approached the yellow stucco building that now housed St. Francis's church. Gospel music escaped the sanctuary, tugged at my heart and silently begged me to release my burdens and come. *Come up the steps. Come through the door. Just come.*

Flora Washington stood in the open doorway, the heavy wooden portal flung to one side and anchored against the stucco wall by a wrought–iron hook. The metal work of the door was crafted of blackened iron, which gave the place the look of a medieval fortress.

"Well, what you waitin' for, girl? A special invitation from Reverend Morris hisself? Come on in, Sister Esther. Come on in and feel the healin' waters of baptism and the sanctifyin' power of the holy table."

I walked up the stairs and stood next to my friend.

"Thank you for inviting me."

"It wasn't me, honey. It was the Lord. He's the one you should be thankin'. He's the one callin' out to you. You ready?"

I nodded and followed Flora Washington into the noisy, joyful and calamitous church.

FORTY-TWO

The AME Church reintroduced me to the Bible. I'd studied scripture as a child, at home and under my mother's tutelage, but never in a structured setting. After that first Sunday service, when the music lifted me and Reverend Morris spoke so plainly and eloquently – reciting the parable of the sower as written by St. Mark, one of the verses of the New Testament that I knew intimately, having loved it as a child when Mom used to read it to Lilith and me – I was in rapture.

This is home, I thought to myself as the service ended with piano, guitar, drums and bass thumping out a distinctly unchurch–like version of "Will the Circle Be Unbroken." *This is where I need to be.*

I learned soon enough that St. Francis's counted more than a few recovering addicts and alcoholics as members, and that it was not uniformly and completely black, though most of the two dozen whites in the congregation were married to or living with partners of color. But there were a few white parishioners who simply loved the music, the theology and the community of St. Francis's, who came to church and tithed in spite of the history of the denomination.

Being raised Catholic, I knew virtually nothing about the AME Church; that's why I joined the Beginner's Group. Meetings were on Wednesday nights, leaving me free to attend Narcotics Anonymous sessions on Tuesday and Thursday evenings, my twice–weekly attendance being part of my post–treatment after–care and probation. Once I started attending the Wednesday night sessions, I rarely missed unless I was sick, working a night shift at the hospital, or stuck at Castleton's fulfilling some obligation to the halfway house.

In the Beginner's Group, I learned that the African Methodist Episcopal Church was formed shortly after the American Revolution, when blacks perceived that the Methodist Church wasn't living up to its Christian ideals. The AME grew out of the desire of Richard Allen, Absalom Jones and other free black men to worship God in their own ways. In 1787, at St. George's Methodist Church in Philadelphia, black worshipers were pulled from their knees during worship, setting off angry dissent that culminated in St. George's black parishioners forsaking the Methodist denomination. At first, the secessionists wanted to affiliate with the Protestant Episcopal Church, the American branch of Anglicanism, but the dissenters eventually gravitated back towards Methodism, which means that AME doctrine, unlike Catholicism or Anglicanism, recognizes only two sacraments: baptism and Holy Communion. I learned that, despite the name of the denomination and the fact that free blacks founded the Church, the tenets of the faith – some twenty–five in number – don't restrict AME membership to people of color. I also learned that many of the fundamental principles of Catholicism – principles I was indoctrinated to love and adore, including the concepts of sanctification by works, purgatory and transubstantiation – are rejected by the AME as not having a foundation in scripture.

This makes so much sense. That's what I thought after a few classes with Reverend Morris. The simplicity of the AME faith was an attractive alternative to the complex, inexplicable and, even for me (as a college–educated adult woman), indecipherable doctrines of my mother Church. I knew, as I sat in class, asking questions, digging for answers and pondering my beliefs, that my Irish Catholic grandmother would not have been pleased – but then again, this was not *her* life. It was not her spirit that needed solace. I would not be swayed from exploring a faith that seemed to make sense to me, out of some vague fear that my family might disapprove.

Lilly will have a bird – she and Richard are so locked into Catholicism and its pomp, circumstance and ritual. There's beauty and a certain comfort in all that – I'll grant you. But it isn't for me. And it's me that's in trouble here. It's me God needs to speak to – not my dead grandmother, not my mother, and not my sister. Me.

As I listened to Reverend Morris outline the history of the AME during the first class, another aspect of the faith hit home. It was, according to the pastor – a tall, thin, angular man of great bearing who had a full head of twisted gray hair, bushy gray eyebrows, and elegantly smooth skin resembling that of a well–tanned golf pro – one of the first Christian denominations to license female preachers, and later, to accept them as full–fledged ministers. I'd always considered the Protestant Episcopal Church progressive, with it having ordained women into the priesthood starting in the early 1970s. Well, by comparison to the AME, Episcopalians are pikers: the AME had first authorized female ordinations in 1948, nearly thirty years before the Episcopalians got with the program. As a female professional, that progressive outlook was not lost on me – I promise you that.

It was during the second or third group session, as Reverend Morris recited a Bible verse, that I was taken aback a bit. It wasn't intentional on the reverend's part, mind you. He hadn't projected his high–pitched scriptural voice as an assault upon me. He couldn't have foreseen the impact that the verse would have on any particular individual and he certainly had no inkling of my connection to the words he uttered.

"As he walked along, Jesus saw a man blind from birth. His disciples asked him, 'Rabbi, who sinned, this man or his parents, that he was born blind?' Jesus answered, 'Neither this man nor his parents sinned; he was born blind so that God's works might be revealed in him.'"

It was the same verse Father Michaels had recited to me. *For some reason*, I thought as I sat in the cool basement of my new church, *I trust Reverend Morris's interpretation of the Gospel a hell of lot more than the priest's.*

Maybe, I contemplated as I listened to the other parishioners' questions and the genteel and dedicated way Robert Morris responded to their queries, *I feel this way out of jealousy. Maybe my animosity towards Thomas Michaels and the Catholic Church isn't because of what happened, but is due to feelings, unresolved and unfulfilled, that I once held for him as a man. Maybe, just maybe, I wanted to be the one in Thomas Michaels' arms on that May evening on the shores of Bennett Lake.*

These thoughts, wholly unchurch–like and venal, occupied my mind and clouded my ability to concentrate as I listened to Reverend Morris share *his* interpretation of the Gospel.

FORTY-THREE

I was surprised that Mason Erickson emailed me. I really didn't think he'd stay in touch. I mean, what was there between us other than one evening of tomfoolery and a few heart–felt conversations? True, he is as solid a man as I've ever met. I, on the other hand, am still a work in progress. Why Mason chose to continue a "relationship" with me is puzzling, but continue it he did, almost exclusively via the Internet. It was during one of our chat sessions on Yahoo that he told me about the race.

"you still running?"

"every day. up to five miles now."

"ever thought of running a marathon?"

I knew Mason had been a football player and a wrestler in high school, but I couldn't recall him ever mentioning running as an avocation. The question caught me off guard.

"not really."

"i was checking out where you come from, on the web, and i found an interesting site."

Mmmm, I thought. *So I have a stalker. Not of the dangerous kind, but of the amorous, interested kind. I didn't realize he was* that *interested.*

"what site?"

"the south shore marathon – it starts in cornucopia, follows highway 13 through bayfield, and ends in salmo."

"never heard of it."

"i thought you were from there."

"i am. i mean: i haven't heard of the race."

"this is its first year. they're running it over the fourth of july. thought it might be something you'd want to shoot for, seeing how dedicated you are to torturing yourself."

186

A marathon. What the hell does he think I am, Kenyan?

"i don't know. sounds like a lot of work and a lot of pain."

"i could use that old chestnut of an adage my wrestling coach, coach williams, used to toss out at us when we were slacking off in practice. but I won't."

No pain, no gain, I thought. Still, a marathon does give me a goal, something to work towards. It might keep both my mind and my body occupied. Training would fill up the downtime when I'm not at work.

"if you're interested, i can pass along the website address."

What the hell.

"sure."

He emailed the link to me.

"gotta go. the cows are calling. stay straight. keep running. i'll try to come and visit in a week or so."

Visit? He's awfully sweet, but should I encourage this? I'm going to a black church and meeting single black men. Is this something I want to continue in the face of our differences? I'm not about to up and move to Guthrie Center, Iowa, to become the mistress of a dairy farmer. He knows better. I know better. Still, Mason is one of the nicest men I've ever come across.

"ok."

"i'll call you before i come up, in case you've changed your mind. gotta go."

I didn't reply, and Mason sent no more messages. I felt a distinct and troubling void once the screen was empty. I didn't know whether I was simply in need of male attention (not that I wasn't dodging my share of advances at St. Francis's), or whether Mason's virtual departure triggered a genuine longing for his company. Whatever the emptiness meant, I shut off the halfway house's computer and went downstairs to join the other girls watching *ER*.

187

FORTY-FOUR

There is a ship. Its sails unfurl in the distance. Lines of dark skinned men and women, bound together by rusted chain, iron clasps secured to their necks, hasps locked in place, shuffle forward, their naked bodies shiny and moist beneath an unrelenting sun. Children bawl and whimper as they hold their parents' hands. Drums beat. Strange cries intermingle with the crack of the whip as other Africans, men of opposing tribes, discipline those foolish enough to attempt to run before being locked into the chains. Flies and mosquitoes antagonize the desperate line, feeding upon human flesh and piles of dung left on the beach by the captives. Small boats crash through the surf, propelled by Irishmen working the oars, Irishmen employed to do the bidding of the slavers. The scene I am witnessing is taking place in what is now modern day Senegal. All along the Western coast of Africa, boats bob in emerald blue water and crawl towards ships at anchor. The ships await their human cargo, cargo bound for South America, the Caribbean, and the American South. In my dream, I am naked on the beach and my body is that of a small child. I am fastened to my mother by chain. But though my mother's face looks familiar, it is different. Her skin is not white, but black, like mine. Her eyes are not blue, but brown and sad as she stands exposed to strangers, trying her best to protect the terrified twin girls linked to her by iron, trying to comfort the little lump of dark flesh, my brother David, hiding between her sagging black breasts. My father stands directly in front of us, his chin upright, his nostrils flared. He is proud and undefeated despite the circumstances. His eyes survey the landscape for a means of escape. But there can be no escape. There is no avoidance of the future. We are destined to slavery.

I'd been reading *Kindred* by Octavia Butler, a book labeled as "science fiction" by some, black literature by others, that tells the tale of a young black professional of about my age who is transported, through some mysterious process, back in time to the antebellum South, where she becomes a plantation slave. I thought about the book as I ran along Hennepin Avenue. It was April. My shoes were soggy from melted snow. I was running ten miles a day, every day, seven days a week. After Mason IMed me about the South Shore Marathon, I downloaded and printed an application form off the race's website, mailed the form and the entrance fee to Bayfield, and began training in earnest. I was cruising along in near darkness, with the sun setting and the street lamps beginning to glow, at a nice eight–minutes–per–mile pace. My plan was to run south on Hennepin, cross the Mississippi River at the Nicolette Island Bridge, continue south to Loring Park, loop the park, head north on Central, cross the river again at the Central Avenue Bridge, and end my run on Hennepin.

The book stayed with me. Snow pelted my face. A northwestern wind blew through the Twin Cities. I mulled over how I would've reacted, and what I would've done had I been captured in Africa as a young girl, sold into slavery and shipped across the world to become someone else's chattel. My mind was blank to the concept. I couldn't imagine it other than through Miss Butler's pen. My place in the world, having been carved out for me by my parents as a secure niche in a very tolerant corner of the American Midwest, didn't leave me much room for empathy on a historical scale. I gave up trying to place myself in a situation that seemed remote and concentrated my thoughts on my own recent history.

Things were going well at my job. My supervisors were pleased with my work ethic, despite their original reservations that the position – as demeaning as it is – would prompt me to give less than my best effort. But that's not what I'd learned from my parents: *Hard work. Nose to the grindstone.* I believe in that bullshit and brought it with me every day I worked as a nurse's aide. But I also knew, from visits with Cherise Bennett and Judith Frisk, that they were lobbying the State to let me back into nursing. A review hearing was scheduled with the Minnesota Board of Nursing for June 15.

As I ran, I also thought about Dr. Albert Priestly, an African American professor of political science at the University of Minnesota. Thirty–six years old, Albert had recently lost his wife. He'd joined the Beginners Group at my church to confront his spiritual angst over his wife Amelia's death from lung cancer. We'd hit it off on Albert's first visit to the Wednesday night sessions, what with his sharp intellect, keen sense of fashion and deep brown eyes. True, he was shorter than I was, standing only five–foot–eight, and as a physical specimen, Albert didn't compare favorably to the linebacker's build of Mason Erickson. But he was an

189

intelligent, kind, soft–spoken black man and I was convinced that I needed someone of my own ethnicity to bond with. Mason is many things, but black he surely isn't – at least, that's the way I was thinking at the time. I felt compelled by what I'd read and recently considered to make an effort to accommodate my African heritage. Flirting with Albert was one way to begin that journey.

We'd gone to Rudolph's for ribs and chicken one Wednesday evening. Reverend Morris wasn't feeling well, so he sent us off to contemplate the Gospel on our own. Albert and I did plenty of contemplating in a booth in a dark corner of the restaurant. Little of what was said concerned religion, though the conversation between us was lively and soulful. When Albert drove me home – my belly full of sweet barbeque and my head full of sweeter thoughts – and walked me to the front door of Castleton's to ensure my safety, I felt the warmth of human companionship flowing through my veins. I didn't resist when Albert kissed me, full on the lips, though a peck on the cheek would probably have been more appropriate. His mouth was urgent, a little more so than it should have been, but respectful all the same. I smiled, said "goodnight," and left him standing in the sub–zero cold, watching my rear–end sashay into the parlor of the old house.

The one thing I clearly noticed about Albert that night was his diminutive hands – and as a woman of some experience, I knew what *that* meant. Whether my assumption about Albert's manhood would hold true, I left for another day. I had come to the point in my life where I desired a bond, a union, which I'd not required before. Maybe not marriage, but something akin to it – I was after a solid, practiced, dedicated linkage of souls and hearts and minds that were committed to negotiating life's obstacles together. If it could be found without marriage, I wasn't abhorred by the idea; if it included a wedding, so be it.

I made my turn at Loring Park, my eyes riveted on the windswept ice of the tiny pond.

Definitely not Lake Superior, I mused.

Nightfall arrived but there were so many streetlights and neon signs glowing against the low clouds, I had no trouble seeing. As I headed towards the Nicolette Mall, I heard gunfire, then sirens, high–pitched, loud and closing. I quickened my pace. I pulled my stocking cap down on my head. I tucked my hair beneath the wool cap, leaving the back of my neck exposed to cold. My hands began to sweat inside my choppers. There was little foot traffic on the sidewalk. I moved rapidly through the shopping district. As my shoes struck Washington, I caught the profile of a police cruiser, its lights and siren on, swing in behind me. I blocked the cruiser from my mind and sprinted. Faster. Faster. Faster I ran. I crossed the Central

Avenue Bridge and headed towards Hennepin Avenue. The sound of tires humming across the bridge deck seemed ominous.

It's almost as if they're chasing me.

Honestly, with the howling wind, my hat pulled over my ears, and my concentration so intense, I didn't hear the command to stop. The Tazer caught me square in the back and brought me to my knees before I knew what hit me.

FORTY-FIVE

Flora Washington shoved aside the crowd and tried her best to establish herself as a person of authority.

"Whatcha think you're doing?"

A long–necked Minneapolis patrolman, the skin of his hands, throat and face red and splotchy, tossed his department–issue winter gloves onto the cement sidewalk next to me. He looked up at Flora, turned sternly to his partner – a black man who was shorter, more solid and a few years older than the white officer – and barked, "Keep that woman back, ya hear? The suspect might still be armed."

The black cop placed his body between Flora and me.

"You heard Sergeant Williams. Ma'am, you need to stand back some. Let us do our jobs."

"Your job, young man," a familiar voice said from the crowd, "is to protect your people, not assault them. Now let me minister to my parishioner."

Reverend Morris made his way through the mostly black throng. I was conscious; I could hear and see, but I couldn't move. The Tazer had taken me down so abruptly, I had no opportunity to protect my face. I felt a trickle of warmth on the left side of my forehead where my skull had hit the curb. The odor of blood was nauseating; I felt my stomach clench, as if I were going to vomit.

"Now see here, reverend," Sergeant Williams said, rising from my side, "this young man is a suspect in an armed robbery of a pay day loan center near Loring Park. He'll be arrested and processed. If you want to visit him or make his bail, you can take that up in court."

My eyes fluttered. I focused on the reverend's face.

"Son, you're in a world of trouble," Reverend Morris said. "That 'young man,' as you say, is Miss Esther DuMont, a nurse who is out for her evening run. Training for a marathon, she is. If you bothered to look a little closer, you'd realize you made a mistake. You took down an innocent woman, sir – that's the plain and simple fact of the matter. And you and your department will pay for this – oh yes indeed, you will."

The black cop, Officer Johnson, bent down and pat–searched me for weapons. "Shit, Williams, he's right. She's a woman. What the hell?"

I'll grant you that with the hooded sweatshirt, watch cap and bulky sweat pants I was wearing, my gender was concealed, but there were curves that could be seen fairly easily – distinct curves not found on a man's body, if one were really to look. My twitching muscles were starting to relax. The shock of the Tazer was wearing off, but I was still in handcuffs.

"You assholes better get yourselves lawyers," someone in the crowd muttered.

I sat up, my hands secured behind my back. The blood on my face had slowed to a drip.

"Here, let me get those," the sergeant said flatly, removing the handcuffs.

"Too much 'shoot first, ask questions later,'" a new voice said from inside the crowd, a crowd that had increased to several dozen onlookers, nearly all of whom were black.

"You got that right. These white cops, and their Uncle Tom apologizers, they think any black man walking the street is a gangbanger. Think they've got the right to violate our God–given civil rights. Abe Lincoln would be turning over in his grave, he would, if he could see what's goin' on."

Reverend Morris helped me to my feet, wiped the blood from my face with a clean white handkerchief, and nodded in the direction of the white cop.

"He apologize to you?"

I was slow to respond.

"Not in so many words," I finally managed.

"The 911 call said that the store had been robbed, shots were fired, and that a young Native American male, age twenty or so, was seen fleeing the area on foot, dressed in a blue windbreaker and wind pants. Five– four, one hundred and twenty pounds. When I shouted for the suspect to stop and he – I mean she – didn't comply, I used the Tazer. Standard procedure."

Williams made no further attempt at an apology. He was in defense mode, seeking to deflect blame for his mistake.

"Well, you made an error in judgment, officer. Miss DuMont is obviously not Native American, not male, not wearing a blue windbreaker, and clearly not five–foot–four," the reverend observed, holding my shaking body tightly to his own, allowing me to borrow his warmth against the gathering wind.

"That's right! You tell him, rev," a man shouted out. "He not only got the wrong color, he got the wrong sex!"

"Says here that Miss DuMont is on probation," Officer Johnson related from the passenger's seat of the idling squad car, red emergency lights rotating slowly against the darkened sky. "Fifth degree possession."

The realization that the police had information about me that only my pastor, my closest friends and my family were privy to, was startling.

"Doesn't change the fact that she did nothing wrong, officer. You gonna stand up for what's right or are you gonna try to sanitize this thing?"

Reverend Morris left me in the care of Flora Washington, who, being a head shorter than me, was the perfect prop to hold me up. The pastor peered into the police cruiser as he challenged the black officer to do the right thing.

"She's got no warrants or holds on her. She's not holding. I think we'd best cut her loose."

Sergeant Williams stood eye–to–eye with me, his warm breath reeking of onion and salami.

"You're free to leave."

There was no apology, and no recognition that he'd Tazered the wrong person. That, more than anything else, convinced me to make an appointment to see a lawyer. It was the first time in years that I could remember being singled out simply because of the color of my skin.

That experience taught me that, more than any other situation I'd encountered, there were aspects to my ethnicity that I needed to understand and that I needed to get a handle on, if I were going to be the person God intended me to be. I knew that bringing a lawsuit against the City of Minneapolis wasn't going to solve the complex questions of personal identity I'd been considering; that wouldn't be the purpose behind making a claim. Deterrence: that's what I was after. If my actions in taking on the police department made one officer stop and think as he or she acted in haste because of skin color, then I felt I was doing something positive.

When the City of Minneapolis issued its check, there were a lot of questions, the most repeated of which was why I'd accepted the paltry sum of ten thousand dollars in the settlement of my claim. After all, my tumble to the concrete had resulted in a permanent scar. I'd obviously been traumatized and, given the public nature of the event, been made a spectacle of, all without any probable cause or reasonable suspicion. Those were my lawyer's words, not mine. Cherise Bennett didn't handle my case; it wasn't something she was equipped to do. She hooked me up with Sue Holden, the president of the Minnesota Bar Association, who urged me to press for more compensation. As I said, however, that wasn't what I was after.

FORTY-SIX

Albert Priestly and I took in a few shows, mostly dramas at the Guthrie, the Theater in the Round and the Jungle Theater. We shared some intimate moments, including some serious discussions about the War in Iraq. (He was for it, a firm believer that Saddam was within a whisker's breath of achieving nuclear weapons; I was against it, convinced we'd been duped into picking a fight we were destined to walk away from.) We also talked about the underlying reasons behind September 11 (Albert thought it was economic and political jealousy that drove the terrorists; I believed it was fear of our country's political and military power), and the right to choose (on this subject Albert was more liberal than I, due to our different religious upbringings. He was raised Episcopalian). We exchanged a few kisses and some relatively tame embraces. I liked him, liked his quick mind and his seriousness, and his devotion to reason. But I knew, after spending a few dinners with the man, that he and I were not right for each other. There was a defined and consistent soberness about Dr. Priestly, perhaps the result of watching his young wife waste away from disease and being powerless, despite his mental prowess, to make any sense of it all. It wasn't that he didn't get a joke if he heard one; Albert was very much capable of laughter. But there was an unspoken aspect of seriousness that seemed to haunt Albert, a veil that cloaked his every word and was found in every gesture. This quirk of his was troubling, off–putting, and impacted the time we spent together. As quickly as we started seeing each other, it was over. A month of companionship ended in a simple and mutual understanding that it wasn't meant to be.

During my stay at Castleton's, I was inundated with emails and IMs from Mason. He wrote me every day, revealing bits and pieces of farm life, updating me on the latest treatment center gossip, sharing the shenanigans and antics of the new girls. His messages were like the breaths of a newborn – something both precious and precarious.

I thought about Mason as I ran my route on a rainy summer day in early June. My hair was wet, my chest constricted by a sports bra, and my legs bare. My thighs and calves were growing stronger with each stride, and my arms were becoming more toned and firm from the fifty pushups I insisted on doing each morning and the fifty more I did before going to bed. The iPod I'd bought with my hard–earned salary as a nursing assistant played a John Gorka tune as I pushed myself past St. Mark's Episcopal Cathedral near Loring Park. I sped by gays and lesbians walking hand–in–hand around the perimeter of the park's pond, and smiled. My position on same–sex love had changed dramatically due to a letter I'd received a month earlier from my old friend Amy Olson, now Dr. Amy Olson. Amy was in the last year of her residency in Family Practice in Duluth when she wrote to me. She'd tracked me down through my mom. It was in her first letter to me in quite some time that Amy revealed she was a lesbian.

Now, understand, my position on this subject didn't mature due to some deep philosophical or religious awaking. For my entire adult life, at least on a superficial level, I felt queasy when I detected sexual innuendo between women, but Amy's revelation, along with her announcement that she would attend our high school reunion in July (the same weekend as the marathon) and that she'd be bringing her partner (her word, not mine), Sarah Miles, with her, started my mind to working. After some consideration, I simply accepted Amy's news. She's my best friend. What else could I do?

Love is love, I repeated to myself as I sped up Nicolette past the Barnes & Noble bookstore, dodging throngs of early–morning lawyers, secretaries and day–traders on their way to work. *It isn't for me to decide what sort of love between two consenting adults is sacred and honorable. That's God's province, praise the Lord, not mine.*

Phrases of worship were sneaking with some regularity into my thoughts. Three months of attending Beginner's Group, listening to Pastor Morris's enthusiastic sermons, and regaling in the celebratory music of St. Francis's congregation had made their mark. Whether I remained a parishioner of St. Francis's or found a spiritual home in some other denomination, the religion I'd experienced because of Flora Washington's invitation – much like that tiny mustard seed described in St. Mark's Gospel – had taken hold. Conversion? Born again? I dislike those labels, seeing how I was raised Christian and never really stopped believing. So even though I consider what happened to me to be a spiritual tune–up and not a major overhaul, the change wasn't fleeting or transitory. It was real and it ran deep.

Tell me the truth, what are you living for
Tell me why, why you are near
'Cause if you cannot make yourself a good noise
Then tell me what you're doing here.

The Gospel beat of John Gorka's music propelled me across wet sidewalks, my feet splashing joyfully through small puddles in my way. There's a sexiness, an earthy sensuality to Gorka's voice that hints of lazy afternoons spent naked in bed sipping fine wine and eating fattening desserts. I felt something alter – some part of me underwent an inner shift – as I listened and as I ran. And ran. And ran.

Now we all got the hand for the gimme
We all got the mouth for the much obliged
But when it comes down to giving back
We give the eye to the other guy.

Oh it seems that so much trouble
Is simply caused by the angry word
Although silence can be a virtue
I say it's a good noise that's preferred.

By the time I reached St. Francis's, orange and red shards of light outlined the haggard steeple of the structure as the sun sought to rise above the horizon. I walked the last hundred yards to Castleton's as part of my cool down; my face was streaked with sweat, my legs were sore and my feet ached. I'd done my ten miles in a virtual sprint. Not world class, and not fast enough to frighten a cross–country star.

As I caught my breath, I couldn't avoid day–dreaming about a certain Norwegian American dairy farmer. What would become of my speculations about him was anybody's guess.

FORTY-SEVEN

Cherise Bennett met me at the Minnesota Board of Nursing in St. Paul, in an office building that flanked the state capitol building. It was a sultry day in June when Cherise stood before the Board and presented a request for relief from the Board's prohibition against my working as a registered nurse. My probation officer, Julia Frisk, showed up to support my request. It was an interesting trio of women who confronted the board that day, I'll have to say: an African American registered nurse–turned–drug addict, a male–to–female transgender lawyer (and not a bad looking one at that) and Ms. Frisk, whose dark eyes were fixed in a humorless gaze, staring down, in finest matriarchal fashion, the six white women and men sitting across the table.

"You say that Miss DuMont has maintained sobriety – *complete* sobriety?"

Edward Parks, a thin, bald, man, an accountant by trade, was one of the citizen members of the review panel interrogating us; he spoke first, once introductions and Cherise's opening remarks had been made. The Board was represented by Ellen Wong, a Chinese American attorney working for the Minnesota Attorney General's office. Despite her heritage, Miss Wong was no China doll: she was thick–necked, thick–limbed and relatively tall, she was my physical equal and all business as she sat at the head of the conference table and took notes.

"That's correct. She's had over sixty urine and blood tests. Every single one has been clean." Julia Frisk confirmed my compliance with little emotion. Her eyes were lowered, her reading glasses sitting low on her nose as she studied my file.

"I understand there was an incident," Sally Hastings, one of the nurses on the Board, brought up.

Damn, I thought. *I was hoping to avoid getting into that mess.* I swallowed hard.

"It was a mistake, on my part, to trust the person I was with. I thought we were going to her mother's house to pick up a few things – things she was bringing to the Cities for our stay at Castleton's."

"Castleton's?"

"The halfway house she's living in, Miss Hastings," Ms. Wong stated.

"Oh. Sorry for the interruption. Please continue."

"As it turned out, the woman knew all along there was going to be a party at her mother's place. I tried to get her to leave. When I felt uncomfortable, what with what was going on and all, I called a friend. He came and got me."

"What was going on – at the party, I mean, Miss DuMont?" Miss Hastings fixed her nondescript eyes on me as she asked the question.

I took a breath, and continued. "Drugs. Alcohol. Just about anything you can think of. I felt I was in trouble so, as I'd been taught, I called for help."

"And help came? Before you did anything you would regret?" One of the other men on the panel, a guy whose name I didn't catch, had jumped in.

"That's only partially true. I regret being there. But I didn't know what was going to happen. I had no inkling there'd be trouble."

The panel seemed satisfied with my answer and the questioning moved on. In the end, after my lawyer and Ms. Wong conferred in the hallway, a compromise was reached: I was going back to nursing, albeit with constraints regarding my access to medications and a clear understanding that I could not, until two years passed, work as a lead or supervisory nurse. That was fine with me, given that I was still jittery and fighting off the residual desire to use. I knew that I wasn't perfect, and that there still existed, in a distant corner of my being, a longing to use meth. I could live with the limits imposed by the Board. In fact, I welcomed them.

When the Hennepin County Medical Center wouldn't hire me as an RN, I walked into the human resources office and handed in my identification badge that very day. It wasn't like I wanted to quit my job. Like I said, I needed to work to keep my mind off using. But I wouldn't starve. I had a roof over my head. My parents were funding my stay at Castleton's. Dad had taken out a loan against his beloved Chris Craft runabout to pay the cost of my aftercare, and I told him I'd pay him back. Every dime. He told me I didn't have to, but I was determined to make it right. And I'm a stubborn girl when it comes to things like owing folks money. It just feels wrong, if you know what I mean – even if the people you owe are your parents.

In the last week of June, the week before my ten–year high school reunion and the South Shore Marathon, I went back to work as a registered nurse. Pastor Morris found me a job at the Metropolitan African Women's Clinic, just up the street from St. Francis's. The Clinic treats poor women; most of them are black and from West Africa: Liberia, Senegal, Guinea, Sierra Leone, and the Darfur region of Sudan. Getting that job meant more to me than just having a reliable source of income. Because of my new job and responsibilities, Judge Patrick – God bless his soul – saw fit to give me additional freedom. He let me leave Castleton's early, and though I was still on supervised probation, I had the ability to begin life anew in my own place – so long as I stayed clean, made regular telephone calls to my probation officer and submitted to urine and blood tests when asked. But before I could take advantage of Judge Patrick's largess, there was something I needed to do. And I had to go to Guthrie Center, Iowa to do it.

FORTY-EIGHT

I was just another black woman on her way home. At least, that's how it seemed, I'm guessing, to the other riders on the Greyhound bus. I was dressed in ripped jeans, a festive yellow and blue silk blouse, and flats; my reconstituted hair was done up in dreadlocks, the result of numerous visits to a salon and hours of twisting by an African lady I met at the Clinic.

Choosing to put my hair into tightly woven spires, with the knowledge that the only way dreadlocks can be removed is by shearing the hair at the roots, was a decision I hadn't come to lightly, especially given my lifelong envy of Lilith's straight hair. But after the perm worked itself out, changing to dreads felt right, felt like I was recovering some part of me, my ethnicity. Whether Mason Erickson would appreciate the tie between my hair and my ancestry wasn't something I'd considered.

My make–up consisted of hints of rouge, lipstick and eyeliner. I'd packed an extra pair of panties. An extra white bra, nearly new – a JC Penny purchase, I think. A pair of white athletic socks, though, since I was wearing sandals, it was unlikely I'd need the socks. My toiletry kit filled out the extent of what I'd brought along for the trip to Guthrie Center, except for the book.

I asked Mom to send me *Jubilee*. The novel arrived in the same condition I'd shelved it in my room seven or eight years before. On the ride from Minneapolis to Des Moines, I pulled the book out of my backpack, opened it and rediscovered the letter. My fingers held fragile paper up to the morning light that was unimpeded by clouds. I studied Father Michaels's handwriting. An old lady in the seat next to me slept, mouth agape, snoring loudly and oblivious to the world, as I considered the priest's words.

Dearest Lilith,

If you are thinking I am a wicked man who intends to take your innocence and then retreat into cloister, you are mistaken. I am in love with you, Little One. Deep, serious, passionate (you know how passionate) mature love. I have tried to reach you but, for obvious reasons, I have not attempted to send messages through your sister. I fear that she would not handle well what we have and how we are connected, given the spark of interest I've witnessed in her eyes when she and I talk. Honestly, I do not hold the same feelings for her that I hold for you – not even remotely close. Esther is a fragile soul in some ways, strong as the north wind in winter in others. I think we should avoid taking her into our confidence at present, given her obvious infatuation with me. That said, I have sent this letter through someone I trust, someone loyal to me, rather than through Esther.

I am sure you are asking yourself: "Just what is 'our situation'?" I am afraid I have no easy answer for that. I am a priest. I have broken more than one vow by what transpired between us. It should be easy and right and in accordance with my calling to make my confession to the Bishop and agree never to see you again. But I find that I cannot put you out of my mind. Not just the physical you, but your tenderness, your giving nature, your soul. I am in love, Lilith, in love with you. I need to see you. I want to see you.

Though I am no poet, perhaps this slight verse will compel you to initiate contact with me. My heart would leap for joy if that occurred. But I understand. I will abide by your silence, if that is what you wish. You will have to be the one who contacts me in the future.

Here is the poem:

Thoughts
Are you the lantern
And I the moth?
Are you the lighthouse
And I the lost?

Is this a fiction
From some lost page?
Is this a story
From some past age?

Are you my savior
Or my demise?
Are you the promise
Or mere surprise?

Please get word to me that things are okay and that we can see
each other again. You are the light and I am a mere moth.
    Love,
    T

I had found the letter in Lilith's wastebasket, her reaction to the priest's audacity plain in the manner she'd ripped the paper in two. Why I'd retrieved the thing, taped it together and hid it in Miss Walker's book, I still don't understand. I think it had something to do with my own grieving process. Having witnessed the carnality of their connection, having longed for the handsome priest to ravish me in the same way, and having come to understand, from the content of his letter, that I was not desirable, I know that I felt loss. Why Lilith didn't reveal her pregnancy to force the priest's hand, I can't say. All I know is that she chose a different route, a route neither of us ever discussed after that miserable drive to Duluth. Maybe, like I've said before, Lilly is smarter than I give her credit for. Maybe she knew that, even if her girlish charms compelled the priest to do the right thing by her, in the end, such an act would turn on her and crush her beneath the burden of a relationship born of simple lust.

As the Greyhound bounded south, venturing further and further into a land dominated by new corn, sprouting soybeans, plowed fields, flat terrain and endless sky, the old lady next to me snorted, scratched her nose, but remained asleep. I watched farms whirl by at dizzying speed as I tried to understand why I was bound for Guthrie Center.

Am I playing the fool, traipsing off to the middle of the Corn Belt to beg a man I have so little in common with, a man whose idea of music is Journey and Van Halen and the occasional female country western star, whose politics mimic those of John McCain and whose idea of art is staring at those weird little 3D puzzles in the Sunday comics – to love me? What is it about Mason Erickson that drives me to him, that forces me to show my hand?

I was sitting in a window seat, and I had a clear view of the countryside, of America, passing me by. The nightmares of slaves and slaving I'd experienced after finishing *Kindred* had abated. I was content in the knowledge that my father's people had come here under great duress and hardship, receiving the lash and the branding iron as human cattle, but persevering. Indeed, in the case of my father, his line had excelled and become integrated into the fabric of American life despite the intentions of the masters to keep his people down, to reduce *niggers* to mere bits and pieces of personal property. These were thoughts that I'd never touched upon as a child growing up along the rocky shores of Lake Superior. No one – not my father, nor a teacher, and certainly not my Irish-Finnish mother – had ever broached the subject of my slave heritage. There had been no need, in my father's version of reality, to consider the issue. I was Wisconsin–born, American blooded, and the daughter of immigrants on both sides of the parental equation – albeit on my father's side, his African ancestors had not come to America by choice.

My eyes moistened. Visions of Del and me on our mattress in our basement bedroom, our limbs entwined, with the light, the dark, the diversity of our skin reduced to a mere happenstance because of our passion and affection for each other as human beings. Sure, there was wrong in what we'd done. I know that now, and I likely knew it then. But there was no wrong in the "us"; only comfort, kindness and tenderness. Whatever problems we had, whatever faults we displayed, whatever disasters we fell into, I would not allow them to displace the truth of what Del and I meant to each other.

Love.

It was and is that simple. Colors and shapes and sizes and accents and all the other quirks and niceties of body and persona have importance, but all of them can be overcome by true affection.

Race? What does race have to do with any of it? There is no such thing as "pure blooded" anymore. My own parents can't boast of racial purity in their veins. My father, though he looks the part of a racially intact black man, has the blood of the Irish, at the very least, and perhaps other ethnicities, tied up in his past. And Mom? Half Irish, half Finnish, at least, that's what she claims. Consider that the Danes, the Icelanders and the Norwegians raided Ireland. The blue eyes and the blond and red hair so revered in Irish beauty didn't come from dark–featured Celts. And the Finns? Ruled by the Swedes for 600 years and by the Russians for another 100, what level of ethnic purity can they boast?

It's plausible that I possess Sami blood, traces of intercourse between my mother's Finnish ancestors and the indigenous people of Lapland, and that it flows from my heart to my limbs. Beyond skin color and the artificial labels of culture and ethnicity, we are all human beings sharing the same dreams, wishes and fate. The same red blood flows inside each of us. Skin color means very little; it cannot gauge the true measure of a person, nor can it trace a person's heritage beyond the obvious. One could assume, from the color of my skin, that I have African blood. And, I must confess, I do long to know the origins of that pigmentation. But the realities of time and distance are such that I will never know the name of the African village my ancestors came from. There are no records, no writings to tell me that. Such things are mysteries and they will always remain as such.

"Nothing ventured, nothing gained," I muttered into the hot glass of the bus window as I considered how to approach Mason Erickson, once I pulled into Guthrie Center to complete what seemed like a fool's errand.

The bus entered town. The heat was sweltering. Tufts of white flitted across the blue prairie sky as I left the bus, my backpack slung across my left shoulder. As I stood on Iowa soil for the first time since February, I realized that my crazed pilgrimage lacked any sort of calculated resolve.

I have no plan.

That's what I thought as I began to walk the two miles from Guthrie Center to Mason's farm. I hadn't emailed the man. I hadn't called. But I knew he'd be at the farm – he was always there. He was a dairyman. His cows needed him. There was no reason to make an appointment.

As I passed the bay window of the café where I once worked, I saw him. He was sitting in a booth, dressed in a clean white shirt, wearing his light blue tie, the only necktie he owned, and black dress slacks. He wasn't alone. He was with a woman and a little boy. I recognized them from the photographs I'd seen in Mason's farmhouse.

His ex–wife. His son.

The woman smiled familiarly, as if she'd never up and left Mason for the Canadian prairie; as if she had never uprooted their child and run off with another man. I stared through the dusty film coating the window, watching helplessly as the man to whom I'd come to bare my heart reached across the Formica tabletop and placed his hand on the pale wrist of the woman who had once shared his bed.

FORTY-NINE

Lilly and I talked as her little yellow BMW convertible raced across western Wisconsin. We drove east until we came to US Highway 53, an expressway running north to Superior. I felt like getting ripped in Superior, a town famous for its bars, but even catching Mason Erickson on familiar terms with his ex–wife couldn't trip me up. One drink, the lowering of inhibitions, and I'd be back out on the street, looking for meth. I'd be doomed. I wasn't going to let one disappointment erupt into a full–blown catastrophe. No way was I going back there – not for Mason Erickson, and not for any man.

What did I expect? I thought as the sports car raced over asphalt, the BMW's cruise control set at seventy–five, the radar detector activated, music (a CD by Nelly) blaring from the six–speaker disc player. *They have a history. They're from the same place, the same background. They have a son. It was only a matter of time. I should have known better. God, I am such a fool.*

I had immediately turned around and run as fast as my sandals would allow, to the convenience store where the bus was refueling. I convinced the Greyhound driver, by a cascade of tears and the inconsolable shuddering of my body, to let me ride to Council Bluffs without a ticket. I sat in the bus station in Council Bluffs for a few hours, having myself a good cry and setting my mind against Mason, before buying a ticket back to the Twin Cities. I wasn't rational. I didn't accord to the dairy farmer's side of things the fact that I'd arrived without warning, with no claim on him other than a few somewhat suggestive emails, one night of naked hilarity in his truck, and a few passing moments between a recovering addict and a cook in the kitchen of a treatment center. None of those things mattered to me as I added up the weight and heft of what I took to be, despite no evidence to support my position, Mason's calculated move to disparage my feelings. It didn't matter at all that he had no clue I was there, spying on the scene between him and Virginia, and that he couldn't possibly have orchestrated the event to hurt me. None of it mattered one iota; I was pissed. I was determined to forget Mason Erickson and move on.

"You still thinking on that man?" Lilly smiled as she turned her head. The wind tousled her hair in the cockpit of the open car, but it had little impact on the dreadlocks under my Minnesota Twins baseball cap.

"You got that right."

"You still pissed off at him for being with his old lady?"

"Wouldn't you be? I dropped everything, wasted good money on a ticket, and came down to settle things between us in a positive way, only to find him playing patty–cake with his ex–wife. That's not how the script was supposed to be written."

Lilly smiled. "Problem is, you're not the only playwright in your little drama."

"Bastard."

Lil laughed the sophisticated laugh she'd adopted since moving to Apple Valley. She didn't feign such a laugh when she lived on the East Side of St. Paul, where she once worked as a receptionist in the medical clinic where she would meet her future husband. She met Richard when he interviewed for a position with the clinic. The doctors Lilly worked for made Richard an offer that he ultimately turned down. The way Lilly tells it, Richard just about fell over his shoes trying to leave the office, as smitten as he was with her on that first meeting. When he called the clinic later that same afternoon, she assumed he was calling to accept the job offer. He wasn't; he was calling to ask her out. She agreed to a date. The rest, as they say, is history.

Once Lilith Ann became a doctor's wife, she changed in subtle but palpable ways. I don't think she realizes just how much her new life has changed her. Maybe, like a chameleon changing colors, she's simply adapted to her surroundings as a way of surviving. She has been, after all, cast into a world of wealth and intellect that comes with being a surgeon's wife; she's had no education beyond high school and possesses little more than beauty and feminine instinct to defend herself in the societal shark pool she's now immersed in.

I shouldn't be so hard on her. She's had to enter a world she's never been a part of, not even with Dad being a doctor. The pace of life, the allusions to prestige, wealth and power – none of those things were part of our life in LaPointe. Mom kept it real and made us humble. She insisted on it. But such allusions are part and parcel of the life Richard has crafted for them. Lil's had to adapt, through whatever means possible, to feel comfortable in her new place, in her new role.

"I think you're being unfair. How could he know you'd be standing on a street corner in his hometown, eyeballing him? Get over it, girl. Either talk to him about it or move on. And given the differences between you, I'd say movin' on makes good sense."

"Differences?"

"He's white, you're black. That's for starters. I know, I know. Mom and Dad, Dad and Mom. Well, just because it worked for them, isn't an endorsement it'll work for you. Why not start thinking about someone you can make beautiful little African American babies with? Trust me. There are a lot fewer complications when you marry a colored man."

"'Colored man'? What the hell has gotten into you, Lilith? You sound like someone from *Gone with the Wind*."

"Okay, African American man, black man, take your pick – someone of your own race."

I mentally revisited the aspects of race I'd considered during my bus ride to Iowa. I saw no point in waxing philosophical with my sister.

"I've tried."

"One time, with some boring professor from the U. There are lots of handsome, well–mannered, fine black men in the Twin Cities, if you'd only open your eyes."

I sighed. Wisconsin eskers passed by, their crowns concealed by the shiny new leaves of summer oaks and maples. A flock of trumpeter swans, their wings and breasts starkly white against the midday sun, followed the highway. I was tired of thinking about my failed errand to Iowa. I changed the subject.

"I hope I do well tomorrow."

Lilly's mood lightened.

"You'll do great. Wish I had your drive. It's all I can do to force myself onto the treadmill three times a week."

I suspected that, hidden in Lil's statement, was a kernel of fear: fear that, if she became fat and past her prime, Richard's eyes might wander, eventually causing other parts of his athletic body to follow. I detected an undercurrent of apprehension in her words. Maybe it was imagined. Maybe not.

We stopped for lunch at Barker's Island Marina in Superior. We watched yachts move in and out of their berths as we sipped ice tea and ate Caesar salads. It was past three by the time we sped out of town. A few miles south of Superior, we turned onto Highway 13 and followed the South Shore. The sun remained brilliant, and as the car slowed for Cornucopia, the little fishing village that marked the beginning of the marathon course, my stomach felt queasy. A hill loomed just beyond the race's starting line. My eyes fixed on the ascending highway. I realized that I hadn't trained for hills and that my run would likely be reduced to a plodding crawl. The thought of four hours of humiliation made me forget all about Mason Erickson and his ex–wife.

FIFTY

Modesty vanishes for folks running a marathon. What I mean is: before, during and after a race, women can be seen with their sports bras pulled down, their hands rubbing Vaseline on their breasts; men wander off into minimal foliage and urinate in public; and both sexes have been known to shed clothing, including chafing underwear, without modesty over the course of a race. Before the race, I made sure my tender parts were lubricated and that band–aids protected my nipples. It's not that I'm a prude, but I'm modest around strangers, and exposing myself – especially with the scarring and all – well, that just isn't in my constitution. Even if my body were perfect like Lil's, exposing my parts in public isn't something I'd do.

The night before the marathon, I slept in my old bed with full knowledge that I'd be hurting when I showed up at my class reunion after the race. I realized that I'd be worn to the bone from the marathon and that there'd be looks – and stares for sure – thrown my way. Bayfield's a small place, and all of my classmates would have heard versions of my story. I'd have to keep my wits about me, but I wasn't about to get dragged into cat fights over unfounded perceptions of who I'd become or where I'd been.

Morning. A cool northeastern breeze blew across the lake. The temperature was forty–five degrees. The sky was a quilt of impenetrable gray. Lil rose with me. We showered and dressed in darkness. I had trouble finding my running shoes until I realized that Mom had tucked them under my bed.

She hasn't changed a lick. Always the organizer.

I worked bee's wax through my dreads before putting on my baseball cap and brushing my teeth. Without waking our parents, we ate a light breakfast before leaving the house.

Though an inaugural event, the South Shore Marathon had received considerable attention. Of course, the race wasn't on par with Grandma's Marathon, a tradition for decades in nearby Duluth. Marathons don't achieve that sort of following the first time out. Still, by the time Lil and I arrived in Cornucopia, a significant crowd was in attendance. Over a thousand folks had entered the race, and by the size of the group milling near the starting line, most of the entrants had shown up.

"You run fast, you hear me?" Lilith said as we walked away from her BMW, the top up, the alarm activated, the car parked in the gravel lot next to the Cornucopia village marina and fishing museum.

Gulls wheeled against the charcoal backdrop of the low sky. Gobs of cold rain, precursors to a deluge, struck us as we walked towards shuffling, stretching, jogging–in–place runners who were antsy to get under way. Volunteers in orange t–shirts with "OFFICIAL" silk-screened on the fronts and backs weaved in and out of the crowd, directing traffic, finding ointment for the unprepared, answering questions. Mom and Dad planned to watch me run through Red Cliff, at the twenty–mile mark, when the reality of the race would be taking its toll.

"Esther? Esther DuMont?"

The voice was familiar. Though I hadn't heard it in awhile, I knew in an instant that it belonged to Amy Olson. Amy walked towards me in the company of a willowy black woman with a shorn head and spindly limbs wearing a singlet and running tights. The black woman was built to run: her considerable length was all sinew from head to toe. She had virtually no chest or hips, but possessed a gorgeous face. All that remained of the woman's coarse African hair was a carpet of nubs glistening with drizzle. Amy looked the same as she always had; she hadn't aged one iota. Her face was cherubic, her body solid and compact. Her hair was the same mousy brown, cut to the shoulder, shifting and bouncing in time to her girlish gait. It was if she'd walked off the basketball court in our senior year, taken a shower and then suddenly appeared ten years later, with not an age–line to her detriment and not an extra pound on her frame.

"Amy!"

We hugged. Amy smelled of perfume and her hair felt soft against my face. Though not romantically inclined to my own gender, in that instant, I understood why women might desire Amy Olson.

"Lilly," Amy said, releasing me and hugging my sister, nearly buckling the poor girl in two. "This is Sarah Miles, my partner."

The implications of that term drifted into my mind and then disappeared. From the look on my sister's face, the connection between the women didn't register with Lil.

"Pleased to meet you," I said, extending my hand.

For a rail of a girl, Sarah Miles had a significant grip.

"Likewise. Amy has told me a lot about you two."

At that, Lilith giggled – not the stage giggle she'd developed while living in the Twin Cities, but an actual snicker that harkened back to high school.

"I hope she didn't bore you to death," I interjected, preventing Lilith from saying something rash.

My eyes took in the black woman. Everything about Sarah Miles said "speed." Then it dawned on me: *Sarah Miles. Olympic 10,000-meter champion. Sarah Miles!*

My face must have betrayed the recognition.

"Yes, she's *that* Sarah Miles. Now that she's over thirty, Sarah's concentrating on longer distances. She wants to run the marathon in Beijing. We've been a lot of places together, but never to China. We'll have an excuse to visit China, if she makes the team."

Lord, I thought, *what have I gotten myself into? Running against an Olympic champion? Maybe I bit off more than I can chew.*

Sarah shifted her long feet, which were covered in five–hundred–dollar running flats. I could sense that, despite her notoriety, Sarah Miles was shy, making her a perfect complement for Amy's exuberance.

"We'll see if I can make the transition. There's a world of difference between being fast over 10,000 meters and being fast over twenty–six miles. You been running long?"

Her question, asked in a near whisper, the breathy texture of her voice surely one of the reasons Amy fell for her, caught me unawares.

"Uh, not so long. I started training around Christmas."

"Intervals?"

"Endurance. I didn't really have the time to train for speed. I was in treatment for most of my training."

Amy studied me. "I heard about that. I'm sorry about your friend."

She means Del. Yes, "friend." That's discreet. But he was *a friend, amongst all the other things he was to me. "Friend" suits Delmont Benson just fine.*

"It was hard on Es," Lilly said. "She and Del were getting on pretty well. Dad didn't much care for the man. And Mom, well – you don't want to know what she thought of that man."

White trash – that's the plain and simple truth of what Mom thought of Delmont Benson.

"Looks like they're getting ready to give us final instructions," Sarah said quietly, her eyelashes batting at the mist. "Good luck, Esther. It was nice to meet you."

I expected her to give me some last words of sage advice – you know, some sort of prophetic message from the goddess of running. Instead, she and Amy simply headed towards the starting line, and Lilly and I followed. My heart was pumping too hard; I knew enough about my body to realize I needed to relax. I drew a deep breath and rubbed my left knee. I'd capped my longest training run at twenty miles a month before the race. I'd tapered my runs to four miles every other day until a week before the race, when I stopped running to allow the knee time to rest. It was a matter of overuse, not injury. I wasn't worried about my left knee holding up; I was as strong as I'd ever been, I was young and I'd lost the weight I'd gained at New Beginnings.

"You ready for this?" Lilly asked as we made our way through the crowd.

"Ready as I'll ever be."

"Don't try to keep up with the champion," Lil said through a smile.

"Hadn't even considered it."

"That's good. That's real good," Lilly added, pecking me on the cheek before turning to leave.

"Thanks," I shouted over the din of runners making nervous conversation.

Lilly didn't turn around. My sister vanished into the throng of milling spectators and I was on my own.

FIFTY-ONE

Sheets of cold rain pummeled me as I climbed out of Cornucopia. My white anklets were saturated, and my t–shirt and running shorts soaked. My dreadlocks hung free of my ball cap and were heavy with water. I was miserable but comforted by the knowledge that others shared my tribulations. Now *there's* a good Biblical term for you: *tribulations.* Seems all those old–time prophets, Job, Moses, Noah and the like, experienced tribulations. I was in good company

Why not me? I'm no prophet, and surely no saint. Life is hard, and tribulations are part of that hardness, along with other maladies described in the Old Testament: war, pestilence and sin. I've never been to war. I've only seen pestilence from a distance. But tribulation and sin? Now those *are concepts I can relate to!*

I reached the top of the first hill. My instincts told me to push. I stretched my legs. As I passed the five–mile marker, I glanced at my stopwatch.

The rabbit syndrome.

Adrenaline had caused me to abandon my game plan of running nine–minute miles. Running nine–minute miles would allow me to finish in just under four hours. I wasn't out to break records or qualify for Boston; if I survived and enjoyed myself, then I'd set loftier goals. Having never run track or cross–country in high school, I had no idea what to expect. I'm not built like Sarah Miles or my sister. Lilith has a perfect runner's build: lanky with little body fat, a small chest, and diminished hips. I'm built to play women's soccer or lacrosse, though I've never played either. My body is more akin to those of Venus and Serena Williams than Flo Jo (Francis Griffith Joyner). She's passed away but, in spite of the fact that I'd never been a track star, she'd been one of my idols. She was someone like me, and she'd made a big impression on the world when I was growing up.

Talk about tribulations, I thought as I caught up with a pack of runners moving along at my pace. *To win three Olympic gold medals, to be the world's fastest woman, in the best of shape, and to die from a heart attack at 38 years old – that, indeed, is tribulation.*

The rain stopped and the wind lessened. The sky remained gray and close, but the day began to warm. The group I was running with consisted of three men and two women. We were keeping an almost perfect pace, running nearly in unison, as we passed mile ten.

So far, so good.

I adjusted my running bra and shook my hair, my dreads swinging from side to side, in an attempt to throw off moisture, much like a dog does after coming out of a lake. I wasn't wearing jewelry. There was no need for finery, no need for display. I had a job to do: a gritty, dirty, exhausting job that required my full and undivided attention. At mile thirteen, I felt a twinge in my left knee.

Shit. If this gets worse, I may end up walking.

I said the word "walking" to myself as a reminder that I would not, unless hit by a truck and killed, fail to finish the race. I would not, like folks I'd heard about over the years, run twenty miles, only to walk off the course. Failure wasn't part of my itinerary. It wasn't like I was doing this for Del or for David or for that long distant line of black, Finnish or Irish ancestors in my history. And I certainly wasn't running the marathon for my parents, my sister or Mason.

Mason.

I thought about the farmer as I passed a watering station at mile fifteen. I grabbed a Dixie cup of cold water in each hand and tossed the contents down, splashing more water on myself than I swallowed. I scanned the highway. Runners were strung out for miles. I had no idea where the leaders were. I glanced at my watch; I'd been at it for two hours. The road ahead was crowded with runners wearing colorful singlets and other clothing; an assortment of shorts, sports bras, t–shirts, and there were a few runners in wind pants and sweats. Paper cups littered the asphalt for hundreds of yards past the watering station. Behind me, a line of stragglers extended back towards Cornucopia for as far as the eye could see. My group passed runners engaged in acts of self–preservation: disrobing and discarding unneeded clothing; puking; defecating; urinating.

Timing is everything.

There were satellite toilets every five miles, just past the tables holding the neat rows of paper cups filled with water, but runners are impatient. Bodily systems cry out for immediate attention and runners respond.

Mason got me into this.

That was the thought that crossed my mind as I entered Red Cliff, as I felt cramps attack my leg muscles. Ache? That would be too mild a term. Anguish? Too severe. Somewhere in–between those two concepts was what I felt as I struggled to make the summit of the hill. I'd fallen behind the pack I was running with. I tried to keep within striking distance of a stocky white woman whose hair was dyed a silly shade of red, and whose ass was large and cumbersome in running tights, with excess fat jiggling over the waistband of her tights.

I will not lose to that woman.

Please understand: I didn't know her. It wasn't anything personal. I'm not claiming I targeted her because she lacked fortitude. (There's another one of those Biblical words.) *Fortitude* was keeping her just ahead of me as we crested the hill onto the Reservation, but I wasn't about to let some fat woman best me.

"You go, girl!"

Lilly's words were welcome encouragement as I slogged my way past the Indian gaming casino. I looked up from the roadway at the sound of her voice. Mom, Dad, Lilith and Billy and April Cadotte were lined up along the roadside, cheering me on. All of them except April were animated. April, true to her shy nature, barely smiled. I didn't hold it against her. I was too focused on keeping my feet moving to consider petty things like that.

"Keep it up, daughter," Dad shouted, his head held high, his chest puffed out as if I'd just won the Miss America pageant.

"Only six more miles to go," Mom added. "You're looking great."

"Thanks," I muttered between draws of warming air. The day's humidity was beginning to assert itself, and the sun was beginning to burn away the clouds. "I'll see you in Salmo."

As I left my little fan club behind, I realized that the one person I really wanted to see at milepost twenty was likely five hundred miles away.

He's got his life. I have mine. Best to keep focused on the task at hand. Lamentations aren't going to get me to the finish line.

Lamentations. Another term from the Old Testament. Why that word popped into my head, given the extreme fatigue lodged in my diaphragm and legs, I can't say, but it did. The fat girl swayed back and forth on her ample legs. I pushed myself and tried to close the gap between us, a gap that had, despite my best efforts, widened. I wanted to use the woman as a marker for my finishing push. After passing her, I intended to pick out other struggling runners and pass them, one by one, like rungs on a ladder. But I had to catch her first.

Dig deeper. You're in the state championship. There's a minute left. Amy passes you the ball. You pass it back. Coach has made it clear: you're

216

to take the shot. Madison Catholic is ahead by two. You need to shoot the three and make it, with no time left for them to run the floor. You move to your left and shake a defender. They're in a zone. Amy passes the ball to Debbie Thomas. Debbie hesitates, allowing you to clear a screen. You're free – for a second, you have no one on you. The ball sails through the air. Your hands feel leather, but like you've practiced a million times in your driveway, you spin and shoot. The ball barely rotates as it leaves your hands. Swish.

My feet felt like cement blocks. Through sheer willpower, I overcame my body's natural reluctance to move forward. The fat woman was fifty yards ahead, the rump of her black–and–red running tights sashaying back and forth like a bull's–eye. I set my sights on her ass and pushed.

At twenty–four miles, after climbing into Bayfield, winding through the village and heading downhill past the fish hatchery, I caught up with the woman. I pushed and pushed and pushed going down that hill, thrashing my big feet against the pavement in an uncontrolled scurry. I pulled even with my prey. Her face was drawn in pain and sweat slurried down her cheeks. She clutched her right side as if someone had shot her. The woman's eyes widened as I drew next to her. She feigned a smile.

"I'm about done in," she whispered.

"You're almost there."

"I don't think I can make it."

"Sure you can," I said as I passed by.

Another hill. Highway 13 climbed one last maple and oak studded ridge before descending to the finish line. My legs fought the incline. As I started up the hill, I looked back. You might call it a mistake, or *providence*, another of those holy words. Whatever you call it, what I saw crumpled my resolve. The fat woman *was* all done in. She was walking, with both hands on her hips, her hair stringy and limp; her pace, incredibly slow, fought against the weight of the landscape. It was if she'd landed on a planet where gravity exponentially increases your weight.

Christ.

"Sorry, Lord," I mumbled.

I drew a breath. My eyes looked uphill. There were at least a dozen runners struggling ahead of me.

Easy pickings.

I glanced back. The woman had stopped. I knew I had no choice in the matter – no choice at all. I turned around. My legs objected. In short order, I found myself jogging in place beside the woman.

"You can't give up. You've only got two miles to go."

217

"I *want* to finish...worked two years for this...had surgery...lost...hundred pounds...broke my foot last year...couldn't run the Twin Cities Marathon...took a year to get back in shape."

The words came out haltingly. She was hatched; still, what she said moved me. I didn't want her to fail.

"Look here: you've come this far. I'll walk you to the top of the hill. Then we'll see if you can't pick up those feet and jog the rest of the way."

Her eyes blinked.

"You don't even know me."

I smiled. "And you don't know me. But that's what it's all about, right? Folks helping folks. Whaddya say?"

She nodded, removed her hands from her hips and began to walk. I had the urge to run, to free myself from the obligation of being with her, but I walked with her, urging her on, until we stood at the crest of the hill.

"Can you jog?"

Runners were passing us in droves as we stood in the gathering sunlight, the gray canopy dissipating with the arrival of late morning. I'd stopped looking at my watch. There was no way I'd break four hours. I was okay with that – disappointed to a degree, but willing to bear that disappointment if the fat woman made it to Salmo.

The woman nodded. We began a labored trot.

"I didn't get your name."

"Esther. Esther DuMont."

"Marilyn Samuels. Pleased to meet you, Esther."

My leg muscles cramped and Marilyn's side ache reasserted itself. We slowed to a walk. After a few hundred yards, Marilyn began to move her feet in something approximating a shuffle. I picked up my pace and stayed by her side. The finish line was in view, and the crowd of spectators at Salmo was a mass of color; reds, yellows and oranges were visible from a distance. I wanted to sprint to the finish line, to pass the fifteen or so tortured bodies in front of us and salvage some feeling of athletic superiority by besting people at the end of the race. But Marilyn wasn't in a condition to pass anyone. We moseyed towards the finish line as runner after runner went past us.

It seemed that Marilyn sensed my internal dialogue. "You go on ahead," she gasped, her teeth clenched in determination. "You finish the race the way you want to."

I shook my head.

"Great job, Esther," a familiar voice called before I could respond to Marilyn.

It can't be.

218

A thousand things distracted me and competed for my attention. My heart thumped. The urge to pass the folks between me and the end of the race, the finishing line defined by yellow police tape draped across wooden saw horses, tempted me again. But I held back. Marilyn and I went through the finish line side by side, her pale freckled hand clasped in my dark palm, both of us exhausted and sweaty from the ordeal. Volunteers unpinned the numbers from our chests and placed them in a notebook in order of our finish as we stumbled through the crowd.

"God bless you, Esther DuMont," Marilyn said, her eyes brimming as we found an open space near the medical tent to gather our wind.

The woman hugged me with a residual strength I didn't think she could possess. I hugged her back and shed a few tears of my own. A rotund, middle–aged man waddled towards us, and two plump children followed the man through the throng, their side–to–side wobble making them teeter like human versions of the Weeble people my niece Abby loves to play with.

"You did great, honey. I am so damn proud of you," the man said, planting a kiss on Marilyn's flushed cheek.

"Mommy, Mommy," the kids yelled, surrounding the woman with their arms, hugging her waist as if they'd been lost in the forest for days.

Marilyn stepped back from her family and pointed to me.

"I...she did it. I was...ready to quit. At twenty–four miles...couldn't make it up that last hill. This woman picked me up...literally...figuratively...and carried me home."

I extended my arms over my head to stretch out a kink in my back, but said nothing.

"Thank you ma'am," the man, whom I took for Marilyn's husband, said. "She's been working so hard. If she didn't finish, it would've killed her."

Before I could object, the man planted a sloppy wet kiss on my cheek and hugged me like I'd never been hugged before.

"It wasn't me. It was your wife. All I did was give her a little encouragement," I said, using my hands to gently create distance between us.

"Hamilton, you could at least introduce yourself and the kids to Miss DuMont."

The man looked sheepish.

"Sorry, ma'am. I'm Marilyn's husband, Hamilton – Hamilton Samuels. These two scallywags are Moses and Ruth."

Is someone trying to tell me something? I thought. *More Biblical references.*

"Pleased to meet you."

The awkwardness of the moment, of what would happen next – whether they'd invite me to lunch, or give me their phone number and invite me to visit them in their home, or whatever, for my small kindness – was dispelled when a familiar figure approached.

"Esther, I am so glad to see you," Mason Erickson said softly as he cleared the crowd and stood beside me.

FIFTY-TWO

We walked beneath a gloaming sky, our hands at our sides and our attitudes nonchalant and noncommittal. That is to say, there was an air of impermanence about us in the way we carried ourselves and acted towards one another, and it was neither real nor truthful. I think we both knew that we were simply posturing.

When I looked up and saw Mason Erickson at the finish line of the marathon, my first impulse was to do what I'd done on the main street of Guthrie Center: run. But I was so winded and sore that I simply held my ground and stared at the man who had saved my life.

"Mason...."

Mason had smiled. He hesitated, as if unsure of whether he should approach me or not. Thankfully, his apprehension passed.

"Great run," he said.

"Thanks."

Awkward doesn't begin to describe what I felt at that moment. The last time I'd last laid eyes on Mason, I'd been standing on the downtown sidewalk of his hometown, scrutinizing him, his ex–wife and their child through the dirty window of a diner. Ashamed at my naiveté, I'd turned on my heels and fled without so much as a word.

But he doesn't know that, I surmised. *He's here now. Don't blow this!*

My underarms were drenched with sweat and, despite the growing warmth of the day, my body was beginning to chill. My teeth chattered. Lilith came to my rescue. She approached with a silver space blanket hanging over one arm – one of several hundred stacked in front of the medical tent for use by the runners. She unfolded the blanket and slipped the foil garment over my shoulders.

"Hello, Mr. Erickson," Lilith said cooly.

"Nice to see you, Mrs. Culver. Your sister here ran a heck of a race."

Lilith gave me a hug.

"Yes she did. We are all *so* proud of her."

My eyes locked on Mason's. There was much I wanted to ask him, and so much I wanted to say, but serious conversation between us would have to wait. Out of the corner of my eye, I saw Mom and Dad, Richard and Abby, Billy and April, and Amy and Sarah approaching. Sarah had a medal hanging from a ribbon around her neck. As she moved closer, I could see that the medallion was bronze.

"Wonderful run," Mom said as she hugged me with such force, I thought she'd break my spine.

It was a very foreign sensation. Mom's embrace brought me to an understanding that had eluded me since David's death. A vision of Mom, Lilly and I, in the kitchen. Lilly and I are ten or eleven years old. Mom is laughing. We're making Christmas cookies – cutouts, I think. Somehow, in the middle of what was surely a very serious enterprise, Mom dipped her hands into a bowl of white flour and lightly slapped first Lil, then me, in the face, causing clouds of flour to erupt into the warm air of the kitchen. I remember studying Mom, thinking she had gone nuts. Lilly had the same look on her face; an uncertainty of what was happening was etched strongly across her narrow features. Instinctively, I picked up a bowl of egg yolks. Slowly, very ceremoniously, like I was a tribal priestess participating in an ancient ritual, I dumped the slimy mess on top of Mom's head, the yolky glob sliding over her blond hair, pulled up as it was in a ponytail off her shoulders. Instantly, food was flying across the room. It was as if three nuts from an asylum were ransacking an institutional kitchen. When it was over, there was egg, flour, sugar, milk, nutmeg and assorted shades of food coloring splattered across the room. That's when Dad made his entrance, having driven home from Ashland on a weeknight to surprise us. But it wasn't *us* who were surprised when Dr. DuMont walked into the kitchen.

Someone capable of orchestrating a food fight with two little girls is someone who can forgive. I feel it. I feel forgiveness flowing through Mom's strong arms. I see it in her eyes. There is no reason to say the words. She knows it. I know it.

Dad didn't wait for Mom to end her embrace, but simply joined in, which was an immediate invitation for Abby to do the same. Our group hug lasted a few moments and drew nearly every ounce of breath from me.

"We are so damn proud of you," Dad whispered, kissing my sweaty cheek and patting me on the shoulder as he withdrew. There were tears, honest to goodness tears, pouring out of his eyes, something that occurred about as often as a full solar eclipse.

"You run slow," Abby observed, her blue eyes reflecting the sun, her head cocked to one side in concentrated scrutiny of her auntie.

Everyone laughed and when I heard Mason's distinctive chuckle, I realized he had been left out of the camaraderie.

"Mason, come on over here."

He reluctantly stepped closer.

I turned to my family. "You all remember Mason Erickson, my friend from Iowa? He drove all the way from Guthrie Center to see me run, isn't that right?"

Mason nodded. I reintroduced him to my family despite the fact my family had met Mason at the graduation ceremony. The scrutiny Mom gave the man was something; her hazel irises fairly burned their mark on the Iowan's face. Thankfully, Dad's demeanor more than made up for Mom's directness.

"Nice to see you again, Mr. Erickson," my father said in a non–threatening tone while offering his hand. "We're headed to the Rittenhouse for brunch. You're all welcome to join us," Dad added expansively to everyone within earshot.

"I'd like that."

Mason's response was like his personality: quiet and reflective. Amy, on the other hand, was unable to restrain herself. As I introduced her and Sarah Miles to Mason, my girlfriend broke free of her partner and nearly knocked me to the ground with her exuberance.

"You are awesome," she whispered into my ear as she pulled our bodies together and gave me a soft, warm kiss on my right ear. "And he is really, really cute."

I felt my face burn from embarrassment. I bowed my neck so as to conceal the two of us in my dreads, the thick fibers smelling of sweat and rain.

"You think so?"

"I *know* so!"

Our conversation, mere whispering inside my shaggy hair, was entirely private. As we embraced, Billy and April walked up. Billy patted me on my left hip. Amy moved aside.

"Great job. We'd like to take your Dad up on his offer for brunch, but we've got to get back to the kids. Mom's watching them. Are you up for the reunion?"

"I'll be there."

"Bring your suit, so I can toss you in the pool," Billy chided, referencing the fact that the site of the party, the community center, has a swimming pool.

"You best watch yourself around Esther," Lilith called out after the departing couple. "She'll whoop your ass."

"Lilith," Mom said disapprovingly.

"Butt," Lilly quickly corrected. "'She'll whoop your butt' is what I meant to say. Sorry."

My attention became fixed on the medal hanging around Sarah Myles's neck.

"Third place?"

The woman nodded shyly.

"She was with the woman from Winnipeg until that last hill. She just ran out of gas," Amy said, placing an arm around her companion's waist in a fashion that was discreet yet tender. "The Estonian was, like, a half–mile ahead. But the Canadian…my girl had a shot at second until that damn hill. Sorry, Mrs. DuMont – 'darn' hill."

Snickers.

"You ready for something to eat?" Dad asked.

I nodded.

"I need to go to the school and take a shower. I'll meet you at the Rittenhouse. Amy, you and Sarah will be there, right?"

"I'd never pass up spending some of Dr. DuMont's money," Amy said.

Dad laughed.

"Mason, you're coming, right?"

He nodded.

"Can someone give me a lift to the high school?"

"We're headed that way," Sarah Miles replied.

Standing beneath the warm water of the shower in the girls' locker room, I tried to keep from staring at Sarah's body; it was impossible. She was so dark – darker even than me – the color of coal from West Virginia, the place she called home; she was so tall, so statuesque. Her small breasts sat high on her narrow chest, the nipples black, pink and perfect; her tuft of intimate hair was thick but neatly trimmed; her eyes were closed and her chin thrust forward, causing warm water to cascade over her African beauty like molten silver poured into a jeweler's mold. I couldn't avoid gawking. Thankfully, I had the prescience of mind to avert my eyes when she reached for a bar of soap.

"You ran a good race," Sarah remarked in a quiet voice.

"I wanted to break four hours."

She raised one of her thin arms, the hair of the armpit unshaven, thick and curly in its natural state, and rubbed the bar of Ivory up and down the length of the limb.

"And you would have, if you hadn't stopped to help that woman."

How does she know that? She was miles ahead of me, finishing the race in two hours and thirty–two minutes – nearly two hours ahead of my paltry effort. How in hell does she know that?

"You're wondering how I know about it, right?"

Water danced across my scalp. I rinsed shampoo from my dreadlocks, my eyes closed tightly to avoid the sting, and nodded.

"Word gets around. One of the volunteers saw it, who told someone else who told someone else." Sarah paused as she rinsed off. "I was at the finish line with Amy, trying to figure out where I'd made mistakes along the way. I wanted to beat Christine Swaggle so damn bad; that Canadian ate my dust in nearly every 10,000–meter race we were in. But she got me good today. She's a great marathoner. Much better than I am at this point. And then there's that Estonian, Marta Manderheim. She's in her own world, running by herself in nearly every race."

Sarah's speech was the most I'd heard from her since meeting her, like someone had opened up a tap and let water pour out.

"You'll get the Estonian eventually," I said, turning off the shower and reaching for a towel.

It was then that I saw Sarah staring at my scars, though not in an unkind way. But she *was* staring.

"I'm sorry," she whispered as she too shut off the water and began to towel off. "It was rude of me to stare."

I shrugged. "I'm used to it. No apology necessary."

"Amy told me what happened."

Did she now. I wonder what Amy's version of that Labor Day picnic might be. Does she know more or less than I do, about what happened that day?

"It was a long time ago."

Sarah Myles and I left the shower area, towels wrapped around us, terrycloth shifting as we walked into the locker room to dress.

"Still, it must be a painful memory."

I tried to be nonchalant about the whole thing as I dried the thick ropes of hair hanging free of my head.

"It is."

Fast–forward to the Inn, where we all enjoyed a hearty meal. My father was taken with Mason, but Mom continued to discreetly measure the man; after Del, I guess she was being cautious. When the meal was over and Mason and I had survived our first public moment together, we took leave of each other. I accompanied my family to the island while Mason went off exploring the farms and orchards surrounding Bayfield.

You can take the farmer out of...

Later that evening, Mason and I walked the breakwater of the Bayfield Marina; the day was fading and the oranges, pinks and purples of the dusky sky were gorgeous and surreal above the emerald hillside rising behind the town. We'd done the obligatory class reunion walk–through. I'd talked to my classmates and their spouses and partners, and a number of assorted gatecrashers from other classes we'd gone to school with. My class had thirty–two graduates; thirty–one were present. The only member of the class of 1995 who was absent was Tina Miller; she'd died of breast cancer a week before the reunion. Tina had been a loud, stupid girl, someone I'd never liked all that much. I know I shouldn't speak ill of the dead, but it's the truth. Still, her passing put a damper on the evening. I felt it, and I'm sure Lilly did, too. We didn't talk about it, but the empty chair was there, as real as the multi–colored sky above Mason and me as we walked Bayfield's pier. Maybe the pall of Tina's death was omnipresent because she was so young, and she had left behind a husband and a little girl. Maybe it's just the nature of reunions themselves – a time for introspection and the taking of personal inventory. Whatever it was, Tina Miller's absence made a larger impression on me than her presence ever could have.

You live, then you die – what else is there?

All I'd vocalized to Mason was the fact that Tina was the only member of my class who had passed away. What I was mulling over in my mind, however, wasn't Tina Miller and the life she had so recently left – left for an unknown and unseen eternity – but something I'd noticed as Mason and I stood around the community pool watching Lilith and Richard dive in and out of the water in brilliantly colored swimming suits like two teenagers on their first date. What I noticed was this: Mason was drinking Sprite – not that I'd ever seen him drink alcohol. Our relationship up to that point, as I've explained, consisted of stolen moments at New Beginnings, a place completely devoid of libations, a few vividly embarrassing moments together in the front seat of his Ford, and a couple of isolated instances when I'd visited his farm with others from the treatment center. Why I noticed he wasn't drinking at the reunion is beyond me. But I did.

"Can I ask you something?"

We stopped on the breakwater and looked east, towards Madeline Island. LaPointe, the place I call home, was out there, across darkening water, hidden from view.

"Sure."

I didn't make eye contact. I fixed my eyes on a ferry churning towards us over flat water. The vessel's deck was loaded with vehicles, and small batches of passengers were wandering the confines of the boat, waving to folks walking on the boat docks, piers and the breakwater of Bayfield Harbor.

"You don't drink?"

Mason riveted his eyes on the near–distant island as he answered. "Used to. Don't anymore."

I mulled over his comment. "May I ask why?"

The dairy farmer stroked his chin. "I thought it best."

Oh, oh. He's got demons in his own personal closet of secrets, I thought. "How's that?" I asked.

Mason Erickson leaned against the concrete breakwater and, without so much as looking at me, said, "I thought it best, considering I've fallen in love with someone who appreciates sobriety."

Understand, by that time, we'd already covered my sorry visit to Guthrie Center and my cowardly retreat. Seems that one of the waitresses at the restaurant had seen me, plain as day, gawking at Mason, his ex–wife, and their little boy through the picture window. Seems that the waitress told Mason she'd seen me, but by the time he excused himself from the table and made it outside, onto the sidewalk, all he caught was a glimpse of me high-tailing it onto the Greyhound. He'd explained, when he and I walked from his room at Gruenke's earlier that evening – me dressed in my best short skirt and a gauze top, my bust suggested, my height reduced by the flat-soled sandals I wore to keep me from being taller than my date, and Mason dressed as Mason nearly always is when he goes to town, in Wrangler blue jeans, a short–sleeved polo shirt and freshly polished brown deck shoes, that Virginia and their son were in town for her father's funeral. When I'd seen them at the restaurant, they were simply having breakfast. The way Mason explained it, Virginia – or "Ginny," as he called her – felt the death of her father in a way that, despite the pain and sadness of it all, had done her some good.

"She grew up," was the way Mason put it. "It doesn't change the past, but since Edward's death, we've been able to talk like we never talked during our marriage. Jacob will be the better for it."

He must have sensed that I was becoming uncomfortable talking about his ex–wife.

"Like I said, it doesn't change what happened. It's just that we've got three lives to deal with...."

Three lives...his, his wife's and Jacob's, I thought.

"Mine, hers and ours together as parents. We'll never get back together – if that's what's bothering you – but we *are* parents and that's something that can only be improved by Ginny's sudden maturation."

Fallen in love with.

The words struck me like a thunderclap crashing on a hot summer's night as we stood silently watching the ferry pass by.

He's talking about me. About us. Love. But is love something I'm ready to declare? I don't know. Affection, yes. Respect, certainly. Passion?

227

Without a doubt. I'm so ready, so horny, I could rip those loose–fitting, straight–legged jeans off Mason Erickson out here, in the middle of Bayfield, step out of my mini skirt, and let him have his way with me. But love? That's beyond where I am, I'm afraid, at this point.

Now, I know what you're thinking: *Fickle girl. Chases after the man, tries to throw herself at him in his own hometown and now, when he makes a declaration of purpose – when he lays his heart on the table – she steps back and reconsiders her options.* But that's not how it was. I can't really explain it other than to say: my mind and my gut told me to move slowly, to take my time. After all, it had been less than a year since Delmont had passed, and in that year, I'd fought off the demons of methamphetamine, dedicated myself to becoming physically and mentally fit, and acquired a new purpose in my professional life by working with African women. What I saw there, what I'd learned, was enough to give one pause, regardless of the specters in one's past.

I told you earlier how I had devoured the books that Wanda Jones gave me. I also told you that one of the starkest, most intimate, most telling of those books, and the one that stayed with me with total clarity, was *Possessing the Secret of Joy*, the novel about female circumcision. Well, despite the greatness of Ms. Alice Walker's prose, until I actually saw the results of a village matriarch's handiwork, I had no real concept of what female circumcision entailed.

Hannah Ojakandi was the first patient I treated who had undergone the procedure. Hannah came to Minneapolis from Senegal as a political refugee, conversant only in her local language, Diolla, and French, the language of the colonial power that had once occupied and controlled her native land. She came to escape the fighting between separatist guerrillas and government troops. Bright and quick to learn, Hannah's English two years after her arrival was better than some folks I've met who claim to be American–born. Short, squat and powdery brown, like a fresh cocoa, she wore her coarse hair tight and close, loved to display the gold jewelry she'd inherited from her grandmother, and dressed in colorful African patterns. When Doctor Thomas, the physician who runs the Clinic, called me into the examination room after the Certified Nursing Assistant, Olivia Pratt, had taken Hannah's vital signs, history, and the like, I was immediately taken by Hannah's calm resolve and lack of recrimination over what she'd endured as a ten–year–old girl at the hands of her mother's sister.

I'll not describe here what I saw during my examination of Hannah. To do so would be to invade her privacy unnecessarily. You can read elsewhere detailed descriptions of what all is involved in an infibulation, the most destructive form of the procedure. But what I will say is this: there was nothing left down there that bore any resemblance to adult female genitalia

228

that I've ever seen. It was shocking, horrific, and disgusting – and it was all done by another woman who had professed to love Hannah.

Now, my immediate reaction – as would be the reaction of any sane American woman of any color – was one of utter horror, then rage. But, under the careful tutelage of Dr. Thomas, Miss Pratt, and the others who worked at the Clinic, I began to understand the cultural differences between my world and Hannah's. Once I recognized that we come from two very different cultures, I was able to put aside my personal opinion and help Hannah begin to heal emotionally from the trauma her young body had sustained.

During the short time I worked at the Clinic, I was able to counsel and refer Hannah and a half–dozen other women to a plastic surgeon who donated her time to perform corrective procedures. Those procedures gave back to the women their sexual identities and, in nearly every case – as Ms. Walker so aptly observed in her book – the ability to experience sexual joy.

Working with these women, I began to comprehend (I think) why God had dragged me through the experiences I'd endured. I was prepared, having lived through personal tragedy, to counsel and advise these African women who'd suffered at the hands of people they loved.

But again, I digress.

My mind weighed Mason Erickson's declaration. I pondered it fully, but I didn't know how to respond to Mason's profession of love.

Before I could formulate a reply, I saw Billy Cadotte, a manila envelope in hand, walking towards us on the breakwater.

"Hey," I said plaintively.

I'm quite sure Mason didn't appreciate Billy's intrusion, especially after what he'd just said to me, but if Mason was upset, he contained himself.

"This is for you. I meant to give it to you earlier."

Billy handed me the envelope.

"What is it?" I asked, accepting the package, the paper smooth and dry in my sweaty palms.

"Some old paperwork, from when David passed away. From the investigation."

My eyes narrowed; I'm certain that my frown was visible to both men. The story of that day wasn't one I'd shared freely with Mason. He knew some of what had taken place: how David and I both ended up on fire, how David died and I hadn't. But the details of that day and my recovery – well, I hadn't seen any reason to go into them with Mason yet. That could wait until something larger came of our connection.

"Where'd you get this?"

Billy shifted his weight inside his shiny black rattlesnake skin cowboy boots and folded his arms nervously across his chest before answering.

"We're converting old records to digital. We're getting rid of boxes stored in the basement of the courthouse. Got no need for these; they've already been scanned. Thought you might want them."

My hands massaged the paper as I contemplated whether I really wanted to know what was inside the envelope.

"Thanks." My response was tentative. My mouth was suddenly dry; my voice, strained.

"I'd best get back to April," Billy replied. "I think she's had a few too many glasses of wine. You never know: she might be skinny–dipping in the pool by now."

We all grinned, but the awkwardness of the moment was clear, despite the levity. Billy turned on his heels and walked back towards shore. I drew the envelope into my chest, my shoulders shaking. My eyes closed as I faced fear rising inside me.

What is in this? What details, facts and opinions are contained in these papers that I don't already know? I should toss the whole lot over the wall and into the water. Or better yet, I should burn it like David and I were burned. What good does this serve? What use is this to me or anyone else?

"You okay?"

Mason's voice was calming. I nodded and turned towards him, my eyes slightly moist. My arms had fallen to my sides and the package was now tight to my left hip – the hip that bears evidence of that Labor Day.

"Could we get a cup of coffee?" I asked quietly.

Mason's eyes displayed sympathy. He hugged me. The embrace conveyed this message: *I'll wait. You take your time. I'll be here.*

FIFTY-THREE

What the documents said. You've probably already guessed what they said, if you've been reading this and paying attention. God Bless Billy Cadotte. God Bless him, even though he left me lying in a hospital bed in Duluth eleven years ago to take up with the girl who would become his wife. Rather than burden you with the entire contents of the envelope, I'll let you read what was on the one piece of paper that meant something.

Bayfield County Sheriff's Department
Bayfield County Courthouse
Washburn, Wisconsin

To: Investigator Gene Stampf
From: Deputy Edward Walters
Re: Death of David DuMont (DOB - May 25, 1993)
ICR No.: BAY20352503
Date of Incident: September 5, 1994
Date of Report: November 10, 1994
Date of Interview: September 6, 1994

Supplemental Investigative Report
On September 6, 1994, I, Deputy Walters, conducted a follow-up interview with a person of interest (witness): Kevin Delmore (K. Delmore; DOB - February 2, 1978), 223 Ambrose Lane, Bayfield Wisconsin. K. Delmore was one of the juveniles at the party held at the DuMont home on Madeline Island where the injuries to David DuMont and Esther DuMont (DOB - April 4, 1977) occurred. Initial investigation into the incident done by Deputy Roger Crow revealed that Esther DuMont (E. DuMont)

inadvertently left a gasoline canister used to ignite a charcoal grill on the back patio at the DuMont residence, in an area accessible to her young brother David. Deputy Crow's conclusion, after interviewing those in attendance at the party (with the exception of E. DuMont, who was unable to speak to authorities due to her injuries, and K. Delmore) was that E. DuMont used gasoline to ignite the fire and returned the canister to the basement of the home, and that David DuMont (D. DuMont) found the canister and spilled gasoline in the basement of the home. The pilot light of the home's liquid propane hot water tank then ignited the gasoline fumes, causing the fire and the resulting injuries, ultimately culminating in D. DuMont's death.

Before closing the file, I determined that K. Delmore, the only guest who had not been interviewed (he was out of the area when previous interviews were conducted), needed to make a statement. I contacted K. Delmore's parents and arranged to meet their son at the Bayfield Police Department on September 6.

After explaining to the parents and K. Delmore that he was not in trouble, not in custody and free to leave at any time, K. Delmore agreed to speak with me. I did not tape record the interview.

K. Delmore's statement agrees with those of the other witnesses, except as to one point. K. Delmore has a clear recollection from when he was sitting on a chair on the DuMont patio, watching E. DuMont light the charcoal. E. DuMont started the charcoal and then returned the gasoline canister to the shelving in the walk–in portion of the home's basement. This scenario differs from a statement given by Miss Lilith DuMont (L. DuMont; DOB - April 4, 1977), E. DuMont's twin sister.

In addition, K. Delmore was quite certain that, after starting the grill, E. DuMont then went inside the house. While E. DuMont was inside, L. DuMont came onto the patio. K. Delmore recalls very clearly that, at that time, the fire in the grill had extinguished itself and that, in response, L. DuMont walked into the basement, retrieved the gasoline can and reignited the grill. Whether or not L. DuMont returned the canister of gasoline to the shelf, or left it within reach of the child, K. Delmore is unable to say, as he left the patio just as L. DuMont was returning the gasoline to the basement of the home.

While no other witness has indicated that L. DuMont was the last person to use the gasoline canister, K. Delmore has a very clear recollection of the day's events. It is highly likely, in this officer's opinion, that L. DuMont, and not E. DuMont, was negligent in not returning the gasoline canister back to a safe place, resulting in the fire, the injury to E. DuMont and the death of David DuMont. Whether there is a sufficient factual basis to bring charges against L. DuMont for criminal negligence *resulting in injury and/or death is for the District Attorney's Office to determine.*

D.D.W.

There was also a handwritten note at the bottom of the report. The note, apparently written by the District Attorney, consisted of four words in cursive: "No Probable Cause Found" followed by an indecipherable signature, presumably that of the D.A, with the date "11/14/94" scrawled in the same poor penmanship.

You might want to know what I was thinking as Mason and I sat in a booth in a Bayfield coffee shop after I read the contents of the envelope. You might get the idea that, having carried with me the shame, guilt and responsibility of David's death, only to discover that my beloved twin sister was to blame – and likely knew she was to blame, and never said one damn word of recompense to me – I was ready to knock her on her ass. But I wasn't. That wasn't at all what I felt when I finished reading the file Billy Cadotte had given to me.

Like I told you before, I had had an inkling that I wasn't the one at fault. So the report wasn't, in itself, earth–shattering. But I won't lie: for an instant, as I slid the documents back into the envelope, I considered going back to my class reunion and causing a scene. That notion faded as quickly as it formed.

What the hell good would that do? It's years after the fact. Even if folks could be convinced to believe what's in these papers, what's the end result? Will it bring David back from the dead? Will it rid me of my scars?

"What's all that stuff say?"

Mason's question broke up my internal dialogue. I looked up from the table, my hands tight around the coffee mug that sat on the oak planking between us. I studied the man sitting across from me. Like I said, there was simply no reason to change history. I'd borne the cross of David's death for so long, I was comfortable in the role I'd been chosen to fill. Not that I was happy with my lot – not at all. But I could manage the part, and had managed the part, for the whole of my adult life. Changing roles with Lil at that point would have done harm to Lilith and no good for me. In a split second, I made the decision you already know I made. I kept my big mouth shut.

"Just copies of the sheriff's report, legal papers, about the fire and David and all. There's nothing worth looking at in here, nothing that changes what you already know."

Granted, what he knew wasn't all that much – just the basics: we'd had a party, there was a grill, I'd used gas, I hadn't put it away, and there was an accident. I lost a brother and some skin. Lots of skin. That was about it.

"Okay."

You see, right there was the reason I considered making love to Mason Erickson the night of my ten–year high school reunion. Other men might have prodded, pushed, cajoled and otherwise dug at me to get more, to discover bits and pieces of privacy I didn't want to divulge. Not Mason. He looked at me and immediately understood that the discussion was over.

FIFTY-FOUR

We went back to the reunion, talked to a few people, had a few more soft drinks, and then, as the DJ played "With or Without You" by U2, a lovely song that is nigh impossible to dance to, we decided to head back to Room No. 1 at Gruenke's First Street Restaurant and Inn, three blocks away from the Bayfield Community Center. Room No. 1 faces east, which means its windows have a nice view of Bayfield Harbor and the island. When Mason and I climbed the rickety staircase inside that historic building, you might think I was contemplating the ethics and morality of what we were about to do. Not so. I was okay, definitely okay, with the fact that we were going to be intimate. The thought of sex wasn't bothering me a bit, not a lick. What was concerning me was that I couldn't remember if Mom was working that evening or not. I felt a huge weight lift from my shoulders when I realized that Mom had the night off.

Until that night, I'd never been upstairs from the restaurant or in any of the sleeping rooms. Mason's room was decorated with Victorian–style wallpaper, antiques and reproductions of paintings appropriate for the late 19th century. With the door to his room open, I stood at the threshold, my body all a twitter and my heart racing, as Mason withdrew the key from the lock. Without speaking, he drew me from the brightly–lit hallway into muted dark. Once Mason shut the door, the only light in the room was the soft glow of streetlamps outside the building filtered through drawn curtains. I entered Mason's room willingly and with longing. I entered his room hopeful that we were about to embark on something that would, to use an oft repeated phrase, "float my boat."

Mason didn't say anything as he stood toe to toe with me in the dark. I was still holding the envelope from Billy Cadotte in my left hand as we considered where we were headed, and what we were about to do. I won't fudge the truth and tell you I wasn't scared. I was. Thoughts – suspicions, really – rambled through my brain as we stood next to each other in silence.

So is this, like, an experiment? I asked him silently. *Your attempt to find out what it feels like to make love to a black woman? I know you're curious. You want to know if all the rumors and hoopla about black women and their lovemaking abilities ring true. Am I right? Sure I am.*

Del, for all his integrated upbringing, wanted to know. And Lord, he surely found out! Is that so bad, to want to know and experience something different? Is our being here something based on love, with a dash of curiosity thrown into the mix for good measure? Does it really matter, Mason?

The lights are low. Our eyes are riveted on each other.

Your upper lip is quivering. My heart is racing. I hope you can't hear it. That I'm as ready and eager as you are for this thing to happen, well, that's not something "good girls" advertise. We're teetering on the brink, and I think we both know where this night is headed. I'm all right with that. Are you? Sure you are. Just look at you. What the hell are we waiting for?

I'd like to tell you that Mason and I disrobed and became entwined in the slow, timeless and tasteful manner of an old movie – you know, the kind that once made our grandmothers blush. But that would be a lie. Once the two of us got over the initial shock of being alone, there wasn't much choreographed or elegant about the way we shed our clothes. Not that Mason ripped my skirt and blouse off me like a kid opening a birthday present. It wasn't quite that bad. He'd obviously learned that the way to a woman's heart involves tenderness, patience and the like. Whether he got that from bedding Virginia or came to it before they ever hooked up is a secret only he can tell. It wasn't that we were hasty about our disrobing. We were simply more pragmatic than poetic.

For the record, once I kicked off my sandals and tossed them cavalierly into a corner, where they landed with a distinct and reassuring thud, and rid myself of the paperwork in my left hand, Mason got busy pulling my panties down my legs with two strong hands, his fingers massaging and caressing my thighs, knees and calves along the way. He was a little quicker with that move than I would have liked. I mean, after feeling virtually nothing for a year, a little more deliberation at each step of the process would have been appreciated, if you know what I mean. When his hands met my ankles, he was careful not to snag my underwear on the gold bracelet I was wearing on my right ankle, which hung just below the tattoo I'd suffered through when Del and I first got together. Mason paused at the rose etched into my skin and kissed it with soft lips. Again, further hesitation on his part would have been perfect. What he did was merely nice.

When he stood up, our bodies mashed together; my heat was clearly rising, and his maleness was at full attention and demanding through the well-worn denim of his blue jeans. My chest flattened against his thick frame, and his fingers found the roundness of my bottom as he lifted me off the floor. My eyes, if you can believe it, were closed so tightly I thought I'd shut off the blood to my brain. It wasn't like I wanted to avoid seeing Mason. No, not at all. I was simply carried away, lost in a corner of myself I hadn't visited for a very, very long time.

It was only a matter of seconds before he had my blouse off and my bra undone. The undergarment eventually came to rest alongside my flimsy top on the hardwood floor of the rented room, the cups of the bra humped up slightly, their fabric shiny in the light cast into the room from outside. Mason caressed my breasts, their newly released weight responding to gravity, my excitement revealed in my nipples, even the left one. (He was able to make something happen there despite the scarring.)

My fingers undid his belt buckle. I pulled franticly on the metal tab of his zipper to release tension. Mason's jeans slid to the floor and clumped around his ankles. He was wearing jockeys, gray and tight to his broad thighs, the pouch of the underwear full and strained. He stepped out of the pile of denim surrounding his feet and attended to me. I opened my eyes. Even in the dim light of the room, it was clear that Mason's body was virtually hairless. Blond wisps and tufts covered his armpits, his chest, his legs, his wrists. The hair was soft, like goose down, and nearly invisible. The contrast of his body hair to my own was bold and stimulating. I like blonds; I think I've told you that. I think the contrast between us also intrigued him. Why else do you suppose he reached up and stroked my dreadlocks with such patience, such reverence?

There were two beds in the room – a queen sized and a single. Feeling a bit rushed, I let Mason know, in subtle ways, that slow is better. I managed to direct the two of us to the larger bed. As my bare rump met cool linen, I realized we'd not spoken. Not one endearment, not one nasty word in preparation for what was to come. I thought about saying something, but decided against it. The moment seemed better served by silence.

We climbed into bed, the quilt folded back to expose tangerine sheets. Mason was still in his underwear; me in the altogether. We lay side by side, facing each other. He kissed me. It wasn't one of those munch–your–mouth and slam–your–tongue kisses; it was slow, this time, exactly at the pace I liked, and soft. *Oh, it was so soft.* Like the touch of a warm summer breeze on your cheek.

I'm not aggressive in bed but I'm also not a sack of flour that a man can simply enter and exit according to his needs. For me. the desire for sex,

237

the desire to become one, is about the coming together of souls, that brief moment when, if everything goes exactly right (an iffy proposition, I'll grant you), both male and female libidos coincide and reach climax in unison. Why, when it happens so infrequently, we humans insist upon mutual orgasm as the gold standard of success, I can't explain; but when it happens, sweet Jesus, there is (drug–induced couplings aside) nothing like it on earth. That had been my experience, anyway, and it was what I was striving for on that July night last year in the work–hardened arms of Mason Erickson, in a tiny room above Gruenke's Restaurant. My scars were showing, my breath was short, my eyes were wide open, the room was hot and the air was still. Sweat beaded on my forehead and my dreads hid the true joy spreading across my face. Union. *I was seeking union with another human being.* Damned if we didn't almost achieve it.

In the morning, after I'd used the shared bathroom down the hall and climbed back under the covers to nestle next to the man who'd made love to me, I thought it all through. Why I was there, with someone whom I'd met in my rehabilitation program, naked, his semen collected in latex and sitting on the nightstand next to the bed. I thought big thoughts and sought to understand my own motivations, all while his broad back faced me, with his face turned towards the flowered wallpaper.

What are we doing? I asked myself as I removed my earrings, my earlobes sore from carrying their weight. I held the hoops in my right hand, my fingernails painted shiny blood red (Lilith's doing) before placing the jewelry on the nightstand. *What is he thinking? I sure as hell don't know. What about seeing each other once this reunion thing is over? He lives five hours away. He's from a world, a place, that isn't mine. It's bad enough I'm stuck in Minneapolis, a city I don't understand, a place where ponds are considered lakes and where folks think that Bayfield is located somewhere above the Arctic Circle. Not to mention what the blacks I've met say about where I come from: no black folks, no black culture, no tribal roots. That's what they say dismissively about where I'm from. But that's not right. My roots are in northwestern Wisconsin. It's where I'm from, and where I belong. I am black. I am white. Both together. This is my home – but it isn't Mason Erickson's home. He's a farm boy from Iowa. How is this all going to work?*

My eyes stared at the textured ceiling.

Orange peel. That's what Dad calls the technique, because of the way the troweled plaster hardens in swirls. Dad had contractors remodel Lilly's and my bedrooms when we were little. The contractors had used the same technique. I'd stared at the engaging pattern for hours as a kid, lying on my back in bed, thinking other big thoughts.

Mason's satisfied breathing prompting me to consider the fact that Lil and I had been raised as Midwestern girls. It's not so unusual in the world I come from, I guess – or for the rest of America, when you think it through. Consider all the little black, Asian and other colored babies who get adopted by well–meaning suburban white couples. These kids become gentrified – Caucasianified, if you will (yes, I made that word up) – despite their parents' best efforts to instill a sense of culture and ethnicity in them. These adopted kids spend 99.9 percent of their time acting white, and in that respect, they're a lot like Lilly and me. I had more to consider on the subject, but my train of thought was interrupted.

"Good morning," Mason said, his thick yellow hair standing nearly stick–straight, our shared musky odor apparent as he shifted his body beneath the bedcovers. "How are you?"

I giggled.

"What?"

I clasped my right hand over my mouth to prevent an outright laugh. Mason caught a glimpse of himself in a mirror across the room and grinned. It was obvious from the sparkle in his icy blue eyes that he wasn't upset with me for guffawing at his hair.

"How are you feeling?"

How indeed? How am I? I'll tell you, Mr. Erickson. I am spent. I am sated. I am happy. But I'm also confused – confused as to where we are going with this intimacy thing. Confused about what I want from you, beyond the sex and the holding and the touching.

Of course, I didn't say these things to my lover. I simply smiled and said: "I'm hungry."

FIFTY-FIVE

Dairy farmers don't take vacations, because asking a neighbor to mind your farm for more than a day or two isn't realistic. Neighbors have their own herds and don't have time to baby–sit someone else's cows. We had a nice breakfast but didn't touch on much of importance before Mason fired up his Ford F–250 to leave. Oh sure, he kissed me. Real pleasant it was, too: a long meeting of lips as we stood outside the driver's door of his pick–up truck and held each other tight. The embrace was a little more public than I might have liked, given the internal turmoil I was going through. But the embrace was expected: we'd just been together for the first time, after all. There was much I wanted to explore and examine about Mason's perceptions of "us," but that would have to wait. Mason's cows had to be attended to.

I'll spare you most of the dialogue that happened between Lilly and me when I returned to the island. Suffice to say, she wouldn't let my evening away from home die a natural death. She had to tease, cajole and prod, like an angry fire ant getting after your toes at a picnic, until I finally tossed her raggedy ass on her bed and held her down, giving her the old "Chinese finger thump" that I used on her when we were kids.

"Stop it," she whined, my knees pinning her arms to the quilt. Her legs dangled off the edge of the bed, and her feet were kicking empty air.

"Not until you stop going on and on about Mason and me."

She was having a hard time breathing as I thumped her breastbone, the flimsy bra she wore insufficient to contain her breasts.

"You rode that pony, didn't you, Es? Rode him good and long and hard. Where'd you do it? In his truck? Tell me you didn't screw that farm boy in the cab of his pick–up truck," she giggled.

I didn't answer my goofy sister. I simply thumped harder.

"Hey, that hurts! I was only teasing. I'll shut up. Really – I will."

240

I stopped pressing fingers to bone, but I continued to hold her down.

"Let me tell you something, Missy," I said in the worst imitation of a household servant from an old movie I could muster, "Mason Erickson is one sweet love. 'Bout that subject, I ain't sayin' no more. As God is my witness, you best lay off or I'll slap your skinny ass back down and hurt you for real."

Lilly's deep brown eyes turned to kindness. I eased off her and sat on the edge of her bed as she adjusted her bra and stood up.

"For real?"

"For real. He's one patient and kind man."

"Seems a little thick around the middle for your taste. A little short and too square, if you know what I mean."

I smiled. I wasn't really interested in revealing details, but I knew I had to toss her a bone to shut her up. Otherwise, she'd dive right back into the teasing and I'd have to lay her out to get her to stop.

"He's got big hands."

Lil smiled. "*Oh.*"

My life returned to its routine. My new apartment was a block off Lyndale, in the Uptown neighborhood of Minneapolis, just two blocks from the place Delmont Benson and I had once called home. I was living on the third floor. The rent was high, but the place was right on the bus line. A grocery store and a pharmacy were right down the street. Lake of the Isles was five blocks away – a place to go running, and a place to find peace and quiet. Throughout July and August, when the humidity rose and the temperature climbed, I sweated sheets riding the bus to and from work at the Metropolitan African Women's Clinic. My work clothes – the pale green nursing uniforms, the slacks and matching tops I wore over clean white cotton men's undershirts to absorb the sweat rolling off my skin – were wringing wet by the time I got home. I had no air conditioning in my apartment, so I took two showers a day. I had little choice if I didn't want to smell like a dead fish in a plastic bag. (Okay, maybe that's a bit of an exaggeration, but you get my point.) My life consisted of working, meeting girls from the Clinic on the weekends for lunch and shopping, running five miles every morning before my morning shower, and trying hard to make sense out of whatever was going on between Mason Erickson and me.

You might think that, having finally achieved a physical connection that seemed, at least to me – and I think, from his reaction, to Mason as well – mutually satisfactory, we'd figure out a way to be together, or at least get together. But the distance and the cows proved to be problematic. A couple of times, I boarded the bus and met Mason in Guthrie Center. We had some sweet moments in his old brass bed. And on his couch. And in the hammock in the screen porch off the kitchen of his old rambling farmhouse, set against the shimmering green corn stalks and soybeans of his farm. We connected, we did, in those brief interludes. And we talked.

As much as I could pull from the quiet Norwegian when we were together, I came to understand that, as I had hoped and prayed, I wasn't simply some whim, some experiment in interracial dating. Granted, I was his first black woman, but that didn't seem to make much of an impression on Mason. I was simply someone he loved. Period. End of discussion. He truly and honestly, so far as I could tell, never really gave my race serious consideration.

As a black woman, even though I "feel" white in many ways, I know better. Incidents I've suffered through in my life, some of which I've disclosed in this memoir, have left their mark on me. Even though such experiences haven't occurred all that often, they did happen. Given such history, I was prepared to deal with Mason suddenly discovering that I wasn't Norwegian, but Mason gave no indications or hints that my skin pigmentation was an issue.

My understanding of our circumstances, as transitory and illusory as they were, was different from that of Emma's, the protagonist in *The Professor's Daughter*, the novel I was then reading. Emma, by running off to Brazil to find a place that would accept her mixed heritage, gave up – gave up on herself, on her place in the world, and on her family. That wasn't something I was prepared to do: play the coward. I talked to Mason about the story, and tried to get him to read it, but it didn't take. Men! I learned with Del that men rarely read fiction and when they do, if bombs aren't exploding, cars aren't crashing, or serious blood isn't being spilled, they're not interested. Non–fiction, like biographies and histories, are books a guy like Mason will crack open and read – but a literary novel like *The Professor's Daughter*? Forget it. I loaned him my copy of the book, a copy I'd bought in a funky little Duluth bookstore, Northern Lights, on my way back to Minneapolis after running the marathon. I saw the novel sitting on Mason's nightstand, a bookmark stuck in the same place, over the summer. I finally asked Mason if he was ever going to finish the damn thing. He admitted he wouldn't, so I reclaimed it. Despite the fact that Mason didn't finish the story, we did talk about the racial components of Emma's journey of self–discovery, and I was comfortable in the knowledge that Mason was seeing me – and bedding me – for love, and not as part of some weird sociological experiment.

Outside of my occasional visits to Iowa, we relied on the telephone, email and instant messaging to stay involved. Once or twice I tried to connect with Mason the old–fashioned way, via the United States Postal Service. I'd write a two– or three–page letter, gushy and juicy with affection, and what would I get in return? A telephone call. So I gave up writing letters and let modern love take its course.

Right here, I should stop and tell you what happened before I got that damned phone call from Lilly. It was early September, and Hurricane Katrina had already happened. I was pissed off at Condoleezza for ignoring her black brothers and sisters trapped in New Orleans after the storm cleared. Instead of helping, she was off shopping (that's what I heard, anyway) – spending money on shoes at some posh store while the people of New Orleans struggled in hundred–degree heat without food, water or adequate shelter. I expected a fly–over from the President; I mean, in spite of his fake Texas drawl, his photo–op wood splitting and his pretense of being a common man, he's an East Coast patrician, born and bred. So I didn't have any illusions that George W. Bush would actually understand or care about the plight of poor folks who lost their homes in Louisiana and Mississippi. But Condi? A smart, educated black woman from the Deep South? I surely expected her to put on a pair of blue jeans and work boots and wade in the floodwaters to help. Hell, even Sean Penn did that much. Anyway, it was as I was fuming over Ms. Rice's betrayal of her people that I had my own little (near) disaster.

I was cleaning out my junk drawer in the kitchen. Exterminators had just fumigated the building for roaches. (How I hate roaches!) I'm okay with ants and bees and even spiders, but ugly beetles crawling in and out of my bread drawer? No thank you! I'd never even seen a cockroach until I lived with Del. The basement apartment beneath the bakery was constantly sprayed for them, but the evolutionary marvels that they are, the bugs always won. Well, at least in my new place, the spraying did some good; it got rid of the bugs for a while. Anyway, again I digress. I was inventorying my catch–all junk drawer, when I came across the envelope Billy had given me. I won't lie and tell you I didn't reread Deputy Walters's report. I did. Several times. But once I had my fill of it, once the memories were dredged up to the point of causing nauseating sadness, I knew what needed to be done.

There's no reason to keep this around. Sure, it's stored somewhere, in some computer. And some folks besides me – Billy, Deputy Walters and maybe a couple other cops – might remember the details. But Lilly doesn't know, and there's no point in saving this.

It was a tad stupid of me to burn the papers in my kitchen garbage can. You see, I forgot about the smoke detector. When the device went off, the piercing scream nearly broke my eardrums. I scatted across the linoleum, grabbed the wastebasket, ran out the back door, and tossed the smoldering mess onto the back lawn of the place, grateful that the complex didn't have a sprinkler system.

That was the day Lilly called. Like I said, it was early September, just after Labor Day – a holiday I should have spent with my family but which I'd instead spent with Mason in Iowa. It was under the starry Iowa night that I finally told Mason, when he turned to kiss me, that I was falling for him. I didn't blurt it out, nor did I use the "L" word – though I did come pretty darn close. So, when Lilly called a few days later, her voice quaking and upset clearly heard in her words, I was still in a generous mood, ready to take on whatever troubles she might need to unload. Even so, what she had to say wasn't something I was ready to hear.

FIFTY-SIX

"I don't know what to do," my sister began, sobs interfering with her speech.

"How so?"

There was a period of deep breathing and more crying before Lil resumed.

"Father Michaels."

"Thomas Michaels?"

"Ah huh."

"What about him?"

I was hoping that Lilly wasn't about to tell me she'd run into the priest and that, through some weird vortex of passion, they'd reconnected.

"He's here."

There wasn't much I could glean from that statement. I mean, was he "here," as in at her doorstep with a bouquet of roses, ready to declare his undying love? Or was he "here" in the Twin Cities? What did she mean?

"Where?"

"In Lakeville."

"He lives there?"

"Uh huh."

I tried to take in the implications of it all.

"Why's that a reason to get upset? I mean, Lakeville's a big place. Surely, you won't bump into each other all that much. And if you do, do you think he'll even remember you?"

I knew when I said that last part, I wasn't helping my sister at all. She'd become pregnant by the priest just after her eighteenth birthday, and she's a stunningly attractive young woman besides.

"Sorry. Of course he'd remember you. How stupid of me."

"It's worse than that."

"How's that?"

There was static on the line. I was using a remote phone – one that often goes dead because I forget to put the handset back on its charger when I'm through talking. The noise cleared. My sister's voice fell to a whisper.

"He's been assigned to *my church* – as the priest–in–charge – by Archbishop Flynn. They say that it's the final step to becoming a bishop in another diocese."

My throat clenched. I couldn't swallow. I understood my sister's despair.

"You've *got* to be kidding me."

"I'm not."

More silence.

"Es?"

"Yes?"

"What am I going to do? I can't confess my sins to *him*."

No shit, I thought.

"Why don't you switch churches? I'm sure Richard will understand."

Lilith wailed.

"I can't," Lilith finally whispered as she regained a semblance of composure.

"Why not?"

"Because."

"How so?"

"Richard doesn't know. I never told him. He's such a strict Catholic, I'm not sure he could love a woman who had had an affair with a priest, much less an abortion."

Shit.

Lilly waited for me to reply. I had no answers; no easy solution to her predicament popped into my head.

"Let me think about it. There must be some way we can spare you from having to tell Richard."

Lilly whimpered. "What other choice do I have?"

I dumped my shift at the Clinic; I needed a short break anyway. I was working with the poor, many of whom were newly immigrated, some of whom were abused. That can wear you down. Many of the women I saw retained little in the way of spirit or hope. Some, like Hannah, were different: in spite of all that life had hurled at them, they still maintained dignity and grace. Mostly, I heard sad tales about the way women were abused by their men – men who had given them diseases or impregnated them, and then cast them aside like damaged goods once their bellies started to round and the sex was no longer sweet. Hearing such stories day after day after day from my patients was disheartening, to say the least. Is it any wonder I welcomed the chance to take a day off, despite the complexity of my errand?

I hailed a cab to St. Paul – to St. Paul's Cathedral, more precisely, where Father Thomas Michaels was posted as assistant pastor, pending his elevation to pastor of All Saints Church, Lakeville. I didn't tell Lilly what I was planning to do because, quite frankly, it would have shocked her sensibilities. I was dressed in my nicest navy blue skirt and powder blue blouse. My hair was shorn to the scalp (upkeep of the dreadlocks having proved too taxing during the summer heat), and I was wearing a fairly sedate set of black pumps, consistent with the maturity and professionalism my mission required. When the taxi stopped in front of the cathedral, the structure's copper dome dominating the skyline of St. Paul, I felt my stomach begin to flip.

Do I have any idea what I'm doing?

"Somethin' wrong Miss?" the cabbie asked, looking at me in the rear–view mirror.

Bile rose from my stomach. I covered my mouth with my left hand.

"Will you wait? I shouldn't be more than a half–hour or so." The nausea passed and I climbed out of the car.

"I have to charge you for the time."

"I understand. Please wait. I won't be long."

I began considering my sister's predicament after I hung up the phone, following her tearful call. I continued mulling over a plan of action the next day as I rode the bus to work. My original idea didn't seem doable: confronting an archbishop with a ten–year–old tale of love and lust between a priest and a parishioner didn't seem plausible, and would likely, given my sister's part in the sorry episode, lead only to trouble for her. True, Archbishop Flynn would likely take action against Father Michaels once he learned what had transpired; after all, the young priest had done more than merely break his vow of celibacy by screwing my sister. He'd taken advantage of a high school girl he was charged with counseling. His conduct was not only spiritually reprehensible; it was, despite Lilly's being an adult at the time, illegal, as he was in position of authority and trust.

The archbishop might, after the priest displayed sufficient remorse and contrition, transfer Father Michaels to another diocese. Father Michaels might end up reciting homilies somewhere remote, like Baudette or Hallock, but it seemed impossible to tell Lilith's story to Archbishop Flynn without revealing her pregnancy, which meant, putting two and two together, someone might deduce the termination of that pregnancy – which could mean scorn would befall (to put the mess in Biblical terms) my sister. I couldn't allow that to happen.

247

My alternate plan was to confront the man who'd done the deed himself. That's why I held the copy of *Jubilee* the priest had given me close to my chest as I walked through the enormous doors of St. Paul's Cathedral. That's why I'd made a copy of the letter Father Thomas Michaels had written to my sister and placed it inside the book, the original safely tucked away in that junk drawer in my kitchen, the tear my sister had caused in anger to the original mended with Scotch tape.

My arrival wasn't a surprise. I'd called ahead. I had an appointment to see the man. Father Michaels knew I was coming, though I doubt he had any clue what I was going to say.

FIFTY-SEVEN

When you're born Catholic, you're born into hierarchy. You're taught to bow to authority and to never second–guess a priest. Lilith has never had a problem with those rules. I, on the other hand, though I toed the line as a kid, always chafed at this harness of authority; once I became an adult and could see things clearly, I broke away from my religion, never to return. It wasn't just the incident between my sister and Father Michaels that steered me away. The reasons for my leaving the Church are multifaceted, though the Church's position on abortion was not one of them. I happen to be pro–life, holding in my heart that abortion is wrong. I'll make exceptions for situations involving rape and incest, but the procedure, no matter how you try to sugar coat it, is brutal and savage and cannot be reconciled with the Gospels. So the Church's position on abortion is not something that I hold against Catholicism.

You'd be right, however, if you guessed that one of the reasons I turned away from Catholicism was predatory priests. I know, I know: every profession and every faith community has its share. It's not that abuse happened within the confines of the One True Church that got to me. It's the Roman Catholic Church's lack of recognition, even after being sued for hundreds of millions of dollars and being pilloried repeatedly by public opinion, of the damage – both spiritual and psychological – that the Church's conduct has wrought over the course of time. This institutional indifference from the Church brought me to the realization that the religion I grew up in, including the rituals I loved, could no longer hold my allegiance. I could also go into the way the Church treats women, or the foolishness of a Church that bans marriage for its priests, but I think I've said enough to let you know where I stand. Still, as I walked the stony hallway of the great cathedral, the secretary leading me towards Father

Michaels's office, I won't lie to you: the majesty of two thousand years of ritual gripped me as surely as if I were walking to the altar for my First Communion: my little sister and I dressed in virgin white, our family, friends, and fellow Catholics sitting in the pews, watching the procession of wee children about to taste the body of Lord Jesus Christ for the very first time.

"Here 'tis," the secretary said, her ancient body nothing more than a sack of wrinkles. The flesh of her arms, neck and jowls hanging free of her bones, as if someone had drawn all the moisture from her body. Her hair was an unnatural ebony, black as boot–polish, and her weak hazel eyes were concealed by thick eyeglasses.

The woman opened a door and we entered a waiting area. She disappeared down a dimly–lit corridor. I didn't sit down, and didn't peruse the copies of *Catholic Digest* resting on a nearby end table. I remained standing, the copy of *Jubilee* clutched to my chest. Father Thomas Michaels entered the room. The old woman led him with such pious reverence; you'd swear he was the pope. I felt my pulse quicken. Though I'd steeled myself against such a reaction, I couldn't help myself.

"Ms. DuMont. How nice to see you!"

The old woman interrupted. "Aye dere, Father. Will ye be needin' anything further, anything a' tall?" she asked in a thick brogue.

"No, I think we'll be fine, Miss Ames."

The woman's eyes bore through me as she exited the room.

"Don't mind her," Father Michaels whispered as the door slammed. "Miss Ames means well, but there's a bit of a rough edge about her."

I was silent.

"Let's visit in my office. I've some fresh coffee – vanilla cinnamon, a nice blend. We can talk more openly there."

More openly? Did he know why I'd come? Had he received some divine premonition about the purpose of my visit?

I followed the priest into his office.

"Coffee?"

Thomas Michaels was dressed in ebony from head to toe, with the exception of the white clerical collar around his pink neck, as he stood next to the coffee maker.

"That would be lovely."

"Black?"

"Thanks."

He poured two cups, adding sugar and whole cream to his own before handing me a cup and saucer – bone China adorned with delicate yellow roses – and bade me to sit in one of two chairs facing his desk. The priest sat down behind his desk. A Tiffany knock–off table lamp provided light. The shades were drawn, preventing daylight from infiltrating the office. I placed the book on the desk and balanced the coffee cup and saucer on my lap.

"It's good to see you," I offered meekly.

"It's been a long time, hasn't it?"

"Over ten years."

The priest smiled. Time had been kind to Father Thomas Matthew Michaels. Other than the fact that Father Michaels had gone to a shorter hairstyle, the only physical changes I could detect were a thickening of the priest's neck, a slight broadening of the waistline, and the appearance of crow's feet around his blue eyes. Everything else about the man's appearance had been preserved as if time had stood still.

"You've grown into a lovely woman."

Though I detected nothing untoward in the priest's observation, I limited my reply to a smile. A moment passed where nothing was said; to fill the awkward void, I scanned the walls of Father Michaels's office, which was decorated with photographs from all the stages of the priest's career. There were pictures taken in seminary; shots of pilgrimages to various holy sites around the world; a large and ornately framed photograph of the interior of St. Peter's, depicting the faithful witnessing the day Father Michaels had an audience with Pope John Paul. I studied the piety in the scene; the young priest kneeling, and kissing the ring of the anointed one; despite my abandonment of the Catholic Faith, I couldn't help but feel the import of that moment. On the wall behind the priest, elegant frames held Father Michaels's degrees: a Bachelor of Arts, a Master of Arts and a recently acquired Doctor of Divinity. There was a family portrait of the priest, his six siblings (ranging in age, it seemed, from about twelve to forty, with Father Michaels being one of the middle children in the mix) and his two aging parents, in a freestanding frame positioned on the desk facing the door.

"You're well?" the priest asked, interrupting my reflection.

I nodded.

"Married?"

He could have figured that one out by simply looking at my left hand.

Maybe priests are taught to avoid staring at a woman's ring finger. That's rich: a man who doesn't inventory a woman's marital status within the first five seconds of meeting her!

I suppressed a chuckle.

"Single. I'm still single, Father Michaels."

"Please. Call me 'Father Tom.' Or simply 'Tom.' There's no need for formality between old friends."

I caught him staring. At first, I thought he was giving me the eye, but then I realized he was staring at the book. It was clear he didn't recognize the gift he'd once given me. As I studied the priest's virile face, I didn't know how to broach the topic of Lilith. Thankfully, the Good Lord intervened and spared me that awkwardness.

"How is your sister?"

I sensed vulnerability in Father Michaels's voice as he asked about Lilith.

"She's a mom, married. In fact, she lives here. Actually, both of us do. I live Uptown, and she lives in Apple Valley."

"Ah. Boys or girls?"

The question threw me, because I was thinking about how I'd corner him and extract a promise from him.

"Excuse me?"

"Your sister. Lilith, isn't it? Does she have boys or girls?"

"One little girl. Abigail. A sweetheart."

I wanted to fire Lilith's aborted pregnancy at the man like an atomic missile, but knew that – unless it were absolutely necessary – I wasn't going to offer up Lilith's sin for conversation. There was another pause as we scrutinized each other. I took a sip of coffee and slurped, a distinctly unlady–like sound coming from a woman as dressed to the nines as I was. I used the corner of a paper napkin to wipe my mouth, smearing my lipstick in the process.

I overdid the lipstick, I thought, touching the edges of my mouth with the paper to return everything to order.

"I see you brought a book with you," Father Tom noted. "What are you reading?"

My throat clenched.

"*Jubilee,* by Margaret Walker."

"Ah. Looking into our heritage, are we?"

I studied the details of the man's face before answering.

"Actually, you gave me the book. I thought you might want to see what you wrote to me back when I was at Miller–Dwan, recovering from the fire."

"So then, this is a nostalgic visit?"

"You might say that."

I opened the book, removed the love letter, and slid the volume to Father Tom.

"Your inscription to me is inside the front cover."

The priest puzzled over the piece of paper I'd removed from the book before accepting the novel.

"I must say, I was a profound young man, wasn't I?" the priest noted with a smile.

"You remember writing it?"

"Sadly, I don't."

252

He pushed the book back to me. The inscription, though he didn't recite it, was clear in my own memory:

This one thing is denied God: the power to undo the past.
Agathon

"Sort of an obscure reference, wouldn't you agree?"

I nodded. Agathon was an ancient Greek poet and playwright; only a few stanzas of his work survive. That both Father Michaels and I knew who the hell Agathon was – well, that proves something about the two of us, doesn't it? What exactly that is, I'm not sure.

"Is there something else?"

To the point.

"There is."

"Are you spiritually troubled?"

Have been for years, Father Tom, have been for years. No, it's you who's about to meet up with some issues – issues you haven't dealt with for a very long time.

I unfolded the Xerox of the priest's letter to my sister and slid it across the desk.

Father Michaels's eyes widened.

"Where in heaven's name...."

I cleared my throat. "Lilith tore up the original. I found it in a wastebasket and saved it. You know why?"

The priest shook his head.

"Because, *Tom,* I wanted to be the one receiving lovely sentiments from my priest. I was infatuated with you. I won't call it 'love,' because who at eighteen knows what love is? But I will say I was smitten with you. That's for certain."

"But why...."

"Now we come to the purpose of my visit. I hear that the archbishop is about to name you to the post of pastor at All Saints, in Lakeville."

"He is."

"That's not something I can allow to take place."

Father Michaels's cheeks reddened. His fingers grasped the letter with vigor. There was a frightening and frightened edge to Father Michaels's voice.

"What are you talking about?"

I set my coffee on the edge of the desk and leaned forward.

"You're not going to take that posting," I said, pausing between each word for effect.

The priest stood up.

"Who the hell are you to tell me what flock I can lead?"

His voice rose to an uncomfortable level. There was more than a bit of threat behind his words, but his demeanor had the opposite impact upon me.

"What are you smiling for? Do you think this is funny?"

It was clear my calm was grating on the man.

"Out with it. What the hell are you smiling for?" he demanded as he returned to his seat.

"I was there."

"What are you talking about?"

"The night of the retreat. Memorial Day, 1994."

Father Tom's eyes flashed concern, though he feigned ignorance. "I don't understand what you're saying."

I smiled more broadly.

"Sure you do, Father. I was there, using the outhouse, the night you raped my sister."

FIFTY-EIGHT

You're attentive – you noticed that I used the term "raped." Forgive me for going over the nasty details, but you'll recall that, at intervals during the priest's debauchery of my sister, Lilith did indeed use the word "no" several times. I heard it, clear as a bell, from a distance. There's every reason to believe that the priest heard it as well. Whether Lilly actually meant it, I'll leave it to you to consider. Legally and ethically, though, the word "no" is a big red stop sign, and Father Michaels chose to drive right through it.

In any case, the fact that she was a parishioner and he was her priest, as I've made clear, violated Father Michaels's vows and any number of laws meant to prevent abuses of clergy power.

"It wasn't rape," Father Michaels said quietly.

"Let's not play games. You and I both know how the Church and the authorities view the sort of thing that took place between you and my sister. They'd do more than just frown upon your actions, I expect."

"She consented."

"Like I said, I heard Lilith protest. But it doesn't matter. What you did is a crime. Separate from that, there's your vow of celibacy to consider."

"What do you want from me?" The priest's voice rose in pitch.

"My sister and her family are parishioners of All Saints."

I watched the man's Adam's apple move in nervous appreciation.

"Yes?" he whispered.

"There's no way the priest who raped her can hear her confession."

The man's eyebrows rose, as if suddenly inspired.

"I won't be the only priest at the church. My associate can hear Lilith's confession and minister to her family."

I chuckled lightly. "That's rich. She'll be there, sitting reverently next to her husband and her little daughter in the family pew, listening to

255

you preach, knowing what she knows, and so long as your underling deals with her, everything will be fine? I don't think so, Father."

"What you're asking – it's not fair."

The priest was really pissing me off now.

"Fair? Listen here, you sanctimonious ass. Is taking advantage of a young girl – a girl who put her trust in you, a man of God, only to have you overstep your role and abuse that trust and screw her blind on a church youth retreat – in any way 'fair'?"

The look on the priest's face, once my diatribe subsided, convinced me that the worst of my fears – that Father Michaels would balk and I'd be forced to reveal Lilly's pregnancy– were unfounded. I allowed some time to pass before resuming.

"Do we understand each other?"

The priest's eyes closed in deliberation.

"We do," he whispered.

"You'll tell the archbishop that the posting at All Saints isn't for you? That the timing isn't right or some such nonsense?"

Father Michaels nodded.

"I need to hear you say the words."

"I'll decline the position."

"Righteous."

Father Tom folded the letter and slid it towards me.

"No. That's for you to keep, as a reminder of your promise."

I stood up from my chair, shifted my skirt so that the hem was even, and reclaimed my book.

"You'll understand if I don't see you to the door?"

"Surely. You've got some thinking to do before you find Archbishop Flynn and explain your sudden change of heart."

I turned and walked towards the door.

"I loved her."

I slowed but didn't stop as I replied.

"Then you should've done right by her. You needed to choose between God and Lilith, Father Michaels, but you did not."

I closed the door on the priest's response. Our little drama, a scene right out of the *Thorn Birds*, Mom's favorite book, had played itself out. I had a taxicab waiting and the bill was likely more than I could afford.

FIFTY-NINE

Lilly rested easily once I told her I'd talked to Father Michaels. I never explained the details of our conversation to my sister – only that we'd met and talked, and that Father Michaels had agreed not to take the position at All Saints. She left things alone – which, given what had transpired at the cathedral, was fine with me.

Attending a Labor Day Picnic on Lake Panorama, the only African American amongst a slew of square–jawed, fair–skinned Norwegians – well, that wasn't an unusual cultural experience for me, seeing how I grew up surrounded by Scandinavians. Mason's sister, Jessica, invited me and, seeing as how close Mason and I had become, I couldn't really turn the woman down now, could I? So I returned to the shores of Lake Panorama for the Erickson Family Picnic. Other than Jana, a dark–skinned Indian beauty from New Delhi married to Mason's brother Edward, I was the only person of color at the party. Everyone else there was white – so white that there should be a separate skin color category just for them.

It's funny. When I was at New Beginnings, I jogged by Jessica and Marvin's cottage on training runs and admired the place, mostly because it reminded me of my parents' home, but I never knew who owned it. As the crow flies, Jessica and Marvin live only a few hundred yards from where Mason and I had our lewd encounter with the deputy.

What I'd really come back to Iowa for on that trip was, I thought, still stored in the machine shed on Mason's farm. I'd purchased an old Nissan two–wheel drive pick–up truck, the body pock–marked with rust, the bed of the box attached to the frame by a system of baling wire and coat hangers that only an engineer could've designed, before returning to Iowa. Despite the truck's rickety appearance, the engine and drive train were billed as being "in excellent condition." (At least that's what the guy who sold it to me claimed, when I noted that there were over 180,000 miles on its odometer.) Anyway, I learned on my own how to shift the truck's manual transmission before I took off for Iowa. My days of riding a bus were over. I'd had enough of babies bawling, of drunks hitting on me, of avoiding gross–looking excrement on the lavatory floors of Greyhounds, for one lifetime.

I showed up at Mason's place, thinking I'd stay a couple of nights. I brought my checkbook, because my plan was to buy the Sonett. With winter only a few months away, and winter being a slower season for dairymen – with the harvest over and the cows hunkered down in the barn – I thought Mason could get the car ready for me by spring. That, as I said, was my plan. But I was in for a surprise.

The air was cooling at dusk, and daylight was graying to black. The yard lights sputtered to life. I'd just come into the barn from the machine shed; to say I was disappointed would be an understatement.

"Mason?"

"Yes?" he asked, his back turned to me. Mason was adjusting a coupling on one of the cows. Suction took over. Milk flowed through plastic tubing to the stainless steel holding tank in the milk house at the other end of the barn.

"Please look at me when I'm talking to you."

Mason stood up. He'd been around me long enough to sense that, despite my normally even–keeled disposition, when I get hot, I'm capable of losing it. I say "sensed," because I hadn't shown my full temper yet in front of him, but there were a couple of times when his stoicism, his calm in the midst of one of my heated diatribes – like my rant driving home that night from Council Bluffs, where I went off about the screwed–up priorities of Congress, the funding of the infamous "Bridge to Nowhere" in Alaska at the expense of Head Start and food stamps, and the Administration's failure to rescue folks made homeless by Katrina – made me see red. OK, here's the deal. What really frosted me was the fact that Mason's entire family, with the exception of Jana and Mason, had weighed in earlier that day on the side of dumping social programs as a necessary sacrifice to waging war. Now, like I said, I kept my anger in check on the long drive to Council Bluffs to watch the fireworks. But once I got in Mason's truck for the trip back to Guthrie Center, well, I let loose. I think Mason knew what I was capable of and had taken great pains to defuse my upset.

"Where's the fucking car?"

It was the first time Mason ever heard that word come out of my mouth. It's not a word I learned at home. My parents don't use it and I certainly don't use it in casual conversation. But, like I said, when my dander is up, I'm capable of many things. Discovering the empty space in the machine shed where the butterscotch–colored Saab once sat – well, that really ticked me off. So I used a word Mason had never heard from me, not even in the depths of passion.

"I should have told you: it was spoken for."

I held my breath like a little girl about to launch into a tantrum.

He doesn't realize how much I looked forward to that car. I scrimped and saved the five hundred bucks for the Nissan and then, hording every penny I could, including the money from my claim against the City of Minneapolis, I came up with four grand for the Saab. I wanted to feel the wind blowing through the open windows of that little car, the purr of the motor, a CD player blaring Lucinda Williams, Seal, Tracy Chapman, or better yet, John Gorka as I found some winding, deserted Midwestern country road to lose myself on. But it's gone. I've saved my money for nothing.

"Spoken for?"

"Someone was interested in it. I should have told you."

"Damn right you should've. You knew how much I loved that car. Damn you, Mason. I thought we had an understanding."

I stood there, acting all bitchy, my hands on my hips. I was dressed in shorts, a revealing halter and sandals; I was braless, so when I raised my voice a notch to make a point, everything quivered. Mason wouldn't engage; he simply refused to be drawn into a petty argument. I stomped my foot on the concrete floor of the barn, stubbing my big toe in the process. I wanted to swear some more, mostly on account of the pain, but I held my breath and tromped out of the barn.

As you might've guessed, we didn't make love that night. In fact, for the first time since I'd been coming to visit Mason in Iowa, we slept in separate beds. Mason stayed in his bed, the one he used to screw Virginia in, which is also the one where he'd had his way with me more than a few times. And me? I slept in the bottom bunk in Jacob's old room. I'll have to tell you, I've slept better. First off, the bed is only a single, so I kept waking up in the middle of the night to catch myself from falling onto the floor. Then there's the issue of comfort. There's no box spring – only a sheet of plywood supports the mattress. Talk about sleeping hard!

In the morning, I sat across the kitchen table from Mason, quietly sipping coffee, containing my disappointment as he read the *Des Moines Register*. I looked like crap, despite having taken a shower and attempted to bring order to my appearance. My stubbly hair was still wet. I'd simply covered the damp nubs with a ball cap, rashly breaking the rule I'd been taught at home about sitting down for a meal with a hat on your head.

"I'm going home today," I announced.

"Thought you were staying until tomorrow," Mason responded without lowering his paper.

"I need to get some things done at home before going back to work."

"Oh."

I wasn't much good at playing the part of the downtrodden, especially when all the man had done was sell off an old car that belonged to *him*. I adjusted my mood to something less onerous.

"Mason?"

"Yes?"

The sports page lowered, and I could see his baby blues. I could tell he was having fun with me. A sheepish grin seeped through his feigned grimace.

"I'm sorry. I had no right to get upset over a stupid car. You named your price months ago and I just assumed you knew I was interested. I should have made myself more clear."

"No problemo," he chirped. "I'll keep my eye out for another one. I can maybe pick one up for cheap. My brother Danny can fix anything, you know."

I *did* know. Danny, a monster of a man with hands the size of pancakes, ran a garage somewhere in West Des Moines. I'd met him once before, and once again at Jessica's picnic.

"Thanks," I replied with a smile, finishing off my coffee. "I think I'd better hit the road."

I stood up from the table and put my dishes into the top rack of Mason's abused dishwasher, its stainless steel insides nicked and dented from hard use. Mason left the table and, before I could react, hugged me in front of the window by the sink.

"Don't ever do that again."

"Don't do what?"

His breath was sour with milk. The pores of his face were clean and absent of whiskers. From his dreamy look, I knew he wanted to make love to me right there, on the kitchen floor, or on the kitchen table, or against the sink. You know what? I wanted to do that, to feel him against me, to feel his strength and his yearning, and to know the essence of him right then and there. But I couldn't. I just couldn't. I don't know why. I just wasn't in the right mood.

"Sleep in my house in a different bed."

I nodded.

"I gotta run."

He held my shoulders loosely and kissed me on the lips. I felt something; of course, what girl wouldn't? But I'd made up my mind. Making love would have to wait.

SIXTY

The telephone call came on a Sunday afternoon in late September. I had just walked into my Uptown apartment in Minneapolis, only moments after experiencing a vehicular catastrophe. My truck's radiator bit the dust on my drive home from church. Vapor boiled out from beneath the Nissan's hood, after which the engine seized up as tight as a baby's fist.

Engine and drive train in excellent condition, my ass.

Despite my truck's desperate condition, I was surprisingly upbeat. Reverend Morris's sermon had been uplifting – something from the Gospel of John, the details of which escape me now, months later, as I write this down. I do recall, however, a sanctifying glow burning inside me as I stepped into my darkened little piece of the world and picked up the receiver to answer the telephone.

"Esther?"

"Yes?"

"Amy. Amy Olson."

I wriggled out of the light jacket I was wearing.

"*Doctor* Olson," I corrected.

"I can hear the sarcasm in your voice, Esther Mary DuMont. I know you too well. Remember that. I know things."

Not everything.

"How you doing?" she asked.

"Fine. Life's good. I could use a break from the Clinic, though. I thought working with the poor – especially women – would be a worthy penance, but there's a limit to my piety, I guess."

Amy laughed, the same exuberant laugh she's always had.

Images came to mind: Amy and I were shooting hoops at my parents' house on a sultry summer day. We were about twelve or so, just in

261

the beginning stages of change. Lilly and another little girl (whose name I can't remember) were skipping rope at the far end of the driveway. Mom was out back, tending to her vegetable patch, and Dad was tinkering with fishing gear in the garage with the door open – an eternal mess of golf clubs, fishing rods, tools and the like exposed for the world to see. (Now that I think about it, Dad has always been disorganized around the house. Seems unnatural for someone whose life work requires precision. But that's Dad.) Anyway, Dad got the idea that he should take Lil and me fishing for bluegills and sunnies on Shoulder Lake. He ended up taking three little girls in his seventeen–foot Grumman square–stern canoe that day. Amy came with. The other girl, for whatever reason, went home. Talk about a hoot: three twelve–year–old girls trying to cast lines without snagging each other's eyes with hooks, tossing squiggly masses of night crawler between lily pads where pan fish schooled in the shade. Dad sat quietly in the back of the canoe, an Ansel Adams–style hat pulled down over his big ears; though he rarely smoked, he was sucking on a pipe, and puffs of sweet tobacco smoke billowed into the air. It's one of those timeless scenes that, whenever I talk to Amy or think about her, always comes to mind. She had such a grand time of it, holding up oodles of fish at the boat landing while Dad snapped our picture, Lilly and I on either side of our friend; the panfish were still flopping, suspended by their gills from the chain stringer. Amy's tanned arms strained from the weight of our catch.

I need to go fishing with Dad, I thought, as I listened to Amy over the telephone.

Another image from another day: Amy and I were sitting on the back porch of Ellie Swartz's house in Ashland. We were in seventh grade and Amy was staying over with me at Grandma Mary's. Lilly was gone, probably off chasing some boy. Ellie, a tall, stoop–shouldered big–hipped girl with bad acne, was the same age as us and lived on the same street as my Grandma. We sat on the front steps of Ellie's house, looking at teen magazines. Neither Amy nor I were much into fashion or fame, but Ellie sure was. Ellie wanted to be a movie star, the next Jodie Foster. She could sing some, but beauty? It didn't seem to be in the cards for that girl. *Unhandsome*, rather than ugly, is how I'd describe her. She just wasn't all that pretty.

Anyway, like I said, as a black girl growing up amongst whites, even though I wasn't the target of many racial slurs, every once in a while, something got said that made the hair on the back of my neck stand on end. I'm not hyper–vigilant or anything because of these isolated situations. I don't walk around expecting the worst from people. But I'll admit to being wary, and to keeping my radar attuned. That's how I knew when it was time to leave Ellie's place – it wasn't Ellie who said it. I overheard a conversation between Ellie and her Dad, who was chewing her out for having "that Negro girl" over. The words were spoken from the kitchen at the back of the house. Amy and I were outside, on the porch, waiting for Ellie to bring us lemonade or something, when Ellie's dad made the comment. Amy, God bless her soul, heard the slur and wanted to march into the kitchen and let Old Man Schwartz have it. Though I talked her out of making a scene, I loved her for the sentiment. We ditched Ellie. I never played with her again. It wasn't Ellie's fault, you understand, but that's what happened. What else could I do? I was just a kid.

"You'll never guess why I called."

"Say what?"

"How would you like to go to Africa?"

"What are you talking about?"

"You remember Sarah?"

"I do. Nice lady."

"Well, she's a Public Health Nurse with St. Louis County. When I transferred to Duluth for my last year of residency to be closer to my folks, Sarah got a job working for the county. She's also the parish nurse of St. Mark's, the African Methodist Episcopal Church in town. Ever heard of it?"

Indeed I have. One of Dad's relatives was once the pastor there.

"Yep."

"Well, Reverend Stone, the pastor, has the church participating in a mission to Liberia that's sponsored by the AME National Church. You know anything about Liberia?"

Not much, I thought to myself, a sense of shame creeping into my mind. *I know it was founded in the 1800s as a haven for freed slaves from America and that the capital city, Monrovia, is named for President James Monroe. I know there's some sort of unrest, some sort of turmoil going on there, much like the rest of sub–Saharan Africa. But that's about it.*

"Not really."

"Since the 1980s, the place has been in chaos. Civil unrest, military coups. The president, Charles Taylor, was indicted for war crimes by the UN and went into exile in Nigeria. Things have settled down, but the place is still in shambles. There's a need for medical care. St. Mark's is sending a group of us to help out. It's a six–month commitment. When Sarah came home with this bombshell in May and suggested that we should go to Africa once I finished my residency, I was intrigued. I finished my training in June and then, of course, my dark–skinned friend, I thought of you."

"Bitch," I said, using the term as an endearment, not a put down.

"You go, girl. I can handle it. But understand, when we're done talking, you'll be hooked up with Sarah and me and you'll be heading to Africa."

I doubted what Amy Olson said. I doubted that my friend, as brilliant and as crafty as she is, could convince me to leave my new position, my apartment and my new romance to minister to sick folks in a place I'd only read about.

"No way."

"Yes way. Listen up: I heard you lamenting about 'roots' and other ethnic crap with Sarah at the reunion. Well, here's a chance to see where part of you came from. The Church has raised money. They'll take care of room and board and pay for your airfare and a small stipend – five hundred a month – if you're a doctor, dentist or nurse. Reverend Stone has already brought in over a hundred thousand dollars in donations for the project. It seems that building that monument – you know, to the black circus workers who got lynched – has opened up more than my fellow Caucasians' eyes. It's also opened up their wallets."

I have to be honest here. I had no idea what the hell was going on anywhere in Africa, much less in some backwater country founded by freed slaves from America. Visions of rape, torture and strife rolled through my mind like snippets from the evening news. Turns out, these portraits weren't too far from the actual truth of what had gone on in Liberia since the late 1980s. Despite the deployment of fifteen thousand UN troops and over a thousand police advisors, the place – according to Amy Olson – was still seething with upset and poverty. Still, as we talked, I felt something tugging at my heart – some part of me accepting what Amy was asking me to do. Why and how her words turned me, I don't know, but turn me she did.

"Okay."

"What was that, Miss DuMont? What did I hear come from that beautiful black mouth of yours?"

Amy could get away with talking like that to me. Despite losing touch with each other for a time, we're as close as sisters. She'd earned the right to be flippant.

"I said I'll go, damn it."

"I thought that's what I heard. You need to meet with Reverend Stone and the screening committee. It's just a formality. With Sarah backing you, you'll have no trouble from them."

"When does this big mistake happen?"

"We're leaving on the first of November. You need to get up here in the next few weeks. And you need to make sure your passport is up to date. You'll need a Liberian visa, but that won't be a problem, since you're with a relief organization. The Church can help you with that. You also need to be vaccinated for yellow fever. I can take care of that. It would be my pleasure."

I'm sure it would. I'm sure you'd just love to stick a needle in my ass. Of course, I didn't say that to Amy. There's a limit to familiarity, even among friends.

"We're set, then?"

"Ah huh."

"When can you meet with the reverend?"

"Shit."

"How's that?"

"I forgot something."

"What?"

"I'm still on probation."

"Is that a problem?"

"I don't know. My probation officer seems to like me. I shouldn't have trouble convincing her. But I'll have to start working on her and get the paperwork signed."

"You do that. And don't be trying to sabotage this, you hear me? We need you. And you need to take this trip. You know you do."

"Ah huh."

Amy Olson hung up. I sat in a hand–me–down easy chair in the living room of my apartment and thought about what I'd just done. Then I thought about Mason Erickson and what I was going to tell him. We were supposed to get together during Bayfield's Apple Festival the first weekend in October. I'd have to conjure up with some clever way of saying to my new lover: "Oh, by the way, Mason, honey, you won't be screwing me blind for the next six months. In fact, it's likely you won't even hear from me. Not by phone. Not by email. Maybe, if the Liberian postal authority actually works, by snail mail, but that's iffy at best. It's all due to the fact that I'll be traipsing off to Africa to find myself. You understand, don't you sweetheart?"

I told you I didn't have much use for the way Emma Boudreaux, the character in *The Professor's Daughter*, left her life in America and ran away to Brazil. Well, now it seemed I was about to do the very same thing.

SIXTY-ONE

What, you ask, was I thinking? You're right of course: I'd gone over the edge by agreeing to up and leave the slightness of my new life and my newfound love.

There. I said the word. I was in love with Mason Erickson. Not just in the physical sense, but in the moral, uplifted, romantic sense of old novels, the way Mom and Dad are in love. Their marriage survived the death of their only son and the near–death of their daughter. Not many couples make it through something like that. It was love that brought them through: tenacious, audacious, outrageous love. Same thing with Lilly and Richard. Their connection may be a bit more selfish, a bit more yuppified. But one look at the two of them together, and you know and understand that these are two people who care deeply for each other. And I've come to recognize that Sarah Miles and Amy Olson have found something just as strong, and just as real. You can't diminish it or tarnish it by turning your head away. You may not agree with what they have, but you certainly can't deny it.

So, you ask: what the hell were you thinking, Esther DuMont, when you, on the spur of the moment and over the telephone, agreed to leave it all and get on an airplane and go to Africa? I'd like to be able to give you some grand pontification, some preachy rationale for my decision, but I can't. All I can tell you is that I said "yes" and that, having agreed to go and being a woman of my word, I was stuck.

I kept my plans to myself. At night, after a hard day at the Clinic, when I emailed or IMed Mason from the ancient Gateway laptop sitting on my kitchen table, I didn't share with him what was about to happen to us. There, I said it: we had, in my mind, become an "us." I hadn't really confirmed it with Mason, hadn't yet said the "L" word to him. He'd said it to me on a number of occasions – mostly during or after sex, but not always. Sometimes, after a hug or some other casual sign of endearment; he'd toss it out for me to hear. He's pretty affectionate for a Norwegian – not at all like the bachelor farmer stereotype depicted on *Prairie Home Companion*. But, like I said, up until I headed north to Bayfield for the Apple Festival – the biggest celebration of the year for folks living around Chequamegon Bay – taking a few extra days off to meet with Amy and Sarah and the other members of the AME Mission group in Duluth, I hadn't yet told Mason that I loved him. I also hadn't told the Clinic that I was about to leave. I was planning on doing that when I came back from Duluth, after making sure I was compatible with the mission group, the pastor and all. Julia Frisk, my probation officer, was on board; she recommended to Judge Patrick that I be allowed to stay in Liberia for the full six months. There was no reason, at least from a legal standpoint, why I couldn't go on the mission trip.

My laptop computer, one Dad bought me for my college graduation, is ancient. Don't ask me what it has in terms of megahertz or gigahertz or whatever. I just know that it's outdated. Still, I was able to pull up information about Liberia and what's been going on there, from international news sources. What I read about Liberia confirmed what I'd thought all along about the Iraq War.

What has Iraq got to do with Liberia, you might ask? Well, let's see. If you accept that Saddam Hussein murdered thousands of his own people, I'll grant you he is one bad man. But you know what? In Somalia, Senegal, Sierra Leone, Rwanda, Sudan and Liberia, the number of women, children, old people and other innocents killed off by dictators, insurgents and revolution since 1970 is in the millions. In Liberia alone, since the civil war there began in the 1980s, a quarter of a million people – as many folks as live in St. Paul, Minnesota – have been killed. And what has America done? Did it invade Liberia and pull Charles Taylor, the brutal dictator of that country founded by freed American blacks, off his ivory throne? Of course it didn't.

Now, I don't know the exact reasons, but it sure seems funny to me that our country, the most powerful democracy on the planet, is ready, willing and able to send troops, planes, tanks and whatever else it takes to protect folks in the former Yugoslavia, but the United States of America won't lift a finger to help people being slaughtered in Africa. Racist? You be the judge. I know that when I found out about this stuff, it set me off. And don't get me started about sending young Americans – many of them reservists and national guardsmen and women from my home state of Wisconsin – off to die because some desert dictator tried to kill the current President's father. Or maybe we invaded for oil. Or so that Dick Cheney's pals could make another zillion dollars. Just don't go there, okay?

I apologize for getting upset. It's just that, probably like me, you likely read a line or two in your elementary school geography or history books about Liberia. It probably went something like:

In 1847, freed blacks from America founded the Republic of Liberia; its capital city, Monrovia, is named after President James Monroe. Monroe and other prominent Americans supported the idea of creating an independent homeland in Africa for freed American slaves.

Beyond such isolated references, you, I, and the rest of the world likely know nothing more about the place. Seeing as how most African Americans trace their roots back to West Africa, this lack of understanding is a real shame. It took Wanda Jones handing me works of fiction written by African American women to get me interested in this stuff. It will take an earthquake to make me stop learning about what my African forefathers and foremothers experienced, or from trying to discover where they came from. Anyway, I learned something positive during my Internet perusal. Please understand: this isn't information I gleaned from reading the *Minneapolis Tribune*. No, I had to find stuff out about Liberia from international news organizations. What I learned was that the country was about to undergo a presidential election, a contest pitting Ellen Johnson Sirleaf, an economist, against soccer star George Weah. I also learned that our plane would arrive in Africa shortly after the election – which, given the country's rocky political history, seemed like precarious timing. To say I was apprehensive about the promise I'd made to Amy would be an understatement.

I drove up from the Cities for the Apple Festival in my battle–weary Nissan, ever watchful for an eruption of coolant from beneath the hood. I'd spent over a thousand bucks repairing the truck. I had little choice; buying another vehicle, what with my trip looming and all, wasn't an option. Mason was driving up separately; we'd rented a room at a local bed and breakfast for the weekend.

Like nearly every Friday morning of nearly every Bayfield Apple Festival I can remember, it was raining when I drove into town. Not cats and dogs, mind you – just a penetrating drizzle with the temperature hovering near forty. I was wearing neon–pink running tights under green corduroy slacks; a black fleece pullover; my omnipresent choppers; a bright green rain slicker, the hood pulled up to keep me dry; and leather Red Wing hiking boots I'd bought at Minnesota Surplus in downtown Duluth the day before. The boots were something I'd need in Africa; tennis shoes or sandals wouldn't do the job against rocks and snakes. The new boots were stiff and uncomfortable. As I walked the wet streets of Bayfield with hot coffee steaming from the openings in my plastic travel mug, I marveled at the furious pace of vendors setting up their display tents against the misty day.

Walking down ManyPenny Lane, I came across a self–published author struggling to pitch a display tent.

"Need a hand?" I asked, noting that the man was having trouble raising the shelter.

"No thanks. I think I've got it."

The man's eyeglasses dripped rain. Though I doubted he could see my gesture, I toasted his effort by raising my coffee cup. I continued walking but didn't get far. The next booth was ready for business. A short white woman with a bouncy personality, her hands covered in fleece mittens and her long hair covered in a stocking cap of knitted wool, engaged me with dark brown eyes.

"Mornin'."

I stopped in front of racks of music CDs. A sad melody played over the speakers, the music a gentle mix of violin and acoustic guitar. The tune piqued my interest.

"Is that one of theirs?"

The woman handed me a CD.

"It's the theme song from *Legends of the Fall.*"

"My Dad's favorite movie," I quipped, studying the compact disc.

"Makes a great Christmas gift."

I smiled.

"You've got a lovely accent," I observed.

"You mean, I don't sound like I'm right out of *Fargo?*"

"East Coast, am I right? And I don't mean of Lake Superior."

The woman laughed. Not a false laugh released gratuitously, in hopes of making a sale, but a genuine laugh – the kind expressed by someone who's really and truly happy.

"You got it."

I picked up my coffee cup and handed the CD to the woman.

"I'm supposed to meet someone. I'll be back."

She nodded and went back to arranging compact discs.

The rain stopped, but the clouds remained low. I continued on. I was browsing shops on Rittenhouse Avenue when I heard someone calling my name.

"Esther!"

Before I could turn around, Mason Erickson was hugging me with such warmth, vitality and love that I was unsure of whether I could ever leave his embrace.

SIXTY-TWO

Mason and I returned to the musician's booth. Like I've said before, Mason isn't much of a folk music fan. I've forced him to listen to the stuff I like, and he's forced me to ride in his truck while he plays Journey, AC/DC, REO Speedwagon and the like, with an occasional Neil Young or Bruce Springsteen song thrown in. That's what Mason considers folk music: Neil Young and Bruce Springsteen! Anyway, we found ourselves riveted: we joined a small knot of customers listening to two men playing acoustic music in forty–degree weather.

"They're good," Mason whispered.

"Ah huh."

I held paper sacks full of gifts. Since I would be gone for Christmas – a reality that Mason was as yet unaware of – I was doing some serious Christmas shopping. The gift I was most proud of was the one I'd purchased for Mason.

Earlier that day, I'd discovered an old man selling homemade knives on Rittenhouse Avenue. He was hunched over his work, with gnarled fingers working steel. The knife–maker's workmanship caught my eye, and his prices seemed fair. I needed a good pocketknife for my trip to Africa, so I spent considerable time at the old man's booth. In addition to selecting a pocketknife for myself, I spied a six–inch hunting blade with a finely crafted bone handle and leather sheath, the perfect gift for Mason. For an extra five bucks, the old man said he'd emboss Mason's initials in the sheath. I didn't buy anything right then. I thought about it for a while, and when Mason was busy visiting the little boys' room, I went back and bought three knives: a pocketknife for myself, a hunting knife for Mason and a fillet knife for Dad.

"You want one of their CDs?" Mason asked.

"I was thinking about getting one for Dad."

"I could buy it for him."

"He'd like that."

"Which one do you think he'd like?"

"This one. He loves the movie *Legends of the Fall*."

Mason picked up the CD entitled *Lonely Land* and read the back cover.

"That's my favorite movie," Mason said, pulling out his wallet.

God, I love this man, I thought as I watched the slow, deliberate care Mason used to count out fifteen one–dollar bills before handing the money to the woman I'd talked to earlier. *Why can't I tell him?*

I turned my back so as not to embarrass myself by letting Mason see that I was crying. It wasn't the after–effects of meth that prevented me from telling Mason how I felt. The drug's impact on me, its stifling of pleasure, had been defeated. Dopamine was flowing – trust me when I tell you that. I mean, there was any number of times when Mason and I slept together that the experience was near what Del and I had shared while high. It wasn't any physical deficit that kept me from saying what needed to be said. I think it was old–fashioned fear. Anyway, by the time I'd resumed listening to Pat Surface sing, my nerves had steadied and the fleece sleeve of my pullover had sopped up my tears.

I'm not going to lose it at the Apple Festival, surrounded by strangers, I insisted to myself.

"Let's get a hot chocolate," I said as Mason finished paying for the CD.

The suggestion seemed to make sense, seeing as how, despite the fact I'd shed my poncho, I was still wearing choppers and you could still see your breath.

"Where?"

"Up the hill. On Rittenhouse, one street over. There's a fudge shop with great coffee and hot cocoa."

"Okay."

We waded through a mass of humanity: the only significant minority presence in the crowd was a smattering of Native Americans. Up on Rittenhouse, the crowd blocked our way; perhaps a thousand people stood in the street, staring at a makeshift stage, gawking and chatting with coffee cups or plastic bottles of beer in their gloved or mittened hands, waiting; waiting for four musicians who had crowded onto the Apple Festival main stage to play music.

"Who are they?" I asked Tim Corbet, a guy I used to work with at the Rittenhouse Inn when we were in high school. Tim stood with a woman in front of Mason and me on the sidewalk.

271

"Well, if it isn't Esther DuMont!" Tim said with a nod, never releasing his arm from around the woman's waist. "Used to be called 'Brule.' Now they're known as the 'American Indian Rock Opera.' Guy by the name of Paul LaRouche is their leader. They're absolutely great."

"Tim, this is my friend, Mason Erickson."

Corbet nodded politely.

"Pleased to meet you. This is my wife, Erika."

"Hi," I replied, eyeing the tall white girl standing beside the red–headed former cook.

A tribal drum began to pound. The thump, thump, thump of leather against skin demanded the absolute attention of everyone within earshot. The drums' ancient rhythm, something akin to the drums Dad's forefathers and foremothers must have heard in African villages, stopped my thoughts.

Suddenly, as if a clap of thunder had been loosened from the sky, the young guitarist on the stage ripped into a long and soaring riff. I stood there, watching the young man; his father, the keyboardist; his sister, the flutist; and a wildly animated drummer craft music inherently spiritual, mystical and physical. The dichotomy of the music superimposed upon the ethnicity of the crowd nearly broke my heart. But it didn't – in fact, my heart seemed to grow stronger as I listened to the music, as I thought about how hard Native Americans, like African Americans, have fought to survive. From the music, I drew courage, and from this courage, I was finally able to whisper into Mason's left ear the three words that I'd been so afraid to say.

SIXTY-THREE

My nakedness was covered by cotton sheets. Mason stood at the mirror in the adjoining bathroom, shaving. It was then that I finally told him that I was leaving – not just him, but everything: my job, my life and my family. It was hard enough to say the words. But what he'd done – the surprise he'd dropped on me the day before – made my disclosure seem all the more cruel.

We'd driven around Bayfield County that Saturday in Mason's truck, touring apple orchards, talking and laughing; we were genuinely and completely in love. But I was troubled – troubled that the illusion we were caught up in would dissipate like reflections on water fade when clouds crowd out the sun. I didn't know how to tell Mason I was about to embark on a journey of self–discovery. I tried hard not to let my hidden agenda interfere with our day. Still, Mason is a perceptive sort. I'm sure he sensed that something was amiss. To his credit, he never pried or picked at what it was that lay just below the surface of our time together.

Late in our drive, we pulled into Hauser's Orchard on the ridge behind town. As Mason eased his truck into the gravel parking lot, my eyes were drawn to a car. Though clouds blocked the October sun, the little vehicle gleamed like a jewel. The two–seater's paint job shone as if it had just come off the showroom floor.

"Hey, that looks like the car you sold."

Mason didn't answer.

"Mason, did you hear me?"

The farmer said nothing.

"Well?"

"I never said I sold it."

I was puzzled. I was certain that, when I'd asked about the Saab, Mason told me he'd sold it.

"Sure you did. Remember that morning? You told me you'd sold it, which pissed me off, if you really want to know."

Mason chuckled. "Oh, don't I know it, Miss DuMont. You think I'm stupid? You think I don't know why we ended up in separate beds in my house that night? Pissed off? You were a hell of a lot madder than 'pissed off.'"

I opened the door, stepped out of the truck, slammed the door and walked over to inspect the sports car.

"She's primo, ain't she?"

An orchard worker, someone I didn't know, made the statement as he approached.

"That she is," Mason replied. "I'm a lucky man to be in love with such a beautiful woman."

The stranger winked at me.

"That too. But I meant the car."

I laughed and looked inside the Saab. The car's interior was flawless. A CD player was installed in the dash. Six speakers were strategically placed around the cockpit. Sheepskin seat covers protected the car's tan vinyl seats. I took it all in, lamenting what I'd missed when Mason decided to get rid of his ex–wife's Sonett.

"I love these cars."

"Wanna take her for a spin?"

The orchard worker was grinning from ear to ear as he spoke.

"Seriously?"

"Sure."

"The keys aren't in it."

"Here," Mason said, tossing me a set of keys.

"What the…?" I said, snaring the keys in mid–air.

Mason's smile was as wide as Lake Superior as the orchard worker wandered off.

"You told me you sold it."

Mason opened the driver's door so I could slide in behind the steering wheel.

"Not true."

"Did too."

"You *are* stubborn, Miss DuMont – but, as usual, you only hear what you want to hear."

I turned the key. The engine purred like a cat being stroked.

"She sounds beautiful."

"That she does. But you're still wrong."

"You told me you sold this car. That's exactly how I remember it."

Mason shook his head.

"What I said, Esther my dear, is that 'it's spoken for.'"

I remembered the conversation. That's exactly what he'd said.

"Danny did one hell of a job on 'er, didn't he?"

I nodded.

"But I don't have the money to pay you. I spent it on that piece of shit Nissan."

That was partly true. I couldn't tell him that I'd allocated the rest of my savings, including my settlement money, to cover my trip. *Hell, he doesn't even* know *about the trip.*

"It's a gift."

My grip tightened on the steering wheel.

"Mason, it's too much. I can't accept it."

"It was collecting dust. It's worthless to me. What am I going to do, cruise Guthrie Center in a Swedish sports car? That'd be sort of a waste, don't you think? No, Esther, it's yours. The title's in the glove box."

I raised myself from the seat, wrapped my arms around Mason's neck, and planted the wettest kiss I could muster on his lips. My body trembled. I didn't want to let go of the man.

"Loosen up, Miss DuMont. Let's take 'er for a spin."

Mason freed himself and slipped into the passenger seat. My left foot slipped as I shifted into reverse, but I quickly found my comfort zone. I eased the Saab out of the gravel parking lot. Once the car's rear tires hit blacktop, it was a different story. I shifted smoothly and the sports car zoomed over rolling hills and through the scarlet, orange and yellow October forest surrounding the rural roads we traveled. I loved the car's ability to hug pavement as it swept in and out of curves. And Mason seemed pleased as he watched me drive because he was smiling ear to ear.

"Push play."

"How's that?"

"On the CD player."

I complied. The song "Fast Car" by Tracy Chapman boomed over the stereo.

"You've been listening."

Mason didn't respond for quite some time. I put the car through its paces before ultimately returning the Saab to Hauser's parking lot.

It was only after the car was fully stopped that Mason responded to my observation.

"Baby, I always listen to you, even when you think I don't," Mason said as we exited the car.

I laughed. "Ya, right."

Then it dawned on me. *How the hell did he get the car here? He drove his truck. He couldn't drive two vehicles.*

"Mason...."

Mason interrupted what I was about to say by pointing at a flatbed trailer parked off to one side of Hauser's parking lot.

"Oh."

That night, Mason did things to me that, well, let's just say I'm too modest to write about. I tried hard to reciprocate – honest, I did. I wanted to approximate his passion, and I think I came close; I wasn't exactly his equal, but I gave it my all. I hope he experienced the same thunder and lightning storm I did. He seemed to enjoy himself. He seemed to have a satisfied, all–done–in look on his face as he fell asleep beside me in our rented bed.

In the morning, I pulled the top sheet over my nakedness and via the bathroom mirror's reflection through the doorway, watched the man I love stroke his lathered face with a razor. I knew I had to tell him what was about to happen to us; I knew that there was no better time.

"Mason," I said quietly, my voice edged with distress.

"Somethin' wrong?"

"We need to talk."

Mason stepped into the bedroom, a bath towel wrapped around his waist, his hairless chest bare to the cool air of the room as he wiped remnants of shaving cream from his face with a hand towel.

"What's up?"

I took a deep breath and sat up in bed. My mind tumbled back to the evening before. I was on top of Mason, sitting on him, with him inside me. In the position we were in, and given that I was already spent, I didn't feel pleasure. I felt satisfaction and obligation and I didn't mind being in debt. When he came, his hands grasping my shoulders and his mouth buried in my chest, it felt damn good to make him happy. His breathing stopped and his legs trembled. I think he got out of our little tryst all that I was capable of giving.

"I'm going away for a while," I finally said.

Mason grimaced. It was the first real sign of temperament that I'd seen from the man in nearly a year of knowing him.

"What are you saying?"

"Come sit by me."

"No. Just tell me what this is about."

I sensed he thought I was going to dump him.

"It's not like that. I told you, I love you. I meant it."

"Then what?"

I sighed and looked towards the ceiling. "I'm going on a trip – with Amy Olson and her partner Sarah."

Mason studied me.

"Where?"

"Liberia."

He pondered my revelation. "That's in Africa."

I inhaled deeply.

"Yes, it's in Africa. It's through Sarah's church. A mission, to build a clinic."

"How long will you be gone?"

"Six months."

"Jesus."

SIXTY-FOUR

Sweltering is the only word I can use to describe this place. It's all I can do to keep my fingers from slipping off the keyboard of my laptop as I conclude my story. Maybe "conclude" isn't the right word. There isn't anything conclusive about what has transpired, about what I've gone through or where I'm headed. I'm only twenty–eight years old, so hopefully there's a lot more of my story to be written. Things will likely happen to me, around me, and inside of me that I don't even suspect. Hopefully, I'll be able to keep it together, make the right choices, remain sober and keep love in my heart. I don't have a clue what the future holds. I can only finish relating the past.

When I met Reverend Stone and the missionaries from St. Mark's and sat for an interview with them, I immediately sensed I'd made the right decision. The reverend was a happy man, about my dad's age, with a fat face, fat arms and legs, a well–nurtured belly, skin as shiny as oil, and an overwhelming disposition. What's weird is that, whereas I normally have this thing against fat people – folks who've let themselves go, so to speak – I don't feel that way about Reverend Stone. It must be the love – he simply and profusely emanates it from every pore of his body. Once I met him and the rest of the mission board, well, there was no question left in my mind at all: I was going to Liberia.

Leaving my job was hard. Patients I'd been seeing for months were bound to lament my departure, as I lamented leaving them. In fact, we did some of that lamenting right in the waiting room of the Metropolitan African Women's Clinic, clutching each other and weeping deeply as we said our goodbyes.

Then, sunglasses adjusted, my head covered by a ball cap, Lilly and I zoomed off in my Saab, intent upon taking one last road trip before I climbed aboard an airplane bound for Africa. We drove the two–lane highway from Minneapolis to Marquette, Michigan, stopping only at a small neglected cemetery outside St. Paul, making the four hundred mile run in a little over eight hours.

About our visit to that cemetery: Del's sister– Cheryl – the only one of Del's siblings who was ever decent to me – gave me directions, and told me where to find Del's gravesite in the cemetery located halfway between Afton and Stillwater. Lilly stayed in the car; she didn't much care for Delmont Benson in life, so asking her to stand with me at Del's grave shivering for warmth against the cold – well, that wouldn't have made a whole lot of sense. I'll not bore you with the details of what I said to Del. I'll only relate that they were my last words to him. That's right: last words, as in: "I have a new life and I can't come back." Suffice to say, my words were honest, tender and heartfelt. There was something between us that, gratefully and sadly, I won't likely find with anyone else. That's just how it was. Pleasure and pain. The good and the bad. That was Del and me in spades.

Lilly and I spent two nights in Marquette. I showed Lil all my old haunts, including places I'd hung out at with college boys whose names I don't remember. We walked by, but didn't enter, bars I'd frequented, rowdy places catering to college kids where the music is loud and hormones rage. We found the quiet spots, too: the city park located on the rocky point beyond the iron ore docks; the boat marina, the wintry black water of Marquette Harbor empty of pleasure boats; the deserted bike and walking path skirting the waterfront; and the fancy houses built by the turn–of–the–century rich standing proud against the lonely sky on the bluff overlooking the lake. Lilly and I, well, we did some catching up as we walked along the waterfront trail, taking in the subtle nuances of the place where I'd gone to school, where I'd learned to be a nurse. There were no startling revelations. I didn't tell her the whole of what I'd learned about David's death. I didn't share with her what had happened between Father Michaels and me. I sensed she knew I'd done something – something a little less than honorable to affect the priest. We didn't get into the details of it, just like we didn't talk about why I'd left the Catholic Church, or why I'd decided to cast my spiritual lot with Protestants. We simply enjoyed each other's company. I was grateful she didn't try to talk me out of going to Africa. She, I think, simply welcomed spending time with me, time away from the expectations that come from being a mother and a high–society wife.

You want to know about Mason and me? Well, that's an interesting situation; it's one that could take any number of turns. Where it's headed, I haven't a clue. Despite all the love and emotion we've poured into and onto each other over the past year, gradually building a connection between us as mature adults do, there are troublesome things that need to be addressed –

things that didn't get addressed before I left. The most telling, of course, is whether our love can survive six months of separation. I'm not too worried about that one; I mean, I was in treatment for a similar period of time and managed to keep my relationships intact. And Mason, as upset as he was when I told him I was going to Liberia, calmed down before he left Bayfield. That doesn't mean we resolved our differences, however; even though we kissed "goodbye," the gesture seemed perfunctory. No, that's not quite right. The kiss felt temporary, like a band–aid trying to hold back blood from a stab wound. Our relationship will likely bear a scar from the choice I've made, but whether or not that scar will be significant and disfiguring, only time will tell. I *will* say this: Mason was gracious enough to call me at my parent's house the night before I left for Africa. We talked, mostly around the edges of things, but we did talk. Even so, things between us remain unresolved: his plans, my plans, whether our respective futures will mesh or clash all remain open for further consideration.

What do I mean by that? Well, for one thing, I'm not sure what I want to do when I come back from Africa. There's an opening at the Red Cliff Clinic for a Nurse Practitioner. I don't have NP certification, but the tribe – through Billy Cadotte's intervention – voiced their willingness to pay for my course work, which I can do at Northland College in Ashland. That would give me the chance to work side–by–side with Dad during my clinical rotation. That's something I've always wanted to do: learn medicine from Dad. But am I ready to come back home to Chequamegon Bay? Maybe, but maybe not. Is Bayfield a place that Mason Erickson could live? He's fairly rooted to the rich earth, oak–crowded hills and undulating pastures of Iowa. Sure, he's got an economics degree, so he could find a job at a bank or credit union, but I doubt that's what he has in mind. He's a man of the soil and the open sky. Sitting at a desk would likely kill him. He could sell his farm and try his hand at raising milk cows and running an orchard near Bayfield. That's a plan that has promise, but we haven't talked about it – and we won't, until I come home. Whether this idea takes root or not, well, I'll leave that to God.

I could live in Duluth where there are nursing jobs galore. With two competing hospital systems, hundreds of doctors and dozens of clinics, the place has become a regional medical center. Amy was badgering me, as we sat next to each other on the 747 flying to Africa, about taking a nursing job at the Family Practice Center in Duluth. Sarah Miles had her own ideas: there was an opening for an RN at Planned Parenthood. I'm not sure about that. I mean, they don't do abortions at Planned Parenthood, but they do referrals for the procedure. Recalling Lilly's experience brings bitterness to my mouth: the taste of copper, the taste of blood. I don't think my heart could handle working at Planned Parenthood, though I understand the need for such places.

280

All the same, I *could* live in Duluth. It's a good compromise between the hustle and bustle of the Twin Cities and the quiet solitude of Chequamegon Bay. But could Mason? There's not much for a farmer to do around Duluth. The growing season is, at best, eighty days long. The soil is either rocky as hell or sandy and subject to frost. There aren't many dairy farmers left around Duluth, and the farms that still operate are mostly hobby farms. I don't know that my boyfriend from Guthrie Center, Iowa could ever consider farming to be a mere hobby.

Then, of course, there's religion. I'm a lapsed Catholic. My mother, the defender of the One True Faith in our family, God bless her, has finally realized that I'm not coming back to her church. She has no way of knowing exactly what it was that convinced me to bolt the Catholic faith. Oh, there have been a few times when we've talked about religion, and she poked and prodded gently at my disdain. There've been times I thought she was on to what had happened between Lilly and the priest. Maybe she found the love letter from Father Michaels that I'd foolishly – though, as it turns out, providently – hidden in the novel, and made the connection. Maybe not. Like I said: Mom's perceptive, and she likely knows more about my and Lil's business than she'll ever let on. But whether she knows the complete story about the priest, I can't say. I get the sense she does, and that nothing is hidden from her eyes. But who knows – that might be unfounded paranoia on my part.

Which brings me to this: I'd love to attend Reverend Stone's little brick church on the steep hillside of Duluth overlooking the blue waters of Lake Superior. The man, when he preached to us before we left for Africa, was a thunderbolt of love, forgiveness and grace. He made murky and dim truths appear clear and precise. But how would Mason, a man used to quiet reflection, take to the noisy faith of my ancestors? Not so well, I'd guess; it would take a lot of convincing from a certain Irish Finnish African American woman to warm him to the idea. And then there'd be the obvious fact that, walking through the solid wooden doors of that little AME church on any given Sunday, only a handful of St. Mark's parishioners would look anything like Mason Erickson. Could Mason, as strong of heart as he is, assimilate into a faith that is fundamentally black? It's an interesting question, I'll grant you.

Liberia: like I said, the place is just north of the equator, and Monrovia, where I'm posted, receives ninety inches of rain a year. The temperature never dips below seventy–five degrees. The good thing is, arriving in November, it's the dry season (though "dry" here is a relative term). With the humidity permanently stuck at ninety percent, I take three showers a day. It's not like we don't have the water; the big galvanized tanks supplying our encampment with fresh water are always full. There's no way we can use too much water in this waterlogged place.

No matter how much Secret I roll under my arms, the antiperspirant doesn't seem to help. This, in spite of the fact I'm not going on my daily runs while I'm here. It's too dangerous for anyone – including Sarah Miles, who has temporarily shelved her dreams of competing in another Olympics – to jog the streets of Monrovia. Of course, the fact that I won't be running for six months has set my own training schedule back some, but I'm young and Boston can wait.

The good news is that *everyone* – even Amy, a girl who barely broke a sweat on the basketball court back in high school – sweats like a pig in this environment. We *all* smell, and no one holds their nose up at their neighbor. And, as it turns out, it was a stroke of genius for me to have my hair cropped. If I were still wearing it long, with or without the dreads, I'd be hacking it off with my new pocketknife about now. Having a nearly shaved head keeps me cool, at least relative to how I'd feel if I were carrying around a mop of thick black hair on my head. It's funny: you'd think that being black, I could handle the sun, the heat and the humidity. I mean, it's genetics, right? You're forgetting that my father's people have lived north of the Mason–Dixon Line for four generations. So, even though I boast some African blood, my kinfolk were all raised in the Snow Belt. Whatever natural protection against the sun and the heat my ancestry once provided has long since been assimilated into oblivion.

It's morning here in Monrovia. We're living and working in a cluster of white tents near the Waterside Market, a big outdoor market that was once the center of daily commerce in Liberia's capital. The market closed during the war and has yet to reopen. The empty marketplace is a gathering place for displaced kids, boy warriors who were recruited and armed by the insurgents and by President Taylor – some as young as ten years old – who've been disarmed. Of course, demilitarizing the children doesn't end the problem; kids who were used as pawns in an ugly game of real–life chess need to be reintegrated into Liberian society. That'll take some doing, I'm afraid, given the fact that unemployment here hovers around eighty percent. Idle young hands need attention, otherwise they'll simply gravitate to trouble. You see clods of preteen and teenaged boys standing on street corners, bored out of their minds, looking for something to do. If the government doesn't figure out how to integrate them into school or the work force, they'll likely end up to no good.

You know, it's funny: one of the UN contingents providing security here is from Ireland. The 94th Infantry Battalion of the Irish Defense Force deployed just as we landed, just as Mrs. Sirleaf was declared the winner of the election. Some of the Irish soldiers are from Galway, and when I learned that, it cracked me up. Here I am, in West Africa, seeking some sort of reconciliation with my African heritage and who protects me? Soldiers from my Irish grandmother's hometown!

Though Monrovia is relatively calm, destruction is apparent everywhere. Buildings remain in disrepair. Every block of the city has been physically touched by war; unlike my own country, part of which was recently ravaged by tropical storms and is slowly (too slowly, as I've already opined) on the mend, Liberia doesn't have the financial muscle to rebuild. Still, despite the crushing poverty, stifling heat and still–fresh wounds of war, Liberians constantly smile. They smile because, for the first time in many years, they have hope of a better life.

All the same, what I don't get, walking around the safe areas of the city (always with an escort of UN soldiers close by), looking at the needs of this place, is why America has turned an essentially deaf ear to the cries emanating from this land. After all, this is a country founded by Americans as a toehold of American–style republican democracy. I've also learned, since coming here, that America used Monrovia's harbor as an important port during WWII, when little Liberia stood up to Nazi Germany and joined America in declaring war on the Axis powers – despite the fact that, if the Germans had wanted to, they could have destroyed this sliver of a country in a heartbeat. Iron ore and rubber from Liberia helped feed the Allied war machine and thus bring about the downfall of the Axis. So why, when the shit hit the fan here in the 1980s, did America turn a blind eye to its ally? I can only surmise it's because Liberia is poor and devoid of oil and populated by black folks. What other reasons could there be?

Just before finishing this passage, I was out along the Atlantic Coast, walking a beach that once served as a vacation spot for Europeans. The beach was empty, and I could see why. Just short of the sand, Monrovians have piled garbage in heaps taller than the height of a small tree. As I passed these impromptu landfills, rats scurried amongst the filth, scattering at my approach, disappearing into labyrinths tunneled throughout the refuse. The stench from the garbage is awful. This blight highlights the fact that Liberia needs help – help in accomplishing the most basic of services, in filling the most elementary of needs.

Amy, Sarah and I met on the beach. We found a spot safely away from the trash and its stench to sit on driftwood and watch waves. Amy and Sarah held hands as the three of us baked in the late afternoon sun. I wiggled my toes into hot sand. A UN soldier stood nearby – his boots polished, his uniform sharply pressed, every button and crease in order, a rifle slung over his shoulder and a cigarette smoldering in his mouth. The Irishman was young (younger than me) and handsome: he stood stony faced, blue eyed and blond, his golden locks reduced to mere prickles beneath the fabric of his blue UN beret by the shears of a military barber.

Too bad he had to cut his hair, I mused, kicking sand into sea–moistened air with my toes. *I love blonds.*

My eyes fixed on the ocean. White froth ebbed and flowed over the stones that defined the edge of the beach. I thought about this place, this land I'd come to, and the West African Shield that supports the landscape of Liberia. At several billion years of age, the basement of West Africa shares a heritage with the black basalt of the Canadian Shield, the foundation of Madeline Island. The Shields are two of the oldest landforms on earth, and they are connected by a shared history, by common origins in the making. Contemplating this geological link, I thought some more about Mason Erickson and me.

Something in our joining makes sense despite all the reasons it shouldn't. It was clear, sitting on the beach just moments ago, that maybe – just maybe–we could figure out a way to be together. There was an understanding, as I stood up to walk back to the mission compound with my friends, that Mason and I could create sweetness, goodness and light together, just like Neil Young (a middle–class white boy from Winnipeg) and Tracy Chapman (a poor black girl from Cleveland) do when they make music. I'd left my iPod in my tent, so I had to rely upon my memory to recreate Ms. Chapman's soulful vocals set against the church–like chords of Mr. Young's piano, the words and music to "All that You Have is Your Soul" churning over and over and over in my mind as I walked.

In the end, I know this: I am a child of water. I was born in a little harbor town on the largest freshwater lake in the world. I am at peace when I can view the world's horizon over the blue expanse of Lake Superior or the churning surf of the sea. I also know that I am loved. This love shines brightly, like the sun reflecting off a sandy beach. It shines here, in West Africa, where I'll stay and lend a hand to my African brothers and sisters for the next six months. And it shines in Guthrie Center, Iowa, where Mason Erickson waits patiently; in Apple Valley, Minnesota, where my sister and her family live; and on Madeline Island, Wisconsin, where my parents grow old.

I feel this love; I know this love, as I type the final words to this chapter in my life.

THE END

284

About the Author

Mark Munger is a lifelong resident of northeastern Minnesota. Mark, his wife René, and their youngest son live on the banks of the wild and scenic Cloquet River north of Duluth. When not writing fiction, Mark enjoys hunting, fishing, skiing, chasing kids and working as a District Court Judge.

Other Works by the Author

The Legacy (eBook in all formats)
    Set against the backdrop of WWII Yugoslavia and present-day Minnesota, this debut novel combines elements of military history, romance, thriller, and mystery. Rated 3 and 1/2 daggers out of 4 by *The Mystery Review Quarterly*.

Ordinary Lives (ISBN 97809792717517 and eBook in all formats)
    Creative fiction from one of Northern Minnesota's newest writers, these stories touch upon all elements of the human condition and leave the reader asking for more.

Black Water (ISBN 9780979217548 and eBook in all formats)
    Now for the first time the essays of Mark Munger appear in one collection. Stories about hunting, fishing, raising kids, gardening, canoeing and life lived large in the great Minnesota out-of-doors.

Pigs, a Trial Lawyer's Story (eBook in all formats)
    A story of a young trial attorney, a giant corporation, marital infidelity, moral conflict, and choices made, *Pigs* takes place against the backdrop of Western Minnesota's beautiful Smoky Hills. This tale is being compared by reviewers to Grisham's best.

Suomalaiset: People of the Marsh (ISBN 0972005064 and eBook in all formats)
    A dockworker is found hanging from a rope in a city park. How is his death tied to the turbulence of the times? A masterful novel of compelling history and emotion, *Suomalaiset* has been hailed by reviewers as a "must read."

Mr. Environment: The Willard Munger Story (ISBN 9780979217524: Trade paperback only)
    A detailed and moving biography of Minnesota's leading environmental champion and longest serving member of the Minnesota House of Representatives, *Mr. Environment* is destined to become a book every Minnesotan has on his or her bookshelf.

Laman's River
(ISBN 9780979217531 and eBook in all formats)
    A beautiful newspaper reporter is found bound, gagged, and dead. A Duluth judge conceals secrets that may end her career. A reclusive community of religious zealots seeks to protect its view of the hereafter by

unleashing an avenging angel upon the world. Mormons. Murder. Minnesota. Montana. Reprising two of your favorite characters from *The Legacy*, Deb Slater and Herb Whitefeather. Buy it now in print or on all major eBook platforms!

Sukulaiset: The Kindred

The long awaited sequel to Mark's masterpiece of historical fiction, *Suomalaiset: People of the Marsh*, this novel-in-progress was a finalist for the 2011 Pirate's Alley Faulkner Award. Due to be published on the 10th anniversary of the release of its predecessor, *Sukulaiset* follows Elin Gustafson Ellison Goldfarb, one of the main characters from *Suomalaiset* as she and her second husband leave America for Karelia during the height of Karelian Fever. A love story. A war story. A story of purges and the Holocaust. Above all, a complex tale of Karelia, Finland, and Estonia during the Great Depression and the Second World War, this book will be as cherished as Mark's previous historical novels. **Coming to a bookshelf or eReader near you in 2014!**

Visit us at www.cloquetriverpress.com.
Order direct from our estore at the website!

Made in the USA
Middletown, DE
27 June 2015